The Books of ELIZABETH BOWEN

These are BORZOI BOOKS, *Published in New York by*

ALFRED A. KNOPF

Early Stories

Early Stories

[*ENCOUNTERS & ANN LEE'S*]

Elizabeth Bowen

1 9 · 5 1

NEW YORK · ALFRED · A · KNOPF

Preface

These stories [*Encounters*], my first published work, were written between the ages of twenty and twenty-three. Their arrangement here is that of the first edition of 1923, in which I had the help of Mr. Frank Sidgwick; the order happens to be, roughly, chronological, though I do not believe that either of us had that in mind. One story, "Requiescat," is certainly out of place, coming higher up in the index than several others I know to be earlier. "Requiescat" has a Lake Como scene, and I did not go to that part of Italy until (as it then seemed) fairly late on.

The greater part of *Encounters* was, therefore, written just less than thirty years ago. I must have re-read the book many times in the months after the first copy reached my hands: to have failed to be dazzled by the apotheosis into print would have been unnatural. (None of these stories had "appeared" before: any magazine editors with whom I experimented had rejected them.) Since that summer, I had not read the collection through as a whole until I undertook to write this Preface. I now hope to be old enough to be clear of those split, heated, and complicated feelings which must surround for the writer his or her early work. All the same, can I, I ask myself, approach

Encounters as dispassionately as if it were a collection of stories by an unknown young writer sent to me for review? I am afraid not. That might be too much to ask.

What I remember about the writing of these stories is, chiefly, the sheer newness of the sensation of writing. It is, of course, to be doubted whether that sensation ever becomes familiar; or, still more, whether the writer ought to desire that it should. The sensation of desperate and overweening enterprise, of one's entire being being forced to a conclusive ordeal, remains constant. What possibly does wear off—or, through familiarity, become less acute—is that uncanny first sense of complicity with one's surroundings, those physical objects, sounds, and lights and shades comprehensively known as "the writing-table." The room, the table, the convulsive and anxious grating of my chair on the floor were made hypersignificant for me, in those early days, by the fact that here were substantial witnesses to my crossing of the margin of a hallucinatory world.

My embarking upon my first story, "Breakfast"—*not* the first I had attempted, but the first I was to bring to its end—had the character of a last hope. I had already, at twenty, failed to be a poet and was in the course of failing to be a painter. The scene was the top of a house at Harpenden; an attic of which the window was set high— only when I stood up could I see gardens, apple trees, a blur of open country beyond. Between the sill of the window and the top of my table intervened a stretch of white wall-paper, lightly mapped by damp which must have percolated in through the outdoor tiling. This, as I sat at the table, was at eye level. The short rose-dotted curtains, which I had too often allowed to blow out into the rain, fretted over my head and smelled slightly musty. Now and then a voice from one of the gardens could be heard. The then Midland Railway main line ran at a right angle to the bottom of the road in which the house stood: from time to time an up or down express roared by; or, more disturbingly, a local train slowed down as it approached the station. I wrote by hand, as distinctly as was possible for me—as when at school, two or three years before, I had been making a fair copy of an essay. As the filling up of sheet after sheet of my lined block proceeded, I had the sense of swinging between two worlds.

The importance to the writer of first writing must be out of all proportion to the objective value of what is written. It was perhaps more difficult then than now to disentangle what was *there*, on the page, from the creative excitement that had given it birth. There could be but one test of validity: publication. I know I shaped every line in the direction of the unknown arbiter; there was still the sensation of "showing up" work. When I say that had I not written with the intention of being published I should not have written, I should add that I did not so much envisage glory as cry out for affirmation. Publication would be the sign that I was not mad; more than that, it was the necessary gateway to being read. I know that I wrote then with no less—though also with no more— difficulty than now: as an occupation writing pleased me, which made it suspect, but also killed me, which made it to be respected. The sensation of struggle was predominant. I saw no point in killing myself for the sake of anything which was not to be a reality. For me, reality was the books I had read—and I turned round, as I was writing, from time to time to look at those books existing, in their unassailable sphere of reality, in the shelves behind me. (This was my own room.) I had engaged, by writing a book myself, to extend the bounds of reality one stage further.

Decision to retreat upon the short story, on the part of a young person who was a poet *manqué*, would today seem obvious. In *my* young days the position of the short story was anomalous. It was not yet—I think I am right in saying—by then recognized as "a form." There had appeared so far, that is to say, little constructive-critical interest in the short story's possibilities and problems. Any such interest as there may have been had not travelled my way—I could not have been further out of the movement. I had not gone to a university; I had no part in any intellectual life. I had read widely, but wildly. I did not know the stories of Hardy or Henry James; I may have heard of Chekhov; I had not read Maupassant because I imagined I could not read French. . . . With regard to the short story, Katherine Mansfield was not only to be the innovator but to fly the flag; since *Bliss* the short story has never been quite ignored. I read *Bliss* when I had completed that first set of my stories which were to make *Encounters*— then admiration and envy were shot through by a profound dismay: I thought: "If I ever am published, everybody will say I imitated her." I was right: this happened.

Did I, then, in writing my early stories, think I was doing something without precedent? I am sure not. I had found examples, which were also incentives—Richard Middleton's *The Ghost Ship*, and E. M. Forster's *The Celestial Omnibus*. Those collections I read at school.

In themselves, the *Encounters* stories are a mixture of precocity and naïvety. I still cannot consider them badly written; the trouble with some of them is they were not well found. But at twenty—twenty-one, twenty-two, twenty-three—where is one to find a story? Stories require people; and principally one is interested in oneself; or, it might be more true to say, one's own sensations. Those appear to be new; actually, what *is* new is one's awareness of them, and one's cultivation of that awareness for its own sake. Literature, in those years, excites one according to its power to reflect, express, altogether magnify awareness of which one is incoherently conscious in oneself. In my own case it would not be too much to say that my attitude to the most noble literature was brigandish: I was waiting to rifle its vocabulary. I was also a pupil, possibly over-quick to be taught to see anything I had not so far seen for myself. I can perceive, now, in the *Encounters* stories how much I was using synthetic language to express something perfectly real to me.

I can see, too, how I was each time using the story as a device, in order to place sensations at one remove from me—and at once to exalt and rationalize them. The characters in the stories—are they, then, stand-ins, stooges? In the main, to them I was ungratefully harsh. It is the harshness and the touches of little-girlish smarty unkindness throughout *Encounters* that today shock me. These creatures, were they materialized that I might score off them? Were there at work the malignancies of a protracted childhood; or had I debts to settle? . . . It seems worth remarking (*a*) that with very few exceptions—the child in "Coming Home," the schoolgirls in "Daffodils," Laura in "Sunday Evening"—all these characters were considerably older than myself, were involved in experiences of which I had no knowledge and often gutted by passions beyond my ken; and (*b*) that not more than three of them bore resemblance to anybody I had encountered in real life. They all the more pleased me, I remember, by having an actuality for which I could not account. They impressed me, even while I mocked at them, by having experience that was none of mine.

I know that I had a snobbery with regard to age. For my generation (possibly the last of which this was true) grown-ups were the ruling class. As an only child I had lived very much among them, noted as closely as possible their ways, and tried in my reading to keep abreast with books they seemed to admire, which were of many sorts. Moreover, I was being continually shifted from household to household, in and out of varying social groups, to and fro between Ireland and England. This made me diplomatic, and imitative. All through my youth I lived with a submerged fear that *I* might fail to establish grown-up status; and that fear had probably reached its peak when I started writing. A writer and a grown-up, it appeared to me, could not but be synonymous. I had embarked on an act of levelling up. As far as I can see (more from these stories, re-read, than from my memory), I was anxious at once to approximate to the grown-ups and to demolish them. At the same time, I was not yet ready to try conclusions with any world I knew, particularly that of my own family. My characters, therefore, lived in houses which, in real life, I had done little more than contemplate from the outside.

The above could be called the social motive. Horror of being at a disadvantage may have worked itself out in my aptness to take my characters at a disadvantage, to snap them (in the camera sense) at moments when weakness, mistrust, falseness, or affectation could not but be exposed. But, one point more: in fairness to the writer of *Encounters* one must allow for literary fashion, and for the psychological climate of a decade. The famous twenties, mocking and disabused, had already set in, though had not yet a name. Though I did not meet writers, I keenly read what was being written. If I was *mal élevée* in my attitude to the human race, so were my betters.

The stories have build, style, and occasional felicities of expression which I must say startle me. Their strong point is visual clarity; and though there is too often a conscious, metallic clang of phrases, on the whole the meaning does not bog down in words. But I find in the best of them something better—an uncorrupted attempt to say something not said before. "Daffodils," "Requiescat," "All Saints," "Mrs. Windermere," "The Shadowy Third," "Sunday Evening," and "Coming Home" engage my respect. As a performance, "The Return" is the most showy, but it has a hollow kernel—a situation I thought up, or borrowed, rather than felt. The truest ring of emotion comes out of "Coming Home"—which was transposed autobiography. "Requiescat" and "The Shadowy Third" make me, now, very clearly see how I used to work: I would posit a situation and then explore it. (Of that method a third, malignant example is "The Evil That Men Do—".)

I was still not clear, while I was writing *Encounters*, as to the distinction between a story and a "sketch." I failed to see that, while it could be emancipated from plot (in the magazine formula sense), a story, if it is to *be* a story, must have a psychological turning-point. A sketch, lacking the turning-point, is little more than knowing, accomplished reportage—"Breakfast" and "The Lover" are examples. When one or two reviewers described the published *Encounters* as "a collection of sketches," I felt this to be derogatory. Actually, it would have been correct to describe the volume as a collection of sketches and stories. I imagine few writers who are today at the age that I then was would have the same blind spot: story-consciousness has gone on maturing. All the same, the point seems just worth noting.

I claim for the *Encounters* stories one other virtue—susceptibility, rendered articulate, to places, moments, objects, and times of year. This shows, at the best, with the naïvety of a deep love. "Daffodils" overflowed from uncontainable pleasure in the streets of St. Albans on one March afternoon; "Requiescat" eased an obsession about Lake Como, and a particular garden I knew above it. Even in the centrally artificial "Return" I see the welling up of a solitary person's love for an empty house; and the scene, if not the characters, in "The Shadowy Third" seems to be dignified by emotion. Granted all this, I see one reason for my springing upon my characters at their most trying moments: their susceptibilities had to be heightened to match my own.

I owed the publication of _Encounters_—had it _not_ been published, what would have happened next?—to three persons. In order of time they were a woman friend, the "M. J." of the dedication, who paid the bill for having the stories typed; Rose Macaulay, upon whose decision as to whether I was or was not a writer I hung my future; and Frank Sidgwick, to whom Rose Macaulay wrote. He not only honoured me by his faith but made what had appeared the most fantastic of my dreams come true by bringing out _Encounters_ in the same series as _The Celestial Omnibus_. The title, which I think did much to further the book, was of his finding.

*   *   *   *   *   *

After _Encounters_, _Ann Lee's_ was first published in 1926. The actual date of the stories is earlier by a year or two; some were written while _Encounters_ was still in press. In the interval between the completion and the appearance of _Ann Lee's_ I wrote my first novel, _The Hotel_.

Encounters had had a better reception than I had dared to hope. How much this might be due to the book's format, and to its place in a series which had maintained distinction since _The Celestial Omnibus_, I had the sense to ask myself. To the serious kindness of critics in 1923 I record my debt. I had, to the full, envisaged being ignored; I had braced myself for a snub; most of all, perhaps, I had dreaded patronizingness. As it was, I received what I most wanted: judgment. Looking back at that year, I realize that very good reviewers were in the field. By goodness in a reviewer I do not mean good-nature or the predisposition to give a beginner the benefit of the doubt; I mean, readiness to search for potential quality in the work of a writer not known before—with which must go insistence, as the writer continues, that he fall not short of his original mark. Up to a point, the young writer's expectations of himself need to be nurtured; only the intelligent critic can guess at the desperation these have to fight. And, on his side, the young writer is not easily fooled; he can measure the perspicacity of the critic. I doubt whether praise *with* judgment ever turned a head. I cannot over-emphasize the importance, to the young writer, of initial reviews. Do I, then, argue that every young writer should be encouraged? I can only be thankful that I was.

Encounters did not sell widely. Sidgwick and Jackson must have sustained loss; for their new author publication had been a gain, a steadying, and an education. If I was cheered up, I also was sobered down. The promotion with amateur status carried certain alarms with it—not only the fear of disappointing, in the future, those who had spoken up for me, but the almost paralysing violence of the incentive to work. To continue to write is as trying as to begin. Every step forward brings one into an area of new dangers, involves a summoning of powers which may or may not be there.

The first of these *Ann Lee's* stories to be written was, I think, "The Back Drawing-Room"; after that came "The Storm." The first has the interest of touching, for the first time, on my native Irish scene; the second (like "Requiescat" in *Encounters*) came out of my infatuation with Italy. "The Contessina" (Como) and "The Secession" (Rome) complete, in this volume, the Italian group. . . . During this term of time my assault on magazine editors continued with renewed force—backed by the not unreasonable hope that the *Encounters* notices might have gained me footing. However, I fared little better than I had done before. "Ann Lee's" itself, it is true, had the distinction of being published (in an abridged form) in the *Spectator,* in July 1924; it was, I believe, the first short story the *Spectator* had ever carried. For that I have to thank John Strachey, who, at that time concerned with the literary side of his father's paper, let me know of the proposed experiment and invited me to submit work. It was he, too, I remember, who urged me to begin going (or rather, going again) to the cinema, which was just then emerging from disrepute. There was much, he suggested, to be learned from the cinema. He was right.

In the autumn of 1924 the *Queen* under Naomi Royde-Smith (who had already printed two of my sketches in the *Saturday Westminster*) took "The Contessina." The support of Ann Pearn, then of Curtis Brown's, gained a place for "The Parrot" in the *London Mercury*, 1925, and for "Making Arrangement" in *Eve*, in the same year; and she succeeded in selling the same two stories in America, to *Everybody's*. Otherwise, silence. For editors did I, I asked myself, carry the mark of Cain? The dismay, in part economic (I needed money), shook my æsthetic faith: *was* I writing nonsense? Also, I doubted the sincerity of editors who, in the beautifully printed manifesto of each new review, professed to be searching for new talent. Looking down their contents lists, every month, I perceived, or seemed to perceive, that Uncle Tom Cobley and all his company still held place—could a newcomer hope to break those ranks? Once one has "a name," I concluded, one can sell anything, anywhere. I cannot remember when it occurred to me that "a name" is not simply donated; it must be earned.

I do not know whether the position of a new short-story writer actually was more difficult then than it is now —if I incline to think so, that may be a sign of age. My own string of failures with periodicals remains, where I am concerned, a historic fact. One explanation—that the work here collected, as *Ann Lee's*, did not quite make a grade—may occur to readers. These stories were, are, half-way between the first bright stage of experimentation and the required next degree of command. They show advance, but advance at any awkward stage—the disarming naïvety of *Encounters* is missing. Though, like the later pieces in *Encounters,* they are of an ambitiousness that deserves respect. What I regret, on behalf of my self of years ago, is not the ambitiousness but the playing safe—which betrays itself, in several of these studies of human extremity and dereliction, in the little smile of one who, herself, knows better. "Ann Lee's," "The Parrot," "The Contessina," "Human Habitation" (though in other ways this is a reputable story), and "Recent Photograph" are cases in point. An author should never feel superior to his characters. The repulsive superiority of young persons needs breaking down—as a rule, life arranges this. It is unnerving to find one's own youthful superiority preserved forever in the amber of print.

The harshness, or human inadequacy, of several of the *Ann Lee's* stories may be forced the more into prominence by their fair technique. The scene-setting has gained in effectiveness since *Encounters;* the dialogue has shape, and the action (always a problem) is under control. These pieces have more texture, fullness, or call it body—in the sense in which I have already spoken of body to a story being desirable—than their predecessors. There is more sureness—the critics, by perceiving what sort of writer I ought to be, had done much to shape me. I was, with rather more confidence, still concerned with exploring the possibilities of atmosphere. One must remember that in the first half of the 1920's, within which my first two books were written, both the name and the sense of potentials of "atmosphere" were still new. I very possibly had not heard of "atmosphere" till I read my press notices. In attempting to register the hazy queerness places and persons had for me, I was bona fide; I cannot accuse myself of being infected by a literary vogue. *These* days, it would be different; by now the thing has been exploited and overworked, used as a cloak for writers' ignorances, negligences or poverties. I still, however, think it would be a pity if a young person's apprehension of psychic atoms were spoilt for him, or if he felt he should not note them in writing. One is in youth most honest in one's surprise at feeling, most natural in one's admission of its force.

There is a good deal of prettiness in the *Ann Lee's* stories —prettiness of hats in a shop, of a parrot on a flowering chestnut tree, of the Contessina's muslin skirts against a glittering lake-scene, of broken Roman brick walls—"*so solid yet with such a silver-pink bloom of impermanence.*" The younger sister of beauty at that time delighted me. I was, as to one particular, still where I was when I wrote *Encounters*—I liked places and objects better than people. My pen was ready enough, as may be seen, to dwell upon scenes of guilt and misery, but it was essential to me that the *locale* should be pleasing, or at any rate picturesque: I did not care to depress myself too far. In fact, I see, I found writing, though harder and harder work, an unexpected outlet for my frivolity. I now do not find the stories the worse for that—would, though, that the priggishness had been more firmly checked!

The major stimulus, during the writing of *Ann Lee's*, was travel: in a sense, everything I experienced was travel. Now that I knew myself to have become a writer, I could look back objectively at my own past: the two childhood stories, "The Visitor" and "Charity," are, I think, the truest in the collection. I was by now located, married, the mistress of a house; and the sensation of *living* anywhere, as apart from paying a succession of visits, was new to me. We were living in the English Midlands, outside Northampton; a flat but reposing view of vegetable gardens stretched away outside the bow window in which my table stood—the nearest high point in *that* direction being, I was told, the Ural Mountains. A canal-side walk inspired "Human Habitation," and a tossing sunny chestnut tree at the corner of our road, with the thought of how comic a parrot would look in it, was the genesis of "The Parrot." Otherwise I drew on the distant rather than the immediate scene. Every now and then I caught a train and went to London; I went to Ireland from time to time to see my father; every spring I went to Italy. Between these journeys I worked, at the table in the bow window, with an uninterruptedness that I envy now.

The writing of these *Ann Lee's* stories was overcast by the idea that I ought to be attempting a novel. One reviewer of *Encounters* had spoken of "these novels in miniature," and Mr. Sidgwick was certain I had it in me. My difficulty, as I had the sense to realize, was that I at that time could not extend my vision outside the range of an hour. I could spotlight, but not illumine steadily. I could expose people, but I was not yet interested in their continuity: I had a flitting mind. My view, to be a view at all, had to be dramatic, and I could not see how interplay between persons was to be sustained throughout the whole of a book—might my characters not begin to exhaust and bore one another just as much as (I foresaw) they might exhaust and bore me? I realized that the prerequisite for a novel was slow combustion, and I could not yet see how to achieve that. This transitional difficulty, for writers who have begun as short-storyists, is no doubt general. I re-read my stories, wondered if any of them *could* have been capable of being extended, always decided not. At the same time I realized that if my adherence to the short story were to become a matter of sheer timidity, or, still worse, of inelastic stupidity, there would be a danger of the short story's coming, in time, to deaden under my hand. I increasingly wished to write a novel—the ideality of hotel life as a stage for one came to me, one afternoon, in a flash. The Italian Riviera, on which I had spent one winter in a hotel, offered—with its social futility, pretty backdrop, and dramatic changes of weather—propitious climate for a first novel of mine.

I do not know whether the mood of æsthetic restlessness in which I wrote them has left any mark on the *Ann Lee's* stories. It possibly made for tenseness, for over-anxiety to justify my medium. I was beating myself against human unknowableness; in fact, I made that my subject—how many times? The stories are questions asked: many end with a shrug, a query, or, to the reader, a sort of over-to-you. The unexplained man in "Ann Lee's"—"*scudded across their patch of visibility. By putting out a hand they could have touched him. He went by them blindly; his breath sobbed and panted. It was by his breath that they knew how terrible it had been—terrible. Passing them quite blindly, he stabbed his way on into the fog.*" The fate of the missing lady in "The Secession" is not hinted at; nor is the belatedness of Willy in "Human Habitation" ever explained. As for the couple in the Tivoli villa in "The Storm," where do they go from there? . . . I cannot consider these to be trick endings; they were the admission of my predicament.

Ann Lee's was, like *Encounters*, received kindly. I wonder how it would fare if it were appearing for the first time today? The short story has grown up, considerably, since 1926. I am glad I wrote them; one or two of them do still give me pleasure. The critic may use them to measure growth (art's, not mine), and for the student writer they may have the value of cautionary tales.

ELIZABETH BOWEN

Contents

ENCOUNTERS

ANN LEE'S

Encounters

Breakfast

"BEHOLD, I die daily," thought Mr. Rossiter, entering the breakfast-room. He saw the family in silhouette against the windows; the windows looked out into a garden closed darkly in upon by walls. There were so many of the family it seemed as though they must have multiplied during the night; their flesh gleamed pinkly in the cold northern light and they were always moving. Often, like the weary shepherd, he could have prayed them to keep still that he might count them.

They turned at his entrance profiles and three-quarter faces towards him. There was a silence of suspended munching and little bulges of food were thrust into their cheeks that they might wish him perfunctory good-mornings.

Miss Emily further inquired whether he had slept well, with a little vivacious uptilt of her chin. Her voice was muffled: he gathered that the contents of her mouth was bacon, because she was engaged in sopping up the liquid fat from her plate with a little dice of bread, which she pushed round briskly with a circular movement of her fork. It was not worth sitting down till she had finished, because he would be expected to take her plate away. Why was the only empty chair always beside Miss Emily?

Last night in the lamplight he had almost begun to think he liked Miss Emily. She was the only lady present who had not beaten time with hand or foot or jerking head while they played "Toreador Song" on the gramophone. But here, pressed in upon her by the thick fumes of coffee and bacon, the doggy-smelling carpet, the tight, glazed noses of the family ready to split loudly from their skins . . . There was contamination in the very warm edge of her plate, as he took it from her with averted head and clattered it down among the others on the sideboard.

"Bacon?" insinuated Mrs. Russel. "A *little* chilly, I'm afraid. I do hope there's plenty, but we early birds are sometimes inclined to be *rather* ravenous."

She added: "There's an egg," but there was no invitation in her tone.

She could never leave a phrase unmodified. He could have answered with facetious emphasis that he was *almost* inclined to believe he would *rather* have enjoyed that egg.

Dumbly, he took two rashers of the moist and mottled bacon.

"And then," Hilary Bevel was recounting, "it all changed, and we were moving very quickly through a kind of pinkish mist—running, it felt like, only all my legs and arms were somewhere else. That was the time when *you* came into it, Aunt Willoughby. You were winding up your sewing machine like a motor car, kneeling down, in a sort of bunching bathing dress. . . ." She dared indelicacy, reaching out for the marmalade with a little agitated rustle to break up the silence with which her night's amazing experiences had been received.

Miss Emily, always kindly, tittered into her cup. She kicked the leg of Rossiter's chair and apologized; and he watched her thin, sharp shoulders shining through her blouse.

Mrs. Russel's eye travelled slowly round the table; there slowed and ceased the rotatory mastication of her jaws. Above her head was a square of white light reflected across from the window to the overmantel. He wished that the sheen of the tablecloth were snow, and that he could heap it over his head as that eye came round towards him.

"Now for it," he braced himself, clenching his hands upon his knife and fork, and squaring his elbows till one touched Miss Emily, who quivered.

"I'm afraid you couldn't hardly have heard the gong this morning, Mr. Rossiter. That new girl doesn't hardly know how to make it sound yet. She seems to me just to give it a sort of *rattle*."

Damn her impudence. She censored him for being late.

"Oh, I—I heard it, thank you!"

They had all stopped talking, and ate quite quietly

to hear him speak. Only Jervis Bevel drained his coffee-cup with a gulp and gurgle.

"The fact is, I was—er—looking for my collar-stud."

"Ah, yes. I'm afraid you've sometimes been a little reckless about buying new ones before you were quite sure you'd lost the others, haven't you, Mr. Rossiter? Only fancy,"—she looked round to collect the attention of the breakfasters; there was a sensation to follow —"Annie found *three* good ones, really good ones, under the wardrobe, when she was turning out your room."

"I can't think how they get there," he protested, conscious of inanity.

"Perhaps they took little legs unto themselves and walked," suggested Hilary Bevel.

"Perhaps the wardrobe got up in the night and sat on top of them," bettered Miss Emily.

There was a rustle of laughter, and she cast down her eyes with a deprecatory titter.

The remark was a success. It was really funny. It was received by Mrs. Russel with a warm benignity: "Really, Emily, you do say silly things." She laughed her gentle breathy laugh, gazing at Mr. Rossiter, who wriggled.

"I say—er—Bevel, when you've finished with that newspaper—"

Jervis Bevel looked insolently at him over the top of the paper. "Sorry, I've only just begun. I left it lying on your plate some time, then I didn't think you'd have much time to read it, being rather rushed."

Rossiter hated Bevel, with his sleek head. He was not aware that he was rushed. What business had Bevel got to tell him so?

"Well, when you *have* finished—"

Hilary Bevel was staring at him across the table as though she had never seen him before. She had eyebrows like her brother's, owl's eyebrows, and long-lidded, slanting eyes; and affected a childish directness and ingenuousness of speech which she considered attractive. Her scarlet, loose-lipped mouth curled itself round her utterances, making them doubly distinct.

"Mr. Rossiter's got another tie on, a *crimson* tie!" said Hilary Bevel.

Rossiter was instantly aware, not only of his tie but of his whole body visible above the table-edge. He felt his ears protruding fanwise from his head, felt them redden, and the blush burn slowly across his cheekbones, down his pricking skin to the tip of his nose.

Mrs. Russel's attention was temporarily directed from himself by a skirmish with Aunt Willoughby. The click of swords was audible to all.

"Oh, but you wouldn't, Aunt Willoughby. Not when they've got five or six rooms to settle up every day, you wouldn't. You see, with you, when poor uncle was alive, it was a different thing altogether. What I mean to say is, in proportion to the size of the family you had more of them, in a kind of way. It was a larger staff."

"Ah then, Rosie, but what I always used to say, 'You do what I expect of you and we won't expect any more

than that. I'm reasonable,' I used to say, 'I won't expect any more than that.' *Annie* could tell you that was
what I used to say to her. As my dear husband used to
say," Aunt Willoughby raised her voice, anticipating
an interruption, "there are those that can get good work
out of their servants and those that can't. We mustn't
be set up about it; it's just a gift, like other gifts, that
many haven't got. I've had such a happy, *happy* home,"
she sighed towards the attentive Miss Emily. "Always
so comfortable, it was."

"Annie *is* a funny girl," reflected Mrs. Russel; "she
said to me—of course I never take the things those girls
say seriously—'I wouldn't go back to Mrs. Willoughby
not for anything you might give me, I wouldn't.' I
said, 'But she spoke so well of you, Annie,' and she
just wagged her head at me, sort of. She *is* a funny girl!
Of course, I didn't ought to tell you, but it made me
laugh at the time, it did really."

"I came down on her rather *hard*," admitted Aunt
Willoughby swiftly. "I was so particular, you see, and
she *had* some dirty ways. Now I shouldn't wonder—
when was it you lost those collar-studs, Mr. Rossiter?"

"I don't exactly remember," said Rossiter, basely. He
felt Mrs. Russel's approval warm upon him, but was
sorry to have failed Aunt Willoughby, who, disconcerted, relapsed into irrelevancy.

Miss Emily harked back.

"Oh, Hilary, you are awful—why shouldn't he?"

"Well, I didn't say he shouldn't, I simply said it *was*

one. They'll be jealous of you at the office, won't they, Mr. Rossiter?"

Mr. Rossiter, eying her contemplatively, supposed that Miss Bevel was a "merry" girl.

"It may mean an *occasion* for Mr. Rossiter," said Mrs. Russel from her Olympia behind the urn. "You shouldn't draw attention to it, girls."

The light glanced on Hilary's waved and burnished hair as she turned her head towards Aunt Willoughby.

"*Nobody* takes *any* notice of little me, when *I* go gadding, do they, Auntie! Why, it's all round the table in a minute if I come down with half an inch of new coloured cammie-ribbon sticking out above my jumper!"

"You wouldn't put it in at all if you didn't think it was going to notice," remarked her brother, without raising his eyes from the *Daily Express*.

"I wouldn't put on anything at all if I was quite invisible, if that's what you mean!"

Miss Emily glanced apprehensively at the unshaken barricade of newspaper.

"Oh, Hilary, you are *awf—*"

Jervis had apparently not heard.

"Hilary!" said Mrs. Russel, "I'm afraid you're shocking Mr. Rossiter!" She lingered on the name as though he were something delicious to eat.

"I believe," thought Rossiter, "they all want to marry me! Is this insight or delirium? P'raps not Aunt Willoughby, but—"

He appraised Jervis round the edge of the newspaper. Surely he was showier, more attractive? Why couldn't he divert some of their attentions; take on, say, Miss Emily and Mrs. Russel? Mrs. Russel was old enough to be the mother of either of them.

A hand shot out suddenly from behind the urn. Rossiter jumped.

"—had your second cup of coffee yet," Mrs. Russel was saying. "You look quite poetic, Mr. Rossiter"—she was referring to his abstracted glare?— "Aren't you going to pass along your cup?"

"Thank you—*half* a cup, if you please."

"There's no *hurry*." She glanced over her shoulder at the round relentless clock-face on the mantel. "You see, you eat rather faster than the others, Mr. Rossiter, though they have had a bit of a start this morning!"

Did he really bolt his food and make, perhaps, disgusting noises with his mouth?

"That's why I always say we'd rather breakfast early —all of us, even the ones who haven't necessarily got to rush. It's so much homier, one feels, than rough-and-tumble modern breakfast nowadays. Everybody sort of rushing in and scrambling and snatching and making *grabs* at things off a table at the side. There's nothing so homely," said Mrs. Russel with conscious brilliance, "as a comfortable sit-down family to breakfast."

"My God!" said Jervis irritably, "there's going to be another strike on that damned railway—they're cutting down the trains again. Why *pretend* railways are a convenience—that's what I should like to know?"

No one could tell him.

He pushed his chair back from the table, impatiently, and crossed his legs.

"Pore old thing, then," trilled Hilary. "Diddums wazzums cwoss."

"They're *not* taking off the eight-forty-seven, are they?"

"Not the eight-*forty-seven?*"

"They are. That means either the eight-twenty-seven or the eight-fifty-three. The *eight-fifty-three!*"

"The eight-twenty-seven," they decided unanimously.

"Then that'll just have to mean breakfast earlier," said Mrs. Russel brightly; "you won't mind, will you, girls?" Her appeal included Aunt Willoughby, who made no response. "You see, we couldn't hardly rush them over their breakfasts, could we?"

This was "home comforts." This was one of the privileges for which Rossiter paid her twenty-four shillings a week. Being sat round and watched while you were eating. Not being *rushed*. He had a vision of a "rushed breakfast," of whirling endlessly through space while one snapped at a sausage with little furtive bites; of munching bread and marmalade with the wind of one's velocity whistling through one's teeth.

Would it be better? Could it be worse?

Not worse than his chair-edge creaking against Miss Emily's; the unceasing consciousness of her unceasing consciousness of him. Not worse than Hilary Bevel, *vis-à-vis;* with her complacent prettiness, her tinkling, laboured witticisms. Not worse than Aunt Willoughby's baffled, bearded morosity; than Jervis Bevel's sleek disdain.

He would escape from Mrs. Russel, her advances, her criticisms, her fumbling arguments that crushed you down beneath their heavy gentleness until you felt you were being trampled to death by a cow. By a blind cow, that fumbled its way backwards and forwards across you. . . .

The "girls" delivered their ultimatum in chorus.

"England expects," declaimed Hilary, turning her eyes towards the ceiling, "effery woman to—er—do—er herr dew-ty."

"It's *nice* to be down early," said Miss Emily earnestly, "with a nice long day stretching out in front of me."

"Breakfast will be at quarter to eight sharp," said Mrs. Russel. "Mr. Rossiter, we really must *try* not to lose our collar-studs."

All his days and nights were loops, curving out from breakfast-time, curving back to it again. Inexorably, the loops grew smaller, the breakfasts longer; looming more and more over his nights, eating more and more out of his days.

Jervis Bevel's eyes swerved over to the mantelpiece. He pushed his chair back further over the bristling carpet pile.

"Well," he said, "I think it's almost time—"

The room broke up, the table grew smaller again as they all rose from their chairs. Mrs. Russel and Aunt

Willoughby gathered themselves together; Hilary seized Miss Emily by the back of the waist and punted her laughingly towards the door.

The coffee and the bacon and the hostility and the Christian forbearance blew out before them into the chilly hall.

Daffodils

MISS MURCHESON stopped at the corner of the High Street to buy a bunch of daffodils from the flower-man. She counted out her money very carefully, pouring a little stream of coppers from her purse into the palm of her hand.

"—ninepence—ten—eleven—pence halfpenny—*a shilling!* Thank you very much. Good afternoon."

A gust of wind rushed up the street, whirling her skirts up round her like a ballet-dancer's, and rustling the Reckitts-blue paper round the daffodils. The slender gold trumpets tapped and quivered against her face as she held them up with one hand and pressed her skirts down hastily with the other. She felt as though she had been enticed into a harlequinade by a company of Columbines who were quivering with laughter at her discomfiture; and looked round to see if anyone had witnessed her display of chequered moirette petticoat and the inches of black stocking above her boots. But the world remained unembarrassed.

Today the houses seemed taller and farther apart; the street wider and full of a bright, clear light that cast no shadows and was never sunshine. Under archways and between the houses the distances had a curious transparency, as though they had been painted upon glass. Against the luminous and indeterminate sky the Abbey tower rose distinct and delicate.

Miss Murcheson, forgetting all confusion, was conscious of her wings. She paused again to hitch up the bundle of exercise-books slithering down beneath her elbow, then took the dipping road as a bird swings down into the air. Her mouth was faintly acrid with spring dust and the scent of daffodils was in her nostrils. As she left the High Street farther behind her, the traffic sounded as a faint and murmurous hum, striking here and there a tinkling note like wind-bells.

Under her detachment she was conscious of the houses, the houses and the houses. They were square, flat-faced and plaster-fronted, painted creams and greys and buffs; one, a purplish-rose colour. Venetian shutters flat against the wall broadened the line of the windows, there were coloured fanlights over all the doors. Spiked railings before them shut off their little squares of grass or gravel from the road, and between the railings branches swung out to brush against her dress and recall her to the wonder of their budding loveliness.

Miss Murcheson remembered that her mother would be out for tea, and quickened her steps in anticipation of that delightful solitude. The silver birch tree that distinguished their front garden slanted beckoning her across the pavement. She hesitated, as her gate swung open, and stood looking up and down the road. She was sorry to go in, but could not resist the invitation of the empty house. She wondered if tomorrow would fill her with so strange a stirring as today. Soon, in a few months, it would be summer and there would be nothing more to come. Summer would be beautiful, but this spring made promise of a greater beauty than summer could fulfil; hinted at a mystery which other summers had evaded rather than explained. She went slowly up the steps, fumbling for her latch-key.

The day's dinner still hung dank and heavy in the air of the little hall. She stood in the doorway, with that square of light and sound behind her, craving the protection and the comfort with which that dark entrance had so often received her. There was a sudden desolation in the emptiness of the house.

Quickly she entered the sitting-room and flung open the window, which set the muslin curtains swaying in the breeze and clanked the little pictures on the walls. The window embrasure was so deep that there was little light in the corners of the room; armchairs and cabinets were lurking in the dusk. The square of daylight by the window was blocked by a bamboo table groaning under an array of photographs. In her sweeping mood she deposed the photographs, thrust the table to one side, and pulled her chair up into the window. "I can't correct my essays in the dark," she asserted, though she had done so every evening of the year.

"How tight-laced you are, poor Columbines," she

said, throwing away the paper and seeing how the bass
cut deep into the fleshy stems. "You were brave above
it all, but—there now!" She cut the bass and shook the
flowers out into a vase. "I can't correct," she sighed,
"with you all watching me. You are so terribly flippant!"

But what a curious concidence: she had set her class
to write an essay upon Daffodils! "You shall judge;
I'll read them all out loud. They *will* amuse you." She
dipped her pen in the red-ink pot with an anticipatory
titter.

With a creak of wheels a young woman went by
slowly, wheeling a perambulator. She leant heavily on
the handle-bar, tilting the perambulator on its two back
wheels, and staring up, wide-mouthed, at the windows.

"How nice to be so much interested," thought Miss
Murcheson, pressing open the first exercise-book. "But
I'm sure it can't be a good thing for the baby."

The essays lacked originality. Each paragraph sidled
up self-consciously to openings for a suitable quotation,
to rush each one through with a gasp of triumph.

> *"And then my heart with pleasure fills*
> *And dances with the daffodils."*

> *"Fair daffodils, we weep to see*
> *You fade away so soon."*

She wondered if any of her class could weep for the
departure of a daffodil. Mostly they had disclaimed
responsibility for such weakness by the stern prefix,

"As the poet says—." Flora Hopwood had, she remembered, introduced a "Quotation Dictionary," which must have been round her circle.

"I must forbid it. Why can't they see things for themselves, think them out? I don't believe they ever really see anything, just accept things on the authority of other people. I could make them believe anything. What a responsibility teaching is— But is it? They'd believe me, but they wouldn't care. It wouldn't matter, really.

"They're so horribly used to things. Nothing ever comes new to them that they haven't grown up with. They get their very feelings out of books. Nothing ever surprises or impresses them. When spring comes they get preoccupied, stare dreamily out of the windows. They're thinking out their new hats. Oh, if only I didn't know them quite so well, or knew them a little better!

"If I had a school of my own," she meditated, running her eyes down the pages and mechanically underlining spelling-mistakes, "I would make them think. I'd horrify them, if nothing better. But here—how ever can one, teaching at a High School? Miss Peterson would—

"They *do* like me. At least, one set does, I know. I'm rather a cult, they appreciate my Titian hair. They'd like me more, though, if I knew how to do it better, and knew better how to use my eyes. Their sentimentality embarrasses me. In a way they're so horribly mature, I feel at a disadvantage with them. If only they'd be a little more spontaneous. But spontaneity is beyond them at present. They're simply calves, after all, rather sophisticated calves."

She dreamed, and was awakened by familiar laughter. Nobody's laughter in particular, but surely it was the laughter of the High School? Three girls were passing with arms close-linked, along the pavement underneath her window. She looked down on the expressive, tilted ovals of their sailor hats; then, on an impulse, smacked the window-sill to attract their attention. Instantly they turned up three pink faces of surprise, which broadened into smiles of recognition.

"Hullo, Miss Murcheson!"

"Hullo, children! Come in for a minute and talk to me. I'm all alone."

Millicent, Rosemary, and Doris hesitated, eying one another, poised for flight. "Righto!" they agreed unanimously.

Miss Murcheson, all of a flutter, went round to open the front door. She looked back at the sitting-room as though she had never seen it before.

Why had she asked them in, those terrible girls whom she had scarcely spoken to? They would laugh at her, they would tell the others.

The room was full of them, of their curiosity and embarrassment and furtive laughter. She had never realized what large girls they were; how plump and well-developed. She felt them eying her stack of outraged relatives, the photographs she swept off on to a chair; their eyes flitted from the photographs to the daffodils, from the daffodils to the open, red-scored exercise-books.

"Yes," she said, "your writings, I daresay. Do you recognize them? I was correcting 'Daffodils' and they made me dreary—sit down, won't you?—*dreary*. I wonder if any of you have ever used your senses; smelt, or *seen* things— Oh, *do* sit down!"

She seemed to be shouting into a forest of thick bodies. They seated themselves along the edge of an ottoman in a bewildered row; this travestied their position in the class-room and made her feel, facing them, terribly official and instructive. She tried to shake this off.

"It's cruel, isn't it, to lie in wait for you like this and pull you in and lecture you about what you don't feel about daffodils!"

Her nervous laughter tinkled out into silence.

"It was a beastly subject," said someone, heavily.

"Beastly? Oh, Mill—Rosemary, have you never seen a daffodil?"

They giggled.

"No, but looked at one?" Her earnestness swept aside her embarrassment. "Not just heard about them— 'Oh yes, daffodils: yellow flowers; spring, mother's vases, bulbs, borders, flashing past flower-shop windows'—but taken one up in your hands and felt it?"

How she was haranguing them!

"It's very difficult to be clever about things one's *used* to," said Millicent. "That's why history essays are so much easier. You tell us about things, and we just write them down."

"That's why you're so lazy; you're using *my* brains; just giving me back what I gave you again, a little bit the worse for the wear."

They looked hurt and uncomfortable.

Doris got up and walked over to the fireplace.

("Good," thought Miss Murcheson, "it will relieve the tension a bit if they will only begin to prowl.")

"What a pretty photograph, Miss Murcheson. Who is it? Not—not *you?*"

"*Me?*" said Miss Murcheson with amusement. "Yes. Why not? Does it surprise you, then?"

"You've got such a *dinky* hat on!" cried the girl, with naïve astonishment.

The others crowded round her.

"You look so different," said Doris, still scrutinizing the photograph. "Awfully happy, and prosperous, and—cocksure."

"Perhaps it was the hat!" suggested Millicent.

"Oh, *Millicent!* No, I'm sure Miss Murcheson was *thinking* about something nice."

"Or somebody."

"Oh, Doris, you are awful!"

They all giggled, and glanced apprehensively across at her.

She wondered why she was not more offended by them.

"As a matter of fact," she enlightened them, "*that*

was because of daffodils. It just illustrates my point, curiously enough."

They were still absorbed.

"Oh, Miss *Murcheson!*"

"*Miss* Murcheson!"

"When was it taken?"

"Last Easter holidays. Nearly a year ago. At Seabrooke. By a friend of mine."

"*Do-oo* give me one!"

"—And me?"

"I'm afraid that's the only print I've got; and that's Mother's."

"Were there more?"

"Yes, various people took them. You see, I haven't faced a real camera for years, so when I got these snaps they were scrambled for by people who'd been asking me for photos."

"People?" She was rising visibly in their estimation.

"Oh yes. Friends."

"Why *daffodils?*" reverted Rosemary.

"Somebody had just given me a great big bunch." She was impressed by their interest. "I wonder if daffodils will ever make any of you look like that."

"It all depends, you see," said Millicent, astutely. "Nobody has ever given us any. If they *did* perhaps—"

"*Really?*" said Miss Murcheson, with innocent concern. "Take all those, if they would really inspire you! No, dears, I'd *like* you to."

She gathered the daffodils together and lifted them, dripping, from the vase.

The girls retreated.

"Oh no, really, *not* your daffodils—"

"We don't mean—"

"Not *your* daffodils, Miss Murcheson. It wasn't *that* a bit."

Evidently a false move on her part. She was bewildered by them; could not fathom the depths of their cinema-bred romanticism.

Doris had put away the photograph and stood with her back to the others, fingering the ornaments on the chimney-piece.

"There are lots of things," she said rapidly, "that you only feel because of people. That's the only reason things are there for, I *think*. You wouldn't notice them otherwise, or care about them. It's only sort of—" She stopped. Her ears glowed crimson underneath her hat.

"Association," they sighed, ponderously.

"That's exactly what's the matter," cried Miss Murcheson. "We've got all the nice, fresh, independent, outside things so smeared over with our sentimentalities and prejudices and—associations—that we can't see them anyhow but as part of ourselves. That's how you're—we're missing things and spoiling things for ourselves. You—we don't seem able to *discover*."

"Life," said Doris sententiously, "is a very big adventure. Of course we all see *that*."

The other two looked at her quickly. All three became suddenly hostile. She was encouraging them to outrage the decencies of conversation. It was bad form, this flagrant discussion of subjects only for their most secret and fervid whisperings.

To her, they were still unaccountable. She had not wished to probe.

"I don't think that's what I meant," she said a little flatly. "Of course your lives will be full of interesting things, and those will be your own affairs. Only, if I could be able, I'm always trying, to make you care about the little fine things you might pass over, that have such big roots underground.

"I should like you to be as happy as I've been, and as I'm going to be," she said impulsively. "I should love to watch you after you've left my form, going up and up the school, and getting bigger, and then, when you've left, going straight and clearly to the essential things."

The tassel of the blind cord tapped against the window-sill, through the rustling curtains they looked out on to the road.

They had awaited a disclosure intimate and personal. The donor of those last year's daffodils had taken form, portentous in their minds. But she had told them nothing, given them the stone of her abstract, colourless idealism while they sat there, open-mouthed for sentimental bread.

"Won't you stay to tea?" she asked. "Oh, *do*. We'll picnic; boil the kettle on the gas-ring, and eat sticky buns—I've got a bag of sticky buns. We'll have a party in honour of the daffodils."

The prospect allured her, it would be a fantastic interlude.

They all got up.

"Doris and Millicent are coming to tea with me, Miss Murcheson. Mother's expecting us, thanks most awfully. Else we should have loved to."

"We should have loved to," echoed the others. "Thanks most awfully."

She felt a poignant disappointment and relief, as standing with her eyes on the daffodils, she heard the children clattering down the steps.

Tomorrow they will be again impersonal; three pink moons in a firmament of faces.

The three, released, eyed one another with a common understanding.

"Miss Murcheson has never really *lived*," said Doris.

They linked arms again and sauntered down the road.

The Return

Mr. AND Mrs. TOTTENHAM had come home.

The moist brown gravel of the drive and sweep bore impress of their fly wheels. Lydia Broadbent listened from the doorstep to the receding gritty rumble of the empty fly, and the click and rattle as the gate swung to. Behind her, in the dusky hall, Mr. Tottenham shouted directions for the disposal of the luggage, flustered servants bumped against each other and recoiled, and Porloch the gardener shouldered the heavy trunks with gasps and lurches, clutching at the banisters until they creaked.

Lydia heard Mrs. Tottenham burst open the drawing-room door and cross the threshold with her little customary pounce, as though she hoped to catch somebody unawares. She pictured her looking resentfully round her, and knew that presently she would hear her tweaking at the curtains. During her six weeks of solitude the house had grown very human to Lydia. She felt now as if it were drawing itself together into a

26

nervous rigour, as a man draws himself together in suffering irritation at the entrance of a fussy wife.

"Were these all the letters, Lydia? I hope none were forwarded to Wickly? Porloch, do be careful of the paint! The fly was very stuffy, Lydia. I wish you'd ordered one of Bicklesfield's. His are always clean."

Mrs. Tottenham had darted out of the drawing-room, swept up her letters from the table, and stood hesitating at the bottom of the stairs.

"You might order tea immediately. Yes, the drawing-room for today." A red shimmer of firelight invited them through the open door. "Herbert, *Her*-bert!"

Mr. Tottenham was clattering in the smoking-room. His face peered crossly at them round the door.

"I wondered if you had gone upstairs. Porloch has been very careless of the paint. You might have watched him, Lydia!" She vanished slowly into the gloom above.

Lydia went into the drawing-room and stood warming her hands before the fire. A servant with a lighted taper passed from gas-bracket to gas-bracket and the greenish lights sprang upwards in her wake. Outside the brown gloom deepened over the November garden. The young distorted trees loomed dark and sullen, the air was thick with moisture, heavy with decay.

Today there had been no time to think. Lydia was aware but dimly of a sense of desolation and of loss. Something was shattered that had built itself around her during these coherent weeks, something violated which had been sacred unawares. Every fibre of her quivered

with hostility to these invaders who were the owners
of the house. She was at odds with herself again, at
odds with her surroundings. She stared at her gaunt reflection in the fireplace and knew that her best companion had drawn back again, forbidding her. She would
be baffled once again by the hostility of Lydia Broadbent, her derision, her unsparing scorn. "I was such
friends with myself when they left us together; we
were so harmonious and at ease with each other, me
and myself and the house. Now we are afraid and angry
with each other again."

Mr. and Mrs. Tottenham were impossible. They
were childless, humourless, and dyspeptic. They were
not even funny. There was nothing bizarre about them,
or tragic or violent or farcical. They neither loved nor
hated each other, there was nothing they did not know
about each other; no mystery or fear between them. In
the early days of their marriage they had been actively
and articulately unhappy. She had had a lover; he had
left her for months together and lived in some drab
wickedness elsewhere. Then her lover had deserted her,
he had been left more money; they had drifted together
again, bought "The Laurels," spun their shams and
miseries around them like a web and lurked within
them. They visited, were reputable and entertained;
and kept a home for Mr. Tottenham's nephew, their
expectant heir.

"Lydia?"

The thin voice fluted over the banisters. Lydia hurried upstairs, flicked at a panel of Mrs. Tottenham's

door, and entered, her footsteps muffled among the woolliness of many rugs. There was a blot of yellow light from a candle on the writing-table. Mrs. Tottenham stood beside the bed, staring at two sheets of close-written paper and an envelope, which she held out fan-wise between rigid fingers, as one holding a hand at cards.

"Did—has my husband taken his mail yet? Did he overlook the letters?"

"I think Mr. Tottenham's post is still lying on the hall table. Is there anything you want to show him?" They had all their correspondence in common; it was quite impersonal.

"No, no, Lydia, shut the door, please. Is tea up? It *is* draughty: I should have liked a fire. You might get the things out of my dressing-bag—there, it's over on the sofa."

This constant attendance was to begin again. Lydia was well schooled to it; why had she forgotten?

She unpacked the combs and brushes, and Mrs. Tottenham fidgeted before the glass.

"Light the gas, please. I hate this half-light!" There was resentment in her glance towards the window, where the last daylight leaked in faintly through draperies of parchment-coloured lace. Why was Mrs. Tottenham so agitated, tugging her hat off and patting at her crimped and faded hair?

She bent to a level with the mirror; haggard-eyed and grinning with anxiety, she searched her bleached and baggy face to find what prettiness was there. Lydia

watched her with apathetic curiosity from where, on
her knees beside the sofa, she unwrapped the shoes and
bottles from their little holland bags.

"Have you seen the photo," asked Mrs. Tottenham
suddenly, "of me when I was twenty-five? On the
chiffonier—the plush-framed one—you *must* know it!"

Lydia assented.

"It's a good one, isn't it? D'you think it's like me—
now, I mean?"

"Quite a likeness, really, considering."

"*Considering?*" (How sharp her voice was!)

"Oh, change of fashions makes a difference, doesn't
it, and, well . . . time, of course."

"Of course I know it wasn't taken yesterday, Lydia.
I don't need telling. But I'm a lot younger than Mr.
Tottenham to look at. There was a gentleman at the
Hydro took us for father and daughter, really he did!"

Her voice was by turns peremptory, confidential, almost appealing. It died out into silence.

The room was restive and disturbed. "Oh, you unhappy house," thought Lydia. "They have broken into
your silence and given you nothing in return."

"Tea will be ready, I think," she reminded. Mrs.
Tottenham turned sharply from the glass, and Lydia
saw with amazement that she had reddened her lips.
They shone with sticky brightness in her sallow face.

Mrs. Tottenham was conscious of her glance.
"Shows rather, doesn't it?" she queried diffidently, and
rubbed her mouth with the back of her hand till the
red was smeared out over her cheeks.

"One looks so washy after a journey. Just a touch of colour—one wouldn't notice it, hardly, if it wasn't for the glare." Her muttered extenuations were not addressed to Lydia.

They heard the tea-tray rattling through the hall. Lydia turned the light out, and they prepared to descend. Mrs. Tottenham pawed her in the twilight. "You needn't mention to Mr. Tottenham I've opened any of my letters. I'll be showing him the rest. This one was rather particular—from a friend of mine, it was." An appeal still quavered in her husky tones which her paid companion had never heard before.

From the drawing-room they saw Mr. Tottenham scurrying across the grass, drawn teawards by the lighted window. There was something quick and furtive about him; Lydia had never been able to determine whether he dodged and darted as pursuer or pursued.

"Wretched evening, wretched." He chattered his way across the crowded room. "Been talking to Porloch—garden's in an awful way; shrubberies like a jungle. Did 'e sell the apples?"

He darted the inquiry at Lydia, turning his head sharply towards her, with his eyes averted as though he could not bear to look at her. At first she had imagined that her appearance repulsed him. She knew herself for a plain woman, but now she had learnt that he never looked at anybody if he could avoid it.

"Oh, he sold them well, I believe. I thought he wrote about them?"

"Oh yes, yes, sharp man, Porloch. Dickie been running round for his things?"

"Not often. He says he wants his letters forwarded to Elham till further notice."

The reference to Elham tickled Dickie's uncle. He put his cup down, giggled, mopped at his mouth and darted a side glance at his wife.

Mrs. Tottenham was not listening. She sat very stiff and upright, staring straight before her, crumbling at her cake.

"Hey, Mollie! Dickie's gone to Elham. Didgehear that? Pore old Dickie's gone to Elham again! Never wrote and told me, never told me anything. The young dog!"

The silence was once more outraged by his falsetto giggles.

He held his cup out for Lydia to refill, and she watched with fascination the convulsive movements his throat made while he drank.

"Hey, Mollie! Don't forget we're going to the Gunnings tomorrow. Write it down, my dear girl, write it down, and tell them about orderin' the cab." He always referred to Lydia obliquely as "they" or "them."

"Gunning's a good fellow," he informed the fireplace.

"This cake is uneatable, Lydia. Wherever did you buy it?" Her grumble lacked conviction; it was a perfunctory concession to her distrust of her companion's housekeeping.

"Birch's. I'm sorry, Mrs. Tottenham. Aren't you

ready for more tea? It's nice and hot for you, isn't it, after the journey?"

Lydia felt as though she had caught her own eye, and was embarrassed and discomfited. She listened with derision to her glib and sugary banalities of speech. "The perfect companion!" taunted the hostile self. "What about all those fine big truths and principles we reasoned out together? Yesterday we believed you were sincere. '*Nice and hot after the journey.*' Bah!"

The mirror in the overmantel now fascinated Mrs. Tottenham. She finished her tea mechanically, laid her cup down and stood before the fireplace, patting and tweaking at her hair. Her husband looked at her contemptuously. "Pretty little daughter I've got!" he mumbled, with his mouth full of cake. It was a bitter comment on the mistake made by the gentleman at the Hydro.

Mrs. Tottenham put her hands before her face and hurried from the room.

Lydia began to gather up the tea things, and a servant darkened the windows with a musty clatter of Venetian blinds. Mr. Tottenham's chair creaked as he stretched his legs out to the fire. The room was hot with the smell of tea and tea-cakes, and the smell of upholstery and wilting ferns was drawn out by the heat.

The hall outside was cold and quiet. The sense of the afternoon's invasion had subsided from it like a storm. Through a strip of door the morning-room beckoned her with its associations of the last six weeks. She saw the tall uncurtained windows grey-white in the gloom.

Her book lay open on a table: she shut it with a sense of desolation. It would never be finished now, it was too good a thing to read while *they* were in the house; to be punctuated by *her* petulant insistent chatter, *his* little shuffling, furtive steps. If only this room were all her own: inviolable. She could leave the rest of the house to them, to mar and bully, if she had only a few feet of silence of her own, to exclude the world from, to build up in something of herself.

If she did not go upstairs now Mrs. Tottenham would call her, and that, in this room, would be more than she could bear. Vaguely she pictured headlines: " 'Laurels' Murder Mystery. Bodies in a Cistern. Disappearance of Companion." The darkness was all lurid with her visionary crime.

Mrs. Tottenham had not been round the house. She did not say the rooms smelt mouldy, and she left the curtain-draperies alone.

Lydia wondered deeply.

"Did you know Sevenoaks?"

The question abashed her. What had Mrs. Tottenham to do with Sevenoaks?

"N—no. Scarcely. I've been over there sometimes for the day, from Orpington."

"A friend of mine lives there—a Mr. Merton. He wrote to me today. He's come back from the Colonies and bought a place there. It's funny to hear from an old friend, suddenly. It makes me feel quite funny, really."

She did not sound funny. Her voice was high-pitched with agitation. Lydia had been told all about Mrs. Tottenham's friends, and seldom listened. But she did not remember Mr. Merton.

"He wants to come and see us. I really hardly like, you know, to suggest the idea to Mr. Tottenham."

"I thought you'd all your friends in common. How well these night-dresses have washed! They must have laundered nicely at the Hydro."

"Ah, but this is different, you see." She laughed a little conscious laugh. "Mr. Merton was a particular *friend* of mine. I—Mr. Tottenham didn't used to know him."

"I see," said Lydia vaguely. "A friend of yours before your marriage."

"Well, no. You see, I was very young when I was married. Quite an inexperienced young girl—a child, you might almost say."

Lydia supposed that Mrs. Tottenham *had* been young. She strained her imagination to the effort.

"I did very well for myself when I married Mr. Tottenham," the wife said sharply. "I must say I never was a fool. My mother'd never brought me up to go about, but we did a good deal of entertaining at one time, Mr. Tottenham's friends and my own, and we always had things very nice and showy. But it was a lonely life."

Mrs. Tottenham's confidences were intolerable. Better a hundred times that she should nag.

"So you liked the Hydro—found it really comfortable?"

"Oh yes. But it's the coming back—to this.
. . . Lydia, you're a good sort of girl. I wonder if I ought to tell you."

"Don't tell me anything you would regret," said Lydia defensively, jerking at the drawer-handles.

"You see, Mr. Merton was a good deal to me at one time; then we tore it, and he went off to Canada and married there. I heard he'd been unhappy, and that there was the rumour of a split. Of course he didn't write or anything; we had ab-so-lutely *torn* it; but I couldn't help hearing things, and she seems to have been a really bad sort of woman—there were children, too. He's bringing the children back with him to Sevenoaks.

"He wants to come and see me. He's been thinking about me a great deal, he says, and wondering if I've changed, and wishing— He always was a straight sort of man; it was only circumstances drove him crooked. I daresay I was a good bit to blame. I've kept his photograph, though I know I didn't ought, but I liked having it by me to look at."

She had unlocked a drawer and held a stiff-backed photograph up beneath the light, scrutinizing it. Lydia listened to a distant surge of movement in the house beneath her; steps across the oil-cloth, windows shutting, voices cut off by the swinging of a door. She felt, revoltedly, as though Mrs. Tottenham were stepping out of her clothes.

"He says he's hardly changed at all. Seventeen years

—they go past you like a flash, he says, when you're working."

"Seventeen years," said Lydia deliberately, "are bound to make a difference to a woman. Did you care for him?"

Mrs. Tottenham made no answer; she was staring at the photograph. Her eyes dilated, and she licked her lips.

"I suppose you'll be glad to see him again?" suggested Lydia. She felt suddenly alert and interested, as though she were watching through the lens of a microscope some tortured insect twirling on a pin.

Mrs. Tottenham sat down stiffly on the sofa, and laid the photo on her lap. Suddenly she clasped her hands and put them up before her eyes.

"I couldn't," she gasped. "Not after all these years I couldn't. Not like this. O Lord, I've got so ugly! I can't pretend—I haven't got the heart to risk it. It's been so real to me, I couldn't bear to lose him.

"It's all gone, it's all gone. I've been pretending. I used to be a fine figure of a woman. How can I have the heart to care when I couldn't keep him caring?"

"You broke it off. It was all over and done with, you told me so. It was wrong, besides. Why should either of you want to rake it up when it was all past and done with seventeen years ago?"

"Because it *was* wrong. It's this awful *rightness* that's killing me. My husband's been a bad man, too, but here we both are, smirking and grinning at each other, just to keep hold of something we neither of us want."

Lydia was terrified by the dry, swift sobbing. She felt suddenly hard and priggish and immature. All her stresses, her fears and passions, were such twilight things.

Mrs. Tottenham stood upright and held the photograph in the flame of the gas jet, watching the ends curl upwards. For all her frizzled hair and jingling ornaments and smudgy tentative cosmetics she was suddenly elemental and heroic.

It was over.

Lydia went quietly out of the room and shut the door behind her.

The place was vibrant with the humanity of Mrs. Tottenham. It was as though a child had been born in the house.

The Confidante

You are losing your imagination," cried Maurice.

It was a bitter reproach. He stood over her, rumpling up his hair, and the wiry tufts sprang upright, quivering from his scalp.

Penelope gulped, then sat for a moment in a silence full of the consciousness of her brutality. She had never dreamed that her secret preoccupation would be so perceptible to Maurice. Unconsciously she had been drawing her imaginations in upon herself like the petals of a flower, and her emotions buzzed and throbbed within them like a pent-up bee.

The room was dark with rain, and they heard the drip and rustle of leaves in the drinking garden. Through the open window the warm, wet air blew in on them, and a shimmer of rain was visible against the trees beyond.

"I never meant—" began Penelope.

"I beg your pardon," said Maurice stiffly. "I suppose I am becoming quite insufferable. I have been making perfectly unjustifiable demands on your sympathy and patience and—imagination. I am an egotistical brute, I daresay. Of course there is not the slightest reason why you—" His indulgence intimated that there was, on the contrary, every reason why she should. . . . "I felt a bit *jarred* just now," he excused himself, with simple pathos.

"I never meant, a bit—" resumed Penelope.

"I know, I know," said Maurice, all magnanimity. The sickly sweetness of this reconciliation overpowered her.

"What a pair of fools we are!" she cried hysterically. "Maurice, dear, we're wearing this thing thin. I'm afraid I've been doing gallery to you and Veronica for the last six months, and you've both played up to me magnificently. But—"

"Veronica—" protested Maurice.

"Oh, yes, Veronica comes here too. She comes and sits for hours over there, just where you are now. There's not an aspect of your emotional relationship that we've not discussed. Veronica's coming here this afternoon," she said abruptly. "She's a chilly person. I'd better light the fire."

"God!" said Maurice.

Penelope was on her knees before the fireplace, her head almost inside the grate. Her voice came hollowly from the dark recess.

"I thought you'd be surprised," she said. ("Damn, it will *not* light!")

"Surprised!" said Maurice. "Penelope"—his tone had

the deadly reasonableness of a driven man's—"I think you hardly realize what you're doing. I know you meant well, my good girl, but really— It puts us in such an impossible position. Surely you must see."

"I see quite well," she assured him. "You and she both breathe and have your being in an atmosphere of conspiracy; it's your natural element, of course. To force you into the straighter, broader courses of the uncomplex would be as cruel as to upset a bowl with gold-fish in it and leave them gasping on the table-cloth. Ooh!" She sat back on her heels and ruefully beheld her grimy fingers.

Maurice tried his hardest to endure her. She heard him breathing heavily.

"It's really quite *unnecessary* to have a fire," she soliloquized. "But it makes a point in a room, I always think. Keeps one in countenance. Humanizes things a bit. Makes a centre point for—"

She became incoherent. Maurice's irritation audibly increased. They were both conscious of the oppression of the darkening, rain-loud room.

"You're forcing our hands rather," said Maurice.

"Forcing you into the banality of meeting each other sanely and normally in my drawing-room, with no necessity to converse in allusions, insinuations, and *doubles-entendres?* With me blessing you both and beaming sympathetically on you from afar? Bullying you into that? . . .

"I'm sorry!" she flashed round on him, impenitently.

"You don't understand," he winced, and looked

round him for his hat. "I think it would be best for me to go."

"I suppose I mustn't keep you," she conceded with polite reluctance. "But I think you really ought to see Veronica. She has—she will have something of particular importance to say to you. I shall go, of course."

"Oh, don't!"

"But surely—?"

"There's nothing we can keep from you. And it makes it easier for both of us—as things are."

"But do you never want to be alone with her?"

Maurice considered.

"I don't believe," said Penelope, swiftly, "that you two have ever been alone together for a second since your—acquaintanceship—began."

"No," said Maurice, sombrely. "There have always been outsiders."

"Audiences," murmured Penelope.

"I beg your pardon?"

"Oh, nothing. Well, you'll be alone this afternoon. I'm going out," she said with firmness.

"But don't you *understand?*"

"Oh, I understand the strain will be colossal—would have been. But there've been developments—suddenly. Veronica'll have a great deal to tell you. Has it never occurred to you she might get free after all? There'll be heaps to say," she said, significantly.

"For heaven's sake—!" He threw up his hands again and paced the room in agitation, stumbling over stools.

"That was why I pulled up just now," she continued.

"Seemed hard, perhaps, apathetic and unsympathetic when you were talking all that about awfulness, refined irony, frustration, and things. I was thinking how soon you'd—if you only knew— And then you told me I was losing my imagination."

"For which I have already begged your pardon," said Maurice, patiently.

Penelope rose from the hearthrug and threw herself on to the chesterfield. Maurice turned to her with a goaded expression, and she regarded him with shining eyes. Then the door opened with a jerk, and Veronica entered stiffly, with a rustle of agitation.

Maurice drew back into the shadow, and Veronica hesitated for a moment in the centre of the room, then groped out her hands towards Penelope, as though she could see little in this sudden gloom.

"Tell me," she cried, without preliminaries, "you, you heard from Victor?"

Penelope, who had risen, glanced across at Maurice. He took his cue.

"Veronica!" he quavered huskily.

Veronica's shoulders twitched. She turned on him in the dusk like a wild thing, with an expression that was almost baleful.

"You!" she said.

"Er—yes," admitted Maurice. "I'd simply no idea that I should . . . I just came in. By chance, you know."

"It's just as well, isn't it?" interposed Penelope. "We've—you've simply got to talk things out, Veronica; tell him. Show him Victor's letter." She moved towards the door.

"Don't go!" shrieked Veronica. "You've got to explain to him. I can't," she said, with the finality of helplessness.

The rain had stopped, and through a sudden break in the clouds the watery sunshine streamed across the garden. Veronica sat down on an ottoman facing the window, and Penelope knelt beside her, looking at her pitifully.

The long, pale oval of her face was marred and puckered by emotion, fair hair lay in streaks across her forehead, her clothes were glistening from the rain. Many tears had worn their mournful rivulets through the lavish powder on her nose. Her gloved hands lay across her lap, in one was clutched a sheet of blue-grey notepaper. She would not look at Maurice, but turned pathetic eyes on Penelope and made appeal with soundless moving lips.

"Veronica has had a letter from Victor," said Penelope, slowly and distinctly. "He releases her from her engagement. He says . . . he explains . . . He is not so blind as you both seem to have thought, and he has seen for some time that Veronica was not happy. He has noticed that she has been listless and preoccupied, and has interpreted her unhappiness—rightly! He is convinced, he says, that Veronica has ceased to care for him, but that she is too scrupulous, or not quite brave enough perhaps, to speak out and make an end of things herself. He knows that her affections are elsewhere, and he believes that he is doing the best thing he can for her by setting her free."

Veronica had turned a little, and set facing Maurice. Penelope saw the golden flicker of her lashes; the blue letter fluttered to the ground from between her writhing fingers.

"The trousseau was all bought," she faltered. "The going-away dress came from Pam's this morning, just before I got that letter."

Penelope could not speak; she felt utterly inadequate. Maurice shifted his position, and stood leaning up against the window-frame; with intensity of interest he turned his head and looked into the garden.

"It's stopped raining," he observed. Veronica did not move; but Penelope saw her eyes slide sideways, following his movements under drooping lids.

"How do you know all this," Maurice asked abruptly, "what Victor says and that, when you've had no time to read his letter?"

"He wrote to me, too," said Penelope. She heard her own voice, self-conscious and defiant.

"To *you!* Why you?"

"But we know each other—rather well. Since much longer than he's known Veronica. And, well, you see I'm her cousin. He thought I'd make things easier for for her. Do the explaining as far as possible. Probably he thought I'd speak to you."

She stealthily touched her pocket and smiled to feel the crisp thick letter-paper crackle beneath her hand. Then she wondered if the sound were audible to the others, and glanced guiltily from one to the other of them. But they sat there silent, embarrassed, heavily preoccupied, one on either side of her.

"So now—," she said with bright aggressiveness. She could have shaken them.

"I do not think," said Veronica, in a small determined voice, "that I am justified in accepting Victor's sacrifice."

"He is extraordinarily generous," said Maurice, without enthusiasm.

"The loneliness," went on Veronica, gazing wide-eyed down some terrible vista. "Picture it, Penelope, the disappointment and the blankness for him. I could never have loved him, but I would have been a good wife to him." (Her voice rose in a crescendo of surprise. She thought "How genuine I am!") "We—we had made so many plans," she faltered; fumbled, found no handkerchief, and spread her hands before her face.

Penelope gave a little gasp, half sympathetic. She was praying hard for tact.

"Veronica," she said, "I don't think you should let that stand between you and Maurice. You mustn't be too soft-hearted, dear. I don't think Victor's altogether unhappy. He's relieved, I know. You see, the last few weeks have been an awful strain for him, as well as— other people."

"How do you know?"

"He told me."

"You've been discussing me. Oh, Penelope, this is intolerable!"

"He had been talking to me; he had no one else. For a long time, I suppose, he put me in the position of a sister-in-law."

"That was going too far!" cried Maurice. "Had you neither of you the slightest idea of loyalty to Veronica?"

Penelope ignored him. She leant suddenly forward, crimson-cheeked, and kissed Veronica.

"Oh, my dear," she said, "did you think that because you couldn't care about Victor nobody else could? Do you expect him to go on giving you everything when you've got nothing to give him?"

They looked at her, dazzled by a flash of comprehension. When she rose from between them she left a gap, a gap she knew to be unbridgeable for both. They were face to face with the hideous simplicity of life. She had upset their bowl and left the two poor goldfish gasping in an inclement air.

"Now at last you two have got each other," she cried, smiling at them from the threshold. "Nothing more to bother or disturb you. Just be as happy and as thankful as you can!"

They sat in silence till the last ironical echo died away. Then, *"Don't go!"* they cried in unison.

But she was gone.

Requiescat

M AJENDIE had bought the villa on his honeymoon, and in April, three months after his death, his widow went out there alone to spend the spring and early summer. Stuart, who had been in India at the time of Howard Majendie's death, wrote to Mrs. Majendie before starting for home and her reply awaited him at his club; he re-read it several times, looking curiously at her writing which he had never seen before. The name of the villa was familiar to him, Majendie had been speaking of it the last time they dined together; he said it had a garden full of lemon trees and big cypresses, and more fountains than you could imagine—it was these that Ellaline had loved. Stuart pictured Mrs. Majendie walking about among the lemon-trees in her widow's black.

In her letter she expressed a wish to see him—in a little while. "I shall be returning to England at the end of June; there is a good deal of business to go through, and there are several things that Howard wished me to

48

discuss with you. He said you would be willing to advise and help me. I do not feel that I can face England before then; I have seen nobody yet, and it is difficult to make a beginning. You understand that I feel differently about meeting you; Howard wished it, and I think that is enough for both of us. If you were to be in Italy I should ask you to come and see me here, but as I know that you will be going straight to Ireland I will keep the papers until June, all except the very important ones, which I must sign without quite understanding, I suppose." In concluding, she touched on his friendship with Howard as for her alone it was permissible to touch. Stuart wired his apologies to Ireland and planned a visit to the Italian lakes.

Three weeks afterwards found him in the prow of a motor-boat, furrowing Lake Como as he sped towards the villa. The sky was cloudless, the hills to the right rose sheer above him, casting the lengthening shadows of the afternoon across the luminous and oily water; to the left were brilliant and rugged above the clustered villages. The boat shot closely under Cadenabbia and set the orange-hooded craft bobbing; the reflected houses rocked and quivered in her wake, colours flecked the broken water.

"Subito, subito!" said the boatman reassuringly and Stuart started; he did not know that his impatience was so evident. The man shut off his engines, let the boat slide farther into the shore, and displacing Stuart from the prow, crouched forward with a ready boat-hook. They were approaching the water-stairway of the villa.

For a few moments after he had landed, while the motor-boat went chuffing out again into the sunshine, Stuart stood at the top of the stairway looking irresolutely through the iron gates. He was wondering why he had come to Italy, and whether he even cared at all for Mrs. Majendie. He felt incapable of making his way towards her under the clustered branches of those trees. If there had been a little side-gate it would have been easier to go in; it would not have been so difficult, either, if he had ever been here with Howard Majendie. But this was *Her* place; she had loved it because of the fountains.

He pushed open the big gate, already cold in the shadow, and followed the upward curve of the avenue among the lemon trees. Beyond the villa disclosed itself, unlike all that he had expected; he was surprised at his own surprise and did not realize till then how clearly he must have visualized it. There was a wide loggia, a flight of steps, a terrace on a level with the loggia running along the side of the hill. Cypress trees rose everywhere, breaking up the view. He passed under the windows, climbed the steps and crossed the loggia, not looking to left or right for fear that he might see her suddenly, or even one of her books. The loggia had an air of occupation; it was probable that on any of those tables, or among the cushions, he might see her book, half open, or the long-handled lorgnettes that Majendie had given her in France.

The servant said that Mrs. Majendie was in the gar-

den. She showed Stuart into a tall, cool parlour and
disappeared to find her mistress. Stuart, distracted by a
scent of heliotrope, made an unseeing circle of the
room; he was standing before a Florentine chest when
the girl came back with a message. Mrs. Majendie
would see him in the garden. It would have been easier
to meet her here; he had pictured them sitting opposite
to one another in these high-backed chairs. He followed
the girl obediently out of the house, along the terrace,
and down a long alley between hedges of yew. The
white plume of a fountain quivered at the end, other
fountains were audible in the garden below. He could
hear footsteps, too; someone was approaching by another alley that converged with his beyond the fountain. Here they met.

She was less beautiful than he had remembered her,
and very tall and thin in her black dress. Her com-
posure did not astonish him; her smile, undimmed, and
the sound of her voice recalled to him the poignancy of
his feelings when he had first known her, his resentment
and sense of defeat—she had possessed herself of Howard so entirely. She was shortsighted, there was always
a look of uncertainty in her eyes until she came quite
near one, her big pupils seemed to see too much at once
and nothing very plainly.

"I never knew you were in Italy," she said.

He realized that it would have been more considerate
to have written to prepare her for his visit.

"I came out," he said, "quite suddenly. I had always

wanted to see the Lakes. And I wanted to see you, but perhaps I should have written. I—I never thought . . . It would have been better."

"It doesn't matter. It was very good of you to come. I am glad that you should see the villa. Are you staying near?"

"Over at Varenna. How beautiful this is!"

"The lake?"

"I meant your garden." They turned and walked slowly back towards the house. "I hope I didn't take you too much by surprise?"

"Oh no," she said. It almost seemed as though she had expected him. "Yes, it is beautiful, isn't it; I have done nothing to it, it is exactly as we found it."

They sat down on a stone bench on the terrace, looking a little away from one another; their minds were full of the essential things impossible to be said. Sitting there with her face turned away from him, every inch of her had that similitude of repose which covers tension. His lowered eyes took in her hands and long, thin fingers lying against the blackness of her dress. He remembered Howard telling him (among those confidences which had later ceased) how though he had fallen in love with the whole of her it was her hands that he first noticed when details began to detach themselves. Now they looked bewildered, helpless hands.

"I took you at your word," he said; "I wanted to help; I hoped there might be something I could do, and in your letter—"

"I took you at your word in asking for help. There is a great deal I must do, and you could make things easier for me, if you will. I shall be very grateful for your help about some business; there are papers I must sign and I don't understand them quite. There were things that Howard had never explained." She looked full at him for a moment and he knew that this was the first time she had uttered her husband's name. It would be easier now.

"He had told me everything," he said quickly, as though to intercept the shutting of a door. "I was always to be there if you should need me—I had promised him." She must realize that she owed him nothing for the fulfilment of a duty. He thought she did, for she was silent, uttering no word of thanks.

"Why did you so seldom come and see us?" she asked suddenly. "Howard had begun to notice lately, and he wondered."

"I was in India."

"Before you went to India." A little inflection in her voice made him despise his evasion.

"There is a time for all things, and that was a time for keeping away."

"Because he was married?"

Stuart did not answer.

"We wanted you," she said, "but you didn't understand, did you?"

She did not understand, how could she? She must have discussed it all, those evenings, with the Majendie that belonged to her; he had not understood either.

"I was mistaken, I suppose," he said. "I—I should have learnt later."

There was a slight contraction of her fingers, and Stuart knew that he had hurt her. If he hurt her like this a little more, it would probably be possible to kill her; she was very defenceless here in the garden that Majendie had bought her, looking out at the unmeaning lake. He had crowded out all tenderness for her, and her loneliness was nothing but a fact to him.

"There were messages for you," she said, turning her head again.

"Were there?"

"He said—," her lips moved, she glanced at him a little apprehensively and was silent. "I have written down everything that he said for you. And I believe he left you a letter."

"Can you remember the messages?" he asked curiously.

"I wrote them down; I have them in the house." She looked at him again with that short-sighted intensity; she knew every word of the messages, and with an effort he could almost have read them from her eyes.

"Did he expect to see me?"

"Yes, once he knew that he was ill. He knew that you could not possibly leave India before April, but he kept on—expecting. I wanted to cable to you and he wouldn't let me. But I know he still believed, above all reason, that you'd come."

"If I'd known, if—"

"You think I should have cabled without telling him?" She thought he blamed her and she evidently feared his anger. Curious . . . He had been so conscious of her indifference, before; he had been a person who did not matter, the nice friend, the family dog—relegated. It was that that had stung and stung. After all he need never have gone to India, it had been a resource of panic. It had saved him nothing, and there had been no question of saving *her*. He wondered why she had not cabled; it was nothing to her whether he went or came, and Howard's happiness was everything.

"Yes, I wonder you didn't cable."

"I am sorry; I was incapable of anything. My resource was—sapped."

He looked at her keenly; it was a doctor's look.

"What have you been doing since?" he asked (as the medical man, to whom no ground was sacred). "What are you going to do?"

"I was writing letters, shutting up the house. And here I'm trying to realize that there's nothing more to do, that matters. And afterwards—"

"Well?"

"I don't know," she said wearily; "I'd rather not, please. . . . Afterwards will come of itself."

He smiled as now he took upon himself the brother-in-law, the nice, kind, doggy person. "You should have somebody with you, Ellaline. You should, you owe it to yourself, you owe it to"—he realized there was no one else to whom she owed it—"to yourself," he repeated. "You must think, you must be wise for yourself now."

She looked, half-smiling, at him while he counselled. He had never achieved the fraternal so completely.

"It's not that I don't think," she said. "I think a great deal. And as for wisdom—there is not much more to learn once one has grown up. I am as wise as I need be —'for myself.'"

"When are you going back to England?"

"If you would do one or two things for me I needn't go back until the autumn."

"You can't stay here all the summer."

"No," she said, looking round at the cypresses—how pitiful she was, in Howard's garden. "They say I couldn't, it would be too hot; I must go somewhere else. But if you could help me a little this autumn I could finish up the business then."

"I may have to be in Ireland then." He tore himself away from something brutally, and the brutality sounded in his voice.

She retreated.

"Of course," she said, "I know you ought to be there now—I was forgetting."

Because he was a person who barely existed for her (probably) she had always been gentle with him, almost propitiatory. One must be gentle with the nice old dog. It was not in her nature to be always gentle, perhaps she had said bitter things to Howard who mattered to her; there was a hint of bitterness about her mouth. At himself she was always looking in that vague, half-startled way, as though she had forgotten who he was. Sometimes when he made a third he had found her very silent, still with boredom; once or twice he had felt with gratification that she almost disliked him. He wondered what she thought he thought of her.

Now it was the time of the Angelus, and bells answered one another from the campaniles of the clustered villages across the lake. A steamer, still gold in the sun, cleft a long bright furrow in the shadowy water. The scene had all the passionless clarity of a Victorian water-colour.

"It is very peaceful," Stuart said appropriately.

"Peaceful?" she echoed with a start. "Yes, it's very peaceful . . . David" (she had called him this), "will you forgive me?"

"Forgive you?"

"I think you could understand me if you wished to. Forgive me the harm I've done you. Don't, don't hate me."

How weak she was now, how she had come down! "What harm have you done to me?" he asked, unmoved.

"You should know better than I do. I suppose I must have hurt you, and through you, Howard. An—an intrusion isn't a happy thing. You didn't give me a chance to make it happy. You came at first, but there was always a cloud. I didn't want to interfere, I tried to play the game. Now that we've both lost him, couldn't you forgive?"

"I'm sorry I should have given you the impression that I resented anything—that there was anything to resent. I didn't know that you were thinking that. Per-

haps you rather ran away with a preconceived idea
that because you married Howard I was bound to be
unfriendly to you. If you did, you never showed it. I
never imagined that I had disappointed you by anything I did or didn't do."

"It was not what you didn't do, it was what you
weren't that made me feel I was a failure." (So *that* was
the matter, he had hurt her vanity!)

"A failure," he said, laughing a little; "I thought you
were making a success. If I didn't come oftener it was
not because I did not think you wanted me."

"But you said just now—"

"A third is never really wanted. I had set my heart
on seeing Howard happy, and when I had, I went away
to think about it."

"Oh," she said hopelessly. She had guessed that he
was putting her off. "Shall we walk a little down the
terrace? There is a pergola above, too, that I should
like you to see." She was taking for granted that he
would not come to the villa again.

They rose; she stood for a moment looking irresolutely up and down the terrace, then took a steeper
path that mounted through the trees towards the pergola. Stuart followed her in silence, wondering. The
world in her brain was a mystery to him, but evidently
he had passed across it and cast some shadows. For a
moment he almost dared to speak, and trouble the peace
of the garden with what had been pent up in him so
long; then he knew that he must leave her to live out
her days in the immunity of finished grief. The silence

of imperfect sympathy would still lie between them, as it had always lain; his harshness could no longer cast a shadow in her world, that was now as sunless as an evening garden. His lips were sealed still, and for ever, by fear of her and shame for his dead loyalty to Howard. The generosity of love had turned to bitterness within him, and he was silent from no fear to cause her pain.

"Beautiful," he said, when they reached the pergola and could look down on lake and garden through the clustered roses.

"Will you be long at Varenna?"

"I don't expect so, no. Some friends want me to join them on Lake Maggiore, and I think of going on tomorrow afternoon."

"That will be better," she said slowly. "It *is* lonely seeing places alone—they hardly seem worth while."

"I'm used to it—I'm going back to India in six months," he said abruptly.

"Oh, I didn't know." Her voice faltered. He had not known himself till then. Her face was whiter than ever in the dusk of the pergola, and her hands were plucking, plucking at the creepers, shaking down from the roses above white petals which he kept brushing from his coat.

"I'm sorry you're going back," she said. "Everybody will be sorry."

"I won't go until I have finished everything that I can do for you."

An expression came into her eyes that he had never seen before. "You have been a friend," she said. "Men

make better things for themselves out of life than
we do."

"They don't last," he said involuntarily.

"I should have said that so far as anything is immor-
tal—" He watched a little tightening of her lips.

"It takes less than you think to kill these things;
friendship, loyalty—"

"Yours was unassailable, yours and his"; she spoke
more to herself than to him. "In those early days when
we three went about together; that time in France, I
realized that."

"In France?" he said stupidly.

"Yes. Don't you remember?"

He remembered France; the days they had spent together, and the long evenings in starlight, and the evening he had strolled beside her on a terrace while
Majendie tinkered with the car. It was a chilly evening,
and she kept drawing her furs together and said very
little. The night after, he had lain awake listening to her
voice and Majendie's in the next room, and making up
his mind to go to India.

"Yes," he said. "Now, will you let me have the papers
and we could go through them now? I could take any
that are urgent back to town with me; I shall be there
in a week."

She twisted her hands irresolutely. "Could you come
tomorrow, before you go? I would have them ready for
you then, if you can spare the time. I'm tired this evening; I don't believe I would be able to understand
them. Do you mind?"

"No, of course not. But may I come in the morning? I am going away early in the afternoon."

She nodded slowly, looked away from him and did not speak. She was evidently very much tired.

"I think I ought to go," he said after a pause.

"If you hurried you could catch that steamer down at Cadenabbia."

"Then I'll hurry. Don't come down."

"I won't come down," she said, holding out her hand. "Good-bye, and thank you."

He hurried to the end of the pergola, hesitated, half turned his head, and stopped irresolutely. Surely she had called him? He listened, but there was no sound. She stood where he had left her, with her back towards him, leaning against a pillar and looking out across the lake.

Turning, he pushed his way between the branches, down the overgrown path. The leaves rustled, he listened again; somebody was trying to detain him. As the slope grew steeper he quickened his steps to a run, and, skirting the terrace, took a short cut on to the avenue. Soon the lake glittered through the iron gates.

She leant back against the pillar, gripping in handfuls the branches of the climbing rose. She heard his descending footsteps hesitate for a long second, gather speed, grow fainter, die away. The thorns ran deep into her hands and she was dimly conscious of the pain. Far below the gate clanged, down among the trees. The branches of the roses shook a little, and more white petals came fluttering down.

All Saints

THE VICAR moved about the chancel in his cassock, thoughtfully extinguishing the candles. Evensong was over, and the ladies who had composed the congregation pattered down the aisle and melted away into the November dusk. At the back of the church somebody was still kneeling; the Vicar knew that it was the emotional-looking lady in black waiting to speak to him as he came down to the vestry; he feared this might be a matter for the confessional and that she might weep. The church was growing very dark; her black draperies uncertainly detached themselves from the shadows under the gallery. As he came down towards her, her white face looked up at him, she made a rustling movement and half rose. A curious perfume diffused itself around her, through the chilly mustiness of the pew.

She murmured a request; the Vicar bowed his head. "I will wait for you in the church porch," she said in a clear voice with a suggestion of a tremolo. "Perhaps we could walk across the churchyard?"

He hurried to the vestry with the sense of a reprieve.

She was waiting in the porch with her hands clasped, and smiled anxiously at the Vicar, who turned to lock the door behind him.

"Such a beautiful church!" she said as they walked on together.

"We consider it very beautiful."

"How the people must love it." Her manner was very childlike; she half turned to him, shyly, then turned away.

"Would you like another window?"

"A window?"

"A coloured window for the Lady Chapel. I would love to give you a window." She made the offer so simply that the Vicar felt as though he was being offered a kitten.

"But, my dear lady, windows like that are very expensive."

"I know," she said eagerly, "but I would be quite able to afford one."

"A—a memorial window?"

"Memorial?"

"Of some relation or dear friend who has passed over?"

"Oh no," she said vaguely, "I know so many people who have died, but I think none of them would care about a window."

"Then you have no particular purpose?"

"I think coloured windows are so beautiful. They make one feel so religious and good."

The Vicar was nonplussed; he wished to say a great deal to her but did not know how to begin. Her ingenuousness half touched and half offended him. She was not young, either; he could hardly explain her to himself as young. Yet standing up so straight among the slanting tombstones she had no congruity with the year's decline; the monotone of twilight, the sullen evening with its colourless falling leaves rejected her; she was not elderly, he thought. She was perennial, there was that about her that displeased the Vicar; she was theatrical. Having placed her, he felt more at ease.

He said: "I will place your very kind offer before the Vestry," and took a few steps in the direction of the lych-gate. She looked up at him with fine eyes that she had once learnt how to use; she was so little conscious of the Vicar's masculinity that he might have been one of the tombstones, but eyes that have learnt their lesson never forget.

"Must you go at once?" she said pathetically. "I want to talk a little more about the window. I would like to go and look from outside at the place where it is going to be."

They retraced their steps a little and took a path that skirted the north side of the church and passed underneath the two east windows.

"I know you are not a resident," said the Vicar. Still a diffident man, he disliked these inquiries; however oblique, they savoured too strongly of parsonic officiousness. But still, one ought to know.

"Do you think of paying us a long visit? The country is hardly at its best just now. Do you like the village?"

"I think the village is sweet—it does appeal to me. So quaint and homely. I am staying here in lodgings; they are most uncomfortable, but I sleep well, and the eggs are fresh. And then I love the country. My real name is Mrs. Barrows."

"Do you intend a long stay?" repeated the Vicar, trying not to feel that her last sentence was peculiar.

"I want to watch them putting up the window. After that, I don't know. I don't think I could bear to be long away from London. Perhaps I might buy a cottage here, if you would help me."

Evidently she was a person of means.

"This is the Lady Chapel window," said the Vicar suddenly.

"Oh," she cried in consternation. "I did not know it was so small. We must make it larger—I think this would never hold them."

"Hold whom?"

"All Saints—I want it to be an All Saints window. I went to church last Thursday; I heard the bells ringing and went in to see. I thought perhaps it was a wedding. I found a service, so I stayed, and you were preaching an All Saints Day sermon. It was beautiful; it gave me the idea. You said 'called to be saints' was meant for all of us; I'd never heard of that idea. I'd thought the saints were over long ago; I'd seen old pictures of them when I was a child. I thought yours was a beautiful idea. It helped me so."

"It is not only an *idea*, it is quite true."

"I know. But it was beautiful of you to think of it."

"Oh dear, oh dear, oh dear," said the Vicar, half aloud.

"But then, of course, I supposed there must still be saints. And I thought of two or three people, then of quite a number. Ladies I have met, who have affected me—most strongly—and one dear boy I know—"

"We have most of us been privileged—"

"Don't you think," she said, with round eyes, "that saints must often seem quite unconventional?"

"In so far as conventionality is error—yes."

"There," she cried, "I knew you'd agree with me. Wouldn't you describe a saint as somebody who, going ahead by their own light—"

"By a light that is given them—"

"That's what I meant—doesn't care what anybody says and helps other people; really makes it possible for other people to go on living?"

"Well, yes." The Vicar hesitated over this definition.

"Don't saints seem always very strong?"

"There is a great strength in them, but there is weakness too; they have a great deal in themselves to combat before—"

"Before they can fight other people's battles."

"Nobody can fight another's battle! We have got to fight our battles for ourselves—against ourselves."

"Oh," she said a little flatly, "now that wasn't my idea. When I'm in a difficulty, or even in the blues, I just go to one of these friends of mine and talk it out, and, well, it's quite extraordinary the difference I feel. I see light at once. It's as if they took a burden off my shoulders."

"There is only One who can do that. Can't you try and get straight to the Divine?"

Her voice out of the darkness—it was now very dark —sounded lonely and bewildered.

"No, I don't seem to want to. You see, I'm not at all good."

"All the more reason—"

She ignored the interruption. "It's power; that's what some people have; they're what I call good people—. saints. And you know, these friends I was talking about; they're not at all conventional and they never go to church, except, perhaps, to weddings. And one or two of them are—oh, *very* unconventional. You'd be surprised."

They walked across the churchyard, just able to see the path by the reflected light on the wet flagstones. The Vicar tried to help her: "And you find that contact with certain personalities brings with it healing and invigoration?"

She grasped eagerly at the phrase. "Healing and invigoration, yes, that's what I mean. It isn't anything to do with love or friendship. When I was younger I thought that loving people was meant to help one; it led me—oh, so wrong. Loving is only giving, isn't it, just a sort of luxury, like giving this window. It doesn't do you any good, or the person either. But people like ——" (she named a notorious lady) "I can't tell you how she's helped me. She's so brave, nobody seems too bad for her. She never despises you. And I've another friend who is a spiritualist."

"Error!"

"She told me all about myself; she was so wonderful, her eyes went through and through. She said, 'You're going the wrong way,' and then it all came to me. She helped me so. And another who was a missionary's wife—"

This seemed simpler, but he wondered what he could get at behind it all.

"She didn't live with him. She had met him first at a revivalist meeting; she said he was too wonderful, but he couldn't have been as wonderful as her. She used to come and see me in the mornings, when I was in bed; I was very lonely then, a dear friend and I had just parted. She never talked religion, but there was something wonderful about her face."

"And all this has really helped you? Force of example—"

"I don't want to copy them: I only want to know they're there."

"What holds you in them isn't of themselves."

"Isn't it?"

"It's simply a manifestation."

She failed to understand him.

"They are able to help you—that is their privilege and God's will. But they can't do everything."

"They do, you see; they see I can't do anything to help myself, and I suppose there must be a great many other people like me. They get at something I can't reach and hand it down to me—I could put it like that, couldn't I? That's what saints have always done, it seems to me."

"Nobody was ever meant to be a go-between," he said with energy. "You've simply no conception—"

"I get everything I want that way," she said placidly. "I'm a very weak sort of person, I only want to be helped. Saints are the sort of people who've been always helping people like me; I thought I'd like to put up a window as a sort of thank-offering to them. Crowds and crowds of people I wanted to put in, all with those yellow circles round their heads, dressed in blue and violet—I think violet's such a beautiful colour. And one big figure in the foreground, just to look like helpfulness, holding out both hands with the look I've sometimes seen on people's faces. When can I know for sure about the window? I mean, when will you tell me if they'll let me put it up?"

"I don't know," said the Vicar, agitatedly, hurrying towards the lych-gate and holding it open for her to pass through. "I'll come round and see you about it. Yes, I know the house."

"Oh, would you?" she said, shyly. "Well, that would be kind. You know, talking about helpfulness, you're one of that sort of people. You don't know what it's

meant to me to hear you preaching. You'd hardly believe—"

"Good-night," said the Vicar abruptly. He raised his
hat, turned on his heel, and fled through the darkness. . . .

The New House

Coming up the avenue in the February dusk he could see the flash and shimmer of firelight through the naked windows of the library. There was something unearthly in those squares of pulsing light that fretted the shadowy façade, and lent to the whole an air of pasteboard unreality.

The scrunch beneath his feet of the wet gravel brought his sister to the doorstep.

"*Herbert!*" she cried, "oh, do come in and see it all. You've been such ages today—what *were* you doing?"

"Your messages," he said; "they delayed me. That stupid fellow at Billingham's had made a muddle over those window measurements for the blinds; I had to go over to the workshop and give the order personally."

Standing in the hall, he was surprised to hear his voice ring out into spaciousness.

"I never realized how big it was," he said with gratification. "Why, Cicely, you're all in the dark. You might have lighted up and made the place look a bit more festive. It's all very well to *hear* how big one's house is, but I'd like to see it with my own eyes."

"I'm sorry," said Cicely; "as a matter of fact I'd only just come in myself. I was out in the garden."

"*Gardening?*"

"No. Just poking about. You never heard anything like the way the thrushes sing. I never knew before they could sing like that. Or perhaps I'd never had time to listen. And the snowdrops are coming out all along the kitchen garden border. Oh, Herbert—"

"I shouldn't have thought that a house-move was exactly the most leisurely time to listen to thrushes. But of course—!"

"But I *had* been working."

His injured dignity was impenetrable, like a barrier of steel. She turned aside from it with a shrug.

"Come in and see what I have done. The library— *Janet!*" she called down a dark archway. "Janet, *tea!* The master's in."

Down the far end of the long room was an open fire-place. His chair was pushed up to the fire and an impromptu tea-table covered with newspaper had been set beside it. His books were stacked in piles against the walls, and their mustiness contested with the clean smell of scrubbed and naked boards.

"A nice room," said Herbert. "On Sunday I shall have a good long day at the picture-hanging. I can't have these windows, Cicely; they're quite indecent. Haven't you even got a dust sheet to pin up across them? Any tramp—"

"I'll see. There won't be much light, though, any-how. The man was in today about the fittings, and he says they won't be able to turn the gas on at the main till tomorrow afternoon. We shall have to do our best by candlelight. I've got some ready."

She folded paper into a spill and lighted a long row of candles, ranged in motley candlesticks along the chimney-piece.

"Tut-tut," said Herbert. "We shall find it very difficult to work. How tiresome these people are."

"Yes," said Cicely.

He resented her tone of detachment. She had blown out her spill and stood twisting the charred ends of paper between her fingers. Long streaks of hair had loosened themselves and hung across her forehead, her cheeks were smeared with dust, her tall thin figure drooped with weariness, but her eyes were shining in the firelight with a strange excitement.

She became conscious of his irritated scrutiny.

"I must be looking simply awful—"

"Yes," said Herbert.

"I'd better try and tidy before tea."

"Yes. If we *are* going to have tea. If it doesn't come at once I really can't be bothered. There's a great deal for me to do, and *I* can't afford to waste any time."

He was a hungry man and peevish, having snatched a hasty and insufficient lunch. He thought that he detected a smile of indulgence as she raised her voice and shouted:

"Janet—*hurry!*"

They heard Janet stumbling up the three steps from the kitchen. She entered with the squat brown tea-pot, one hand splayed against her heart.

"Such a house!" she gasped. "It's that unexpected, really it is!"

They ate in silence. All Herbert's old irritation with his sister surged up within him. She was such a vague, uncertain, feckless creature; the air of startled spirituality that had become her as a girl now sat grotesquely on her middle-aged uncomeliness. He contrasted her with the buxom Emily. Emily would have known how to make her brother comfortable. But, of course, Emily had married.

She spoke.

"I suppose I might take mother's furniture. It really is mine, isn't it? Just that little work-table, and the bookshelf, and the escritoire."

"I don't see what you mean by '*take* it.' It'll all be in the same rooms, in the same house as the rest. Of course, poor mother gave them to you. But I don't see how that makes any difference. I was thinking we might put that little escritoire in the drawing-room. It will look very well there."

Cicely was silent.

Herbert brushed the crumbs out of the creases in his waistcoat.

"Poor mother," he unctuously remarked.

"Come and see the house," said Cicely—she was aware that her quick speech shattered what should have been a little silence sacred to the memory of the dead—

"come and see what you'd like to begin on, and what Janet and I had better do tomorrow. We got the bedrooms tidy, but your basin and jug are odd, I'm afraid. The cases of crockery haven't arrived yet—

"I haven't got a basin and jug at all," she said defensively.

Every step of Herbert's through the disordered house was a step in a triumphal progress. Every echo from the tiles and naked boards derided and denied the memory of that small brick villa where he and Cicely had been born, where their mother's wedded life had begun and ended; that villa now empty and denuded, whose furniture looked so meagre in this spaciousness and height.

He carried a candlestick in either hand and raised them high above his head as he passed from room to room, peering round him into corners, looking up to moulded cornices and ceilings.

Standing in the big front bedroom he saw himself reflected in the mirrored doors of a vast portentous wardrobe, and beamed back at his beaming, curiously-shadowed face. Behind him he saw Cicely seat herself on the edge of the wire mattress, and place her candle carefully beside her on the floor. The mahogany bedroom suite loomed up round them out of the shadows. She sensed his radiant satisfaction with relief.

"It *is* a lovely house," she said. "Oh, Herbert, I do hope you're going to be happy!"

"I hope we both are," he amended kindly. "We must have some people staying, Cicely. The Jenkins, and that lot. Entertain a bit—after all, my dear girl, we can afford it now!"

He was glad when she did not seem to realize how their circumstances had bettered—it gave him the opportunity for emphatic reminders.

They passed out on to the landing, and stood looking down into the depths of the well-staircase.

"I'm sure mother did want us both to be happy," said Cicely, peering over the banisters. Herbert felt eerily as though she were deferring to the opinion of some unseen presence below them in the darkness.

"Of course she wished us the best, poor mother." He clattered a little ostentatiously past her down the stairs.

"She would have loved this house!" Her voice came softly after him, and he heard her limp hand slithering along the banister-rail.

"Damn the gas-man," he muttered, feeling his way across the hall, where his candle-flames writhed and flickered in a draught. It was enough to give anyone the creeps, thus groping through an echoing, deserted house with a ghost-ridden, lackadaisical woman trailing at his heels. If only they'd had the gas on.

Cicely was a fool: he'd teach her!

At the root of his malaise was a suspicion that the house was sneering at him; that as he repudiated the small brick villa so the house repudiated him. That Cicely and the house had made a pact against him, shutting him out.

He was no bourgeois and no parvenu. He, Herbert

Pilkington, was good enough for any house bought with his own well-earned money. He pushed savagely against the panels of the drawing-room door.

This was the largest room in the house. A pale light fell across the floor from the scoops of two great bow-windows, and there was a glimmer in the mirrors—fixtures—panelling the walls.

Herbert put down his candles and stood back in admiration.

"Next year," he said, "we will buy a grand piano; it would look well there, slanting out from that corner.

"The shutters—we ought to shut the shutters." Fussily he wrestled with the catches. For all his middle-aged precision he was like a child delirious over some new toy.

"It needs children; it's a room for children," said Cicely, when the clatter had subsided.

Something in her tone filled him with a sense of impropriety. She was gripping the edges of the chimney-piece and staring down into the grate. Her knuckles stood out white and strained.

"Herbert, Richard Evans wrote to me again yesterday. Today I answered him. I—I am going to be married."

Sitting on the chesterfield, Herbert scrutinized his boots. He heard his voice say:

"Who is going to see about the furniture?"

His mind grappled with something immeasurably far away.

Cicely repeated, "I am going to be married."

Suddenly it flashed across him: he was full of angry light.

"Married!" he shouted, "*married—you!*"

"I thought it was too late," she whispered, "till quite lately. Then, when mother went, everything was broken up; this move came—all my life I seem to have been tied up, fastened on to things and people. Why, even the way the furniture was arranged at No. 17 held me so that I couldn't get away. The way the chairs went in the sitting-room. And mother. Then, when I stayed behind to see the vans off; when I saw them taking down the overmantels, and your books went out, and the round table, and the sofa, I felt quite suddenly 'I'm free.' I said to myself, 'If Richard asks me again—' But I thought he must be tired of asking me. I said, 'If only he asks me again I can get away before this new house fastens on to me.' "

With her stoop, her untidiness, her vagueness and confusion, her irritating streaks of mysticism, he wondered: Could any man find her desirable?

He remembered Richard Evans, thin and jerky and vaguely displeasing to his orderly mind; with his terrible spasms of eloquence and his straggly moustache. He had come in often when they were at No. 17 and sat for hours in the lamplight, with his shadow gesticulating behind him on the wall.

"Nobody needs me," she was saying. "Nobody wants me, really, except him. I see it now, and I've got to—"

"What about *me?* Don't *I* count? Don't *I* need you? What about all these years; the housekeeping?" His voice rose to a wail, "and what the devil am I to do about the move?"

"Of course I'll see you through the move. Really, Herbert—"

"I've been a good brother to you. We've got along very well; we've had a happy little home together all these years, haven't we, and now poor mother's gone—"

His eloquence choked him. He was stabbed by the conviction that she should be saying all this to him. Instead she stood there, mulishly, hanging down her head.

"You're too old to marry," he shouted; "it's—it's *ridiculous!*"

"Richard doesn't think so."

"You don't seem to realize you're leaving me alone with this great house on my hands, this great *barn* of a house; me a lonely man, with just that one silly old woman. I suppose Janet'll go off and get married next! Nobody's too old to marry nowadays, it seems."

"No," she said with placid conviction. "You'll marry, of course."

"*Marry—me?*"

She turned to look at him, pink, self-confident, idiotically pretty.

"But of course. That's what I've been feeling. While I was here— Men are so conservative! But this is no sort of life for you really, Herbert; you want a wife, a pretty, cheery wife. And children—"

"Children!"

"Oh, don't shout, Herbert. Yes, you don't want the family to die out, do you, after you've made such a name for it, done such fine big things?"

He felt that two springs were broken in the sofa, and pressed the cushions carefully with his hand to discover the extent of further damage.

"Damn it all," he said querulously, "I can't get used to another woman at my time of life!"

"Herbert, you've got no imagination." Her tone was amused, dispassionate. She was suddenly superior, radiant and aloof; his no longer, another man's possession.

Her speech chimed in with his thoughts.

"Every man's got to have one woman!"

Taking one of the candles, she turned and left the room.

He sat there almost in the darkness; putting one hand up he fidgeted with his tie. Sleeking down his hair he smiled to find it crisp, unthinned and healthy.

Slowly and cumbrously the machinery of his imagination creaked into movement.

He saw the drawing-room suffused with rosy light. Chairs and sofas were bright with the sheen of flowered chintzes, hung about with crisp and fluted frills. Over by the fire was the dark triangle of a grand piano; the top was open and a woman, with bright crimpy hair, sat before it, playing and singing. "A pretty, cheery wife." There was a crimson carpet, soft like moss, and a tall palm shadowed up towards the ceiling. Muffled by the carpet he heard the patter of quick feet. The little girl wore a blue sash trailing down behind her, and there was a little boy in a black velvet suit. They could do very well without Cicely's escritoire.

Lunch

"AFTER ALL," said Marcia, "there are egoists and egoists. You are one sort of egoist, I am the other."

A ladybird had dropped on to her plate from a cluster of leaves above, and she invited it on to her finger and transferred it very carefully to the rail of the verandah.

"Differentiate," said the stranger, watching the progress of the ladybird.

They were lunching on the verandah, and the midday sun fell through a screen of leaves in quivering splashes on to the table-cloth, the elusive pattern of Marcia's dress, the crude enamelled brilliance of the salad in a willow-pattern bowl, the dinted plate and cutlery slanting together at angles of confusion. The water was spring water, so cold that a mist had formed on the sides of their tumblers and of the red glass water-jug. They considered helpings of cold lamb, and their heads and faces were in shadow.

Through the open window the interior of the coffee-room was murky and repellent; with its drab, dishevelled tables, and chairs so huddled *tête-à-tête* that they travestied intimacy. It was full of the musty reek of cruets and the wraiths of long-digested meals, and of a brooding reproach for their desertion whenever they turned their heads towards it. A mournful waitress, too, reproached them, flicking desultorily about among the crumbs.

From under the verandah the hotel garden slanted steeply down to the road; the burning dustiness beneath them was visible in glimpses between the branches of the lime-trees. Cyclists flashed past, and an occasional motor whirled up clouds of dust to settle in the patient limes. Behind their screen of leaves they two sat sheltered and conversant, looking out to where, beyond the village, the country fell away into the hot blue distances of June, and cooled by a faint wind that crept towards them through a rustle and glitter of leaves from hay-fields and the heavy shade of elders.

The jewels flashed in Marcia's rings as she laid down knife and fork, and, drumming with her fingers on the table, proceeded to expatiate on egoists.

"Don't think I'm going to be clever," she implored him, "and talk like a woman in a Meredith book. Well, quite baldly to begin with, one acknowledges that one puts oneself first, doesn't one? There may be other people, but it's ourselves that matter."

He had relaxed his face to a calm attentiveness, and, leaning limply back in his chair, looked at her with tired, kindly eyes, like the eyes of a monkey, between wrinkled lids.

"Granted, if you wish it for the sake of argument. But—"

"But you are protesting inwardly that the other people matter more? They do matter enormously. But the more they matter to you, still the more you're mattering to yourself; it merely raises your standard of values. Have you any children?"

"Six," said the tired man.

"I have three," said Marcia. "And a husband. Quite enough, but I am very fond of them all. That is why I am always so glad to get away from them."

He was cutting his lamb with quiet slashing strokes of his knife, and eating quickly and abstractedly, like a man whose habits of life have made food less an indulgence than a necessity. She believed that she was interesting him.

"My idea in life, my particular form of egoism, is a determination not to be swamped. I resent most fearfully, *not* the claims my family make on me, but the claims I make on my family. Theirs are a tribute to my indispensability, mine, a proof of my dependence. Therefore I am a perfectly charming woman, but quite extraordinarily selfish. That is how all my friends describe me. I admire their candour, but I never congratulate them on their perspicacity. My egoism is nothing if not blatant and unblushing.

"Now you go on!" she said encouragingly, helping herself to salad. "Tell me about your selfishness, then I'll define how it's different from mine."

He did not appear inspired.

"Yours is a much better kind," she supplemented. "Finer. You have given up everything but the thing that won't be given up. In fact, there's nothing wrong in your sort of egoism. It's only your self-consciousness that brings it to life at all. In the middle of your abject and terrible unselfishness you feel a tiny strain of resistance, and it worries you so much that it has rubbed you sore. It's mere morbidity on your part, that's what I condemn about it. Turn your family out into the street and carouse for a fortnight and you'll be a better man at the end of it. Mine is healthy animal spirits, mine is sheer exuberance; yours is a badgered, hectic, unavowed resistance to the people you love best in the world because, unknowingly, you still love yourself better."

"You wouldn't know the meaning of healthy animal spirits with six children on my income. I suppose what you are trying to say about me, is . . . the turning of the worm?"

"No," said Marcia, "not exactly turning. I wonder if I am making a fool of myself? I don't believe you are an egoist at all. My ideas are beginning to desert me; I am really incapable of a sustained monologue on any subject under the sun. You see, generally I talk in circles; I mean, I say something cryptic, that sounds clever and stimulates the activities of other people's minds, and when the conversation has reached a climax of brilliancy I knock down my hammer, like an auctioneer, on somebody else's epigram, cap it with another, and smile round at them all with calm assurance and finality. By that time everybody is in a sort of glow, each believing that he or she has laid the largest and finest of the conversational eggs.

"Goodness, you've finished. Would you just call through the window and ask that woman if there's anything else to eat? She's been taking such an interest in our conversation and our profiles. Say strawberries, if possible, because otherwise I have a premonition it will be blancmange."

The stranger put his head and shoulders through the window. Marcia studied his narrow back in the shabby tweed jacket, his thinning hair and the frayed edges of his collar. One hand gripped the back of his chair; she thought, "How terrible to see a man who isn't sunburnt." She listened to his muffled conversation with the waitress, and pushed her plate away, deploring the oiliness of the salad.

With flushed face he reappeared, and two plump arms came through the window after him, removed their plates, and clattered on to the table a big bowl of strawberries and a small greyish blancmange in a thick glass dish.

"I wonder if I'm tiring you," said Marcia remorsefully. "I know you came out here to be quiet, and I've done nothing but sharpen my theories on you ever since we made common cause against the coffee-room —it *was* worth while, too, wasn't it? Never mind, I'll let you go directly after lunch, and you shall find the tranquillity you came to look for underneath a lime-tree loud with bees. (I never take the slightest interest in Nature, but I always remember that touch about the bees. I came across it in a book.) I see a book in your pocket. If I wasn't here you'd be reading with it propped up against the water-jug, blissfully dipping your strawberries into the salt and wondering why they tasted so funny. But do let's eat them in our fingers, anyway. I never eat them with a spoon unless there's cream. . . . My husband says he finds me too exhilarating for a prolonged *tête-à-tête*."

He smiled at her with embarrassment, then leant his elbow on the warm rail of the verandah and looked down on to the road.

"It's so hot," he said with sudden petulance, "so beastly *hot*. I didn't realize how hot it was going to be or I wouldn't have bicycled out."

"It's not very hot here, is it? Those leaves—"

"No, but I was thinking about the hotness everywhere else. This makes it worse."

"Fancy *bicycling*. Do let me give you some blancmange; I think it is an heirloom. Did you come far?"

"From Lewisham." He added, "I work in a publisher's office."

"A publisher—how interesting. I wonder if you could do anything to help a boy I know; such a charming boy! He has written a book, but—"

He flushed. "I am not a—an influential member of the firm."

"Oh, then, p'raps you couldn't. Tell me, why did you come here today? I mean why *here* specially?"

"Oh, for no reason. Just at random. Why did you?"

"To meet somebody who hasn't turned up. He was going to have brought a lunch-basket and we were to have picnicked down by the river. Oh, nobody I shouldn't meet. You haven't blundered into an elopement. I've got no brain for intrigue. After lunch we were going to have sketched—at least, he would have sketched and I should have talked. He's by way of teaching me. We were to have met at twelve, but I suppose he's forgotten or is doing something else. Probably he wired, but it hadn't come before I started."

"Do you paint?"

"I've got a paint-box." She indicated a diminutive Windsor and Newton and a large water-colour block lying at her feet.

"I'm sorry," he said diffidently. "I'm afraid this must be something of a disappointment."

"Not a bit." She clasped her hands on the table, leaning forward. "I've really loved our lunch-party. You *listened*. I've met very few people who could really listen."

"I've met very few people who were worth listening to."

She raised her brows. Her shabby man was growing gallant.

"I am certain," she smiled, "that with your delicate perceptions of the romantic you would rather we remained incognito. Names and addresses are—"

"Banality."

The leaves rustled and her muslins fluttered in a

breath of warm wind. In silence they turned their faces out towards the distance.

"I love views," she said, "when there isn't anything to understand in them. There are no subtleties of emotion about June. She's so gloriously elemental. Not a month for self-justification, simply for self-abandonment."

He turned towards her quickly, his whole face flushed and lighted up for speech.

With a grind and screech of brakes a big car drew up under the lime-trees.

Marcia leaned over the verandah rail.

"*John*," she cried. "Oh, John!"

She reached out for her parasol and dived to gather up her sketching things.

"How late you are," she called again, "how *late* you are! Did you have a puncture, or what were you doing?"

She pushed back her chair with a grating sound along the tiled floor of the verandah, and stood looking down bright-eyed at his weary, passive, disillusioned face.

"I was right," she said, "there are two sorts of egoists, and I am both."

The Lover

HERBERT PILKINGTON rang the electric bell and, taking a few steps back, looked up to contemplate the house-front. In the full glare of the westerly sun it all looked trim and orderly enough; Cicely had not done so badly for herself, after all, by marrying Richard Evans. Herbert congratulated himself on having foreseen the whole thing from the beginning and furthered it with tact and sympathy. Of course it had been difficult to get poor Cicely off. . . . The hall-door was opened suddenly by Cicely's nervous little maid, who, flattening herself against the passage wall to allow of his entrance, contrived, by dodging suddenly under his arm, to reach the drawing-room door before him and fling it wide.

Richard and Cicely were discovered seated at opposite ends of the sofa and looking very conscious. Cicely wore a pink blouse; she looked prettier than Herbert could have imagined and curiously fluffy about the head. The white-walled drawing-room, dim in the

90

ochreous twilight of drawn blinds, was hung with
Richard's Italian water-colours and other pictorial me-
mentos of the honeymoon; it smelt very strongly of
varnish, and seemed to Herbert emptier than a drawing-
room ought to be. The chairs and sofas had retreated
into corners, they lacked frilliness; there was something just as startled and staccato about the room as
there was about Cicely and Richard. Poor Mother and
Dear Father eyed one another apprehensively from opposite walls; the very tick of the clock was hardly
regular.

They always gave one a warm welcome; Cicely was
quite effusive, and long Richard Evans got up and stood
in front of the fireplace, delightedly kicking the
fender.

"*Tea!*" commanded Cicely through the crack of the
door; just as she had done at No. 17 and at the New
House, during the few short months of her reign there.

"Hot day," said Herbert, sitting down carefully.

"*Richard's* hot," said Cicely proudly; "he's been
mowing the lawn."

"Home early?"

"Well, yes. One must slack off a bit this weather."

"Idle dog," said Herbert archly.

"*Doesn't* being engaged agree with Herbert!" cried
Cicely, slapping his knee. (She had never taken these
liberties at No. 17.) "Don't you feel wonderful, Herbert? Isn't it not like anything you ever felt before?"

Herbert ran one finger round the inside of his collar
and smiled what Doris called his quizzical smile.

"Only three weeks more," contributed Richard. "And how's the trousseau getting on?"

"My trousseau?"

"Ha, ha! Hers, of course. My dear Herbert, those dressmaker women have got you in their fist. If they don't choose to let her have the clothes in time she'll put the whole thing off."

Herbert was not to be alarmed. "Oh, they'll hurry up," he said easily. "I'm making it worth their while. By Gad, Cicely, she does know how to dress."

"They are most wonderful clothes—she is lucky, isn't she, Richard?"

Herbert beamed complacency. "She deserves it all," he said.

"I think she's getting handsomer every day."

"Happiness does a good deal for us all," said Herbert gallantly.

"By the way," said Cicely, winking across at Richard (an accomplishment he must have taught her), "look carefully round the room, Herbert, and see if you see anyone you know."

Herbert, who had taken Richard's place on the sofa and was sitting with his hands in his pockets and his legs stretched out, turned his head as far as his collar would permit and made an elaborate inspection of the chimney-piece, the whatnot, the piano-top.

"Very well she looks up there, too," he said, raising himself a little with arched back for a better view, then relapsing with a grunt of relief. He had seen what he expected, the portrait of his beloved looking out coyly at him from between two top-heavy vases. "Where did you get that, Cicely?"

"She brought it round *herself*, the day before yesterday. She came in just before supper; I was out, but she stayed a long time talking to Richard. Oh, Richard, look at Herbert getting crimson with jealousy!" Herbert, who never changed colour except after meals or from violent exertion, beamed with gratification. "Never mind, Herbert," said Cicely, "*I'm* jealous, too, you see."

Herbert was often irritated by the way that Richard and Cicely looked at one another across him. He did not enjoy the feeling of exclusion. But of course he and Doris would be able to look at each other across people just like that when *they* were married.

"Do bring it over here, Richard," said Cicely, nodding at the portrait. "I want to look at it again." Tea was carried in, not noiselessly, but quite unnoticed. The brother and sister were looking at the photograph. Herbert leant back, smiling at it with an absent and leisurely pride. Cicely bent forward in eager and short-sighted scrutiny. She seemed to be looking for something in it that she could find.

A young lady with symmetrically puffed-out hair returned both regards from out of a silver frame with slightly bovine intensity. Her lips were bowed in an indulgent smile—perhaps the photographer had been a funny man—a string of pearls closely encircled a long plump neck.

"She has framed it for you very handsomely," said

Herbert. "I said to her when we were first engaged, 'Never stint over a present when it is necessary'—I think that is so sound. 'Of course I do not approve of giving indiscriminately,' I said, 'but when they must be given let them be handsome. It is agreeable to receive good presents, and to give them always makes a good impression.' "

Cicely looked guilty; Richard had insisted on consigning the coal-scuttle that Herbert had given them to the darkest corner of the study.

"Doris always understands me perfectly," continued Herbert, examining the frame to see if the price were still on the back. "I think it will never be necessary for me to say anything to her twice. If I even express an opinion she always remembers. It's quite extraordinary."

"Extraordinary," echoed Richard. His voice had often an ironical note in it; this had prejudiced Herbert against him at first, he seemed rather a disagreeable fellow, but now Herbert knew that it did not mean anything at all. Richard, though not showy-looking, was really a good sort of chap.

Cicely, a little pink (or perhaps it was only the reflection from her blouse), drew up the tea-table and began pouring out. There was a short silence while Richard replaced the photograph; they heard two bluebottles buzzing against the ceiling.

Richard hacked three-quarters of a new cake into slices, placed the plate invitingly at Herbert's elbow and sat down on a music-stool. Lifting his feet from the floor he rotated idly till Cicely passed him his cup, which he emptied in three or four gulps and put down, then sat gazing expectantly at his brother-in-law.

"Marriage is a wonderful thing," said Herbert conversationally, recrossing his legs. "Look at you two now, how comfortable you are. It's all been most successful."

Cicely had never known till this moment whether Herbert really approved of them.

"The most surprising people," he continued, "make a success of matrimony. Of course, people have varying ideas of comfort; everybody does not understand this, therefore there have been, alas, unhappy marriages."

"But the right people always find each other in the end," said Cicely dreamily. "You did sort of feel, didn't you, Herbert, when you first met Doris—"

"Women have these fancies"—Herbert was all indulgence for them—"Doris has confessed to me that she was affected, quite extraordinarily affected, by our first meeting. It made little or no impression upon me. But Doris is a true woman."

"What *is* a true woman?" asked Richard suddenly. Herbert thought it must be very uncomfortable to live with a person who asked these disconcerting, rather silly questions. He supposed Cicely was used to his ways. Cicely sat stirring her tea and smiling fatuously at her husband.

Herbert, after consideration, decided to turn the question lightly aside. "I think we all know," he said, "*when we find her.*" He wished Doris were sitting beside him instead of Cicely; he would have looked at her sideways and she would have been so much pleased. As it was, he looked across the table at the bread and butter, and Richard jumped up and offered him some more.

"Yes, but what does she *consist* of?" asked Richard excitedly, forgetting to put down the plate. Herbert was silent; he thought this sounded rather indelicate.

"*Sensibility?*" suggested Cicely.

"Infinite sensibility," said Richard, "and patience."

"Contrariness," added Cicely.

"Inconsistency," amended Richard.

"Oh *no*. Contrariness, Richard, and weak will."

Herbert looked from one to the other, supposing they were playing some sort of game.

"She is infinitely adaptable, too," said Richard.

"She has to be, poor thing," said Cicely (this did not come well from Cicely).

"Dear me, Cicely," interposed Herbert, blinking; "so you consider women are to be pitied, do you?" Cicely opened her mouth and shut it again. She clasped her hands.

"This does not speak well for Richard," said Herbert humorously. "Doris would be much amused. Now I suppose *Doris* is to be pitied, isn't she?"

"Oh *no*, Herbert," cried Cicely quickly.

"She doesn't seem unhappy. In fact, I believe there are very few young ladies Doris would change places with at present. And I think you are wrong, my dear

Richard; I consider woman most consistent, if she is taught—and she can be easily taught. She is simpler and more childlike than we are, of course. Her way in life is simple; she is seldom placed in a position where it is necessary for her to think for herself. She need never dictate—except, of course, to servants, and there she's backed by her husband's authority. All women wish to marry."

Richard and Cicely listened respectfully.

"A true woman," continued Herbert, warming to his subject, "loves to cling."

"But she mustn't cling heavily, must she?" asked Cicely.

"She clings not only to her husband but in a lesser degree to her household and" —he coughed slightly— "children. Her sphere—"

"—Is the home," said Richard quickly. "But suppose she hasn't got a home?"

"She may now hope till a quite advanced age to obtain a home by matrimony. If she cannot she must look for work. It is always possible for an unmarried woman to make herself useful if she is willing and" —he considered carefully—"bright."

"Do you like women to be bright?" asked Cicely eagerly.

"It depends," said Herbert guardedly. He had hated Cicely when she was skittish; it had sat grotesquely upon her as a spinster, though now that she was married a little matronly playfulness did not ill become her. "Doris is bright, bright and equable."

Remembering with resentment how uncomfortable Cicely had sometimes made him, he raised his voice a little. "She has no *moods*. She has simple tastes. She is always very bright and equable."

"So you really suit each other very well," summarized Richard, twirling on the music-stool. "Appreciation is everything to a woman. I congratulate her."

"Yes," said Herbert simply. "But you should congratulate *me*—it is more usual, I think. But we are past all that now; dear me, how many letters there were to answer! And now there are the presents to acknowledge. A very handsome inkstand and a pair of vases came this morning. And in another three weeks we shall be at Folkestone! . . ."

His sister and brother-in-law were so silent that he thought they must have gone to sleep. They were an erratic couple; matrimony seemed to have made them stupid. Richard sat biting his moustache and staring at Cicely, who, with bent head, absently smoothed out creases in the tablecloth. One might almost have said they were waiting for him to go. It was curious how little of this he had suspected in Cicely, although she was his sister. In the evenings he knew that Richard and she read poetry together, and not improbably kissed; through the folding doors he could hear their cold supper being laid out in the dining-room. How could he have guessed that something inside her had been clamouring for these preposterous evenings all her life? She had seemed so contented, sewing by the lamp while he smoked and read the paper and Poor Mother dozed.

It was wasting pity to be sorry for them; he turned from his anæmic relations to review his long perspective of upholstered happiness with Doris. One might almost say that the upholstery *was* Doris. Herbert, feeling his heart grow great within him, could have written a testimonial to all the merchants of Romance. Having given love a trial he had found it excellent, and was prepared to recommend it personally, almost to offer a guarantee. Dear Doris would be waiting for him this evening; demure, responsive, decently elated; he was going to visit at her home. This intention he communicated to Richard and Cicely, who rose in vague and badly-feigned distress. Herbert had said nothing about *going*, as it happened, but since they had so understood him—well, they were scarcely entertaining; he had been there long enough.

They saw him to the gate and stood together under the laburnum tree, watching him down the road. Richard's arm crept round Cicely's shoulders. " 'But this, ah God, is love!' " he quoted.

And Herbert had forgotten them before he reached the corner.

Mrs. Windermere

****

IN THE DOORWAY of Fullers', Regent Street, they came face to face. Mrs. Windermere grasped both Esmée's wrists, drew them towards her bosom, and cried in her deep tremolo, "*My dear!*"

Esmée had not imagined Mrs. Windermere out of Italy. She had never pictured that little pug-dog face without the background of flickering olives, or of velvety sun-gold walls, with cypresses dotted here and there like the exclamation marks in the lady's conversation. Mrs. Windermere now regarded her with intensity through the long fringes of her hatbrim. She said, "The same Esmée!" and gently massaged the wrists with her thumbs.

"This is splendid," said Esmée inadequately, conscious of a rising pinkness and of the long stream of outcoming ladies dammed by their encounter. "What a funny coincidence!"

"God guided me, dearest!" Mrs. Windermere always mentioned the Deity with confidential familiarity;

one felt she had the entree everywhere. "I meant to have lunched at Stewart's."

"I'm sorry you've *had* lunch."

"I will have more," said Mrs. Windermere recklessly. They pushed their way upstairs and stood over a little table in the window while it was vacated. Esmée untwined the dangling parcels from her fingers and propped up her umbrella in a corner. Mrs. Windermere scanned the menu with the detachment of the satiated, and Esmée confessed that she was hungry. "Then it must be rissoles," said her friend enticingly—"little chicken rissoles. I will have a cup of chocolate and an *éclair*." She gave the orders to the waitress and sat looking at Esmée and tapping a corner of the menu card against her mouth.

"But you don't live in town?"

"No," said Esmée; "I'm up for the day. You would have written, wouldn't you, if we hadn't met? I should have been so much disappointed if we'd never—"

"I hope to come and stay with you."

"That will be lovely," said Esmée, answering the smile. There was a moment's silence. "Do you miss Italy?"

"Ye-es." It was an absent answer; Mrs. Windermere's thoughts were concentrated elsewhere. "There's something *strange* about you, child," she said.

Esmée now remembered how her conversation had been always little rushing advances on the personal. She had a way of yawning reproachfully with a little click of the teeth and a "Surely we two know each other too well to talk about the *weather?*" if one tried to give the conversation an outward twist. Esmée had found their first walks together very interesting, they had had the chilly, unusual, dream-familiar sense of walking in one's skin. "There *is* something strange," said Mrs. Windermere.

"*You* look just the same as ever."

"There's a stillness here," said the other, slipping a hand beneath her fur. "Like the stillness in the heart of the whirlwind. Get right into it, live in your most interior self, and you're unchangeable. You haven't found it yet; you're very young, you've never penetrated."

"I don't think I have, perhaps," said Esmée thoughtfully, under the returning influence of Italy. "Perhaps I rather like *twirling*."

"Ye-es," said Mrs. Windermere, leaning back in her chair. Her lustrous eyes looked out mournfully, contentedly, from under pouchy lids, through the long fringes of her hat; her *retroussé* nose was powdered delicately mauve, the very moist lips had a way of contracting quickly in the middle of a sentence in an unpuglike effort to retain the saliva. Curly bunches of grey hair lay against her cheeks, a string of Roman pearls was twisted several times round her plump throat; her furs were slung across her bosom and one shoulder; her every movement diffused an odour of Violet de Parme. She had not removed her gloves, and opulent rolls of white kid encircled wrist and forearm; her sleeves fell back from the elbow. She was an orthodox London edition of her Italian self.

"Twirling," she repeated, narrowing her eyes. She looked round the mild, bright, crowded room, rustling with femininity, with its air of modest expensiveness. "Simply twirling? How" —with an obvious connection of ideas— "is your husband?"

"Very well indeed. He would like so much—" Esmée could not picture Wilfred meeting Mrs. Windermere. "He would have liked to have come up with me today," she concluded.

"Ye-es," said the other, looking beyond at something. "How did he ever come to let you go to Italy—alone?"

"I wasn't alone, though, was I? I was with Aunt Emma. Someone had to take her and I'd never travelled."

"Spiritually, you *were* alone. You were alert, a-tip-toe, breathlessly expectant. *I* came—but it might not have been I! How did he come to let you go like that? Men of his type are not so generous."

"But he isn't *that* type."

The waitress brought the cup of chocolate, the *éclair*, and the rissoles. Mrs. Windermere stretched out across the dishes, gently disengaged the fork from Esmée's fingers, and turned her hand palm upwards on the table.

"That little hand told me everything," she said. "And do you know, child, you have his image at the back of your eyes. I *know* the type—little loyal person."

"Wilfred likes me to travel," said Esmée feebly. "He finds me rather a tiresome companion when he wants to talk about places, and you see he never has time to take me abroad himself."

"That was a very *young* marriage," said Mrs. Windermere, leaning forward suddenly.

"Oh. Do you think so?"

"But you're younger now, after four years of it. Warier, greedier, more *dynamic*. No children!—*never* to be any children?"

"I don't know."

"So *wise* and yet *so* foolish." She sipped delicately the hot chocolate, put the cup down, and once more slipped her hand under her fur. "The Mother-heart," she said, "is here. It grows and grows—stretching hands out, seeking, *finding*."

"I expect there are a great many outlets," said Esmée, helping herself to another rissole, "even if one never has any children of one's own. But I hope—"

"What you are seeking," said Mrs. Windermere firmly, "is a *lover*." She took her fork up, speared the *éclair*, and watched the cream ooze forth slowly with a smile of sensual contentment. She had been saying things like this repeatedly, all the time they were in Italy. But they didn't, somehow, sound quite nice in Fullers'. Esmée thought she saw a woman near them looking up.

"I don't think I *am*, you know," she argued gently, wondering at what date Mrs. Windermere had arranged to come and stay with them.

"Oh, child, *child*. . . . You can't, you know, there's been too much between us. And the Mother-heart knows, you know; the yearning in it brings about a vision. I see you treading strange, dim places; stumbling, crying out, trying to turn back, but always following —the Light." Mrs. Windermere laid down her fork and licked the cream from her lips. "And then," she said slowly, "I see the Light die out—extinguished."

There was a pause. "Thank you very much," said Esmée earnestly; "it—it saves a lot to know beforehand. I mean if the Light is going to go out there's something rather desperate about my following it, isn't there? Wouldn't it be—"

"The Light," interrupted Mrs. Windermere, "is yours to guard."

"But wouldn't it be—"

Mrs. Windermere bowed her head and drew her furs together.

"Such a *child*," she sighed.

"I think I'll have an *éclair* too," said Esmée timidly. "Won't you have another one to keep me company?"

"*I?*" started Mrs. Windermere. "I? *Éclair?* What? Oh well, if it's going to make you shy, my watching."

Esmée ordered two more *éclairs*. "What," she inquired, "are your plans? Did you think of going back to Italy?"

"With the swallows—not before the swallows. I must smother down the panting and the tugging, because my friends can't let me go. They just rise up and say I mustn't. Commands, of course, are nothing, but *entreaties!* Did I tell you in Italy what some people call me?" She laughed deprecatingly and watched the

waitress threading her way between the tables with the
éclairs. "They call me 'The Helper.' It sounds like
something in a mystery play, doesn't it?"

"Oh yes. It's—it's a beautiful name."

"It does seem to be a sort of gift," said Mrs. Windermere, looking beyond her, "something given one to *use.*
You see, I do see things other people can't see, and
tell them, and help them to straighten out. Well, take
your case. . . . And I've another friend in Italy, the
one I was going to stay with after we parted—I don't
know if I told you about her? Well, she left her husband. She *grew up,* and found she didn't need him any
more. Well, I saw all that for her and was able to help
her. I told the other man how things stood—such a
manly fellow! He'd been hanging back, not understanding. Well, they went. I bought their tickets for
them and saw them off to Italy. They've been having
difficult times, but they'll straighten out—I'm still able
to help them. I've been staying there a good deal. I *am*
able to help them."

"I suppose they did feel it was the right thing to do,"
said Esmée.

"And you," said Mrs. Windermere, bringing her suddenly into focus. "What *is* going to happen to *You?* I
must come down and have a look at this husband of
yours, this Wilfred. Let me see—"

She dived suddenly, her bag was on the floor. She
reappeared with it, and its mauve satin maw gaped at
Esmée while she fumbled in its depths. Out came a
small suède notebook, and Mrs. Windermere, fever-

ishly nibbling the point of the pencil, ran her eye down the pages.

"The twentieth?" she said. "I could come then if you could have me. If not, the fourteenth of the next, for the week-end—but if I came on the twentieth I could stay longer. Failing the fourteenth—"

Esmée pondered, lowering her lashes. "I'm afraid, I'm *awfully* afraid it will have to be the fourteenth of next. All this month there'll be Wilfred's relations."

"Little *caged* thing," said Mrs. Windermere tenderly. "Very well, the fourteenth." She jotted down something in her notebook, looked across at Esmée, smiled, and jotted down some more, still with her head on one side and the little secret smile. "Ideas, ideas, coming and going. . . . And now! You to your shoppingses and I—well, childie?"

"Please, the bill," said Esmée to the waitress. "You *must* let me, please," she whispered to Mrs. Windermere.

"No, I *don't* like— Oh well, well. I haven't got a Wilfred. Thanks, dear child!"

They pushed their chairs back and went downstairs together. At the door, Esmée drew a valedictory breath. "It's been ever so nice," she said. "Lovely. Such a bit of luck! And now, I suppose—"

"Which way? Oh, Peter Robinson's? Well, I'll come with you. It doesn't matter about my little shoppingses."

Firmly encircling Esmée's wrist with a thumb and forefinger she led her down Regent Street.

The Shadowy Third

H<small>E WAS</small> a pale little man, with big teeth and promi-
nent eyes; sitting opposite to him in a bus one would
have found it incredible that there could be a woman to
love him. As a matter of fact there were two, one dead,
not counting a mother whose inarticulate devotion he
resented, and a pale sister, also dead.

The only woman of value to him came down every
evening to meet the 5:20, and stood very near the edge
of the platform with her eyes flickering along the moving carriages. She never knew from which end of the
train he would alight, because, as he told her, it was
only by the skin of his teeth that he caught it at all, and
he often had to jump in at the nearest open door and
stand the whole way down among other men's feet,
with his hand against the rack to steady himself. He
could have come down easily and luxuriously by the
6:05, in the corner of a smoking-carriage, but he gave
himself this trouble for the sake of three-quarters of an
hour more with her. It was the consciousness of this,

and of many other things, which made her so speech-less when they met. Often they were through the bar-rier and half-way down the road before she found a word to say. She was young, with thin features and light hair and eyes, and they had been married less than a year.

When they turned from the road down the tree-shadowed lane he would shift his bag from one hand to the other and steal an arm round her shoulders. He loved her shy tremor, and the little embarrassed way she would lean down to make a snatch at his bag, which he would sometimes allow her to carry. Their house was among the first two or three on a new estate, and overlooked rolling country from the western windows, from the east the house-backs of new roads. It had been built for him at the time of his first marriage, four years ago, and still smelt a little of plaster, and was coldly dis-tempered, which he hated, but they said it was not yet safe to paper the walls.

Today she said, "Come down and have a look at the garden, Martin; I've been planting things." So he put down his bag and they walked to the end of the garden, where a new flower-bed looked scratched-up and dis-ordered, and was edged with little drooping plants.

"Very pretty," he said, looking at her and absently prodding at the mould with his umbrella. "I suppose they'll grow?"

"Oh yes, Martin, they're going to grow right up and hide the board-fence; it's so ugly."

"If they're going to be so tall you should have planted

them at the back and put the smaller things in front. As it is, everything else would be hidden."

"Why, *yes*," she cried, disheartened, "I never thought of that—oh, *Martin!* It seemed such a pity to go walking over the new flower-bed, leaving foot-marks; that's why I put them near the edge—and now I can't unplant them. What a lot there is to learn! Will you take me to the Gardening Exhibition next summer? I was reading about it—there are corners of gardens by all the famous people, and stone seats, and fountains—we might buy a sundial there, and there are lectures you can go to, and prize roses. We should learn a lot."

"Next summer? Well, we'll see," he said. "Meanwhile don't overdo it—all this gardening." They skirted the flower-bed and went to lean up against the fence, resting their elbows on the top. She was half an inch taller than he, and her high heels gave her a further advantage. A little wind blew in their faces as they looked out towards the fading distance. The fields were dotted here and there with clumps of elm; with here and there a farmhouse roof, the long roofs and gleaming windows of a factory.

"This open country stretches for such miles," she said dreamily. "Sometimes, on these quiet misty days, I begin to think the sea's over there, and that if the clouds along the distance lifted I should see it suddenly, shining. And, with this wind, I could be sure I smell and hear it."

"Yes, I know. One often gets that feeling."

"Do *you?*"

"Well, no," he said confusedly, "but I'm sure one does. I can imagine it." Someone had said the same thing to him, just here, three or four years ago.

"You often understand before I say things, don't you, Martin? Isn't it curious? All sorts of woman's discoveries that I've made about this house were nothing new at all to you. Like my idea about a fitment cupboard for that corner of the landing. Fancy that having occurred to you!"

He did not answer. He had taken off his hat, and she watched the wind blowing through his fair hair, as soft and fine as a baby's. Little wrinkles were coming in the forehead that she thought so noble, and his face—well, one could not analyse it, but it was a lovely face. She pictured him swaying for forty minutes in the train, with his hand against the luggage-rack, in order to be with her now, and said, "Oh, Martin, Martin!"

"Let's come into the house."

"No, not into the house."

"Why not? It's cold, you're cold, little woman." He drew her arm through his and chafed her hand.

"Let's stay out," she begged. "It isn't time for supper. It isn't beginning to get dark yet. Do stay out—dear Martin!"

"Why," he said, looking round at her, "one would think you were afraid of the house."

"Hoo!" she laughed, "afraid of *our* house!"

But he was still dissatisfied. Something was making her restless; she was out in the garden too much. And when she was not in the garden she was always walking about the house. One or two days, when he had stayed at home to work, he had heard her on the stairs and up and down the passages; up and down, up and down. He knew that women in her state of health were abnormal, had strange fancies. Still—

Now she was talking about the new sundial; where they were going to put it. Nasturtiums were to be planted round the foot, she said, because nasturtiums grew so fast and made a show. Her mind had a curious way of edging away from the immediate future. Next summer! Why, she would have other things besides sundials to think of then. What a funny little woman she was!

"I wonder you never thought of having a sundial before," she insisted. "Did Anybody ever think of it?"

"Well, no," he said, "I don't think it ever occurred to me."

"Or *Anybody?*"

"No, nor anybody."

She looked up at the house, silhouetted against the evening sky. "It's funny living in such a new house—I never had. I wonder who will come after us."

"We're not likely to move for some time," he said sharply.

"Oh no—only if we *did*. It seems so very much our house; I can't imagine anybody else at home here, we have made it so entirely—you and I. What was it like the first month or two?"

"Very damp," he said, now wishing to return to the sundial.

"Did you have the drawing-room very pretty?"

"Oh yes, there were a great many curtains and things. I had to take down all the pictures, they were going mouldy on the walls. It was always a pretty room, even with nothing in it at all. But it's nothing without *you* in it, Pussy."

"You didn't miss me for a long time," she said, with her cheek against his.

"Always," he said, "always, always, always."

"Oh no," she said seriously, "you know you couldn't have been lonely."

"*Lonely*—I was wretched!"

"Oh, hush!" she cried with a start, putting her hand over his lips.

"Anyway"—he kissed her fingers—"nobody is lonely now. Come into the house."

She hung back on his arm a little but did not again protest; they went in by a glass door into the kitchen passage. As they passed through the archway into the hall he put out his hand to sweep something aside; then smiled shamefacedly. It was funny how he always expected that *portière*. *She* had declared that a draught came through from the kitchen, and insisted on putting it up. *She* had filled the house with draperies, and Pussy had taken them down. When the *portière* was there he had always been forgetting it, and darting through to change his boots in the evening would envelop his head and shoulders ridiculously in the musty velvet folds. Funny how he could never accustom himself to the changes; the house as it *had* been was always in his mind, more present than the house as it *was*. He could never get used to the silence half-way up the stairs, where the grandfather clock used to be. Often he found himself half-way across the hall to see what was the matter with it; it had been a tiresome clock, more trouble than it was worth, with a most reverberating tick. Pussy had put a bracket of china there in its place.

Because it was a chilly autumn evening they had lighted a fire in the drawing-room, the curtains were drawn; what an evening they would spend together after supper! An armchair had been pulled forward and a work-basket gaped beside it; he wondered what Pussy had been sewing. He stood in the hall, looking in through the open door, and remembered *Her* making baby-clothes by the fire and holding them up in her fingers for him to see. Sometimes he had barely raised his eyes from his book—she had never been able to understand his passion for self-education. As she finished the things she had taken them upstairs and locked them away, and sometimes she would put down her sewing and rattle her work-box maddeningly, and look at him across the fire and sigh. . . . It would be wonderful to watch Pussy sewing. He could hear her moving about in the hall—such a Pussy!—hanging up his overcoat, then opening the oak chest and rattling things about in it for all the world as though she were after a mouse.

"I found some pictures," she said, coming up behind him with a stack of something in her arms. "Come into the drawing-room and we'll look." The young fire gave out a fitful light, and they knelt down on the hearthrug and put their heads together over the pictures. "Nursery pictures," said Pussy—she must have been up in the attic, he wished he had cleared the contents of it out of his house. He stared at the smiling shepherdesses, farmer-boys and woolly lambs. "They *are* nursery pictures, aren't they, Martin? I didn't know you'd actually bought the *pictures*. Had—had Anybody chosen the curtains, too? Did you get as far as that?"

"I don't know," he said. "I don't really, Pussy, I don't remember."

"And did you take it all to pieces again? Did you alone, or did Anybody help you? I wonder you didn't leave it, Martin; you didn't want the room for anything else. But I suppose it would have made you sad, or other people sad."

"Have you done anything to the room yet, Pussy?"

"I just pulled the furniture about a little, then I went to look for a fender in the attic and found these pictures. I don't know if there *were* any curtains, Martin; shall I buy some more? I saw some cretonnes specially for that kind of room, all over clowns and rabbits and little scarlet moons."

"I'll bring some patterns—or come up to town some day and we'll choose them together."

She did not answer, she was looking at the pictures.

"Martin, was that one going to have been called Martin too, Martin Ralph?"

"I don't know, it hadn't been decided."

"Didn't Anybody choose a name for him, although he didn't live? He was a real person."

"It had never been decided, Pussy. I'm going to get you a longer sofa, so that you can put your feet up. We can choose it when we choose the chintzes."

"Oh, you mustn't. This one is very comfortable; I never sit in it, but that's because I just don't take to it."

"I hate the look of it."

"Well, get rid of it," she said, smiling, "as neither of us wants a sofa. Did Anybody ever sit on that one?"

As far as he remembered, it was the only thing in the room that she had ever sat on. She had never looked comfortable on it. She had a way of sitting with her head at the darkest end and straining her eyes over her work, then blinking up at him when he spoke. Of course she ought to have worn glasses; he hated women in glasses, and she knew it, but her short-sightedness annoyed him and he had frequently said so. *She* used to come and meet him at the station—he came back by the 6:05 in those days, sometimes by the 6:43—and it had so greatly irritated him to watch her grimacing and screwing up her eyes at the carriages that he had slipped through the barrier behind her and pretended when she came home that he had not known she was there. Perhaps the little chap would have been short-sighted if he had lived. . . .

The maid came in to say that supper was ready, and

they went into the dining-room. Here the curtains were undrawn and they could see the lights twinkling out in the windows of the other houses. He often felt as though those windows were watching him; their gaze was hostile, full of comment and criticism. The sound of the wind among the bushes in the garden was like whispered comparisons. He said they saw a good deal too much of the neighbours, and Pussy said she liked the friendly lights. "I wouldn't like to be shut in all round, but I couldn't live without *any* people. The next-doors have been so kind. She came in with some plants this morning, and stayed talking quite a long time, and said if there was ever anything she could do. . . . She spoke so nicely of you, Martin. She's known you by sight ever since you were a little boy."

"Oh, it's funny to have lived in the same place all one's life. All these people—well, they're sometimes rather tiresome."

"Tiresome?"

"One gets tired of their being the same. Would you like to travel, Pussy?"

"Oh, *Martin!*" Her eyes grew wistful; the prospect seemed remote.

"Well, we will," he said, with energy. "We'll go to Switzerland—some summer."

"I'd rather go to Italy—Venice."

"Oh, not Venice. I don't think you'd care for Venice. It's nothing very much really."

"Have *you* been there?"

"Yes, for a bit. I didn't care about it."

"You never told me!" Her eyes that had been looking into his looked suddenly away, the colour surged up under her clear skin. She began to fidget with the spoons on the table.

"More, Martin?"

"Yes, please—I say, Pussy, you're not eating. You must eat, darling."

"Oh, I *am*, don't bother. I want to talk." She lifted her eyes again and glanced at him, the light glinting on her golden eyelashes and on her hair. "I've been so lonely all day—well, not lonely, but the house was so quiet, I could hear myself think. I went into the east room and sat on the window-seat. It is a cold room; I don't know how we'll ever make it warm enough."

"It has never been used, you see."

"We must have fires there this winter. Has it *never* been used? Didn't Anybody ever sit there or go in and out? Oh, they must have, Martin. It's not an empty-feeling room, like the attic."

"Did you stay there long?"

"No, I didn't, I was feeling restless. The white chest of drawers is locked; I wonder where the key is? We shall be wanting to use it."

"The key's lost," he said in sudden fear. "I know it's lost. I'll go up there some day and force open the drawers myself—they're empty."

"How funny to lock them if they're empty."

"What did you imagine was inside?" he asked uneasily.

"Oh, nothing in particular. . . . Martin, I think I

will go up to town and buy those chintzes myself. And there are other things I want."

He remembered how he had heard Her in the east room those last two months before she went, opening and shutting the drawers. It had disturbed him, working at his desk in the dining-room below, and he had come up angrily once or twice. He could hear Her scuffling to her feet at his approach, and when he entered She was always standing by the window, looking intently out. She used to say, "Yes, all right. I won't, I'm sorry, Martin," and come downstairs after him, humming. She had never seemed to have enough to do; before the child came she had been in an aimless bustle, but afterwards she did nothing, nothing at all, not even keep house for him decently. That was probably what had made her ill—that and the disappointment. All the time he had felt Her watching his face; always on the verge of saying something. . . .

When they returned to the drawing-room the fire had burnt down a little. Martin piled on wood, then sat back in the shadow watching Pussy, who, with a reading lamp at her elbow, had begun to sew. He never read these evenings; a table of bric-à-brac had been pushed up against the doors of the bookcase with the gilt-bound classics and encyclopædias which had beguiled his evenings other years. Books, after all, were musty things, and all the book-learning in the world didn't make him more valuable to Pussy, whose eye wandered when he spoke to her of dynasties or carnivorous plants. He would pull her work-box towards him and amuse himself sorting its contents. One evening he came on a thimble-case which made him start. "Where did you get that, Pussy?" he asked fiercely. It appeared that she had had it since she was a little girl. Strange that it should be the same as another, so familiar once! He confiscated it and brought her a morocco one next day, with a new thimble in it that did not fit.

This evening, watching her head and hands in the circle of light, he could hardly keep at the other side of the hearthrug from her. She was preoccupied, worked very slowly; at intervals she smoothed out her sewing on her knee, with her head on one side. Pussy was long-sighted, and always looked at things from as far away as possible. When he spoke, her intent eyes fixed themselves on him unseeingly.

"What are you thinking about, Pussy?"

She evidently did not wish to tell him. She smiled, looked round the room a little fearfully, smiled again and took up her work.

"*Pussy?*"

"Oh, I don't know; I'm so happy. I'm so glad to have you back. I wonder if anyone was ever so happy."

"Then why do you look so sad?"

"I was thinking it would be so terrible not to be happy. I was trying to imagine what I'd feel like if you didn't care."

"*Didn't care!*"

"I—I couldn't imagine it," she admitted. He could no longer keep the length of the hearthrug between them when she smiled like that. She continued with his arm round her. "You never let me know the feel of wanting. Just the littlest differences in you would make me eat my heart out. I should never be able to ask you for things. I should just look and look at you, trying to speak, and then you would grow to hate me."

"—and then?"

"—Don't look at me like that, Martin—and then I should get ill, and if you didn't want me to come back I'd die. . . . Silly, I was only imagining. You shouldn't have made me talk."

"You shouldn't imagine things like that," he said sombrely. "What makes you do it? It's—it's morbid: you might do yourself a great deal of harm. And besides, it's—it's—"

"Do things like that happen? Could a person go on loving and loving and never be wanted?"

"How should *I* know?"

"I think," she said, "that not to want a person must be a sort, a sort of murder. I think a person who was done out of their life like that would be brought back by the injustice much more than anybody who was shot or stabbed."

"Are these the sort of things you think about all day?"

She looked at his white face, and laid her head against his shoulder and began to whimper. "Oh, Martin, don't be angry. I am so frightened, I am so frightened."

"Hush!"

"We're not safe and I don't believe we're even good. It can't be right to be so happy when there isn't enough happiness in the world to go round. Suppose we had taken somebody else's happiness, somebody else's life. . . ."

"Pussy, hush, be quiet. I forbid you. You've been dreaming. You've been silly, imagining these horrors. My darling, there's no sin in happiness. You shouldn't play with dreadful thoughts. Nothing can touch us."

"I sometimes feel the very room hates us!"

"Nothing can touch us," he reiterated, looking defiantly into the corners of the room.

The Evil That Men Do—

A T THE CORNER by the fire-station, where Southampton Row is joined by Theobalds Road, a little man, hurrying back to his office after the lunch hour, was run over by a motor-lorry. He had been stepping backward to avoid a taxi when worse befell him. What was left of him was taken to hospital and remained for some days unidentified, as no papers of any sort were to be found in his pockets.

The morning after this occurrence a lady living on the outskirts of a country town received a letter in an unfamiliar writing. The appearance of the envelope startled her; it was so exactly what she had been expecting for the last four days. She turned it over, biting her lip. The dining-room was darker than usual, it was a dull, still morning, and she had risen and dressed with growing apprehension. Her husband was away, and the windows seemed farther than ever now that she occupied his place and breakfasted alone. She poured out a cup of tea and raised the plated cover of a dish. The

123

sight of a lonely sausage decided her. She opened the letter.

Before she had read to the end she leant forward to think, with her knuckles doubled under her chin. Other people have that sinister advantage over one of being able to see the back of one's head. For the first time in her life she had the uncomfortable sense that somebody had done so, that somebody had not only glanced but was continuously staring. Her husband did not make her feel like this.

"Fancy," she thought. "Just an hour and ten minutes exactly. Just that little time, and all these years I never knew. Think of living among all these people and never knowing how I was different."

She folded up the letter for a moment, and began betting against herself on his Christian name. "Evelyn," she thought, "or possibly Arthur, or Philip." As a matter of fact it was Charles.

"I know you so well," the letter continued. "Before you drew your gloves off I knew that you were married. You have been living on the defensive for years. I know the books you read, and what you see in the streets you walk in of that town with the terrible name. You live in a dark house looking over a highway. Very often you stand in the light of the windows, leaning your head against the frame, and trees with dull leaves send the sunshine and shadow shivering over your face. Footsteps startle you, you start back into the crowded room. The morning you get this letter, go out bare-headed into your garden and let the wind blow the sunshine through your hair. I shall be thinking of you then.

"Your husband and your children have intruded on you. Even your children hurt you with their little soft hands, and yet you are as you always were, untouched and lonely. You came slowly out of yourself at that poetry-reading, like a nymph coming out of a wood. You came towards me like a white thing between trees, and I snatched at you as you turned to go back—"

Her cheeks burnt.

"My goodness," she cried, biting her thumbnail. "Fancy anybody being able to write like that! Fancy living at 28, Abiram Road, West Kensington. I wonder if he's got a wife, I do wonder." Delicious warmth crept down her. "Poetry! I thought he wrote poetry. Fancy him having guessed I read it!"

"I am going to send you my poetry. It is not published yet, but I am having it typewritten. When it is published there shall be just your one initial on the dedication page. I cannot bear the thought of your living alone among those strange people who hurt you— familiar, unfamiliar faces and cold eyes. I know it all; the numb mornings, the feverish afternoons; the intolerable lamplit evenings, night—"

"Now," she thought, "I'm sure he has a wife."

"—and your wan, dazed face turning without hope to the first gleams at the window—"

Ah, guilty, guilty, that she slept so well!

The cook came in.

When the meals for the day were ordered and her

breakfast half-surreptitiously eaten with the letter tucked inside the tea-cosy, she went upstairs to her room and tried on the hat she had worn in London, folding the side-flaps of the mirror round her so that she could see her profile. She leant forward gazing at a point in space represented by the prismatic stopper of a scent-bottle. With a long, slow breath she went slowly through the action of drawing off a glove.

"Living," she said aloud, "for years and years on the defensive." She looked into the mirror at the neat quiet room behind her, with the reflected pinkness from curtains and carpet over its white wall, and the two mahogany bedsteads with their dappled eiderdowns. There were photographs of her aunts, her children, and her brother-in-law's wife along the mantelpiece, a print of the Good Shepherd above the washstand, and "Love among the Ruins" over the beds. On a bracket were some pretty vases of French china Harold had given her at Dieppe, and a photogravure of the Luxemburg gardens she had given Harold. In a bookcase were several selections from the poets, beautifully bound in coloured suède, and another book, white with gold roses, called "The Joy of Living." She got up and slipped a novel from the local library into the bottom of a drawer.

"What on earth would be the good," she reasoned, "of going out into the garden when there is no sun and no wind and practically no garden?" She considered her reflection.

"I don't feel I could go down the High Street in

this hat. There must be something queer about it. Half-past nine: Harold will be back at half-past eleven. I wonder if he's bringing me anything from London."

She put a good deal of powder on her face, changed her hat and ear-rings, selected a pair of half-soiled gloves from a drawer, and went downstairs. Then she ran quickly up again and wiped off all the powder.

"Like a wood nymph," she murmured, "coming out of a wood."

When she was half-way down the High Street she found that she had forgotten her shopping-basket and her purse.

Harold came home at half-past eleven and found his wife still out.

He whistled for some minutes in the hall, looked vainly into her bedroom, the kitchen, and the nursery, then went round to the office to put in some work. Harold was a solicitor. Coming in again at lunch-time he met her crossing the hall. She looked at him vaguely.

"Why, you *are* back early!"

"I was back two hours ago," said he.

"Did you have a nice time in London?"

He explained, with his usual patience, that one does not expect to have a nice time when one goes up to London on business.

"Of course," he said, "we're all out to get what we can out of London. We all, as you might say, 'pick it over.' Only what I'm out for isn't pleasure—I leave that to you, don't I?—I'm out for other pickings."

"Yes, Harold."

"This is very good beef."

"Yes, isn't it," she cried, much gratified. "I got it at Hoskins'—Mrs. Peck deals there, she told me about it. It is much cheaper than at Biddle's, tuppence less in the pound. I have to cross over to the other side of the street now when I pass Biddle's. I haven't been there for three days, and he looks as though he were beginning to suspect—"

She sighed sharply; her interest flagged.

"Ah, yes?" said Harold encouragingly.

"I'm tired of buying beef," she said resentfully.

"Oh, come, tired of going down the High Street! Why what else would you—"

She felt that Harold was odious. He had not even brought her anything from London.

"All my day," she cried, "messed up with little things!"

Harold laid down his knife and fork.

"Oh, do please go on eating!"

"Yes," said Harold. "I was only looking for the mustard. What were you saying?"

"Got any plans this afternoon?" he said after luncheon, according to precedent.

"I'm going to write letters," she said, pushing past him into the drawing-room.

She shut the door behind her, leaving Harold in the hall. There was something in doing that, "living on the defensive." But were there any corners, any moments of her life for the last eight years which Harold had not pervaded? And, horrible, she had not only lived with him but liked him. At what date, in fact, had she ceased liking Harold? *Had* she ever—?

She put her fingers quickly in her ears as though somebody had uttered the guilty thing aloud.

Seating herself at the writing-table, she shut her eyes and thoughtfully stroked her eyebrows with the pink feather at the tip of a synthetic quill pen. She drew the feather slowly down the line of one cheek and tickled herself under the chin with it, a delightful sensation productive of shivers.

"Oh," she sighed, with a shuddering breath, "how beautiful, beautiful you are."

The top of a bus, lurching and rattling through obscurer London, the cold air blowing on her throat, moments under lighted windows when their faces had been mutually discernible, the sudden apparition of the conductor which had made him withdraw his hands from her wrist, their conversation—which she had forgotten. . . . "Ride, ride together, for ever ride." . . . When the bus stopped they had got down and got on to another. She did not remember where they had said good-bye. Fancy, all that from going to a poetry-reading instead of a picture-house. Fancy! And she hadn't even understood the poetry.

She opened her eyes and the practical difficulties of correspondence presented themselves. One could not write that sort of letter on Azure Bond; the notepaper he had used had been so indefinably *right*, somehow. She did not know how to address him. He had not begun with a "Dear" anything, but that did seem rather abrupt. One could not call him "Dear Mr. Simmonds" after an hour and ten minutes of such bus-riding; how could you call a person Mr. Simmonds when he said you were a nymph? Yet she couldn't take to "Charles." Everything practical, she found, had been crowded into the postscript of his letter—people said that women did that. He said he thought it would be better if she were to write to him at his office in Southampton Row; it was an insurance office, which somehow gave her confidence. "Dear Charles," she began.

It was a stiff little letter.

"I know it is," she sighed, distressfully re-reading it. "It doesn't sound abandoned, but how can I sound abandoned in this drawing-room?" She stood up, self-consciously. "The cage that is," she said aloud, "the intolerable *cage!*" and began to walk about among the furniture. "—Those chintzes are pretty, I am glad I chose them. And those sweet ruched satin cushions. . . . If he came to tea I would sit over here by the window, with the curtains drawn a little behind me— no, over here by the fireplace, it would be in winter and there would be nothing but firelight. But people of that sort never come to tea; he would come later on in the evening and the curtains would be drawn, and I should be wearing my—Oh, 'like a nymph.' How trivial it all seems."

And Harold had wondered what there would be left for her to do if she didn't go down the High Street. She would show him. But if she went through with this to the end Harold must never know, and what would be the good of anything without Harold for an audience?

She again re-read the letter she had written:

"—Of course my husband has never entered into my inner life—" and underlined the "of course" with short definite lines. It was quite true; she left books of poetry about and Harold never glanced at them; she sat for hours gazing at the fire or (as Charles said) out of the window and Harold never asked her what she was thinking about; when she was playing with the children she would break off suddenly and turn away her face and sigh, and Harold never asked her what was the matter. He would go away for days and leave her alone in the house with nobody to talk to but the children and the servants and the people next door. But of course solitude was her only escape and solace; she added this as a postscript.

Harold entered.

"I left this," he said, "down at the office this morning by mistake. I thought I had forgotten it in London—I should not like to have done so. I was very much worried. I did not mention the matter as I did not want you to be disappointed." He extended a parcel. "I don't know whether it is pretty, but I thought you might like it."

It was the most beautiful handbag, silver-grey, with the delicate bloom on it of perfect suède—darker when one stroked it one way, lighter the other. The clasp was real gold and the straps by which one carried it of exactly the right length. Inside it had three divisions;

drawing out the pads of tissue paper one revealed a lining of ivory moiré, down which the light shot into the shadows of the sumptuously scented interior in little trickles like water. Among the silk folds of the centre compartment were a purse with a gold clasp, a gold case that might be used for either cigarettes or visiting cards, and a darling little gold-backed mirror. There was a memorandum-tablet in an outer pocket, and a little book of *papier poudre*.

They sat down on the sofa to examine it, their heads close together.

"Oh," she cried, "you don't mind, Harold? *Papier poudre?*"

"Not," said Harold, "if you don't put on too much."

"And look—the little wee mirror. Doesn't it make me have a little wee face?"

Harold breathed magnanimously over the mirror.

"Harold," she said, "you *are* wonderful. Just what I wanted. . . ."

"You can take it out shopping tomorrow morning, down the High Street."

She shut the bag with a click, brushed away the marks of her finger-tips, and swung it by the straps from her wrist, watching it through half-closed eyes.

"*Harold*," she sighed ineffably.

They kissed.

"Shall I post your letters?" he inquired.

She glanced towards the writing-table. "Would you wait a moment? Just a moment; there's an address I must write, and a postscript."

"My little wee wife," said Harold contentedly.

"P.P.S.," she added. "You must not think that I do not love my husband. There are moments when he touches very closely my *exterior life*."

She and Harold and the handbag went as far as the post together, and she watched the letter swallowed up in the maw of the pillar-box.

"Another of your insurance policies?" asked Harold.

"Only just to know the general particulars," she said.

She wondered for some time what Charles would think when he came to the last postscript, and never knew that Fate had spared him this.

Sunday Evening

I T WAS six o'clock, the dusky sky was streaked with
gold behind the beech-trees and the bells were already
beginning; they had sat like this since tea. Mrs. Roche
had turned half-round to watch the sunset, her hands
were clasped along the back of her chair and her chin
rested on her interwoven fingers. She blinked a little
in the level light, and all the little lines were visible
about her eyes and round her puckered mouth. Laura
May and Mrs. McKenna sat on the low window seat,
faintly aureoled, their empty cups beside them on the
floor. Archie Manning was somewhere on the sofa,
away among the shadows of the room, leaning back
with his legs so twisted that his big feet stuck grotesquely out into the light. They had almost forgotten
his existence, and his masculinity did not obtrude itself
upon the conversation.

Cups and silver held the last of the sunlight, the tall
room gradually obscured itself; here and there a frame
or mirror gleamed on the shadowed walls.

They were talking about the First Woman; something had been said of her in the sermon that morning, and the thought had germinated in their minds all day.

Little Mrs. McKenna had had, so far, most to say; now she paused to light another cigarette, and Mrs. Roche turned her eyes in Laura's direction—she did not move her head.

"Laura has been nothing but a dusky profile. What is she thinking about that makes her so silent?"

"Laura is one of these primitive women," said Mrs. McKenna, inhaling smoke; "she doesn't think, she communes."

Laura was a big fair girl; her silences made other people talkative, her virginal starts and blushes stimulated Mrs. McKenna. She sat twisting and untwisting a gold chain round her neck, and said:

"Oh, I don't know really. I am very unoriginal, you know."

"But nobody is original," said Mrs. Roche, in her deep voice. "It's no good, really; all the oldest ideas are the best. But I was thinking, children, looking at the sunset, of her despair, on that first night, watching the light go out of the world. Think how it must have felt."

"I expect Adam was reassuring," said Mrs. McKenna; "he'd seen it happen before."

"No, he hadn't; they were born on the same day— that is, weren't they? Bother, look it up in Genesis."

"Yes, they were," said Laura conclusively. She was full of information.

"So Adam had no time to be lonely—that was a pity.

It would have made him so much more grateful—"

"—Psychologically," interrupted Mrs. Roche, "how interesting it all is, supposing it were true. Eve, of course, was at first no practical assistance to him. There were no chores, no mending. They didn't wear fig-leaves till after the Fall."

"That must have been nice," said Mrs. McKenna— "I mean the no fig-leaves. But inexpressive—"

"—Yes, inexpressive. I was going to say, rather impersonal."

"Oh, come, Gilda, if one's own skin isn't personal, what is!"

"I don't know," said Mrs. Roche slowly. "I don't think it's very personal. After all, it's only the husk of one—unavoidably there. But one's clothes are part of what one has got to say. Eve was much more herself when she began putting flowers in her hair than when she sat about in just—no fig-leaves. And she was much more herself than ever when she had got the fig-leaves on, and you and I are much more ourselves than she was."

"Then do you think covering oneself up is being real?" asked Laura. She entered the conversation with heavy, serious grace, as she would have entered a room.

"I don't know," said Gilda Roche. "The less of me that's visible, the more I'm there."

Laura, looking at Gilda's face so nearly on a level with her own, believed that it was one of the dearest on earth, with those satirical eyes. It was in this belief that she came to stay for long week-ends, and was hurt by

Mrs. Roche's other incomprehensible friends. "That's your mind?" she said. "You mean you feel a deeper sense of identity behind reserve?"

Mrs. Roche looked at her for a moment, then out over her head at the sunset. Mrs. McKenna fidgeted; she disliked this interchange of the personal note. "I don't agree with you," she said, raising her voice to drown the insistence of the bells. "I'm for off with everything—clothes, pose, reserve."

"Oh, now, Fanny, keep a little pose."

"Perhaps," she conceded unblushingly, "a little. Just a flower in the hair. Then to walk about among things like Eve among the trees, and feel them brushing up against me."

"But the world is so crowded, Fanny," said Gilda, who seemed to be enjoying Mrs. McKenna. "Just think, wherever you went it would be like walking in the park."

"I am rather mixed," said Laura; "are we speaking metaphorically, or not?"

"*Not*," said Mrs. McKenna, poking her. "Oh, decidedly not." She had been longing to poke Laura for some time, every line of the girl's anatomy annoyed her.

The bells came pealing chime after chime, their echoes pervaded the darkening room. Archie stirred on the sofa.

"Don't they make one feel holy," he said.

Laura, who had blushed for Archie during the parts of Mrs. McKenna's conversation—one never knew what that little woman was going to say, her mind flickered about like a lizard—thought that it might now be possible to turn the current. "I like them," she asserted.

"I hate them! I *hate* them!" cried Mrs. McKenna, putting her hands up over her ears and stamping her foot.

"They've been ringing for the last half-hour and you didn't seem to mind," said Gilda Roche, bending down to knock the ash off her cigarette into Laura's tea-cup.

"Yes, but they come in at the pauses so reprovingly; like Wilson putting his owl's face round the door. He longs to clear away the tea-things, but you give him no encouragement, and he is afraid of tumbling over Archie's feet. He's been in three times."

"I know," said Gilda penitently. "But if he takes away the tea-things it will leave us all sitting round in an empty circle, with no particular *raison d'être*."

"Archie is feeling holy," said Mrs. McKenna, looking across at the sofa not without respect. "I wonder what it feels like. At present his mind is in the past. When this present is the past it will linger longest in *this* particular part of the past (how difficult that was to say). Seven or eight Sundays hence, Archie, when you are in Africa, very lonely and primæval, leaning on your gun, you will think back to one Sunday evening in the country, in Gilda's drawing-room, and you'll try and hum the chimes (unconsciously you're learning them now). You'll shut your eyes and see the big windows and the beeches, and Laura and me, and think what sweet women we were."

"Oh, shall I?" said Archie in a discouraging tone.

Fanny McKenna was coming a little too near the mark; she was a discordant person altogether, and would have been better away. He was very happy with his head in the dark, listening to Gilda and watching Laura listen—he had been curiously attracted lately by the movements of her big head and big, rather incapable-looking white hands.

"I should like a life in the wilds," said Mrs. McKenna thoughtfully. "It's a pity I can't go with you."

"Yes," said Archie politely.

"But it wouldn't suit me; I should be terrible—luxuriate, over-develop."

"I thought that was what you wanted, Fanny," said Gilda unwisely. " 'Off with everything,' you know."

"Not when there was nobody about. What would it matter if everything was off or on? Nobody would be the better for it. What's the good of being sincere when there's nobody to be sincere at?"

"There'd be Archie."

"Well, anyway, there's William," said Mrs. McKenna conclusively. "And I can't go. I'm afraid I don't love Archie enough. But he will be very lonely—won't you, Archie?"

"Oh, I don't know," said Archie evasively, rolling his head about among the cushions. "I suppose so. I suppose one will live a good bit in the past and future if one has got too much time to think and not enough to do in the present."

"What future, Archie?" said Mrs. Roche with curiosity.

"Oh, I don't know. Coming back, I suppose. I ought to be back in four years. I wonder where everybody will be."

"I shall be here, a little greyer-haired, perhaps, and stupid; several of my friends will have given up coming down to see me, including Fanny—who will be wherever William isn't. Laura will probably be married—"

"Oh?" said Laura consciously.

"—and you will come down once or twice, and be very retrospective and sweet, Archie, then drift away too. Perhaps you will bring the girl you are engaged to down to see me, and she will kiss you on the way home and say I am a dear old thing, and not be the least bit jealous any more. . . . I know I shall be very stupid some day; I can feel it coming down on me, like mist from the top of a mountain."

"Laura will often come and see you," consoled Mrs. McKenna, "and bring all the babies—"

"We must all write to Archie," interposed Gilda. "He will never answer, but he will expect the most enormous posts. It's queer that we three who have been talking so much about primæval simplicity should have nothing much in front of us but drawing-rooms and gardens for the next four years, while Archie, who never asks for anything better than a sofa—from all I've seen of him—should be actually going out into the wilds to do things."

"Why, yes," said Mrs. McKenna, "Archie is actually going to revert. Laura would do that easily too. Now for you and me, Gilda, life is much more perilous. Archie and Laura would camp out quite happily, compassed about by a perfect cloud of lions, and so long as they weren't eaten—well, they'd just go on living. But for us the next four years are going to be most terribly dangerous. I have been feeling so happy lately that I know I must be terribly insecure, right at the edge of something. The struggle for life—they'll never know the meaning of it, will they, Gilda? The feeling that if you stopped for a moment you'd go out."

Gilda's eyes narrowed. "Yes, it's desperate, Fanny, isn't it? You contesting every inch and I longing to grow old beautifully—"

"And murdering," said Fanny intensely, "smothering your youth!"

Gilda began to laugh. "I don't think you're right in saying that Archie and Laura live—just negatively. They are a great deal more than not dead. And you're very sweeping, Fanny; nobody likes to be dismissed as incomplex. Archie is a man of action, strenuous in his mind, and Laura is reposeful—which needs energy. That is why we love her."

"Yes, don't we," said Fanny generously, "but we can't think how it's done."

"Oh, all big things are reposeful," said Gilda; "look at the beech-trees."

"I am a very wiry Scotch fir," said Fanny with relish. "I stand against the skyline and cry out for gales. When they come I ecstasize. Gilda, you are a larch tree planted in a windy place. You look down and think you long for a valley, but every inch of you undulates. In a calm you'd go quite limp. *You* in a calm—!"

"It's all I want," said Gilda. She raised her chin from her hands and leant back to look round the shadows of the room, her hands still resting on the back of the chair. She had an eternal youthfulness in gesture and repose. Archie, watching her silhouette against the fading sky, thought she was like a girl of nineteen.

"Hurry, hurry, hurry, hurry!" intoned Fanny suddenly, echoing the church bell, which was now ringing for late comers with a little note of urgency. "Don't you think we might take Archie to church? It would give him some more to remember. We might arrive before the second lesson, if we started now, and he could sit between Laura and you in rather a dark pew, and share a book, and sing 'Lead, Kindly Light'—"

"Oh, don't, Fanny!"

Fanny had wondered how much of this they were going to stand. She loved to see Gilda defending her lambs. "Oh, it's only that tiresome little Mrs. McKenna," she assured them. "Terribly flippant, isn't she?" She sighed. "I wonder if anyone will ever think of me on Sunday evenings?"

"Only if they want a fourth at bridge," said Archie

brutally. It was extraordinary how nice boys could hurt.

"I've never been to evening church. I know nothing about it; is it poignant?" asked Gilda. "Laura, we will go next time you're here."

"You might go about eight weeks hence," suggested Archie disinterestedly. "When I shall be—*there*, you know. It would be rather amusing. And I say, suppose you always write on Sunday evenings—no, of course you couldn't; the house is always full of people. It's awfully funny to think of those bells going, and all these chairs and sofas here, and people in them, and not me. It's funny to think of everywhere going on without one, and still going on if one never came back."

"I'll keep your corner of the sofa for you, Archie. No one else shall sit in it."

"Yes, you might." The room was getting so dark that it did not matter what one said. Laura leant back with her head against the window frame and sighed. Fanny, with her arms folded, peered down at her own little feet. Archie began to whistle under his breath. " 'Turn down an empty glass,' " he said.

"Four years will fly," said Laura.

"All depends," said Fanny. "Four years hence—" She shivered.

"Funny if we all met here again," said Archie.

"We won't," said Fanny with conviction.

"Who knows, who knows?" said Gilda.

"Who *wants* to know? We'd never dare go on."

"Oh, Fanny, *dare?* . . . We've got to."

"We want to," said Laura quietly.

"Yes, by Jove," said Archie. "It's all been jolly good so far; one feels They wouldn't let one down."

"*They?*" cried Fanny impatiently. "They *who?* How dependent, how pitiful, how childish!"

"Well, you don't believe we're in the dark for ever now the sun's gone down," said Gilda uncertainly.

"We guess it may come up again. We chance it. We're such optimists, such cowards!"

"Well, what do you believe?"

"Believe? I wouldn't *sell* myself."

"I think *that's* pitiful," said Laura.

The door opened.

"Yes, Wilson," said Gilda, "I think you might come in and take away the tea." They heard Wilson fumbling for a moment, then the room sprang into light. They blinked a little, suddenly aware of the furniture, each other's bodies, and a sense of betrayal. Mrs. McKenna rose briskly.

"We might have had some bridge," she said. "What a pity some of us can't play."

She looked down at Laura.

Coming Home

Aʟʟ ᴛʜᴇ ᴡᴀʏ home from school Rosalind's cheeks burnt, she felt something throbbing in her ears. It was sometimes terrible to live so far away. Before her body had turned the first corner her mind had many times wrenched open their gate, many times rushed up their path through the damp smells of the garden, waving the essay-book, and seen Darlingest coming to the window. Nothing like this had ever happened before to either her or Darlingest; it was the supreme moment that all these years they had been approaching, of which those dim, improbable future years would be spent in retrospect.

Rosalind's essay had been read aloud and everybody had praised it. Everybody had been there, the big girls sitting along the sides of the room had turned and looked at her, raising their eyebrows and smiling. For an infinity of time the room had held nothing but the rising and falling of Miss Wilfred's beautiful voice doing the service of Rosalind's brain. When the voice dropped to silence and the room was once more unbearably crowded, Rosalind had looked at the clock and seen that her essay had taken four and a half minutes to read. She found that her mouth was dry and her eyes ached from staring at a small fixed spot in the heart of whirling circles, and her knotted hands were damp and trembling. Somebody behind her gently poked the small of her back. Everybody in the room was thinking about Rosalind; she felt their admiration and attention lapping up against her in small waves. A long way off somebody spoke her name repeatedly, she stood up stupidly and everybody laughed. Miss Wilfred was trying to pass her back the red exercise-book. Rosalind sat down again thinking to herself how dazed she was, dazed with glory. She was beginning already to feel about for words for Darlingest.

She had understood some time ago that nothing became real for her until she had had time to live it over again. An actual occurrence was nothing but the blankness of a shock, then the knowledge that something had happened; afterwards one could creep back and look into one's mind and find new things in it, clear and solid. It was like waiting outside the hen-house till the hen came off the nest and then going in to look for the egg. She would not touch this egg until she was with Darlingest, then they would go and look for it together. Suddenly and vividly this afternoon would be real for her. "I won't think about it yet," she said, "for fear I'd spoil it."

The houses grew scarcer and the roads greener, and

Rosalind relaxed a little; she was nearly home. She looked at the syringa-bushes by the gate, and it was as if a cold wing had brushed against her. Supposing Darlingest were out . . . ?

She slowed down her running steps to a walk. From here she would be able to call to Darlingest. But if she didn't answer there would be still a tortuous hope; she might be at the back of the house. She decided to pretend it didn't matter, one way or the other; she had done this before, and it rather took the wind out of Somebody's sails, she felt. She hitched up her essay-book under her arm, approached the gate, turned carefully to shut it, and walked slowly up the path looking carefully down at her feet, not up at all at the drawing-room window. Darlingest would think she was playing a game. Why didn't she hear her tapping on the glass with her thimble?

As soon as she entered the hall she knew that the house was empty. Clocks ticked very loudly; upstairs and downstairs the doors were a little open, letting through pale strips of light. Only the kitchen door was shut, down the end of the passage, and she could hear Emma moving about behind it. There was a spectral shimmer of light in the white panelling. On the table was a bowl of primroses; Darlingest must have put them there that morning. The hall was chilly; she could not think why the primroses gave her such a feeling of horror, then she remembered the wreath of primroses, and the scent of it, lying on the raw new earth of that grave. . . . The pair of grey gloves were gone from the bowl of visiting-cards. Darlingest had spent the morning doing those deathly primroses, and then taken up her grey gloves and gone out, at the end of the afternoon, just when she knew her little girl would be coming in. A quarter-past four. It was unforgivable of Darlingest: she had been a mother for more than twelve years, the mother exclusively of Rosalind, and still, it seemed, she knew no better than to do a thing like that. Other people's mothers had terrible little babies: they ran quickly in and out to go to them, or they had smoky husbands who came in and sat, with big feet. There was something distracted about other people's mothers. But Darlingest, so exclusively one's own. . . .

Darlingest could never have really believed in her. She could never have really believed that Rosalind would do anything wonderful at school, or she would have been more careful to be in to hear about it. Rosalind flung herself into the drawing-room; it was honey-coloured and lovely in the pale spring light, another little clock was ticking in the corner, there were more bowls of primroses and black-eyed, lowering anemones. The tarnished mirror on the wall distorted and reproved her angry face in its mild mauveness. Tea was spread on the table by the window, tea for two that the two might never . . . Her work and an open book lay on the tumbled cushions of the window-seat. All the afternoon she had sat there waiting and working, and now—poor little Darlingest, perhaps she had gone out because she was lonely.

People who went out sometimes never came back

again. Here she was, being angry with Darlingest, and all the time . . . Well, she had drawn on those grey gloves and gone out wandering along the roads, vague and beautiful, because she was lonely, and then?

Ask Emma? No, she wouldn't; fancy having to ask *her!*

"Yes, your mother'll be in soon, Miss Rosie. Now run and get your things off, there's a good girl—" Oh no, intolerable.

The whole house was full of the scent and horror of the primroses. Rosalind dropped the exercise-book on the floor, looked at it, hesitated, and putting her hands over her mouth, went upstairs, choking back her sobs. She heard the handle of the kitchen door turn; Emma was coming out. O God! Now she was on the floor by Darlingest's bed, with the branches swaying and brushing outside the window, smothering her face in the eiderdown, smelling and tasting the wet satin. Down in the hall she heard Emma call her, mutter something, and slam back into the kitchen.

How could she ever have left Darlingest? She might have known, she might have known. The sense of insecurity had been growing on her year by year. A person might be part of you, almost part of your body, and yet once you went away from them they might utterly cease to be. That sea of horror ebbing and flowing round the edges of the world, whose tides were charted in the newspapers, might sweep out a long wave over them and they would be gone. There was no security. Safety and happiness were a game that grown-up peo-

ple played with children to keep them from understanding, possibly to keep themselves from thinking.
But they did think, that was what made grown-up
people—queer. Anything might happen, there was no
security. And now Darlingest—

This was her dressing-table, with the long beads
straggling over it, the little coloured glass barrels and
bottles had bright flames in the centre. In front of the
looking-glass, filmed faintly over with a cloud of powder, Darlingest had put her hat on—for the last time.
Supposing all that had ever been reflected in it were
imprisoned somewhere in the back of a looking-glass.
The blue hat with the drooping brim was hanging over
the corner of a chair. Rosalind had never been kind
about that blue hat, she didn't think it was becoming.
And Darlingest had loved it so. She must have gone out
wearing the brown one; Rosalind went over to the
wardrobe and stood on tip-toe to look on the top shelf.
Yes, the brown hat was gone. She would never see
Darlingest again, in the brown hat, coming down the
road to meet her and not seeing her because she was
thinking about something else. Peau d'Espagne crept
faintly from among the folds of the dresses; the blue,
the gold, the soft furred edges of the tea-gown dripping out of the wardrobe. She heard herself making a
high, whining noise at the back of her throat, like a
puppy, felt her swollen face distorted by another par-
oxysm.

"I can't bear it, I can't bear it. What have I done? I
did love her, I did so awfully love her.

"Perhaps she was all right when I came in; coming home smiling. Then I stopped loving her, I hated her and was angry. And it happened. She was crossing a road and something happened to her. I was angry and she died. I killed her.

"I don't know that she's dead. I'd better get used to believing it, it will hurt less afterwards. Supposing she does come back this time; it's only for a little. I shall never be able to keep her; now I've found out about this I shall never be happy. Life's nothing but waiting for awfulness to happen and trying to think about something else.

"If she could come back just this once—Darlingest."

Emma came half-way upstairs; Rosalind flattened herself behind the door.

"Will you begin your tea, Miss Rosie?"

"No. Where's mother?"

"I didn't hear her go out. I have the kettle boiling—will I make your tea?"

"No. *No.*"

Rosalind slammed the door on the angry mutterings, and heard with a sense of desolation Emma go downstairs. The silver clock by Darlingest's bed ticked; it was five o'clock. They had tea at a quarter-past four; Darlingest was never, never late. When they came to tell her about *It*, men would come, and they would tell Emma, and Emma would come up with a frightened, triumphant face and tell her.

She saw the grey-gloved hands spread out in the dust.

A sound at the gate. "I can't bear it, I can't bear it. Oh, save me, God!"

Steps on the gravel.

Darlingest.

She was at the window, pressing her speechless lips together.

Darlingest came slowly up the path with the long ends of her veil, untied, hanging over her shoulders. A paper parcel was pressed between her arm and her side. She paused, stood smiling down at the daffodils. Then she looked up with a start at the windows, as though she heard somebody calling. Rosalind drew back into the room.

She heard her mother's footsteps cross the stone floor of the hall, hesitate at the door of the drawing-room, and come over to the foot of the stairs. The voice was calling "Lindie! Lindie, duckie!" She was coming upstairs.

Rosalind leaned the weight of her body against the dressing-table and dabbed her face with the big powder-puff; the powder clung in paste to her wet lashes and in patches over her nose and cheeks. She was not happy, she was not relieved, she felt no particular feeling about Darlingest, did not even want to see her. Something had slackened down inside her, leaving her a little sick.

"Oh, you're *there*," said Darlingest from outside, hearing her movements. "Where did, where were—?"

She was standing in the doorway. Nothing had been for the last time, after all. She had come back. One could never explain to her how wrong she had been. She was holding out her arms; something drew one towards them.

"But, my little *Clown*," said Darlingest, wiping off the powder. "But, oh—" She scanned the glazed, blurred face. "Tell me why," she said.

"You were late."

"Yes, it was horrid of me; did you mind? . . . But that was silly, Rosalind, I can't be always in."

"But you're my mother."

Darlingest was amused; little trickles of laughter and gratification ran out of her. "You weren't *frightened*, Silly Billy." Her tone changed to distress. "Oh, Rosalind, don't be cross."

"I'm not," said Rosalind coldly.

"Then come—"

"I was wanting my tea."

"Rosalind, *don't* be—"

Rosalind walked past her to the door. She was hurting Darlingest, beautifully hurting her. She would never tell her about that essay. Everybody would be talking about it, and when Darlingest heard and asked her about it she would say: "Oh, that? I didn't think you'd be interested." That would hurt. She went down into the drawing-room, past the primroses. The grey gloves were back on the table. This was the mauve and golden room that Darlingest had come back to, from under the Shadow of Death, expecting to find her little daughter. . . . They would have sat together on the window-seat while Rosalind read the essay aloud, leaning their heads closer together as the room grew darker.

That was all spoilt.

Poor Darlingest, up there alone in the bedroom, puzzled, hurt, disappointed, taking off her hat. She hadn't known she was going to be hurt like this when she stood out there on the gravel, smiling at the daffodils. The red essay-book lay spread open on the carpet. There was the paper bag she had been carrying, lying on a table by the door; macaroons, all squashy from being carried the wrong way, disgorging, through a tear in the paper, a little trickle of crumbs.

The pathos of the forgotten macaroons, the silent pain! Rosalind ran upstairs to the bedroom.

Darlingest did not hear her; she had forgotten. She was standing in the middle of the room with her face turned towards the window, looking at something a long way away, smiling and singing to herself and rolling up her veil.

Ann Lee's

Ann Lee's

ANN LEE'S occupied a single frontage in one of the dimmer and more silent streets of south-west London. Grey-painted woodwork framed a window over which her legend was inscribed in far-apart black letters: "ANN LEE—HATS." In the window there were always just two hats; one on a stand, one lying on a cushion; and a black curtain with a violet border hung behind to make a background for the hats. In the two upper stories, perhaps, Ann Lee lived mysteriously, but this no known customer had ever inquired, and the black gauze curtains were impenetrable from without.

Mrs. Dick Logan and her friend Miss Ames approached the shop-front. Miss Ames had been here once before two years ago; the hat still existed and was frequently admired by her friends. It was she who was bringing Mrs. Dick Logan; she hesitated beneath the names at the street corner, wrinkled up her brows, and said she hadn't remembered that Ann Lee's was so far from Sloane Square Station. They were young women with faces of a similar pinkness; they used the same swear-words and knew the same men. Mrs. Dick Logan had decided to give up Clarice; her husband made such a ridiculous fuss about the bills and she had come to the conclusion, really, that considering what she had to put up with every quarter-day she might have something more to show for it in the way of hats. Miss Ames, who never dealt there, agreed that Clarice *was* expensive: now there was that shop she had been to once, Ann Lec's, not far from Sloane Street—

"Expensive?" Mrs. Dick said warily.

"Oh well, not cheap. But most emphatically worth it. You know, I got that green there—"

"O-oh," cried Mrs. Dick Logan, "that *expressive* green!"

So they went to find Ann Lee.

It was an afternoon in January, and their first sensation was of pleasure as they pushed open the curtained door and felt the warm air of the shop vibrate against their faces. An electric fire was reflected in a crimson patch upon the lustrous pile of the black carpet. There were two chairs, two mirrors, a divan, and a curtain over an expectant archway. No hats were visible.

"Nice interior!" whispered Mrs. Logan.

"Very much *her*," returned Miss Ames. They loosened their furs luxuriously, and each one flashed sidelong at herself in a mirror an appraising glance. They had a sense of having been sent round on approval, and this deepened in the breast of Mrs. Logan as their waiting in the empty shop was prolonged by minute after minute. Clarice came rushing at one rather: Mrs. Logan was predisposed to like Ann Lee for her discreet indifference to custom. Letty Ames had said that she was practically a lady; a queer creature, Letty couldn't place her.

"I wonder if she realizes we're here," whispered Letty, her brows again faintly wrinkled by proprietary concern. "We might just cough—not an angry cough, quite natural. You'd better, Lulu, 'cause you've got one."

Mrs. Logan really had a slight catarrh, and the sound came out explosively. They heard a door softly open and shut, and the sound of feet descending two or three carpeted steps. There was another silence, then close behind the curtain one cardboard box was placed upon another, and there was a long, soft, continuous rustling of tissue paper. One might almost have believed Ann Lee to be emerging from a bandbox. Then the curtain twitched, quivered, and swung sideways, and someone gravely regarded them a moment from the archway. "Good afternoon," she said serenely, and "Good afternoon."

Her finger brushed a switch, and the shop became discreetly brilliant with long shafts of well-directed light.

"I've come back again," Miss Ames brought out a shade dramatically, and Ann Lee nodded. "Yes, so I see. I'm glad, Miss Ames. I had expected you." She smiled, and Mrs. Dick Logan felt chilly with exclusion. "And I've brought my friend, Mrs. Dick Logan."

Ann Lee, with delicately arched-up eyebrows, turned to smile.

She was slight and very tall, and the complete sufficiency of her unnoticeable dress made Mrs. Dick Logan feel gaudy. Her hands were long and fine, her outspread fingers shone against her dress—on a right-hand, non-committal finger she wore one slender ring. Her face was a serene one, the lips a shade austere, and her hair was closely swathed about her head in bright, sleek bands. There was something of the priestess about her, and she suffered their intrusion with a ceremonial grace. She was so unlike Clarice and all those other women that Mrs. Logan hardly knew how to begin, and was gratified, though half-conscious of a solecism, when Miss Ames said, "My friend would like so much to see some hats. She's rather wanting two or three hats."

Ann Lee's eyes dwelt dispassionately on Mrs. Logan's face. She looked questioningly at the eyebrows and searchingly at the mouth, then said with an assumption that barely deferred to her customer, "Something quiet?"

Something quiet was the last thing Mrs. Logan wanted. She wanted something nice and bright to wear at Cannes, but she hardly liked to say so. She put forward timidly, "Well, not *too* quiet—it's for the Riviera."

"Really?" said Ann Lee regretfully—"how delightful for you to be going out. I don't know whether I have—no, wait; perhaps I have some little model."

"I rather thought a turban—gold, perhaps?"

"Oh, a *turban*—? But surely you would be more likely to find what you want out there? Surely Cannes—"

This made Mrs. Logan feel peevish. Even if a person did look like a Madonna or something, it was their business to sell a hat if they kept a shop for that purpose. She hadn't followed Letty quite endlessly through those miserable back streets to be sent away disdainfully and told to buy her hats in France. She didn't care for shopping on the Riviera, except with her Casino winnings; the shops expected to be paid so soon, and Dickie made an even worse fuss when he saw a bill in francs. She said querulously:

"Yes, but haven't you got anything of that sort? Any goldish, sort of turbany thing?"

"I never have many hats," said Ann Lee. "I will show you anything I have."

Lulu glanced across at Letty, breathing more deeply with relief at this concession, and Letty whispered, as Ann Lee vanished momentarily behind the curtain: "Oh, she's always like that; like what I told you, queer. But the *hats*, my dear! You wait!"

When Ann Lee returned again carrying two hats, Mrs. Logan admitted that there had indeed been something to wait for. These were the hats one dreamed about—no, even in a dream one had never directly beheld them; they glimmered rather on the margin of one's dreams. With trembling hands she reached out in

Ann Lee's direction to receive them. Ann Lee smiled deprecatingly upon her and them, then went away to fetch some more.

Lulu Logan snatched off the hat she was wearing and let it slide unnoticed from the brocaded seat of the chair where she had flung it and bowl away across the floor. Letty snatched off hers too, out of sympathy, and, each one occupying a mirror, they tried on every single hat Ann Lee brought them; passing each one reverently and regretfully across to one another, as though they had been crowns. It was very solemn. Ann Lee stood against the curtain of the archway, looking at them gently and pitifully with her long pale eyes. Her hands hung down by her sides; she was not the sort of person who needs to finger the folds of a curtain, touch the back of a chair, or play with a necklace. If Mrs. Logan and her friend Miss Ames had had either eyes, minds, or taste for the comparison, they might have said that she seemed to grow from the floor like a lily. Their faces flushed; soon they were flaming in the insidious warmth of the shop. "Oh, *damn* my face!" groaned Miss Ames into the mirror, pressing her hands to her cheeks, looking out at herself crimsonly from beneath the trembling shadow of an osprey.

How could Lulu ever have imagined herself in a gold turban? In a gold turban, when there were hats like these? But she had never known that there were hats like these, though she had tried on hats in practically every shop in London that she considered fit to call a shop. Life was still to prove itself a thing of revelations, even for Mrs. Dick Logan. In a trembling voice she said that she would certainly have *this* one, and she thought she simply must have *this*, and "Give me back the blue one, darling!" she called across to Letty.

Then a sword of cold air stabbed into the shop, and Lulu and Letty jumped, exclaimed, and shivered. The outer door was open and a man was standing on the threshold, blatant in the light against the foggy dusk behind him. Above the suave folds of his dazzling scarf his face was stung to scarlet by the cold; he stood there timid and aggressive; abject in his impulse to retreat, blustering in his determination to resist it. The two ladies stood at gaze in the classic pose of indignation of discovered nymphs. Then they both turned to Ann Lee, with a sense that something had been outraged that went deeper than chastity. The man was not a husband; he belonged to neither of them.

The intruder also looked towards Ann Lee; he dodged his head upwards and sideways in an effort to direct his line of vision past them. He opened his mouth as though he were going to shout; then they almost started at the small thin voice that crept from it to say "Good evening."

Ann Lee was balancing a toque upon the tips of her fingers, an imponderable thing of citron feathers, which even those light fingers hardly dared to touch. Not a feather quivered and not a shadow darkened her oval face as she replied, "Good evening," in a voice as equably unsmiling as her lips and eyes.

"I'm afraid I've come at a bad moment."

"Yes," she said serenely, "I'm afraid you have. It's quite impossible for me to see you now; I'm sorry—I believe that hat is *you*, Mrs. Logan. I'm sorry you don't care for black."

"Oh, I do like black," said Mrs. Logan unhappily, feasting upon her own reflection. "But I've got so many. Of course, they do set the face off, but I particularly wanted something rather sunny looking—now that little blue's perfect. How much did you . . . ?"

"Eight guineas," said Ann Lee, looking at her dreamily.

Mrs. Logan shivered and glanced vindictively towards the door. Ann Lee was bending to place the toque of citron feathers on the divan; she said mildly over her shoulder, with one slight upward movement of her lashes, "We are a little cold in here, if you don't mind."

"Sorry!" the man said, looking wildly into the shop. Then he came right in with one enormous step and pulled the door shut behind him. "I'll wait then, if I may." He looked too large, with his angular blue cloth overcoat double-buttoned across the chest, and as he stuffed his soft grey hat almost furtively under his arm they saw at once that there was something wrong about his hair. One supposed he couldn't help it waving like that, but he might have worn it shorter. The shoes on his big feet were very bright. Fancy a man like that . . . Lulu allowed a note of injury to creep into her voice as she said, "I beg your pardon," and reached past him to receive another hat from Letty. The shop was quite crowded, all of a sudden. And really, walking in like that . . . He didn't know what they mightn't have been trying on; so few shops nowadays were hats exclusively. He didn't see either herself or Letty, except as things to dodge his eyes past—obstacles. The way he was looking at Ann Lee was disgusting. A woman who asked eight guineas for a little simple hat like that blue one had got no right to expose her customers to this.

Letty, her hair all grotesquely ruffled up with trying-on, stood with a hat in either hand, her mouth half open, looking at the man not quite intelligently. One might almost have believed that she had met him. As a matter of fact, she was recognizing him; not as his particular self but as an Incident. He—It—crops up periodically in the path of any young woman who has had a bit of a career, but Ann Lee—really. Letty was vague in her ideas of Vestal Virgins, but dimly she connected them with Ann. Well, you never knew. . . . Meanwhile this was a hat shop; the least fitting place on earth for the recurrence of an Incident. Perhaps it was the very priestliness of Ann which made them feel that there was something here to desecrate.

Ann Lee, holding the blue hat up before the eyes of Lulu, was the only one who did not see and tremble as the square man crossed the shop towards the fireplace and sat down on the divan beside the feather toque. He was very large. He drew his feet in with an obvious consciousness of offence and wrapped the skirts of his

overcoat as uncontaminatingly as possible about his
knees. His gaze crept about the figure of Ann. "I'll
wait, if you don't mind," he repeated.

"I'm afraid it's no good," she said abstractedly, looking past him at the toque. "I'm busy at present, as you
can see, and afterwards I've orders to attend to. I'm
sorry. Hadn't you better—?"

"It's four o'clock," he said.

"*Four o'clock!*" shrieked Lulu. "Good God, I'm due
at the Cottinghams!"

"Oh, don't go!" wailed Letty, whose afternoon was
collapsing. Ann Lee, smiling impartially, said she did
think it was a pity not to decide.

"Yes, but eight guineas." It needed a certain time for
decision.

"It's a lovely little hat," pleaded Letty, stroking the
brim reverently.

"Yes, it's pretty," conceded Ann Lee, looking down
under her lids at it with the faintest softening of the lips.
They all drew together, bound by something tense: the
man before the fire was forgotten.

"Oh, I don't know," wailed the distracted Mrs.
Logan. "I must have that little black one, and I ought to
get another dinner-hat—You know how one needs
them out there!" she demanded of Miss Ames reproachfully. They both looked appealingly at Ann Lee. She
was not the sort of person, somehow, that one could
ask to reduce her things. There was a silence.

"It *is* four o'clock!" said the man in a bullying, nervous voice. They jumped. "You *did* say four o'clock," he repeated.

Ann Lee quite frightened the two others; she was so very gentle with him, and so scornfully unemphatic. "I'm afraid you are making a mistake. On Thursdays I am always busy. Good evening, Mr. Richardson; don't let us waste any more of your time. Now, Mrs. Logan, shall we say the blue? I feel that you would enjoy it, though I still think the black is a degree more *you*. But I daresay you would not care to take both."

"I'll wait," he said, in a queer voice. Unbuttoning his overcoat, he flung it open with a big, defiant gesture as he leaned towards the fire. "Oh, the *toque!*" they screamed; and Ann Lee darted down and forwards with a flashing movement to retrieve the frail thing from beneath the iron folds of the overcoat. She carried it away again on the tips of her fingers, peering down into the ruffled feathers; less now of the priestess than of the mother—Niobe, Rachel. She turned from the archway to say in a white voice, her face terrible with gentleness, "Then will you kindly wait outside?"

"It's cold," he pleaded, stretching out his hands to the fire. It was a gesture: he did not seem to feel the warmth.

"Then wouldn't it be better not to wait?" Ann Lee softly suggested.

"I'll wait today," he said, with bewildered and unshaken resolution. "I'm not going away *today*."

While she was away behind the curtain, rustling

softly in that world of tissue paper, the man turned
from the fire to look round at the contents of the shop.
He looked about him with a kind of cringing triumph,
as one who has entered desecratingly into some Holiest
of Holies and is immediately to pay the penalty, might
look about him under the very downsweep of the sacer-
dotal blade. He noted without comment or emotion the
chairs, the lustrous carpet, Mrs. Logan's hat, the ladies,
and the mirrors opposite one another, which quad-
rupled the figure of each lady. One could only con-
clude that he considered Miss Ames and Mrs. Logan as
part of the fittings of the shop—"customers" such as
every shop kept two of among the mirrors and the
chairs; disposed appropriately; symbolic, like the two
dolls perpetually recumbent upon the drawing-room
sofa of a doll's house. He stared thoughtfully at Miss
Ames, not as she had ever before been stared at, but as
though wondering why Ann Lee should have chosen
to invest her shop with a customer of just *that* pattern.
Miss Ames seemed for him to be the key to something;
he puzzled up at her with knitted brows.

"Perhaps it would be better for us to be going?" said
Miss Ames to Mrs. Logan, her words making an icy
transition above the top of his head. "I'm afraid it's
difficult for you to decide on anything with the place
crowded and rather a lot of talking."

Mrs. Logan stood turning the blue hat round and
round in her hands, looking down at it with tranced
and avid eyes. "Eight—sixteen—twenty-four," she

murmured. "I do think she might reduce that little toque. If she'd let me have the three for twenty-two guineas."

"Not she," said Letty with conviction.

The man suddenly conceded their humanity. "I suppose these are what you'd call expensive hats?" he said, looking up at Mrs. Logan.

"Very," said she.

"Several hundreds, I daresay, wouldn't buy up the contents of the shop, as it stands at present?"

"I suppose not," agreed Mrs. Logan, deeply bored— "Letty, when *is* she coming back? Does she always walk out of the shop like this? Because *I* call it . . . I shall be so late at the Cottinghams, too. I'd be off this minute, but I just can't leave this little blue one. Where'll we get a taxi?"

"First corner," said the man, rearing up his head eagerly. "Round on your left."

"Oh, thanks," they said frigidly. He was encouraged by this to ask if they, too, didn't think it was very cold. Not, in fact, the sort of weather to turn a dog out. "I'm sorry if I've inconvenienced you any way by coming in, but I've an appointment fixed with Miss Lee for four o'clock, specially fixed, and you can imagine it was cold out there, waiting—" The rustling of the paper ceased; they thought the curtain twitched. He turned and almost ate the archway with his awful eyes. Nothing happened; the sleek heavy folds still hung down unshaken to the carpet. "I've an appointment," he repeated, and listened to the echo with satisfaction and a growing confidence. "But I don't mind waiting—I've done so much waiting."

"Really?" said Miss Ames, in the high voice of indifference. Determined that she must buy nothing, she was putting her own hat on again resignedly. "She's bound to be back in a jiff," she threw across reassuringly to Lulu, who sat bareheaded by a mirror, statuesquely meditative, her eyes small with the effort of calculation.

"I don't suppose either of you ladies," said the man tremendously, "have spent so much time in your whole lives trying on clothes in shops of this kind, as I've spent outside just this one shop, waiting. If any more ladies come in, they'll just have to take me naturally, for I'm going to sit on here where I am till closing time."

Miss Ames, fluffing her side hair out in front of the mirror, repeated "Really?" bland as a fish.

"I'm quite within my rights here," said he, looking down now with approval at his feet so deeply implanted in the carpet, "because you see, I've got an appointment."

"There was no appointment, Mr. Richardson," said Ann Lee regretfully, standing in the archway.

Mrs. Dick Logan, catching her breath, rose to her feet slowly, and said that she would have all three hats, and would Ann Lee send them along at once, please. It was an immense moment, and Miss Ames, who knew Dickie, thought as she heard Mrs. Logan give her name and address in a clear unfaltering voice that there *was*

something splendid about Lulu. The way she went
through it, quarter-day after quarter-day . . . Miss
Ames glowed for their common femininity as she
watched her friend pick up yet another hat and try it
on, exactly as if she could have had it too, if she had
wished, and then another and another. Ann Lee, writing languidly in an order-book, bowed without comment to Mrs. Logan's decision. And Letty Ames
couldn't help feeling also that if Ann Lee had wished,
Lulu would have had that other hat, and then another
and another.

Mrs. Logan stooped to recover her own hat from the
floor. Ann Lee, looking down solicitously, but making
no movement to assist her, meditated aloud that she was
glad Mrs. Logan was taking that little black. It was so
much *her*, to have left it behind would have been a pity,
Ann Lee couldn't help thinking.

As they gathered their furs about them, drew on their
gloves, snapped their bags shut, and nestled down their
chins into their furs, the two ladies glanced as though
into an arena at the man sitting on the divan, who now
leaned forwards to the fire again, his squared back towards them. And now? They longed suddenly, ah, how
they longed, to linger in that shop.

"Good afternoon," said Ann Lee. She said it with
finality.

"Good afternoon," they said, still arrested a second
in the doorway. As they went out into the street reluctantly they saw Ann Lee, after a last dim bow
towards them, pass back through the archway so gently

that she scarcely stirred the curtains. The man beside the fire shot to his feet, crossed the shop darkly, and went through after her, his back broad with resolution.

There were no taxis where they had been promised to find them, and the two walked on in the direction of Sloane Street through the thickening fog. Mrs. Dick Logan said that she didn't think she dared show her face at the Cottinghams now, but that really those hats were worth it. She walked fast and talked faster, and Miss Ames knew that she was determined not to think of Dickie.

When they came to the third corner they once more hesitated, and again lamented the non-appearance of a taxi. Down as much of the two streets as was visible, small shop-windows threw out squares of light on to the fog. Was there, behind all these windows, someone waiting, as indifferent as a magnet, for one to come in? "What an extraordinary place it was," said Mrs. Logan for the third time, retrospectively. "How she ever sells her things . . ."

"But she does sell them."

"Yes." She did sell them, Mrs. Logan knew.

As they stood on the kerbstone, recoiling not without complaints from the unkindness of the weather, they heard rapid steps approaching them, metallic on the pavement, in little uneven spurts of speed. Somebody, half blinded by the fog, in flight from somebody else. They said nothing to each other, but held their breaths, mute with a common expectancy.

A square man, sunk deep into an overcoat, scudded across their patch of visibility. By putting out a hand they could have touched him. He went by them blindly; his breath sobbed and panted. It was by his breath that they knew how terrible it had been—terrible.

Passing them quite blindly, he stabbed his way on into the fog.

The Parrot

WHEN MRS. WILLESDEN'S parrot escaped, it rocketed in a pale-green streak across the sky and settled in the chestnut tree at the foot of the garden, where it became invisible among the branches. Invisible, that is to say, to Maud Pemberty and Eleanor Fitch, who stood staring up under their hands into the glare of the morning, until Maud located his head, a vermilion blot borne up and down like a buoy, slowly, by the undulations of a lower layer of the foliage. The chestnut tree blazed all over in the sunshine with candles of wax blossom. The scent of the pollen gave Eleanor Fitch shivers; about the end of May she would pass the tree on any pretext, sighing for something that she could not remember. Maud was in love, and chestnut flowers meant nothing to her; besides, as parlour-maid, she had more to do in the house than Miss Fitch, who was only a companion.

Now they both stood looking up at the parrot piteously, fearfully; Maud who had left the window open, and Eleanor who had been cleaning the cage. They advanced towards the tree unconsciously, step by lingering step, as though attracted; still with that mesmeric upward stare.

The parrot took no notice of them. It wobbled along the branch, peevishly disentangling its wing and tail feathers from the long-fingered leaves. Its tongue was in one corner of its beak; its head turned and its eyes rolled from side to side in a mixture of ecstasy and apprehension. Once or twice it lost its balance and tilted right forward with a muffled squawk until it was hanging nearly upside down. It would recover itself, look reproachfully down at its claws, and totter along further, till another clump of leaves swept down to assault it. It wore an air of silly bravado, and looked what it was, thoroughly idiotic.

Mrs. Willesden had no brothers, cousins or lovers: none certainly who were sailors, and none of these, therefore, had brought the parrot home to her from Indian seas. Dark-faced men may have dazzled it, against the purple of the ocean, with the swinging gold of their earrings, and held it up to stroke the sleek vermilion of its head. This Eleanor would have wished to believe, and Mrs. Willesden even playfully asseverated; but the parrot had not, somehow, the aroma. It had no pedigree; Mrs. Willesden had bought it at an auction at the other side of London: a very new-looking parrot, newer-looking even than the complete edition of Lord Lytton, or the mahogany chest of drawers. It was a guaranteed talker, but its conversation was neither entertaining, relevant, nor profane. It would mutter "Poll, Po-oll, Pol-pol-pol" for hours, in an ecstasy of intro- spection, or say "Lead, kindly Light"—just that, no more of the hymn. If one spoke to it, besought it, cursed it, wooed it, it would blink at one in a smoulder of ma- levolence, and say, "Minnie? Minnie! Tom? Minnie!"

Mrs. Willesden loved the parrot, and would sit beside it for hours in the afternoon. It was carried into the dining-room to meals, and its cage was placed beside her at the head of the table, on a butler's tray. Eleanor hated the parrot, and used to come down and clean its cage early in the morning before breakfast, so as to get that over. Thus it was that the parrot had escaped at a quarter past eight, before Mrs. Willesden was awake, while yellow cotton blinds still unflickeringly sheathed her windows. Mrs. Willesden slept late today; one did not care, one did not dare to wake her. Eleanor and Maud stood sodden-footed out in the dew, with now and then a backward glance up at Mrs. Willesden's window, and their hands burnt and their fingers twitched with the desire to grab the parrot by its scaly legs and its wings and thrust it shrieking back into its cage.

Eleanor's mind went whirling round like a wheel on the hub of this moment. She knew that what had brought her here to be Mrs. Willesden's companion had also brought about the escape of the parrot—her own immense ineffectuality. She knew that she was a clever girl, or she might possibly have loved Mrs. Willesden; she knew that she was a wise girl, or she

could not so continuously have tolerated her. She knew
that she must be a nice-looking girl, or Mrs. Willesden,
whose sense of beauty had found its culminating expression in the parrot, would never have engaged her.
She knew, however, that she could not be dangerously
attractive, because although she was quite ready to
marry anybody who seemed at all suitable, and thus
escape from life with Mrs. Willesden and the equally
odious alternative of using her brains, nobody, even of
the most unsuitable, had so far presented himself. She
never thought about men, because she fully agreed with
Mrs. Willesden that this was not nice; she merely wondered sometimes when Mrs. Willesden would have become a thing of the past. It was while thus wondering
that she had turned away from the parrot's cage to look
in a mirror, and, thus looking, had heard the unlatched
door swing open and the silken sound of the flight. As
things were now, Mrs. Willesden might very soon become a thing of the past; and a swift nostalgia for security made the sky blur and glitter, and the chestnut
candles swim.

"Well, it's no good crying, Miss," said Maud. "It
doesn't get us out of anything, what I mean."

"I'm not," said Eleanor quickly. "Poll, pretty Polly-
poll, come downsey!"

"Come downsey!" echoed Maud. ("Yah, get out of
that, you dirty beast!) Well, he doesn't understand,
Miss. He's just stupid."

"Go into the house and get the cage, Maud. Stick a
banana between the bars, so's he can only get at it from

the inside, and put it down on the grass with the door open. Go quickly and—hush!"

Maud went, and Eleanor stood staring, still mesmerically, up at the parrot, while the imagined eyes of Mrs. Willesden burnt into her back. She stared up at the parrot, but Polly was preoccupied with his feat of balance and was perpetually in profile. He was not to be mesmerized, and just as Maud emerged from the house with the cage held at arm's length and the door invitingly open, he toppled forward urgently, beat for a moment with his wings, then flopped into the air. He did not rise very high this time, but after describing one or two lopsided circles, as though with wings unevenly weighted, he skimmed the top of the garden wall, glittered for a second above it in poised uncertainty, and vanished.

"There!" said Maud, and Eleanor gathered her skirts together, gave one calculating glance, and was up and on to the top of the wall like a cat.

The parrot ambled slowly through the air, with, as it were, the jog of a fat pony translated into flight. It clumsily attempted a landing on some branches in the next garden and slid off again, its claws ripping the leaves. All along, in the pleasant irregular gardens of the road, glass-houses sparkled, flashing out rays, geraniums in the beds made neat little cubes of coral and scarlet, violas grew in great mauve cushions. A furtive young wind spilt the petals from the fruit trees on to the grass, stirred the pools they made, then crept away, frightened. Eleanor, equally furtive, knelt up on the

wall, looked all round her, and tucked her skirts down.
She calculated that the parrot must without fail come
wheezily to earth at either the Cuthbertsons' or the
Philpots'.

It would have a long way to fly before it reached the
poplars of the one garden which she could not possibly
enter to retrieve it. The poplars tapered above all the
trees of the gardens with a sort of elegant irresponsibil-
ity; they swayed towards one another and glittered
with mirth. They rose from out of the four walls of the
Lennicotts' garden, and within these walls no one in
the road had set foot since the occupation of the Lennicotts.

Towards the poplars the parrot leisurely proceeded,
as one in good time for an appointment, and somewhere
down below them came to earth.

Mrs. Willesden had told Eleanor that it was better
not to ask about the Lennicotts, and that it was all very,
very sad. Indeed, the less one knew the better, everybody felt, and ladies flinched as they told one another
in low voices things about the Lennicotts which one did
not care to say, but which demanded to be said. Mrs.
Willesden told Eleanor that sin was becoming, alas,
very prevalent (though one did not care to talk to an
unmarried girl about these things) and that she was
thankful that her mother had not lived to see these days,
and that her dear husband had also been spared. "It is
not even known," she said, "that they are the Lennicotts, but *he* is a Lennicott, and she is *called* Mrs. My
library does not keep his novels, and that nice young

man there looked very much surprised when I asked
for them. Mrs. Cuthbertson lent me a copy of one of
them, but I found it very difficult to read, and so did
she."

"Was it improper?" asked Eleanor, in a low voice,
winding wool quickly.

"One may be sure of that," Mrs. Willesden had replied, "but as I tell you, I did not finish the book; it was
so very dull. As far as I got, I did not see anything in it,
and I glanced through to the end and did not see anything either. However, I should not have dreamed of
keeping a book like that in the house with a young girl
like you about—Eleanor, you had better rewind that
wool, you are winding it too tightly. . . ."

Even in London, it was said, many people would not
know the Lennicotts, so they had come here, doubtless
in the hopes of making nice friends. The road deplored
the Lennicotts, and the neighbourhood envied the road.
In the evenings, long shafts of blistering whiteness
streamed out from the headlamps of cars and lent an
unseemly publicity to the comings and goings of everybody's cats. These cars drew up perpetually outside the
Lennicotts' with a long faint sound like a sniff. Though
they entertained, the Lennicotts were not rowdy; one
heard only, sometimes, low excited laughter of the kind
that made one wish to stop and listen; and, very rarely,
Mrs. Lennicott's voice, which was very beautiful, came
floating down among the trees of the road as she sang
to her guests after dinner.

The parrot dropped down among the poplars, and Eleanor's heart dropped with it, like a stone. She heard a slight rattle at the upstairs window, and knew that Mrs. Willesden's blind was up, and that soon everything would be over. She gathered herself together, her tongue curled back in her mouth with terror, and leapt from the top of the wall into the lane full of nettles that ran along the backs of the gardens, past the Willesdens', past No. 17's, 18's, and 19's, till it broadened out under the Lennicotts' poplars into a small patch of common. As she turned the bend of the lane and heard the rustle of the poplars above her, she heard also, very distinctly and monotonously, the parrot saying "Minnie? Minnie!" down in the garden inside the walls. Had it encountered anybody, or was it merely talking to itself?

Eleanor did not believe that early rising could possibly be compatible with moral obliquity. An outraged sense of fitness was therefore added to her astonishment when, having adjusted her pince-nez, she found herself looking down from the top of the Lennicotts' wall on to the unswerving centre parting of Mrs. Lennicott's marmalade-coloured hair. The parrot sat biting its nails on one end of a pergola, and Mrs. Lennicott did not notice it because she was reading a book of poetry with large print and smoking a cigarette in a long holder. She sat in a deck-chair with her feet on a recumbent watering-can, and wore, as might have been expected, coloured leather shoes. When she heard the scratching sound of Eleanor's toes seeking purchase on the outer bricks, she looked up, smiled vaguely, with the sun on her gold lashes, and said, "Good morning. Have you come to look for a tennis ball? Do come in!"

She had a long chin and a plump, oval, delicately coloured face. Her eyebrows arched very innocently, and she looked at Eleanor uncomprehendingly, but with an air of earnest effort, as though she were a verse of Georgian poetry that one could not possibly understand. "Do come in!" she repeated.

"Thank you," said Eleanor. "I only wanted that parrot." She pointed to the pergola, and Mrs. Lennicott, laying her book face downwards on the grass, turned her head with interest in the same direction. Her hair was braided against her cheek.

"Really," she said, "is that your parrot? It is very beautiful. But do come in and take it away if you want it. I expect it is very valuable. It may have been here for some time, but I did not notice it because this garden is always full of birds, and I am very stupid about natural history."

For the first time that morning the parrot looked straight at Eleanor; for the first time in their acquaintanceship it had a gleam of intelligence in its eye. "Take me," it seemed to say. "I am an old sick bird, beaten out and weary. I have aspired and failed—it is finished. Take me." A white sheath rolled up over its eyes; its feathers drooped.

Eleanor had an idea that if she did not breathe very deeply, if she walked lightly on the tips of her toes, taking as few steps as possible, and if she did not look quite straight at anything, especially Mrs. Lennicott, she might, having entered the Lennicotts' garden, yet leave it uncontaminated. She therefore sprang from the wall, alighting on her hands and on the balls of her feet, as she had been taught at school, at the very brink of a flower-bed. As she stood upright she half saw, then turned irresistibly to watch, Mrs. Lennicott rise with one ripple from the deck-chair and walk as though entranced towards the pergola, holding up her hands. Her dress hung ungirt from her bosom and swept the grass, so that its hem was dark with dew.

"Oh, how beautiful you are!" she sighed. "How your head flashes! You must forgive me," she said to Eleanor, "but I have never looked very closely at a parrot before."

Polly was obviously gratified. He ducked his head and fluttered his tail-feathers, and swayed a little from the claws. He conveyed by a multiplicity of innuendoes that Mrs. Willesden and Eleanor were a pair of old frumps, and that even Minnie had left much to be desired, and that he knew a woman of distinction when he met one. Had Mrs. Lennicott been allowed to engage him further in conversation, his capture from the rear might easily have been effected, but Eleanor was too precipitate. Her outstretched hands cast a shadow; Polly felt them coming and soared into the air with spread wings like a phœnix. He squawked derision at Eleanor, and steered a zig-zag course to the verandah drain pipe, from the pipe to an upper window-sill, from the window-sill to a tank, from the tank to the ridge of the roof between two chimney pots.

"Oh, how terrible for you!" cried Mrs. Lennicott, in real distress.

Eleanor's cheeks burnt; little wisps of hair came down and frisked in the light wind, tickling the back of her neck. The tides of her spirit were slow, drawn by the slow moon of her intelligence, but now anger stirred in her; she drew a gasp which shook her, and locked her fingers together.

"I'm going to catch that parrot," she said, turning to Mrs. Lennicott. "I'm going to catch it so's to wring its neck."

"*Have* you ever wrung anything's neck?" asked Mrs. Lennicott in an awed voice.

When Eleanor admitted that she hadn't, Mrs. Lennicott, with obvious relief, invited her to come into the house and catch the parrot. "It would be very easy," she said, "to get out on to the roof from the window of my husband's room. He has often talked of doing so when there was too much noise in the house, but the roof is not flat enough to hold a writing-table. I don't think he is awake, but if he were he would be delighted to help you."

The shadow of the house fell cold on Eleanor as she left the wind and glitter and innocence of the morning behind and walked with Mrs. Lennicott towards the steps of the verandah. Afterwards, there was so much lilac in the drawing-room and the place was so heavy with it that her other impressions were blurred, except that the room with its low and very many sofas lurked on sufferance round the great jutting triangle of the piano. She was still drawing shallow breaths and walking delicately, and had the sense of passing down a long low shining tunnel of wickedness, to where at the end she saw the parrot, a speck faintly visible against a familiar sky. Because it was on the west side of the house the room was in pale shadow, but beyond a great gold slab of sunshine lay across the pavement of the hall. Not thus fell the sunshine through the glass panels of a similar door on to Mrs. Willesden's oilcloth.

"You are one of the thin family, aren't you?" said Mrs. Lennicott. "There are girls on bicycles—so nice-looking—with rather a sharp-looking little dog that runs behind—though I am sure he is a dear little dog, and so faithful—no, the stairs are straight ahead, through that archway. Shall I go first?"

Eleanor said no, that she was not a Philpot.

"There are a great many people in this road, aren't there? I never knew there were so many people who didn't live in London. Of course, one sees the houses, but it is difficult to realize, isn't it, that they have insides and that they really mean anything!"

Mrs. Lennicott preceded Eleanor with a displaced shimmer of the skirts, a fragrant swish. She was not the sort of woman who rustles. The stair carpet crunched under one's feet with a velvety resistiveness; it had, at the first contact, a sinister sleekness. There were prints on the staircase from which Eleanor turned away quickly, tingling. It was as though the earliest darts assailed her armour. She was here in those Lennicotts' very house; its shadows and scents were surcharged for her, every contact was intolerably significant.

Then a door opened above, and Mr. Lennicott came out from his bedroom on to the landing.

Eleanor stopped dead and pressed back against the wall; her shoulder caught one of the picture-frames and made it swing wildly. She shut her eyes, and at the end of that shining and inexorable tunnel the parrot quivered and receded. She was menaced; the tunnel was narrowing down upon her; she wanted to go back.

"Who in God's name!" cried Mr. Lennicott.

"It's a lady come to take away a parrot, darling."

"Parrot?" said Mr. Lennicott despairingly. "When did we get a parrot? Why didn't you pay for it? Where's all that money I gave you? I told you this would happen again. You know they came and took away the sundial. Not that I care whether you had a sundial or parrots or an apiary, but the people who come to take them away are full of moral indignation —and you know—"

"It's *her* parrot," said Mrs. Lennicott, "and it's on the roof. Do come up," she added, turning back to Eleanor, "and let me introduce my husband, Miss . . . oh, I am so stupid!"

"Fitch," whispered Eleanor, and feeling her tongue curl back in her mouth again looked up slowly. First she saw Mr. Lennicott's ankles, very thin with big bones and covered with black hairs. Then came yards, it seemed, of his dressing-gowned figure, a long thin strip, bent slightly and bulging where his hands went into his pockets; then his long chin with a blue bloom on it, then his quizzical Spanish face. "If there's anything I can do——?" said Mr. Lennicott, and his teeth glimmered.

"*Is* there anything he can do?" asked Mrs. Lennicott, sweeping round and leaning towards Eleanor, as she came up step by step, with such eager bright expansiveness that she almost embraced her. Her eyes were of that clear blueness which almost is not when they are empty of expression; they took colour like water. She was eager and impersonal.

The sun streamed in through the staircase window, and Mr. Lennicott's dragons glowed; he might have stepped out of a cathedral window, and had indeed even that air of ornate asceticism.

"You could get out along my gutter," he said, grasping the situation quickly, "my room has an attic window, and from there to the ridge of the roof it's just a hoist."

He wrapped his dressing-gown further round him with a big gesture, re-knotted the cord at the waist with an air of resolution, and, shuffling a little in his Turkish slippers, went back across the landing and held his door open for Eleanor.

"I expect the parrot isn't there any more," said she. "I——I expect it's gone. . . . I won't mind about it to-day, thank you very much."

"But it's such a *pity* to lose such a beautiful parrot!" wailed Mrs. Lennicott.

"I think really I won't. . . ."

"Oh, come on," said Mr. Lennicott's deep voice suddenly. "A girl like you ought to be able to climb like a cat. No, look here, upon my word, you don't, though —I'll go up and collar the thing, and you lean out of the window and grab it."

"You ought to put it *into* something," said Mrs. Lennicott. "Just wait, I'll get a bandbox." She brought a bandbox which was striped with many colours, and had a French name scrawled across the top. It was so big that Eleanor had to open her arms wide to embrace it, and tucked the lid, for better balance, under her chin. The wind was blowing in through Mr. Lennicott's open window; his curtains rushed to meet them as Eleanor, contracted into an aching knot of terror, followed the bedragoned back, leaving behind her Mrs. Lennicott, the landing, and (save death) the only way of retreat. The room smelt of cigarettes and masculine unguents and had sloping ceilings. She remembered all those terrible books and pressed the bandbox closer to her chest, feeling morally as well as physically embuttressed by it.

Mr. Lennicott, breathing through his teeth, grasped the window-sill and flung one leg over it on to the outside gutter. Eleanor wondered if she would have to appear at the inquest, and whether by that she would be compromised; she watched Mr. Lennicott anxiously as, doubled like a brave on the warpath, he picked his way along the gutter, till he had passed the window and was out of sight.

Mrs. Lennicott came in and sat on the bed, which made Eleanor feel better. She lit a cigarette and said that Trotsky never killed himself, and that it was a lovely day, and that Trotsky never took enough exercise, and that Eleanor mustn't worry. They heard a hoist and a scramble, and knew that Mr. Lennicott must now be up on the roof.

"If you would hold the bandbox," said Eleanor, "I think I'll go too, as it's my parrot." She didn't want the Lennicotts to think she was afraid of *that*.

"*Do*," said Mrs. Lennicott, and, with her cigarette holder cocked skywards from one corner of her mouth, relieved Eleanor of the bandbox. Eleanor, leaning towards the roof, followed Mr. Lennicott along the gutter.

"Hallo-o!" hailed Mr. Lennicott from above. "That's sound. Come on, up here. Where's Piggy? Piggy coming too? It's—it's simply immense up here; you'd never believe. Come on—hoist!"

He gripped both her hands and hoisted. He was sitting astride of the roof, and Eleanor sat side-saddle, tucking down her skirts round her legs. White clouds had come up and bowled past before the wind like puffballs; the poplars swayed confidentially towards one another, then swayed apart in mirth. One of the Philpot girls was mending a bicycle down in their garden,

but she did not look up. Her bowed back looked narrow and virginal; Eleanor half-laughed elatedly, and
smoothed her hair behind her ears.

"And the parrot?" she said, quickly recalling herself
and looking from left to right.

The wind ruffled Mr. Lennicott's hair, but he sat immobile, following the clouds with his eyes and smiling
to himself. "Parrot?" he echoed, starting violently.
"What parrot? Where? . . . Oh, by Jove, yes; where
is it?"

"Here," whispered Eleanor, for the parrot had come
sidling down the roof towards them, and now sat down
beside her. Its feathers were dishevelled, its eyes furtive,
its head, dimmed seemingly in colour, drooped a little.
It looked sadder, smaller, less of a buffoon. It pecked
wearily and perfunctorily at Eleanor's fingers as they
closed upon it, but said nothing as she tucked it under
her arm.

"Poor beast," said Mr. Lennicott. "I believe, you
know, that the other birds have been nasty to it. They
don't like anything a different colour from themselves;
no one ever does, you know, it's damned funny."

He mused upon this, while Eleanor thoughtfully regarded him.

"Did you *find* the parrot, Trotsky?" inquired Mrs.
Lennicott, putting her head out of the window beneath
them.

"No—I mean, yes!" shouted back her husband.
"We've got the parrot here—not in at all good order,
but giving no trouble at all. Where's the basket?"

Mrs. Lennicott leaned out perilously far, encircling the bandbox with her long smooth arms. The lid was tilted a little sideways; she placed one finger upon it to keep it thus, and gurgled with pleasurable excitement as Mr. Lennicott came sliding down the roof with the parrot under his arm, and crammed the bird into the box among the tissue paper. "Clap down the lid!" shrieked Eleanor, scarlet with excitement. Mrs. Lennicott, having obeyed her, withdrew slowly into the darkness of the room, pressing the bandbox closer to her bosom, and gazing at it awfully as it began to throb with the protests of the parrot.

So that was over, and Eleanor could take the parrot home and snap the door of its cage on it, and all that hour of the day would be gone; a nothing, an irrelevancy; a lost hour that had slipped through a crack in her life and vanished. She came down from the roof nothing but an empty stomach, with an empty head above it, through which desires vaguely hurried like the clouds. She sighed as she so often sighed beneath the chestnut tree, and did not want to leave the sunny landing where Mr. Lennicott, behind her, slanted up against a door-post, and Mrs. Lennicott, kneeling by the bandbox, tied the lid securely down with a length of yellow ribbon. The parrot was very quiet in there; perhaps it did not want to go home either.

"This seems quite safe, I think," said Mrs. Lennicott, handing her the bandbox, "but don't carry it by the string. I hope this hasn't been very tiring for your parrot. I didn't think it looked very well."

Eleanor repudiated the parrot—did she then so reek of what was Mrs. Willesden's? "It's not the sort of thing *I'd* ever keep," she said vindictively, "I'd like to have a greyhound, or a large mastiff. It belongs to a lady, otherwise it wouldn't have mattered at all. Now I must take it home. . . . I—I really ought to take it home before it begins to make a noise again. . . . No, really, thank you very much, I mustn't wait for anything to eat."

"Not fruit?" marvelled Mrs. Lennicott. It was like being held back by a thousand hands, they both so evidently wished to detain her. Nobody had ever reached out for her like that so eagerly; she did not want to go back to that house of shut-out sunshine and great furniture, where the parrot was carried royally from room to room on trays, and she was nothing. But it was useless, not an inch of their way and hers lay parallel; to catch at them would mean, ultimately, only another of these wrenches. They had struck out across the open country, and it was so green there, Eleanor felt her feet aching from the high road.

All that they were suggesting, actually, was that she should go down with them to the dining-room and eat figs there, but it was not without remembrance of Proserpine, that she stood mulishly and shook her head. She had shared a roof and breasted the clouds with Mr. Lennicott, and now she must be home in time to carry up the parrot and the breakfast tray into Mrs. Willesden's room. How world lay overlapped with world;

visible each from the other and yet never to be one! Along the wind, through the trees of the garden, came booming out the Philpots' breakfast gong.

No one spoke of meeting any more; had she, too, been a magical interlude for the Lennicotts, over which their lives would close? They went down to the garden, and the prints all down the staircase, flitting past her eyes regretfully, whispered, "Stay, stay, stay!" And when they were out on the grass, and pointed out the path that ran to the gate standing wide to the road, fear returned to Eleanor. Should she come forth publicly out of those gates into the now awakened road, carrying this radiant bandbox?

"I think the back way would be really shorter," murmured Eleanor.

"Back way?" said the Lennicotts.

"Over the wall. . . ."

Mrs. Willesden shut her windows on going to bed at night, and it was Eleanor's duty to open them next morning, just a very little, when she brought in the parrot. Entering Mrs. Willesden's bedroom for this purpose, it was difficult to believe that the winds and dews of May were a reality, or that there was running water anywhere and the shining bodies of bathers, or vigorous laughter, or open country—or roofs. The room was dim with seemly crimson curtains, and Mrs. Willesden's wrappings lay ready to be put on, sheath by sheath.

"Polly's looking very well today," said Mrs. Willes-

den as usual, following the cage across the room with
her eyes because she could not turn her head among the
shawls. "Pretty Polly, pretty little Poll-poll."

"It got out," said Eleanor abruptly. Mrs. Willesden
would have to know, lest otherwise she might find out;
and she was, moreover, one contemptuously knew, a
kind old lady.

"Dear me," said Mrs. Willesden, with placid admiration. "The naughty pretty. Did he go flying far away?"

"I brought him back," said Eleanor; "he flew round
and round the garden."

"Looking for his banana trees and coral reefs, poor
pretty boy," sighed Mrs. Willesden. "And so you
caught him, Eleanor? That was very smart of you, with
nobody to help. No one knows where he mightn't have
flown to: he might have met the most terrible people
and never have come home again. And if strange people
had caught him, even people quite respectable and honest, it would have put me in an embarrassing position—
under compliment, I mean. I know it may be foolish
and old-fashioned of me, but I do very much dislike
being under compliment. So you caught him all alone?"

"Yes," said Eleanor. "He didn't give me much trouble. I—I caught him all alone."

The parrot, rising on its perch, beat its wings and
cried in a hoarse voice, "Minnie, Minnie, *Minnie?*" It
ended on a note of regret and bewilderment.

And Eleanor put down its cage quickly and walked
over to the window. It was like the crowing of the
cock.

The Visitor

ROGER was awakened early that morning by the unfamiliar sound of trees in the Miss Emerys' garden. It
was these that had made the room so dark the previous
evening, obscuring the familiar town lights that shone
against the wall above his bed at home, making him feel
distant and magnificently isolated in the Miss Emerys'
spare-room. Now, as the sky grew pale with sunless
morning, the ceiling was very faintly netted over with
shadows, and when the sun washed momentarily over
the garden these shadows became distinct and powerful, obstructive; and Roger felt as though he were a
young calf being driven to market netted down in a
cart. He rolled over on his back luxuriously, and lay
imagining this.

But the imagination-game palled upon him earlier
than usual, defeated by his returning consciousness of
the room. Here was he alone, enisled with tragedy. The
thing had crouched beside his bed all night; he had been
conscious of it through the thin texture of his dreams.

He reached out again now, timidly, irresistibly to touch it, and found that it had slipped away, withdrawn into ambush, leaving with him nothing of itself, scarcely even a memory.

He had never slept before in anybody's spare-room; theirs at home had been wonderful to him: a port, an archway, an impersonal room with no smell, nothing of its own but furniture; infinitely modifiable by the personality of brushes and sponge-bags, the attitude of shoe-trees, the gesture of a sprawling dress across a chair.

The Miss Emerys' spare-room had long serious curtains that hung down ungirt beside the window, fluted into shadows. One never touched the curtains; if one wanted to make the room dark, one drew a blind that had a lace edge and was stamped all over with a pattern of oak-leaves. Miss Emery, when she brought Roger up to bed last night, tried to do this, laid one hand on the acorn of the blind-cord, but Roger prayed her to desist and she desisted. She understood that no one liked to see the sky from bed. She was a sympathetic woman, and made Roger increasingly sorry for all the things he used to think about her blouses.

The furniture was all made of yellow wood, so shiny and one knew so yielding, that one longed to stab and dint it. There were woollen mats that Miss Dora Emery had made—she had even promised to teach Roger. She had promised this last night, while Roger sat beside her in a drawing-room that positively rocked and shimmered in a blinding glare of gaslight. A half-finished rug lay across her knee and rolled and slid noiselessly on the floor when she moved; the woolly, half-animate thing filled Roger with a vague repulsion. "I'm doing the black border now," she had explained, tweaking the clipped strands through the canvas with a crochet hook and knotting them with a flick of her wrist. "Soon I'll be coming to the green part, the pattern, and I shall work in some touches of vermilion. You really must watch then, Roger, it will be so pretty, you'll really be amused." Roger wondered if she would have come to the vermilion, even to the green, by the time his mother died. Miss Emery was not a quick worker. "How much more black will there be before the pattern?" he inquired. "Three inches," said Miss Emery, and he measured out the distance with his finger.

There were paintings on the spare-room wall of moors with Scotch cattle, and over the chest of drawers there was a smaller picture in a green-and-gold frame called "Enfin—Seuls." French. It depicted a lady and gentleman holding each other close and kissing in a drawing-room full of palms; they seemed to be glad of something. The paper had a pattern on it, although Roger's father and mother had said that patterned wallpapers were atrocious. Roger looked at it, and jumped with his mind from clump to clump—they were like islands of daisies—pretending he was a frog who had been given a chance of just eight jumps to get away from a dragon.

A clock ticked out in the passage; it must be a very big one, perhaps a stationmaster's clock, given the Miss

Emerys by a relation. It had no expression in its voice; it neither urged one on nor restrained one, simply commented quite impartially upon the flight of time. Sixty of these ticks went to make a minute, neither more nor less than sixty, and the hands of the clock would be pointing to an hour and a minute when they came to tell Roger what he was expecting to hear. Round and round they were moving, waiting for that hour to come. Roger was flooded by a desire to look at the face of the clock, and still hearing no one stirring in the house he crept across to the door, opened it a crack, quite noiselessly, and looking down the passage saw that the clock had exactly the same expression, or absence of expression, as he had imagined. Beyond the clock, a rich curtain of crimson velvet hung over the archway to the stairs, and a door painted pale blue stood open a little, showing the bathroom floor.

Roger had never believed that the Miss Emerys or any of the people he and his mother visited really went on existing after one had said good-bye to them and turned one's back. He had never expressed this disbelief to his mother, but he took it to be an understood thing, shared between them. He knew, of course, with his *brain*, that the Miss Emerys (as all the other people in the roads round them) went on like their clocks, round and round, talking and eating and washing and saying their prayers; but he didn't *believe* it. They were, rather, all rolled up swiftly and silently after one's departure and put away for another occasion, and if one could jump round suddenly, taking God by surprise, one would certainly find them gone. If one met a Miss Emery on one's walks, one assumed she must have sprung up somewhere just out of sight, like a mushroom, and that after one had passed her, nothingness would swing down to hide her like a curtain. Roger *knew* that all the doors round the Miss Emerys' landing opened on to rooms, or would do so if he walked through them when he was expected. But if he opened a door when he was not expected, would there be anything beyond it but the emptiness and lightness of the sky? Perhaps even the sky would not be there. He remembered the fairy tale of Curdie.

The spare-room opened off a very private little corridor that had no other door along it but the bathroom's. The Miss Emerys could not fully have realized the charm of this, or they would have taken the room for their own. Roger had an imaginary house that, when it was quite complete in his mind, he was some day going to live in: in this there were a hundred corridors raying off from a fountain in the centre; at the end of each there was a room looking out into a private garden. The walls of the gardens were so high and smooth that no one could climb over into anybody else's. When they wanted to meet, they would come and bathe together in the fountain. One of the rooms was for his mother, another for his friend Paul. There were ninety-seven still unappropriated, and now it seemed there would be ninety-eight.

Somebody in a room below pulled a blind up with a rush, and began to sweep a carpet. Day was beginning in a new house.

The Miss Emerys' breakfast-room was lovely. By the window, they had a canary in a cage, that sprang from perch to perch with a wiry, even sound. Outside, the little early-morning wind had died; the trees were silent, their leaves very still. Since there was no sun this morning, the breakfast-table held without competition all the brightness, to radiate it out into the room. No sun could have been rounder or more luminous than the brass kettle genially ridiculous upon a tripod, a blue flame trembling beneath it. There were dahlias, pink and crimson, and marmalade in a glass pot shaped like a barrel cast a shadow of gold on the tablecloth. There was a monstrous tea-cosy, its frill peaked intelligently; and Miss Emery smiled at Roger over the top of it. There were parrots printed on the cosy—they battled with one another—so brilliant one could almost hear them screech. Could a world hold death that held that cosy? Miss Emery had pinned a plaid bow-tie into the front of her collar. Could she have done this if what Roger expected must soon happen to Roger? Must it happen, mightn't it be a dream?

"Come in, dear," said Miss Emery, while he revolved this on the threshold, and Miss Dora Emery, who had not come to help him to dress (perhaps she was not allowed to), forced a lump of sugar quickly between the bars of the canary's cage, and came round the table to greet him. Roger eyed her cheek uncertainly; it was pink as a peach, and against the light its curve showed downy: he wondered what was expected of him. They eyed one another with a fleeting embarrassment, then Miss Dora jerked away a chair from the table, said "And you sit there, in Claude's place," and pushed back the chair with him on it, pausing over him for a second to straighten a knife beside his plate.

On the table, the hosts of breakfast were marshalled into two opposing forces, and a Miss Emery from either end commanded each. The toast, eggs, bacon, and marmalade had declared for Miss Dora; but the tea-pot and its vassals, the cruet and the honeycomb—beautifully bleeding in flowered dish—were for Miss Emery to a man. The loaf, sitting opposite to Roger, remained unabashedly neutral. Roger looked from one Miss Emery to the other.

"Plenty of milk? I expect so; Claude always liked plenty of milk in his tea. What I always say is—little boys like what's good for them, don't you worry, grown-ups!"

"Two pieces of bacon? Look, if this egg's too soft, mop it up with your bread; I should. They *say* it isn't polite, but—"

"Yes, please," said Roger, and "thank you very much, I will." What jolly ladies the Miss Emerys were!

They were looking at him anxiously; were they afraid he was not quite pleased and comfortable? Perhaps they did not often have a visitor. They were aunts; they had once had a nephew called Claude, but he had grown up and gone to India, leaving only some fishing-tackle behind him and a book about trains which had been given to Roger. Were they looking piteously at him in the pangs of baffled aunthood? But were they perhaps wondering if he *knew*, how much he knew, and whether they ought to tell him? They were ladies with bright eyes that would fill up easily with emotion, white, quick hands and big bosoms. Roger could hear them saying, "Little motherless boy, poor little motherless boy!" and they would snatch him and gather him in, and each successively would press his head deep into her bosom, so deep that perhaps it would never come out again.

Roger shrank into himself in fearful anticipation: he must escape, he must escape. . . . Yesterday had been one long intrigue for solitude, telling a fib and slipping away from his little sisters, telling a fib and slipping away from his father. Father didn't go to work now but walked about the house and garden, his pink face horribly crinkled up and foolish-looking, lighting cigarettes and throwing them away again. Sometimes he would search anxiously for the cigarette he had thrown away, and when he had picked it up would look at it and sigh desolately to find it had gone quite out. Father was an architect: he would go into his study, tweak a drawing out of a portfolio, run to his desk with it, pore over it, score it through; then start, look back at the door guiltily, return to stare and stare at the drawing, push it away, and go on walking about. Up and down the room he'd go, up and down the room, then dart sideways as though at a sudden loophole and disappear through the door into the garden. But he always came back again to where Roger was; he couldn't let one alone. His presence was a torment and an outrage. Roger disliked people who were ridiculous, and he had never cared to look long at his father. Father had dark-brown hair, all fluffy like a baby's, that stood out away from his head. His face was pink and always a little curly, his eyebrows thick and so far away from his eyes that when one came to them one had forgotten they ought to be there. Lois and Pamela loved him; they thought he was beautiful, so it was all quite fair; and Roger thought *she* was wonderful, the way she had always tolerated him and allowed him to kiss her. Always the best hour of the day for her and Roger had been when the little girls had gone to bed, and *he* had not yet come in. Now the pink face was curled up tight, and the eyes were scared and horrible, and the hands always reaching out to Roger to grab him with "Come on, old man, let's talk. Let's talk for a bit." And they had nothing to say, nothing. And at any moment this man who had no decency might begin talking about *her*.

Now, suppose the Miss Emerys were beginning to— no, the thing was unthinkable. And besides, perhaps they didn't even know.

"What's Roger going to do today?" Miss Emery asked her sister.

"We-ell," said Miss Dora, considering. "He could help you garden, couldn't he? You know you wanted somebody to help you sort the apples. You know you were saying only yesterday, '*If only I had somebody to help me sort the apples!*' Now I wonder if Roger likes sorting apples?"

"Well, I never have," said Roger, "but I expect it would be very nice."

"Yes, you'd love it," said the Miss Emerys with enthusiasm. "Claude loved it, didn't he, Doodsie?" added Miss Dora. "Do you remember how he used to follow you about at all times of the year, even in March and April, saying, 'Aunt Doodsie, mightn't I help you sort the apples?' How I did tease him: I used to say, 'Now then, Mister, I know what you're after! Is it the sorting, or the apples?' Claude was very fond of apples," said Miss Dora, very earnest and explanatory, "he liked apples very much. I expect you do too?"

"Yes, very much, thank you."

"Do you look forward to going back to school?" asked Miss Emery, and her voice knew it was saying something dangerous. Back to school. . . . When Mother had died, Father would send him away to school with all the other ugly little boys with round caps. Father said it was the best time of one's life; Father had liked school, he had been that kind of little boy. School *now* meant a day-school, where one painted flowers and mothers came rustling in and stood behind one and admired. They had a headmistress, though they were more than half of them little boys, and there were three older than Roger. Father said this wasn't the sort of school for a grown man of nine. This was because

Father didn't like the headmistress; she despised him and he grew fidgety in her presence.

"Which school?" said Roger disconcertingly, when he had swallowed his mouthful of bread and honey.

"We-ell," hesitated Miss Dora, "the one you're at now, of course," she said, gathering speed. "It seems to me a very nice school; I like to see you going out to games; and that nice girl behind you with the red hair."

"Yes," said Roger, "that's Miss Williams." He masticated silently, reflecting. Then he said provocatively, "I should like to stay there always."

"O-oh!" deprecated Miss Dora, "but not with little girls. When you're a bigger boy you'll think little girls are silly; you won't want to play with little girls. Claude didn't like little girls."

"How long *do* you think I'll stay?" asked Roger, and watched her narrowly.

"As long as your father thinks well, I expect," said Miss Dora, brightly evasive—"Doodsie, do call poor Bingo in—or shall I?—and give him his brekky. I can hear him out in the hall."

Roger ignored the liver-coloured spaniel that made a waddling entrance and stood beside him, sniffing his bare knees.

"*Why* my father?" he pressed on, raising his eyebrows aggressively at Miss Dora.

"—Bingo-Bingo-Bingo-Bingo-*Bingo!*" cried Miss Dora suddenly, as in convulsive desperation, clapping her hands against her thighs. The spaniel took no notice of her; it twitched one ear, left Roger, and lumbered over to the fireplace, where it sat and yawned into the empty grate.

Roger spent the morning with Miss Emery, helping her sort the apples and range them round in rows along the shelves of the apple-room, their cheeks carefully just not touching. The apple-room was warm, umber, and nutty-smelling; it had no window, so the door stood open to the orchard, and let in a white panel of daylight with an apple tree in it, a fork impaled in the earth, and a garden-hat of Miss Dora's hanging on the end of the fork, tilted coquettishly. The day was white, there were no shadows, there was no wind, never a sound. Miss Emery, her sleeves rolled up, came in and out with baskets of apples that were too heavy for a little boy to carry. Roger, squatting on the ground, looked them over for bruises—a bruised apple would go bad, she said, and must be eaten at once—and passed up to her those that were green and perfect, to take their place among the ranks along the shelves. . . . "That happy throng" . . . It *was* like the Day of Judgment, and the shelves were Heaven. Hell was the hamper in the musty-smelling corner full of bass matting, where Roger put the Goats. He put them there reluctantly, and saw himself a kind angel, with an imploring face turned back to the Implacable, driving reluctantly the piteous herd below.

The apples were chilly; they had a blue bloom on them, and were as smooth as ivory—like dead faces are, in books, when people bend to kiss them. "They're cooking apples," said Miss Emery, "not sweet at all, so

I won't offer you one to eat. When we've finished, you shall have a russet."

"I'd rather, if I might," said Roger, "just bite one of these. Just bite it."

"Well, bite then," said Miss Emery. "Only don't take a big one; that would be only waste, for you won't like it."

Roger bit. The delicate bitter juice frothed out like milk; he pressed his teeth deep into the resisting whiteness till his jaws were stretched. Then in the attentive silence of the orchard he heard steps beginning, coming from the house. Not here, O God, not here! Not trapped in here among Miss Emery and the apples, when all he wanted when *that* came was to be alone with the clock. If it were here he would hate apples, and he would hate to have to hate them. He looked round despairingly at their green demi-lunes of faces peering at him over the edge of the shelves. His teeth met in his apple, and he bit away such a stupendous mouthful that he was sealed up terrifyingly. The fruit slipped from his fingers and bumped away across the floor. Not a bird or a tree spoke; Miss Emery, standing up behind him on a chair, was almost moveless—listening? The steps came slowly, weighted down with ruefulness. Something to hold on to, something to grip! . . . There was nothing, not even the apple. The door was darkened.

"The butcher *did* come, Miss. Are there any orders?"

But that settled it—the apples were intolerable. Roger asked if he might go now and play in the garden.

"Tired?" said Miss Emery, disappointed. "Why, you get tired sooner than Claude—he could go on at this all day. I'm afraid that apple disappointed you. Take a russet, dearie, look, off that corner shelf!"

She was kind; he had no heart to leave behind the russet. So he took it, and walked away among the trees of the orchard, underneath the browning leaves. One slid down through the air and clung against the wool of Roger's jersey; a bronze leaf with blue sheen on it, curled into a tired line. Autumn was the time of the death of the year, but he loved it, he loved the smell of autumn. He wondered if one died more easily then. He had often wondered about death; he had felt in *her* the same curiosity; they had peered down strangely together, as into a bear-pit, at something which could never touch them. She was older; she ought to have known, she ought to have known. . . .

The grass was long and lustreless; it let his feet pass through reluctantly. Suppose it wove itself around them, grew into them and held them—Somebody's snare. He began the imagination game.

Miss Dora was leaning over the gate talking to some ladies; a mother and daughter, pink, and yet somehow hungry-looking. They turned their heads at the sound of his footsteps in the grass; he dropped his eyes and pretended not to see them. They drank him in, their voices dropped, their heads went closer together. He walked past them through the trees, consciously visible, oh, every line of him conscious—this was how a little boy walked while his mother was dying. . . . Yes, they had been great companions, always together. Yes, she was to die at any moment—poor little boy, wouldn't it be terrible for him! . . . He turned and walked directly away from them, towards the house. Their observation licked his back like flames.

Then he hated himself: he did like being looked at.

After lunch, Miss Dora took him down to the High Street with her to buy wool. His mouth was still sleek with apple dumpling, his stomach heavy with it, though they had given him a magazine with horses in it, and sent him off for half an hour to digest. Now they walked by a back way; Miss Dora didn't want to meet people. Perhaps it was awkward for her being seen about with a little boy who half had a mother and half hadn't.

She walked and talked quickly, her hands in a muff; a feather nodded at him over the edge of her hat, the leaves rustled round her feet. He wasn't going to remember last autumn, the way the leaves had rustled . . . running races, catching each other up. He barred his mind against it, and bit his lip till he was quite sick. He wouldn't remember *coming in to tea*—not that.

"What's the matter, darling," said Miss Dora, stopping short concernedly. "Do you want to go somewhere? Have you got a pain?"

"No, oh no," said Roger. "I was just imagining those white mice. How awful losing them, how awful. Do go on about them, Miss Dora, go on about Claude."

"—And when he was packing up to go back to

school, *there* was the little nest, at the bottom of his play-box, and the little mother mouse, curled up, and Claude said . . ." Miss Dora continued the Saga.

When they got to the town they saw far down at the other end of the High Street the two scarlet tam-o'-shanters of Lois and Pamela, bobbing along beside the lady who had taken *them*. Somebody had given Lois a new hoop; she was carrying it. Pamela was skipping on and off the kerb, in and out of the gutter. She didn't look as if she minded about Mother a bit. Pamela was so young; she was six. He wanted to go and tell Pamela that what she was doing was wrong and horrible, that people must be looking at her out of all the windows of the High Street, and wondering how she could.

"There are the little *sisters*, Roger—rrrrun!"

People would all say, "There are those poor little children, meeting one another!" and tell each other in whispers, behind the windows of the High Street, what was going to happen. He didn't want to be seen talking to his sisters, a little pitiful group.

"Go—on, rrrrun!"

He hung back. He said he would go round and see them after tea, he thought. "Shy of Mrs. Biddle?" asked Miss Dora swiftly. He allowed her to assume it. "Well, of course she *is* a little . . . I mean she isn't quite . . ." said Miss Dora. "But I expect the little girls like her. And I didn't think you were a shy little boy."

Back at the Miss Emerys' by half-past three, Roger found that it was not tea-time, and that there was nothing to do, nothing to escape to. That walk with Miss Dora had shattered the imagination game; it wouldn't come back to him till tomorrow, not perhaps for two days. He leaned against an apple tree, and tried sickly to imagine Claude. A horrid little boy, a dreadful little boy; he would have pulled Roger's hair and chaffed him about playing with his mother. Mercifully, he had passed on irrecoverably into the middle years; he was grown up now and would smile down on Roger through the mists of Olympus. Roger didn't get on with other little boys, he didn't like them; they seemed to him like his father, noisy outside and frightened in. Bullies. The school he was going to would be full of these little boys. He wondered how soon he would go to school; perhaps his father was even now writing to the schoolmaster—while Mother lay upstairs with her eyes shut, not caring. Roger thought Father would find this difficult; he smiled at the thought in leisurely appreciation. "Dear Mr. Somebody-or-other, my wife is not dead yet, but she soon will be, and when she is I should like to send my little boy to your school. . . . If it is not too expensive; I am not a rich man." Roger's father often said, "I am not a rich man," with an air of modest complacency.

Home was not so far away from Roger as he stood in the Miss Emerys' garden. It was twenty minutes round by the road; from the top of an apple tree one should be able to see the tall white chimneys. There had been something wonderful—once—about those chimneys, standing up against the distant beech trees, dimming the beech trees, on a quiet evening, with their pale, unstirring smoke. From up high, here, one would be able to see the windows of the attics; see whether the windows were black and open, or whether the white blinds were down. If he sat from now on, high in an apple tree, he could watch those windows. Night and day, nothing should escape him. When the blinds came down gently and finally to cover them, Roger would know. There would be no need to tell him, he would be armoured against that. Then he could run upstairs to the Miss Emerys' landing, and be alone with the clock. When they came up after him, puffed with a deep-drawn breath to impart *that*, he could just turn round and say calmly, rather tiredly, "Oh, it's all right, thank you, I do know." Then they would look mortified and go away. Really-kind Miss Emery, really-kind Father *would* look mortified; they wouldn't like having the thing snatched away from them.

Roger gazed up into the apple tree. The branches were big and far apart, the bark looked slippery. "I'm afraid," he thought, and tried to drown it. He was a little boy, he was afraid of the pain of death. "I don't dare go up, and I don't dare go back to the house. I *must* know, I can't let them tell me. Oh, help me, let them not have to come and tell me! It would be as though they saw me see her being killed. Let it not have to be!"

And now it would be and it must be, even while he deliberated and feared. Roger saw his father open the gate of the orchard and stand hesitatingly, looking round at the trees. He was hatless, his face was puckered up and scared—Oh, to run, to run quickly to somebody who would not know, who would think his mother was still alive, who need never know she was not! To be with somebody comfortable and ignorant, to grasp a cork handle through which this heat couldn't come blazing at him. Horrible footsteps, horrible grey figure coming forward again, and now pausing again desolately among the trees. "Roger?" called the voice, "Roger!"

Roger pressed back. He too was grey like the tree-trunks, and slimmer than they; he urged himself against one, hopelessly feigning invisibility, trying to melt. "Roger!" came the voice continuously and wearily, "Old man? Roger!"

Now he was coming straight towards one, he couldn't fail to see. He would drink one in and see one defenceless, and draw a big breath and say IT. No Miss Emery, no cook, no death, no refuge, and the tree shrinking away from before one.

"*Ah*, Roger!"

He thrust his fingers into his ears. "I *know*, I *know!*" he screamed. "Go away, I can't bear it. I know, I tell you."

The pink face lengthened, the scared eyes of his father regarded him, as he stood there screaming like a maniac. A voice was raised, did battle with the din he made, and was defeated. Roger leaned with his arms flung round the girth of the apple tree, grinding his forehead into the bark, clamouring through the orchard. When his own voice dropped he heard how silent it was. So silent that he thought his father was dead too, lying in the long grass, till he turned and saw him beside him, holding something towards him, still standing.

He was holding out a picture-postcard; he meant Roger to take it. "Steady, old man," he was saying; "steady, Roger, you're all jiggy: steady, old man!"

"What, what, what?" said Roger, staring wildly at the postcard. It was glazed and very blue; blue sea, infinitely smooth and distant, sky cloudless above it; white houses gathered joyously together by the shore, other white houses hurrying from the hills. Behind the land, behind everything, the clear fine line of a mountain went up into the sky. Something beckoned Roger; he stood looking through an archway.

"It came for you," said Father, "it's from Aunt Nellie; it's the Bay of Naples."

Then he went away.

This was the blue empty place, Heaven, that one came out into at last, beyond everything. In the blue windlessness, the harmony of that timeless day, Roger went springing and singing up the mountain to look for his mother. He did not think again of that grey figure, frightened, foolish, desolate, that went back among the trees uncertainly, and stood a long time fumbling with the gate.

The Contessina

THE CONTESSINA arrived at the hotel one Friday evening, with an aunt and uncle from Milan. It seemed so odd to everybody else to meet Italians staying on Lake Como; their arrival created quite a stir, and fanned many smouldering conversations into life again at tables where married couples and family parties sat. Even honeymoon couples were set gently bobbing as the ripples of interest widened and spread. The Contessina sat looking very demure, and ate her dinner like a little cat between the mat black mountain of her uncle and the glazed black mountain of her aunt.

There was general though unexpressed disappointment when the new arrivals, filing duck-like from the salle à manger, compressed themselves into the lift forthwith, and were shot bedwards without so much as a glance about the lounge.

Next morning the uncle and aunt made no appearance, but the Contessina sauntered through the lounge at about eleven o'clock carrying a cerise parasol; stood a moment hesitating in the doorway, then stepped across the road to the hotel terrace that overhung the lake. Here four young English ladies, all in white, were seated in a row along the parapet watching Mr. Harrison and Mr. Barlow going out for a row. Their backs were turned to the road, and they dangled eight beautifully shod white feet over the reflecting water that rose and fell in the shadow of the parapet as evenly and gently as a bosom.

The Contessina, leaning over, looked for some time thoughtfully at the row of feet, then down at her own, which were by three sizes smaller than any of them. The four young ladies, all unconscious, waved their hands and called out jolly things as the boat with the orange awning slid away across the water. Mr. Harrison and Mr. Barlow rowed beautifully; every second day they took a boat out, and the other mornings they played golf. They took each other on at tennis at five o'clock every evening on the hotel court, while people from the other hotels watched admiringly through the railings. The Contessina seated herself also on the parapet, shaking out her fluffy skirts round her; her parasol unfurled magically as though it had been wings. When Mr. Barlow turned his head for the last time she was not even looking at the boat, but away beyond it to the opposite hills, cold purple in the shadow. Mr. Barlow observed this with annoyance.

Two of the girls went off together, arm in arm, and the other two, producing their embroidery, moved back on to an iron seat under the shade of a chestnut tree. These trees, clipped low till they spread out into umbrellas, followed for some distance the line of the shore. The Contessina, now their *vis-à-vis*, eyed the couple unabashedly with the naked curiosity of childhood. She studied their dresses and their attitudes, and took in the embroidery they were doing stitch by stitch. Conversation between the two was desultory; they had known each other for three days, and were entering upon that interesting phase in a hotel acquaintanceship where small talk dies, commonplaces falter, and confidences begin. The Italian girl disturbed them; her very sitting there was calculated to disturb them, even had they been quite certain that she understood no language but her own.

In this they would have been mistaken. "Good— *morn*ing," said the Contessina.

"Oh? Good morning."

"Ah speak English," she continued, nodding encouragingly at them. Two dimples flickered, dints of rosy light in the warm twilight of her parasol. Her eyes, usually of amber, caught here and there a glint of red that danced between the disconcerting flickers of her lashes. A queer little face, so foreign.

"Really?" said Ursula; and Jenny, smiling, said, "How nice!"

The Contessina once again nodded, gathering her forces. She was about sixteen evidently, and this was odd, because no English girls of sixteen had figures like that. She revealed herself against the sunny water, a thing of neat assured little curves. She had wrists and she had ankles, her waist had already decided itself, and it would have been evident to the discerning eye that there were many more dimples. Jenny and Ursula hated to seem rude and—well—*English*, but she really would be very difficult to talk to. Their next move should have been, traditionally, "How do you like Italy?" But they could not ask her that.

"Have you been to England?" Ursula inquired.

"Oh, no-o!" tittered the Contessina, and tittered again in scorn. *England*—the very idea!

Jenny, who was very intellectual, suggested, "Then you read English, I expect?"

"Oh, yes. Marie Corelli."

"Oh, yes."

"She is fa-ine."

"Oh, yes. Do you play tennis?"

"Oh, no, I think it is terrible. Do you like Italian men?"

"I don't know any," said Jenny, with indifference. After a moment's pause she smiled kindly at the Contessina, funny little thing. Ursula said that she had once had a most interesting friendship with an Italian lady; she had been really charming. The Contessina looked at her in wonder. "But do you like ladies at *all?*" she asked.

They were spared further of this, for a voice behind them from the other side of the road shrilled out abruptly, "*Serafinetta, vien' qui!*" To the first call, and its repetition, the Contessina remained blandly deaf. As these persisted and were reinforced and bound together by a positive Niagara of sound, the Contessina at length responded, "*Vengo subito*," and did not stir. "*Adesso*," the voice implored, and the aunt, immensely canopied by a parasol of sombre lace, appeared in full sail from the hotel followed by the uncle. She did not look angry nor at all excited; foreigners simply could not help talking like that. The Contessina rose and shook her skirts out, smiled, sighed, shrugged, and nodding to her new acquaintances, went off to meet her aunt, her parasol tilted quite ineffably.

After lunch, the aunt, the uncle, and the Contessina got into the hotel boat, assisted by the concierge, and were rowed up and down for an hour by the two hotel boatmen, not far out and parallel with the shore. The Contessina could be seen leaning out from under the awning to trail her fingers in the water. At five o'clock, people began to gather round the tennis-court, and by the time Mr. Harrison and Mr. Barlow had at last appeared, the aunt, the uncle, and the Contessina were there too, sitting close together on a seat. The uncle had sunk deep down into his stomach, the aunt deep down into her bosom, and the Contessina's glances flitted about like butterflies, never pausing long. All three looked happy and contented, and the aunt was smiling with the most profound indulgence at the English ladies dressed for tennis with their large, flat feet. Mr. Barlow, down the Contessina's end of the court, walked springily about on the balls of his feet, while his opponents took their places; hacking, slashing, and undercutting with his racquet at the air with science and ferocity. He bit his lip, the air whistled through his teeth, his head, as he recovered from a lunge, jerked sideways and remained there, for he caught the eyes of the Contessina looking up at him. Her parasol was not up, for she was sitting in the shade, and her eyes, now merely amber, studied with a mild inquiry the foolishness of Mr. Barlow.

He played quite brilliantly that evening; everybody sat alert to watch him, and the crowd beyond the railings thickened. His partner, a lady of a disenchanted spirit, reported afterwards that he was poaching more than ever, and had made three foot-faults. When the final set was over he pulled on his sweater over his shirt, buttoned his blazer over his sweater, and strolled, just casually, past the seat where the Italian family were sitting. They were still there; the aunt was slumbering like a lady of lineage, and the uncle had disappeared behind the *Popolo*. The Contessina was looking sideways at the view: the evening light upon the hills was indeed very beautiful, but perhaps she had not been looking at it long. Mr. Barlow dropped his racquet—most annoying—at the Contessina's feet.

The Contessina looked down at the racquet in surprise, as though it had fallen from heaven. Mr. Barlow's hand, arm, shoulder, and flushed bent neck came within her field of vision; she started violently. "Thank you," he said, rising, though she had done nothing to assist him. She bowed, and he beheld the dimples. "Do you play tennis?" he asked softly.

"But no. But I do *wish*, I *wish* . . ." It was inexpressible; she caught a sharp breath. Her whipped-cream ruffles shifted, swelled, and sank.

"It's a good game," murmured Mr. Barlow, still more softly, glancing stealthily towards the aunt.

"It is like . . . you do resemble . . . gods!"

"Oh, *well*," laughed he, and looked about him. Everybody hurried to escape the chill of dusk; the court was being rapidly deserted. "Would you care to take a little stroll?" he suggested. She evidently failed to understand his idiomatic English. "I mean, a walk." She ducked to see if any wakefulness still gleamed beneath the eyelids of the aunt, while he, with arched eyebrows, peered over the *Popolo* to see what the uncle was doing. He nodded to reassure her, and she giggled. "A *leetle* walk!" she stipulated. "Oh, as little as anything," agreed the delighted Mr. Barlow. "The sun's just setting; come as far as the edge of the lake."

They watched the sunset together, standing on a little jetty. Beneath their feet the water lapped and gurgled. When they turned to go in Mr. Barlow sighed. He did not take her back the shortest way.

That night his wife was more impossible than ever. He was as nice as anything to her, at the beginning, asked her twice if she had had a pleasant day, and said, "Oh, come," encouragingly, when she responded that she hadn't. Everything was always wrong with Mrs. Barlow's days; she made a point of this, it was her little triumph. But she was such a tired woman now, these little triumphs made her feel no better. Tonight she would not talk and would not eat; the waiters, humane men, waxed openly solicitous, and this annoyed her husband. Their table was beside an open window; beyond, the dark-blue velvet night hung like a curtain; one felt the sleeping presence of the lake, and on the water somebody with a guitar began to sing. It was a night of breathless heart-beats and of beating pulses, a night for love. A night to kiss a satin skin as warm as great grape-clusters hanging in the sun. No one round him, Mr. Barlow knew, as much as glimpsed the possibilities of such a night. Married couples, family parties —even the honeymoon couples looked bloodless; besides, once the woman was one man's wife one ceased, as it were, to be a Gentleman and became a Player. The Contessina's table was in view, if one leant a little sideways to avoid a pillar, but the Contessina was making an excellent dinner, and had no time left to look about her. Scents crept in from the bushes in the garden, met the smell of dinner, did battle with it and retreated; but Mr. Barlow had them, and his nostrils twitched. Now that the chill of dusk had passed, the night was very warm and grew to the accustomed eye still more astonishingly blue.

Mrs. Barlow waved away the *Canneton sauté*, then recalled the waiter, and after much deliberation and hovering of the fork and spoon, selected half a dozen peas. These she floated in a pool of gravy and looked down upon despairingly, while her husband looked despairingly across at her. For the last half-hour they had hardly spoken, and the unmarried girls at the next table, a merry party, pressed each other's feet and discreetly giggled. They had all so often told each other marriage was like that. Mr. Barlow was good-looking; the shape of his head was pleasant, and his sleeked-back hair defined it. His forehead, jaw, and ears were squared perfection, and his sulky mouth was beautifully cut. Mrs. Barlow raised three peas to her lips, then recoiled from them.

"I shan't be able to digest *these*," she said, and looked across at him with the solemn eyes of someone standing on the brink.

"Then why eat them?" said Mr. Barlow. "Oh, but I *must* eat," said she; then her chest twitched with a miserable hiccup, as it came over her suddenly that any other woman's husband would have been saying this to *her*. "Oh yes, of course," agreed Mr. Barlow, and he hummed very softly and tried to look away from her. The electric light poured down upon his wife; even her pink dress looked *triste* and faded, though it was new and expensive, and far too beautiful for the occasion. As for her fair hair—Mr. Barlow always had preferred dark women, and he had realized long ago that it is never wise to make exceptions to one's rules of life.

After dinner the older people gathered on the verandah, while the girls went off together two by two. They would come up out of the dark like moths, glitter under the lights in their pale dresses, then vanish again. Harrison and a Mrs. Pym announced that they were going to look for glow-worms, and a whole bevy of girls went after them. The Contessina sat with her relations in a little isolated group at the glassed-in end of the verandah. When Barlow, searching very diligently round them for a newspaper he had forgotten, jerked his head interrogatively towards the lake, she turned away and simply did not see. So he went down to the edge of the lake alone, swung his legs over the parapet, and sat listening to the water sucking at the stones beneath him. He lighted cigarette after cigarette, and allowed each to slip from between his relaxed fingers into the water. Each sizzled, then was silent. It was a pity one couldn't put oneself out like that. The Bellagio lights twinkled very near him, on a level with his eyes; the lake was, after all, so narrow. He longed to row somebody over in a boat, and climb with her into the inviolable dark beneath the trees of Serballoni Hill.

Harrison and Mrs. Pym were coming up behind him; he could recognize their voices, talking very low. "Lovely night," he said, without turning. "Oh, lovely," said Harrison, with a jump. "Lovely day tomorrow!" he continued. "Look here"; he turned his head over the other shoulder, to where he knew Mrs. Pym was standing. "I want to take that little Italian kid out tomorrow over to San Giacomo. She's an awfully nice little kid; I promised and she's awfully keen. I said I'd take her over in a boat."

"The little kid?" said Mrs. Pym, grinning in the dark. "They'd never allow her."

"Yes, but look here, you work it. Oh, be a sport, woman! You talk their lingo, it'll be your show, you're taking her along, and Harrison and I just come along to row you."

"Ah, yes," said Mrs. Pym evenly.

The Contessina's aunt found Mrs. Pym quite charming. They discovered that they had several friends in common, in Milan and other parts of Italy. She said that it would be delightful for Serafinetta to go for an excursion with the English lady; she loved English ladies, and had had an American governess for three years. At four o'clock on Sunday afternoon, the Contessina was therefore delivered over by her aunt into the hands of Mrs. Pym, who explained that English friends of her own had volunteered to row them. It was difficult to hire boatmen on a Sunday afternoon.

Mrs. Pym was a fair, burnt-out young woman of twenty-five, who spoke in a deep hoarse drawl, wore pale-grey flannels for boating, and had beautiful feet. She never looked hot. Harrison faintly amused her— she had been Barlow's partner too often at tennis— though nobody, of course, was amusing beyond a certain point. She had reached this point earlier than usual with her husband. The Contessina was allowed to steer; she tugged the wrong rope systematically, looking about her, glinting all over with contentment and mirth. She was fascinated by the swing and dip of the sleek oars over the water. Around them, the blue sky and the blue water blazed; a quivering light struck up into their faces and beat against the underneath of the awning. Once a steamer passed them, slanting over to Bellagio; the boat was sucked into her wake and rocked madly, round her oily shadows slid and spread and darted. The Contessina clutched the sides of the boat and screamed with fear and joy.

The bay of San Giacomo was still golden in the late afternoon, as they grounded their boat on the little strip of beach under the tea-house. Above went up the great sheer sweep of the hill; tree-trunks crowded endlessly, impenetrably, up into the sky. Cars along the road to Milan shrieked like birds, high, high among those unseen branches. Stepping from the boat, the ladies stood looking up into the queer ribbed dusk of the tree-trunks, while the others carried up the oars to the tea-house and put them away for safety. The place was very still, the coast of the lake seemed for miles entirely deserted. Barlow returned and loomed above the Contessina speechlessly. She said, "Let us go among the trees."

The others fell away from them. Her ridiculous little feet were useless to her; the high heels flung her whole weight forward on to the blunt little toes, and these scrabbled unavailingly upon the baked, bald earth of the hill. Sometimes she missed her footing altogether, and her whole weight would swing from Barlow's arm. When he had dragged her up about ten feet, she said she would like to come down again, pulled him after her, and they slid the whole way. They skirted the hill and walked for some distance along the edge of the lake, in the opposite direction to that which the others had taken. When they came to a bank of cushiony grass she sat down, and he sat down beside her, tilting his panama over his eyes.

"This is very nice," said Mr. Barlow, looking at the Contessina. She had on a dress of heliotrope organdie, with a fichu folded across the bosom with that best discretion for the display of pretty curves. Her skin was very dark against the heliotrope, as fresh as a young petal, as brown as old, old ivory. Her white Tuscan hat enhanced this peculiar deliciousness, and the little loops of hair corrugated against the curves of her cheeks looked almost blue. Her puffed sleeves were very short, and there was a dimple on each elbow. "This is very nice, you know," repeated Mr. Barlow, stooping to kiss one of the dimples.

"Oh, yes," agreed the Contessina, looking down at the elbow.

"You know," said Mr. Barlow, "you're just the sort of little girl I like; just the sort of little pal I've always wanted—"

"Leetle *what?*"

"Pal—little friend, you know. Amie."

"Oh, yes. Do you like Italian girls?"

"Don't know about *girls*," said Barlow, stressing the plural. She supposed, with a sigh, that like everybody else he preferred them married.

"No," said Mr. Barlow, looking at her tenderly, "not married. No, not *married*, you know."

"I think," said she, "that Englishmen are beautiful. They are like gods."

"By Jove!" said the intoxicated Mr. Barlow. Then he

added, with a sigh: "Some day, perhaps, you'll marry an Englishman."

"Oh, no. I will marry an Italian gentleman, and then we will go and live in England."

"But it would be too late then."

"Oh, yes," said the Contessina, looking thoughtfully at Mr. Barlow. She smoothed the folds of her fichu, and spread the light flounces of her dress about her over the grass.

"Meanwhile," said he, "this is wonderful."

"Oh, yes," agreed the Contessina, "it is like Heaven."

They both paused and looked down at the lake. The Contessina was a little too much of the child that sits with its mouth open, confidently waiting for lollipops. Each lollipop being assimilated, she would thank him prettily, look up with candid greed, and wait for another. And this necessity for direct, unidiomatic English embarrassed Mr. Barlow, master of innuendo and *doubles-entendres;* this was more than throwing lollipops, it was spiking buns to an insatiable little eager bear at the end of a stick. But he couldn't resist her; he slid across the last intervening inches of grass and put his arm round the Contessina's waist. Anyone standing at an upper window of their hotel with a pair of field-glasses could have watched them from across the lake, but Mr. Barlow decided to risk it. His arm tightened —"Oh, please!" she said perfunctorily—and he kissed the Contessina a great many times. She turned her head from side to side, and once he caught her full on the mouth. "Is that still like Heaven?" he whispered ardently, cupping her chin in his unoccupied hand. "Oh, yes," she said politely, just perceptibly wriggling her head.

There was another silence; this time he felt it wonderfully sympathetic. Then the Contessina, whose waist he still encircled, asked him how he liked his wife. Mr. Barlow told her; he explained that life was sometimes very difficult.

"Oh, yes," said the Contessina. "I wonder how she does like you?"

"Oh, well . . ."

"How many children have you?"

"None," said Mr. Barlow indignantly.

"Oh, that is a pity," she sighed, looking down into the lake.

"A pity?" said he, picking up a little hand whose fingers curled in his like a baby's. He looked down at it hungrily, while she too watched from under her lashes her hand and the approach of his lips; then he kissed it twice and crushed it up against him. "It is a pity you have no son," she sighed. "He would be like a god."

"Oh, he would, would he?" said Barlow, indisposed to abdicate.

"Yes," she said regretfully. "Who takes your wife in a boat? Does your wife like Italian men?"

"Really, I don't know. Wouldn't it be more interesting to talk about ourselves for a little? Do you know, if I had had a little girl like you to go through life with, I think everything would have been different. A dainty little thing, you know, a little, a little humming-bird."

"But if I had gone through your life I should be fat," said the Contessina.

She was adorable. "You lovely little thing!" he cried, "you *are* a lovely little thing!"

"You are very very kind," she said, nestling against his arm like a kitten. "When I came here I thought it would be so *triste* because there was nobody young but the ladies, but now I shall not have been dull."

"You'll have something nice to remember. Now I'm going to give you some more to remember." She uncoiled like a spring and was on to her feet in a flash. "Oh, no," she cried, jumping about with delight, and clapping her hands at him as though he were a puppy. "That is enough to remember, that is enough!"

"Is it, indeed!" quoth Mr. Barlow, turning pink with pleasurable excitement. He grabbed at her diaphanous skirts that swirled about her like a ballet dancer's. There was an angry sound of tearing muslin. "Yah!" shrieked the Contessina, and Mr. Barlow recoiled momentarily in dismay. He fell back from sitting posture on to his hands and crouched looking up at her; then, realizing the disadvantages of this position, drew in his long legs and sprang to his feet. The Contessina, breathless even beyond the point of shrieking, swept her mauve skirts round her and went tottering along the beach towards the promontory. She staggered with laughter, her whole body curved upon itself, bowed beneath her weight of mirth.

"Ha!" cried Mr. Barlow, making after her with long strides. The air whistled between his teeth, he grinned;

this was better than tennis. She was now within the compass of his extended arms, and he leaned forward to enclose her, a happy and confident gurgle rising in his throat. The Contessina ducked with a yelp of delight, sprang ahead surprisingly, and missed her footing. She spun round, wavered, beat the air for a second, then came down, *smack*, on to her outstretched palms. Mr. Barlow stopped short. "God!" he whispered, and clapped his hand to his mouth.

The Contessina did not remain prone. Before her cavalier had recovered himself, she was sitting back on her heels to stare at her little bleeding and earthy palms that reared up into her gaze indignantly. Her pose might have been called "Astonishment." Then, while he yet beheld, the ivory of the face and neck now visible to him darkened, her open mouth, eclipsing her face, became a cavern into whose menacing profundity Mr. Barlow's horrified eyes looked down. A shriek like a needle-point, rounding to a sustained boo-hoo, rent across the silence of San Giacomo. As in response, a stone from miles above dislodged itself and came hurtling down through the trees into the lake. This increased the panic of Mr. Barlow, who made a frightened sound and looked about him furtively. She clamoured on without pause, shrieking and sobbing.

"Little darling—" he tendered, dropping on his knees beside her.

"A-ah," shrilled the Contessina. "*Va via*. I hate you. Go!"

"But look here, listen—"

"Aie, go; you are wicked. You have been wicked with me; it is not so you should behave with a young girl. A-ah!"

She was such a child. Mr. Barlow, in a rush of paternal emotion, gathered her against him. "*There*," he murmured, "there—there—there!"

But the Contessina positively roared, and disengaging her fists assailed his breast and shoulders with a rain of blows. One of these caught him on the chin, and he released her sharply. Above the intimidating cavern of her mouth, between the smears and crumples of her face, two slits of eyes blazed out upon him icily. Those eyes were pale with contempt. Mr. Barlow was appalled by them.

"Yah!" resumed the Contessina. "Old stupid! Wicked old man!"

"You *are* a little devil," said Mr. Barlow wonderingly, getting up.

The Contessina rose also, with remarkable agility. The front of her dress was soiled irreparably, cut right through at the knee and stained with blood. "You have killed my dress," she yammered, grimacing down at the torn flounces miserably. "If it had been the most old and the most ugly I would not have spoilt it for *you*. You are not young, and you are not funny, and you have a hot face, and you do not behave well with a young girl. It is not right. There is no *young* man, an English or an Italian, who would behave so, it is *old* men who are stupid and devils. Let me go to the boat!"

"Oh, all right," said he very coldly. "Go on. *I* don't

mind where you go. You are a silly little thing to spoil your dress like that, your aunt will be angry." He wondered, as he spoke, whether she would involve him in a duel with the Italian uncle. With bowed head and heaving shoulders, she preceded him along the beach, sobbing and sniffing. "Such a hullabaloo!" said Mr. Barlow indignantly. "I never take out a little girl if she doesn't know how to behave." He followed at a distance.

Mrs. Pym and Harrison appeared from round the opposite promontory. Mrs. Pym looked vaguely at the Contessina. "But dear *child*—" she said, in faint expostulation, raising her eyebrows. "Oh, I *say!*" said Harrison, "Oh, I say, that's too bad. I say, *Barlow!*"

Barlow explained that she had slipped and fallen while engaged in throwing stones into the lake. Harrison did not hear; he was comforting the Contessina, murmuring things into her ear and patting her little heaving shoulders. The petal-curves of the big Tuscan hat drooped towards him.

"Oh, please," she gasped, "if you would be so kind . . . I would like to go back. . . . Oh, please . . . Oh, please!"

Barlow, his neck burning scarlet, strode to the tea-house to reclaim the oars, and strode back in disdainful silence. The Contessina could no longer see him; it was as though he had slipped out of her vision down a crack, and the crack had closed above him for ever.

Going home, Harrison changed places with Barlow, and sat *vis-à-vis* to the Contessina. She blinked her tears away, the dimples came out tremulously, her lashes were still wet and the lower lashes clung to her cheek adorably. The sun was going down, the lake was of liquid flame with great cold blue shadows like swords stabbing across it. The hills were blue and sharp, the air crystal. The sleek oars swung and dipped to their reflections rhythmically, and Harrison's sleek head beneath the eyes of the Contessina bowed to the rhythm. The level sunshine crept along the air and brimmed with gold the little dints of mirth and pleasure in the Contessina's cheeks, and drew a curve of gold along the brim of her hat.

"You row like a god," the Contessina said to Harrison. "Do you like Italian girls?"

Human Habitation

F OR THE TWENTIETH TIME, as the wet dusk became impenetrably charged with darkness, Jefferies looked distrustfully up at Jameson and challenged him: "I suppose you *are* sure we're going the right way?"

Jameson, the tall man, was carrying the map; he took one step to every one and a half of Jefferies, and thus their footsteps made an uneven, shuffling sound, unutterably wearisome, on the mud and shingle of the towpath. For the last hour they had walked, save for Jefferies's interpolations, in complete silence. Now and then a pebble bounded slantwise from the impact of foot, cleared the sedgy brink of the canal, and spun with a *plonk*, vindictively, into the silent water. It was late September; not a breath of wind; the fine rain stung the air.

Jameson's thin profile had faded from against the darkening sky; his voice came from so uncannily high up that Jefferies started when it said, "Well, my dear fellow, if you don't believe me, take the map yourself."

"I've got no matches," he remarked, craning up his head sullenly to give emphasis to his words. "You said I couldn't possibly have finished my matches before we came to Middlehampton. Now I have finished them. I suppose you can lend me your matches when I want another pipe?"

Jameson stopped, stooped, fumbled, and tucking the map under his arm brought out his match-box and shook it anxiously. They both stood still to listen. "There's not many more," he said unnecessarily. It did not sound as though there were more than three in the box.

"We'd better not smoke for a bit," he said aggrievedly; "that is, if you want to see the map."

"Oh, well, I suppose if you *know* we're making the right way. But what I can't understand is: why we don't see the lights of Middlehampton."

"Well, the air's so dense with rain."

"Can't be *so* dense. You said half an hour ago that Middlehampton must be three and a half miles off."

They plodded on; collars up, caps down. "Ow, *Lord!*" yelped little Jefferies, stumbling and skidding. "Steady on—the canal."

"Well, I ought to know the canal's there, oughtn't I? After walking beside it for four days."

They had made friends towards the end of the London University session. They were reading Science. Jameson knew he liked walking tours, and Jefferies thought he very likely would. Jameson's bright bird-eyes, set so near together into his long thin nose, fascinated Jefferies. He was an awfully compelling sort of chap. The way he *talked*. . . . So they went a walking tour: it was to be at the end of the summer vacation, that they might return to College fearfully fit. They chose the canals of middle England; "There's a regular network of 'em," said Jameson, "and you see some awfully jolly country. One reads a lot of poetry and stuff against the Midlands, but personally I think they're fine. And from our point of view, entirely undiscovered. Now if you go down West in summer, or even into the Home Counties—and of course Wales is hopeless, besides costing such a lot to get there—you find the whole place simply crammed with rich smart people swishing about in cars. You know, the real rotten sort. Even the smaller pubs are full of them. All the year's their holiday, and yet they come blocking up the place for Us Others *now*. Of course that's all going, but it makes me awfully sick. Girls, you know, absolute butterflies, and fellows who ought to be working."

"Sick'ning," had said Jefferies, who also disapproved of these things.

So they walked the Midlands, following the canals from village to village, making towards the town of Middlehampton, where there were some fine old churches and Jefferies had an aunt. They stayed the nights in public houses which were not comfortable, and in the evenings they used to sit downstairs and try to talk to people in the bar. Jameson said one should get to know the English Country as more than a poetic abstraction and its people as more than a political entity, and Jefferies agreed that this was very true. They did not find the people in the bars interesting, but Jameson said that that would come.

Then it had begun raining. It rained a little on the second day, nothing to speak of, and they laughed and turned their collars up. The third day was nearly all wet, though it cleared towards evening and a fine sunset crimsoned the canal. Today it had come on about lunch-time, a different rain; finer, gentler, more inexorable, that made the air woolly, left a muddy taste in one's mouth, and dulled everything. They trudged; the rain stung their faces to stiffness; their minds grew numb. Since four o'clock they had not passed a village; Jameson, glancing perpetually at the map, promised that there should soon be one, but that village hung ever back from them as they pressed on to meet it. Once, very far away, through a momentary lightening of the dimness, they had seen a church spire pricking through a blur of trees; and about four-thirty they had passed a row of brick cottages, standing uncompromisingly a little bit away from a bridge. Jefferies asked, "Tea there?" and jerked his head interrogatively and wistfully towards them, but Jameson, after scanning the cottages for a moment of uncertainty, had said, "Why, confound it all, man, we can't go bursting into English people's homes and ordering them to give us tea just because we're in a position to pay for it. Well, how'd you like . . . After all, it's not as though we were abroad."

Jefferies had said, "No; oh, no," without conviction,

and remembered that Jameson had eaten twice as much dinner as he had. So they went squelching on.

Since then, there had been nothing. Not even, recently, the looming blur of trees; never a house, never a light; there was not a sound to be heard of a voice calling, a dog barking, or the rattle of a cart. Only, ahead of them along the tow-path, they had the sense of just a possibility that something might approach them. Yes, once two barges had come up to meet them; the horse-hoofs being wrenched after every step from the sucking mud were louder than their impact. The water swished and gurgled under the prows; the smoke trickling from the chimneys of the cabins could not rise through the rain, but hung low and sullenly diffused itself. At the first prow a bargee was visible, dusky and inhuman; another man walked at the head of the first horse. Though it seemed as if for the whole afternoon they had been imminent, the dusk so suddenly disgorged them that Jameson and Jefferies had to spring into the hedge under the very nose of the horse with a violence that sent them sprawling among the prickly branches, to escape the tow-rope that would have mown them from their legs. The steaming flanks of the horses loomed beside them, and Jameson, recovering his balance, shouted from the hedge, "This *is* the way to Middlehampton?" For answer the man leading the horse hailed back to him tonelessly and went by, never turning his head again, as Jameson's clamoured reiteration was drowned by the clopping of the horses' hoofs, the squelching of the mud, the rushing of the water

round the prows. The unlighted cavalcade faded
slowly, and was swallowed up. Nothing else came to
meet the two, and nothing else passed them.

As the walls of rain closed in about him and became
impenetrably dark, Jefferies felt sundered by a world
from the now almost invisible Jameson. There was
nothing beside him but a living organism that breathed
stertorously and struggled on, slanting forward a little
into the rain. And beside that big, mindless body
trudged another smaller body, shuffling, sometimes desperately changing step in an attempt to establish
rhythm. On to these two bodies the dulling eyes of
Jefferies's mind looked out. He thought dimly, "If I lose
consciousness of myself, shall I leave off being? I don't
believe in Jameson, I don't believe he's even there;
there's just something, if I put out my hand, to obstruct
it; something against which I should fall if I fell towards the canal, sideways. Why should the fact that
one of those men's legs ache bother me? I don't believe
in either of them. Curse, how my legs ache! Curse my
legs! There was once a man called Jameson, who asked
a man called Jefferies to walk with him for years and
years along a canal, and—they walked and walked till
Jefferies forgot himself and forgot that he had ever
been. What happened then? I can't remember. . . .
Curse, I'm potty. Oh, curse my legs, they're real anyhow. But are they? Perhaps somebody somewhere else
feels a pain and thinks it is a pain in a man called Jefferies's legs, and so there seems to be a man called Jefferies with his legs aching, walking in the rain. But am

I the person who is feeling the pain somewhere else, or am I what they imagine?" He was, he decided, something somebody else had thought; he felt utterly objective, walking, walking. Such a silence, it might have been a night in May. . . . He put his hand out and brushed it along the hedge; the hedge was always there, and the rain soaked silently through it.

Jameson had stopped walking; Jefferies felt himself shoot suddenly ahead. He arrested himself and asked, "Well?" numbly without turning round. Jameson didn't sound so sure of himself.

"Perhaps we might just look at the map again; it's reassuring—here, you're better with the matches; strike away, old man, and I'll be nippy with the map." He rustlingly unfolded it. Jefferies took the match-box, and before the third match, trembling out, had expired, Jameson, bending his long glistening nose over the map, had seen enough. The last glowing match-head spat as it struck the water, and Jefferies, sucking a burnt finger, looked towards Jameson with a mute and animal expectancy. The other said slowly:

"Well, I'm damned. Well, I *am* damned!"

"Why?" said Jefferies dully.

Jameson explained very quickly and with detachment that they had after all taken the wrong turning when they came to that fork. They *had* somehow; it was jolly queer. Jameson thought it really was most awfully queer. This arm of the canal only seemed to lead to a brickfield; it must be a jolly big brickfield, mustn't it, to have an arm of the canal all to itself. He laughed nervously, and they listened while his laughter died away. Jefferies was very quiet. He asked after some time, as though perfunctorily, what they were going to do.

"I saw there was a road marked from the brickfield, straight to Middlehampton. It goes without any turnings, a class B road, awfully good walking. We might pick up a bus. You see, all we shall have done is simply to have come two sides of a triangle. That is all we shall have done. It's bad luck, isn't it—we *have* had a run of bad luck."

"Yes," said Jefferies. "Let's go on." It tired him worse, just standing there. So they went on walking. They did not believe, perhaps, that they gained very much by walking; everything had slipped away from them. They just kept on for the sake of keeping on, and because they could not talk, they could not think. Jefferies felt as though an effort at coherent thought would bring about some rupture in his brain. He had begun to believe vaguely—the thing took form in his brain nebulously without any very definite mental process—that they had stepped unnoticingly over a threshold into some dead and empty hulk of a world drawn up alongside, at times dangerously accessible to the unwary. There was a canal there, but were there not canals in the moon—or was it Mars? The motionless water silently accompanied them, always just beyond Jameson, a half-tone paler than the sky—it was like a line ruled with a slate-pencil, meaninglessly, across some forgotten slate that has been put away.

"Look over there," whispered Jameson. "I'll swear I see lights." He spoke so softly, as though he feared to scare the lights away, that it came into Jefferies's mind that he must mean people, carrying lanterns. "Why," he cried, looking with narrowed eyes through the rain, "those are house-lights. Quite square, not moving—windows."

"Then there must be a house," deduced Jameson. "There'll be people, you know, and they might let us come by the fire. They'd tell us the way, but I expect they'd ask us to stay for a bit. You know," he said, as they approached, "those are very dull lights—muffled. It looks to me as though they'd got the blinds down."

"Yes, I expect they have; they wouldn't want everybody looking in. There are lights upstairs, too, d'you see? It must be quite a biggish house, if it's got two stories. I expect the people are well-to-do, and live here because they like it. It would be rather a jolly place to live." He saw a picture of the house in summer, white-faced and somehow Continental, blistering a little in the glare from the canal, with sun-blinds, and a garden with a white fence running down to the tow-path, and crimson hollyhocks slanting lazily against the fence. He thought there might be an elm or two, a bit to the side, to give shade to the house and garden: that would be very nice, Jefferies thought. "I expect it must be awfully nice in summer," he said elatedly, turning to Jameson. "Topping," they agreed. "Why, if the weather cleared, I expect it would look topping to-morrow." It was extraordinary how happy they felt as they approached the lights, and how benevolent.

There *was* a little garden, and the gate swung to behind them: the latch clicked of its own accord. This
brought someone to an upper window before Jameson,
standing at the door with raised hand a shade porten-
tously, had had time to knock. A blind swung sideways,
displaced by a body, the window was pushed up with
a rattle, and a woman's voice cried out in ecstasy and
reproach, with a note in it of immeasurable relief, "*Oh,
Willy!*"

So certain was she, that she momentarily unconvinced Jefferies and Jameson of their own identities.
They stepped back a pace or two to see her better: she
leaned against the window-frame, keeping the blind
pushed sideways into folds with one elbow. They saw
her form against the dim, dark-yellow lamplight—
Woman, all the women of the world, hailing them
home with relief and expectation. Something stirred
warmly in both of them; it would be like this to have
a wife. She was up there with her child; they could hear
a burst of thin querulous wailing, at which she did not
turn her head, but only peered out more closely into
the darkness. The rain before the window shimmered
in the outpoured lamplight.

"Well?" she cried. "*Come in.* You're late. Oh,
Willy!"

She was so blind to them down there that they were
fain to stand pretending; till Jefferies, wrenching himself free of something, cried out ruefully, "We're not."
He was so husky, it was doubtful whether she could

distinguish his words, but she started back and stood rigid at the unfamiliar voice. Then she leaned forward to thrust out her head at them.

"Get on with you," she blustered. "Get along, will you! This isn't a public; the Green Man's beyond the brickyard. Don't come bothering here, or I'll send my husband out to you, and if you don't get along then he'll fetch his brother . . ." She listened a moment for the sound of their retreat, then added, "*and the dog.*"

"But, Ma'am, I say!" expostulated Jameson in a cultured voice. This was awkward: if she were going to take it like this, how could they ask to come in to her fire? If only she could see them, if only it were not so dark! She was a kind young woman; her arm, with which she now impatiently held the blind back, was round against the light—"Just a minute, if you don't mind. We've missed our way; would you be so kind as to direct us?"

They could feel her frown with the perplexity that was in her voice as she asked: "Who are you? What do you want?"

"We're students, walking; we've missed our way, and we've been walking hours without meeting a soul. Can we speak to your husband?"

"He's asleep," she said quickly, "and his brother and the dog are asleep, too, by the parlour fire. I don't want to wake them. If I stand here calling, the child won't sleep a wink all night. Will you promise you'll give no trouble? Straight? . . . Then I'll come down."

She let the blind swing back, and they heard her footsteps recede towards the door. Then they waited, it seemed interminably. One window below, a bay on the ground floor, was lighted; the blinds were down here too, and were etched over with the symmetrical shadow of curtains. In this lighted, hidden room they heard a door open, and there was the sound of voices—statement, repetition, query, repetition, statement. Someone in there had been listening silently and noiselessly to all they said; now that someone was being deferred to and they knew that judgment on them trembled in the balance.

Though by now indifferent to rain, they had advanced instinctively into the shelter of the porch, and it was standing here that they heard the bolts creak back in their sockets and the rattle of a chain. Jameson had time to whisper, "They're well enough barricaded!" before the woman's face looked round the door at them in a dim slit of light.

As Jameson had expected, and as Jefferies had been secretly convinced, it was not difficult to arrive at an understanding.

"You're what did you say? Students . . . oh, at college? Oh, then, you're quite young fellows." She was easier with them now. "Yes, you've taken the wrong turning miles away back. How did you come to? Very wet. It's a bad night; I'm sorry for anyone that's out. Yes, you've still got a good bit before you. You must follow the track across the brickfield; that'll bring you out on to the Middlehampton road. Six miles, my husband reckons it, or six and a half. Yes, the buses do run on Wednesdays, but you'll have to wait now till the nine-thirty. It's about twenty minutes' walk from here to where the buses stop. No, there's no village or anything, just a cross-roads. We're in a lonely place."

"Thanks," said Jameson, reluctantly, "then we'll be getting on. I dare say we shall find some shelter in the brickyard?"

She hesitated, playing with the bolt inside the door and peering urgently into their faces in the uncertain light.

"If you'd like to come in . . ." she said at last slowly, "I know I can trust you not to make a noise and disturb the child—and my husband and his brother. You can come into the living-room, there's only Aunt in *there*."

They followed her in.

Revealed in what then seemed to them the dazzling glory of the lamplight, the young woman showed pleasant of feature, with shy, perturbed but not un-friendly eyes. Her back was still very straight; she was quite a girl, no older than they were. It seemed strange that it should have been her child that they had heard crying upstairs. She wore a pink blouse, a string of corals round her neck; and gave the impression of hav-ing recently adorned herself, but of being now so pre-occupied that she was unaware of her finery. In her eyes there was a look of the anguished evasion of some dread; she seemed to the two young men to be fever-ishly aware of them yet not to care whether they were there or not. The lamp stood on the waxed covering of the table; beside the lamp, a little behind the girl, sat a very stout elderly woman immobile, her hands folded under her bosom, looking dispassionately across the pool of lamplight at the two young men. They stood caps in hand, their cheeks burning in the sudden warmth, their eyes blinking in the brightness, looking from the young woman to the older one, round at the pictures, furniture, and ranged china of the room with an avidity perfunctorily concealed. Here was a Wife . . . an Aunt . . . a Living-room—*home*.

"I asked the gentlemen in, Auntie."

"Ah," said Auntie, of whom only the eyes were mobile, summing them up. "Yes. They're very wet— did they come far?" Though she did not directly address him, she looked inquiringly at Jameson, who replied obliquely, addressing himself to the niece, that they had been walking since two o'clock, since leaving Pidsthorpe. "Then they can't have had no tea," deduced the old lady with obvious pleasure. Well no, they admitted that they hadn't.

Auntie was the soul of hospitality. She now released a smile which rippled out slowly, and embedded itself in her cheeks. She invited them to sit down, and asked them if they wouldn't like to take their coats off and hang them by the fire. When they had done this, had hung their coats up on two empty, two somehow significantly empty pegs, they seated themselves opposite her and smiled politely, and Jameson blinked his bird eyes and ruffled up his hair. The great plane of Auntie's bosom was heaved up and shifted by a sigh as she said, *she* wouldn't mind a cup of tea, if anybody else were having it, as they had had to wait already more than an hour for their suppers, and it was likely that they would have to wait some hours more—Lord only knew how long. She dwelt upon them with her eyes benevolently, and said she did like a bit of company. "I really can't think," she said, tilting her whole bulk confidentially towards them, "I really can't think what's become of William. He's very regular, he's never missed his tea before. Oh, I do hope nothin' hasn't happened."

The girl had slipped out of the circle of lamplight and was standing by the window, listening intently for something outside. She turned round slowly with her eyes dilated as her aunt reiterated: "I *should* feel bad if anything had happened."

"Oh, *Aunt*," she deprecated, "how you do go on! *Happen*—what should have happened? He's just been delayed."

"Nothing hasn't ever delayed him before," the other mused inexorably. "I don't remember any other occasion when he's been delayed. *I'd* never believed he'd been going to the public, but *really*—"

"*Ooh*," cried the girl, writhing her shoulders, as though intolerably stung.

"But I thought—" objected Jameson eagerly, and broke off because Jefferies had kicked him under the table. They both remembered suddenly that they had seen only one window lighted on the downstairs floor. The realization that she had lied to them in fear made them both feel very large, forgiving, and protective. The old lady twinkled at them knowingly and hospitably, doing the honours of her niece's emotion as she did the honours of her niece's house. "It's very anxious for her," she said, inviting their appreciation with a gesture. She turned her eyes to the girl, after a few seconds' pregnant silence, and said, "Well, Annie, let's have the supper on the table, and have a little tea and a little bit of something tasty, anyway. What I always say: expectin' and expectin' somebody and holdin' everything over for them's not the way to make 'em come. If he's coming, he'll come; and all the sooner for not being waited for."

"*If he's coming!*" echoed the girl, turning round from the dresser where she was taking some plates down off a rack. "*If* he's coming to his own home! Anyone would think you thought he'd fallen into the canal," she cried excitedly, and then caught her breath, assailed with terror by her own words as though someone else had spoken them.

"Ah," said Auntie, like the dropping of a stone.

The plates were of white earthware with a gilt border and a gilt flower in the middle. Jefferies, bending to study them, thought they were significant and beautiful as, having lifted the lamp for a second to wipe over the table, she ranged them round mechanically, at regular intervals, as though she were dealing out the counters for a game. It did seem to Jefferies a game that they were all playing, a game that for her life's sake she must win; and every dish and bowl and knife that she put down to glitter under the lamp seemed a concession she was making to opponents, a handicap she was accepting. She passed to and fro between the table and the dresser mechanically, yet with a faint air of deliberation, and sometimes she would pause and grope a little blindly along the dresser with her fingers. The Aunt, looking into the lamp, tucked in her lips, refolded her hands with precision, and settled down into her bosom. A clock with a big round face ticked loudly on the mantel; the dull scarlet fire rustled and twitched, and all at once the kettle began singing, so loudly and so suddenly that Jefferies started.

"Now you've only got to make the tea," the Aunt prompted inexorably, "and take those kippers out of the oven. Oh, those *was* good kippers; it'll be too bad if they're dried."

Were Jefferies and Jameson to eat William's kippers? The girl knelt down before the fire, opened the little oven and half took out something the savouriness of which crept towards them. Then she slid back the dish with a clatter, and softly, deprecatingly, but very firmly shut the oven door. She remained kneeling on the hearthrug, her face to the fire, in an attitude of prayer; and said, without turning round, "There's eggs, Auntie; I'll just do up a few eggs."

"And yet it does seem a pity not to eat the kippers!" said Auntie thoughtfully.

This was horrible, something was being violated. "It would be very kind," said Jefferies, "if you'd let us have a cup of tea and a bit of bread-and-butter. We oughtn't

to have supper till we get to where we're going to at
Middlehampton; they'll be keeping supper for us
there."

"Oh?" asked Jameson, looking at him dully.

"Yes," said Jefferies with increased conviction.
"They'll be keeping supper for us there."

So Auntie's kipper was brought to her on a plate, and
the girl came slowly to take her place at the table,
carrying the enormous teapot in both hands. As she
bent to place it on its saucer, she started violently, the
saucer clattered, and she straightened herself, and
dammed with tense face and upraised hand the flow of
Auntie's conversation. Auntie had already told Jameson she had a nephew in London, and now she was telling him how nice the nephew was. They all started and
hung poised: then they only heard the child upstairs
faintly and fitfully crying. "Going up?"

"Oh no, it makes him worse, it makes him cry all
night," the mother said listlessly.

The tea steamed in the cups and was fragrant. Jefferies, gazing down into the brown translucency,
watched the sugar he had spooned in generously dis-
solve before he dimmed the clearness with a cloud of
milk. He laced his fingers round his cup, and their tips,
still numb, slowly thawed. The girl cut the loaf into
slices very methodically, and slid the butter-dish towards him from across the table. He looked into her
distraught eyes with nostalgia for something that they
held.

Jameson, a creature of more easy expansions, had

thawed visibly to his very depths. He beamed; his lips, slimy with excitement, glittered in the lamplight; he held the table. Aunt said "Well, I never!" to him when she paused to take another slice of bread, or push her empty cup across to be refilled; the girl, while part of her mind (to Jefferies's understanding) still stood sentinel, leaned towards Jameson with startled eyebrows over the teapot. He painted that new Earth which was to be a new Heaven for them, which he, Jameson, and others were to be swift to bring about. He intimated that *they* even might participate in its creation. They gazed at it, and Jefferies gazed with them, but it was as though he had been suddenly stricken colour-blind. He could see nothing of the New Jerusalem, but the infinite criss-cross of brickwork and Jameson shouting at the corner of the empty streets. A sudden shifting of his values made him dizzy; he leaned back to think but could visualize nothing but the living-room: it expanded till its margin lay beyond the compass of his vision. After all, it all came back to this—individual outlook; the emotional factors of environment; houses that were homes; living-rooms; people going out and coming in again; people not coming in; other people waiting for them in rooms that were little guarded squares of light walled in carefully against the hungry darkness, the ultimately all-devouring darkness. After all, here was the stage of every drama. Only very faintly and thinly came the voice of Jameson crying in the wilderness.

Whatever you might deny your body, there must

be always something, a somewhere, that the mind came back to.

Jameson did not refuse a third cup; he reached out across the table for it eagerly, still talking. "Live?" he was saying: "Why, we'll all live, live till we turn to the wall in a sleep of splendid exhaustion and never wake up again. You've seen a great perfect machine, how it roars round in an ecstasy? Well, that could be *us*—just realize it; there's nothing between our something and *that* something, cohesive, irresistible, majestic, but our *un-wills*, the feebleness of our desires. If every hand of the race were once, just once, outstretched unanimously, there would be nothing that those hands, that hand—I mean the *common* Hand—couldn't grasp; nothing too high, nothing too great. I—I always think that's an awfully solemn thought. Why, you know, there's a cry for life on the lips of every child, and we —you—people *stifle* it, because they're afraid of living. They think living's too *big*—Thanks, only half a slice, really." He looked round vaguely for the butter-dish, and Jefferies thought that very much thus must have spoken Zarathustra.

"Well, you *do* talk!" said Aunt, with pacific enjoyment.

The girl had dropped away from Jameson; she leaned back once more, her folded hands lying listless and forgotten on the table before her, and looked up at the ring of lamplight on the ceiling. Her face was tilted back into the shadow; only her chin gleamed, and her thin throat. She didn't want what Jameson was offering her, she did not understand it. One could not feel she was a stupid girl; it was possible that she merely thought Jameson noisy. One felt that she had built up for herself an intricate and perhaps rather lonely life, monotone beneath the great shadow of William. Jameson was tapping out his points with his spoon against his cup and clamouring about cohesion, but he would be unable to understand the queer unity which had created and destroyed Annie. She might have been leaning now into the yellow circle, all one sparkle, laughing at them and flashing her eyes, a desirable and an acquirable thing.

"You know," said Aunt archly to Jameson, "that's Socialism you've been talking. Of course I wouldn't say I thought you meant anything of the sort by what you've been saying, but it might give some people considerable offence. It doesn't do sometimes to go talking Socialism, even for a bit of fun. But what I always say —boys will be boys, and young men too. I like a bit of fun."

So Jameson began again: he was determined to do Auntie justice.

"Oh!" cried the girl unconsciously, beneath her breath. She turned her head and looked as though beseechingly at Jefferies, who stared back, and felt quite sick because he could do nothing for her. "I've been listening all the time, too," he whispered.

"Yes. You can hear steps for a long time, coming down the path."

"Didn't you hear ours were double?"

"Yes, I did hear that. But I sort of didn't want to."

"No. Would you like me to go out and meet him?"

"Oh no, you couldn't. He'd be angry I'd been letting on."

"We'll have to be going now. Can't I do anything to help you?"

"Well, you can't, can you? I've just got to wait."

"I wish I could make it be next morning," he said violently, not quite knowing what he meant.

"What?" she asked dully. A tear trickled down her face.

"It's awful for you to be afraid."

"Afraid? There's nothing to be afraid of; he's just— he's just late."

"Yes, of course." He felt there were things that could have been done to make it easier for her; he wanted to muffle Aunt's head up and wrench down the ticking clock. He could do neither of these things, so he said, "Well, we must be getting on for that bus now," in a loud voice, pushed back his chair, and looked across at Jameson.

It was difficult to leave the living-room; they felt like candles wavering, soon to be extinguished. They hitched down their coats and struggled on with them, leaving the pegs by the fire empty and attentive for William's coat. Annie brushed her hand along Jameson's wet sleeve and sighed; then she preceded them to the door. Auntie sat amazed and plaintive at the disruption of the supper-table; after they had said good-bye she followed them with one long, hard, regretful

stare, then let her eyes return to where they loved to
rest. At their last glimpse of her she sat again immobile,
her hands folded under her bosom, staring into the
lamp.

Jefferies muttered, brushing against Annie in the
doorway, "If we pass him, is there . . . could
we . . . ?"

"Oh no," she said, with a desolate half-laugh, "there's
nothing you could say. If you pass him he'll be coming
home."

"Good-bye," boomed Jameson abruptly, holding out
his big hand. "You've been awfully good. Thank you
ever so much for the tea and—and everything. You've
been awfully good."

"Oh no," she said vaguely, and vaguely held out her
hand to Jefferies. He started at the chilly contact, said
"Good-bye" gruffly, and dived past her into the cave of
darkness beyond the threshold. Jameson stumbled after
him and the door was abruptly shut. They heard the
bolts creak forward and the chain rattle as they went,
with hands before them, blindly down the path. They
paused to let the fence and the canal take form again,
which they did with an even greater dimness; then
stepped down on to the tow-path, gently closing the
gate. They went forward again, briskly, breathlessly,
shuffle-shuffle; never quite in step. The air seemed
colder, the rain heavier and finer. The tow-path still
went on, it seemed so infinitely that, when hearing the
sound of their footsteps suddenly constricted they
found themselves approaching the looming masses of

the brickfield, it was incredible that the path could have an end.

"Doesn't tea make one feel better?" said Jameson, speaking for the first time.

"Heaps. . . . What a queer house!"

"I wonder when he'll be back?"

"Yes. We shall never know."

They became aware half by instinct of a gap, a brief cessation in the hedge, and turned through it up a cart-track, splashing in the ruts, stumbling in the mud.

"She said the track was not long. We outstayed our time—think we'll get the bus, old fellow?"

"Don't know. Jameson, shan't we ever know if he came back?"

There was no answer.

They stumbled forward in the dark with tingling minds.

The Secession

A ROOM at the Pension Hebe, falling vacant un-
expectedly, was allotted to an English lady who had
made a standing application for admittance earlier in
the season. She arrived on foot one morning—the
Signora only knew from what obscure hotel—her
luggage wheeled behind her on a barrow. The Pension
occupied the two top floors of a palazzo on a hill; from
the Piazzi Berberini one ascended thither by a little
steep street flanked by garden walls as high as battle-
ments. Behind, one could hear fountains spattering
among the leaves; and wistaria brimming over like
froth down the sides of a mug reached its purple, pendu-
lous fingers down to the pavement. Seen in any light, the
English lady recorded in her diary, the Roman streets
are very mysterious, and seen from above (her window
commanded everything, and she paid a supplementary
ten lire a day for the city's generosity) the roofs and
gardens of Rome are scarcely less so. She had arrived
at the blank hour of eleven, and she spent the remainder

of her morning spread-eagled on her window-sill, looking out from a height which would have made another
woman dizzy at a panorama which should have abashed
her. At lunch-time she presented herself a shade too
punctually; she was already seated at her table against
the wall when the other visitors, chiefly American,
returned from sight-seeing.

She looked about her alertly, sifting everybody
through as though expecting an acquaintance, and returning curious glances with dark, disconcerting pen-
etration. She seemed more than thirty, with a long, fine
nose that drooped a little over a short upper lip—a
curious indentation sometimes flickered above her nostrils—and eyes set too close together beneath the slight,
definite curves of her eyebrows: at some angles they
had the appearance of a cast. She ate intelligently; her
knife and fork poised and flitted, and she would pause
to savour everything with a slight, critical compression
of the lips. Once or twice she jerked her head up
irrepressibly as though her thoughts had flamed into
something precious, which she must tell at once to a
vis-à-vis; then, disconcerted, she would question the
blank air before her as though somebody had vanished.
This was hardly marked enough to be noticeable; she
seemed not an eccentric but a diffident, cultured person,
with a thin back and shoulders, who would have visited
Shelley's grave.

After a day or two, having had the good taste to
make no advances, she began to know people in the
Pension Hebe. She was asked to join one or two ex-

peditions, and her tone, glance, and manner, rigid with expectation of the right reply, would ask, "How much do you really want me?" She did not often accept. She was a very independent woman, sat a good deal in her own room, and must have known Rome very well, since one never met her in the accepted places. She dismissed acquaintances, but was "out" for intimacies; she was as avid for them as she was for letters. The way she would pounce, drop hawk-like, on to her letters was remarkable; to read them publicly seemed scarcely delicate. For these, from the manner of her reading, were the kind of letters which should have been tucked away and taken to her room.

She did at length form an intimacy with a blond, milk-white American lady, a Miss Phelps, whom one might say that she perpetually ambushed. Miss Phelps, first merely paralysed by her, warmed to gratification, then to reciprocal emotion; she was a person who came quickly and frothily to the boil, like milk. She told her travelling-companions, two other ladies from whom she never entirely detached herself, that Miss Selby was extremely cultivated, well-read, and very refined; and she would report the matter if not the detail of their conversations faithfully. With all that Miss Selby scarcely ever went out: wasn't it funny? She had not "done" any of the places; she was "*keeping*" Rome. For when, for whom, was she keeping it? One didn't like to ask. That was Miss Selby's secret, which, like a soap-bubble at the end of a pipe, would bulge, subside, waver, wobble iridescently, and subside again. Later, among the

trees of the Pincio, it transpired that she was keeping
Rome for Somebody. Ah, really? Miss Phelps found
this beautiful. Miss Selby interrupted her sigh to con-
fess that she allowed herself daily small rations; she
would stand looking, for instance, through the railings
of the Forum without going in. Miss Phelps hoped
aloud that the Somebody were imminent; she feared the
strain of abstinence for one of Miss Selby's so strong intellectual appetites.

Next morning Miss Selby sought out her friend, half
aghast; her morning's letter, thin sheets of fine scrawled
writing, trembled in her hand. "I am expecting my
friend quite soon now," she said. "In a day or two"—
she made a show of referring to the letter—"the end of
the week. He finds he has been detained unnecessarily.
It was too bad, keeping him all this time."

"Oh, a gentleman?" deprecated Miss Phelps, smiling
gently. She had not failed, from the other's reticence,
to assume this.

"A family friend, a Mr. Humphrey Carr. He has
lately retired. He asks—that is, I wanted to ask you
. . . Of course, it would be unheard of, wouldn't it—
that is, I suppose it would not be possible for—No, I
quite see it wouldn't. . . . But I just thought I'd ask
you . . ." She faltered. The question was finally referred to a committee of Miss Phelps's married friends,
who delivered the ultimatum: if the Signora had a va-
cancy *in the other flat* for Mr. Carr; if *he* sat in the salon
after dinner in the evenings while *she* immediately retired, and if she joined their party at meals, leaving him

to occupy the small single table, the situation of Miss Selby *vis-à-vis* to Mr. Carr would be above reproach.

When Miss Selby began to wish that she had sent Humphrey to another hotel, to spend her days in his less distributed society, it is not known; but certainly she never betrayed herself. She would watch—perhaps with just the faintest compression of the lips as though some new strange dish had been placed before her— Humphrey dividing his attention scrupulously between the three American ladies, who as scrupulously passed him round. The dints above her nostrils would deepen and linger as she watched Miss Phelps's blue, calm, level-lidded eyes encounter briefly, but not too briefly, those of Mr. Carr. Mildred Phelps seemed to her, she records, more than ever beautiful, with her wide calm gaze and classic breadth of brow. She was not young, the brows were sometimes wistful, and at dinner after a long exhausting day her face would often show drained-out and colourless beneath the glare of lights. She said, as they all said without reserve, that Mr. Carr was so very nice, so cultured, so considerate. And what an archæologist he was! She even added, he was charming.

Miss Selby having so long withheld herself now fell upon Rome in a kind of fury. She was tireless—she asserted this to Humphrey with a smile; he need not spare her. Sometimes she crept out alone, often they would join the others, but they two made at least one expedition a day by themselves. By these they both profited; he knew more, but she was quicker to apply her knowledge. Humphrey was a tall, pink, reserved man, a retired schoolmaster, who looked out at the world a shade distastefully through pince-nez. Always stooping, he would incline further to her deferentially as they went down the shady side of the streets together, or stood still in the dazzle of a piazza. She, quicker in motion, was quicker to arrest herself; she was eagerly sensitive— it was as though her every sense flung out unseen, quivering tentacles to draw in what they might. She would stop short, a hand on his arm, a finger to her lips as though they were to surprise something, with: "Hark, Humphrey, listen to the fountain!" or, "See, Humphrey, through that archway there—how blue!" He would say, "Yes, oh, by Jove, yes!" a little uneasily. He felt her measure his appreciation; not the finest shade, the finest lack of a shade, could escape her.

Round her big straw hat she had knotted a Roman scarf; the ends, a striped cascade, hung down on one side of her face. Once, between these, he caught her watching with a bright, bird eye; though her head was scarcely turned in his direction. He was touched, he still remembers, by some quick emotion; behind the gaudy silk she was like some palpitating wild thing, a bird half-seen in a thicket. The emotion slipped away and left him numb; he was so much ashamed to have caught her unawares that he turned away his head and did not speak for two or three minutes: still he felt her eyes beseeching his return. He was numb; and worse, vacant and hollow. That, he supposed, was why he was so alive to other contacts, those American women. . . . He echoed to their tapping like an empty jar. Ever since he had come to Rome he had been like this; something had died as he entered the salon of the Pension Hebe and she rose up to greet him from among her friends. He could not discharge himself of what he had come out to say: it was no longer there. It was horrible that this should be so, that nothing was to happen to her here, in Rome.

For himself, he felt bereaved; it was almost as though she were dead: his thoughts, having lost their bourne of many years, wandered in confusion.

From that day on, the others, and Mildred Phelps in particular, more and more frequently accompanied them. Lena's suggestion, his consent, was not enough; she would reopen the question again and again insistently. "You don't *mind*, do you, Humphrey? they have been so good."

"Well, no-o, if you wish. Oh no," he would concede, carefully reluctant.

"It does so please them."

"As you wish, my dear."

"Oh, I don't *wish* . . . but we don't mind, do we?" She would dwell a little on the pronoun, considering it. Then it would be always: "You do like my friend, Mildred Phelps, don't you? I wanted you to meet each other. Don't you think she's sweet-looking, really rather beautiful?" If she asked this once, she asked a hundred times. And he, after a little surprised pause of self-interrogation, would repeat: "Miss Phelps? Oh yes, very sweet-looking!"

Miss Selby sought out the earliest opportunity to

make her friend aware of Mr. Carr's admiration. One evening, when they had all returned from an expedition, she took Miss Phelps's arm, coming down the corridor, and drew her into her bedroom. "We haven't seen each other for so long," she said. "Let's be together, shall we, until dinner? Watch my sunset!" She unlatched and pushed open the window, and, side by side, they leant out over Rome. The sun was melting down into a sea of yellow mist; soon the long blade of hills behind the Vatican would rise to cut away the brightness. Under the clear depths of yellow which dusk coming up from the gardens gradually infused and clouded, the grave polished faces of the buildings shone. Domes and campanili, the crest here and there of a hill or the tips of cypresses, had the air of floating buoys upon the ebbing tide of light. Miss Phelps and Miss Selby were pressed close together in the narrow frame of the window; their sides and elbows touched, they could have felt one another's hearts beating.

They were silent; Miss Selby's contemplation of that view compelled it. After some minutes of this her companion's placidity was troubled; she stirred with quickened breathing as though she felt the silence as a slip-noose being tightened about her. Miss Selby, turning from the city, focussed her dark gaze myopically on the fair profile now brushed over as with pollen by the evening light. She asked if Mildred had enjoyed their day as much as she had. Mr. Carr, she knew, had enjoyed it. Didn't Mildred find Mr. Carr a pleasant person? Oh yes, Mildred said he was delightful. But

seriously, putting aside all talk of superficial pleasant-
ries, of companionableness, did Mildred *like* Mr. Carr?
Yes, Mildred did indeed.

Miss Selby let out a happy little sigh of relief. "I'm
so glad," she said. "He admires you so much."

"Oh!" said Mildred, and her lashes fluttered. She
could not blush.

"I knew he would. I felt that the moment I saw you.
It's as though," Miss Selby considered, "very close
friendship—sympathy—gave one the same eyes. I
wanted you to meet him so much; I felt it would make
something perfect. And it means a lot to me to know,
now, that you like him, and that he likes you and admires you, because . . ." She paused, as to enjoy in
secret the emotion distilling itself drop by drop from
their silence. It was not with the sense of helping out
confusion or diffidence that Mildred, playing a slow
tune with the fingers of her right hand on the window-
sill, said at last—"Because? . . . Go on."

"He has been for many years my friend," said Miss
Selby. "He has asked me to marry him. I felt I should
like you to share this . . . to know . . ."

"Oh," said Mildred, staring before her, as though
Rome showed itself new and strange to her in the light
of the revelation. "What a beautiful place for it to have
happened in!" The close, dark eyes came closer to her
cheek; their pressure side to side was increased. Keeping her face averted, she still felt herself transparent to
this gaze and knew that her transparency must be darkened visibly by a hurrying shoal of thoughts. "It's dear

of you to share it," she said quickly. "When did— But that's impertinent: forgive me!"

Miss Selby, continuing to search her out, was again for a minute silent. Then she said: "Some years ago Humphrey—spoke. He took me by surprise. I wasn't ready. I did not think, then, that I ever should be ready. I asked him to put that aside, for always. He was wiser than I; he said that some day he believed I would dis-cover myself . . . *different*, and that until then he would be waiting. I never cared for—I feared, disliked —the idea of marriage; but do you know, Mildred, that knowledge was very precious to me. I had only to turn to him in the new way and he would be there. That readiness of his, hidden away from me, from every-body, became the centre of my life. . . . Mildred, he *was* wise. He has a very deep insight. To acknowledge this to him made the moment more precious when I was able to write, 'I am going to Rome. I want you to be there.' And understanding everything, he came."

"Yes," said Mildred Phelps. "When are you going to be married?"

"He hasn't spoken of that," her friend said quickly. "It's the coming nearer to that, every day, that makes these days so precious. It's the perfect understanding, the harmony, that makes your company, your friend-ship, dear, so beautiful to both of us, something that will be always interwoven with the deepest in our lives. I—I wanted you to understand."

The sun had gone down, the night rose, the towers

and domes still held the afterglow. Mildred said, "You must be very happy," and Miss Selby, shivering as though she had suddenly felt the air grow cold, drew her in from the window and closed it, assenting, "Yes, I am very happy," in her gentle, cultivated voice. She was a little late for dinner that evening, having waited to enter something in her diary.

Humphrey Carr, those following days, came to be aware of curious implications in Miss Phelps's manner to himself. The whole party made an expedition to Hadrian's Villa across the Campagna, and when they had entered the garden he and she found themselves walking ahead of the others. As they passed from room to room with their skyey ceilings, over the broken pavements and among the broken shadows of the arches, it was as though some perverse and violent spirit entered into him; he tore aside something from between them and began to question her suddenly, almost to accuse her. Miss Phelps, perhaps less perfectly civilized than it would ever be possible for her to appear, stopped dead, spreading out one hand against the hot brick wall so solid yet with such silver-pink bloom of impermanence; and looked about her huntedly with a delightful tremor of panic. They were quite alone: the archways were empty; the hill above swept up to the skyline unpeopled, netted over with the shadows of olives. Mr. Carr, her Miss Selby's flushed friend, who had stumbled along beside her with the hampered, peering diffidence

of the myopic, now loomed inexorable with his string
of questions—he might even be cruel. She felt that she
was in the power of an emperor.

"Then what has happened?" he was repeating. "Is it
anything I have done?"

"I don't know what you mean."

"Won't you be frank—be true to your nature? If I
have offended, it would not be—*you*—to dismiss me
unheard. And look back at these days. They have been
strange, haven't they, and precious for some of us?"

She repeated dully: "Yes, precious for some of us."
If there were an implication there, he ignored it; he bent
forward eagerly: "Then you've shared—"

"I think," she interrupted, "it is the *colouring*, the
very air of Rome. Even oneself feels intensified. The
white houses and the dark skies, the spurting-up lines
of everything, the cypresses, the fountains. You can't
turn a corner without holding your breath. It's so
crowded . . ."

"Yes, yes," he said, "but you're quoting Lena Selby."
They still stood by the wall, seeing nothing, facing one
another.

"Did she say that to you, too?" she said, startled.

"Very likely; it explains nothing, it does not even
make sense." The very thought of Lena darting about
Rome and that crude scarf with the trailing ends
brought a note of injury and resentment into his voice.
"*You* are not so easily impinged upon. No, there is
something more. Miss Phelps—Mildred—I am intoler-

ably situated. We must understand one another, or there can be no way out."

Her emotion seemed to her so powerful that she could hardly contain it. She would not think, so she shut her eyes and pushed her hand against the wall with all her might. This pressure upon herself was wonderful; she had passed from friend to friend in vain, hitherto— not one of them had known how to apply it. She had heard a raw knife-edge of anger and eagerness in his scholarly English voice, own brother to Miss Selby's. Between her lashes she watched his throat contract as he waited for her to speak.

To her surprise she could not. She did not want him ever to go away, and put her other hand out dumbly, blindly, in a gesture.

He seized at it, with, "Oh, my dear!"

"But you belong; you, you . . ."

"There's nothing. There was never anything. Oh, believe me; you have misunderstood. To be real, there must be two, you know; and she was wiser than I, she would have none of it. I see now how wise she was. I came out to tell her I was free, at last. I know she will be glad. She has such blessed insight. I have everything to thank her for."

"Ah no! Because you came, you came . . ."

"It was an illusion!" he cried. "We both saw. If she does not see now, she has deceived herself. I swear—" He broke off, dropping her hand, which had lain inert in his, because he saw Miss Selby coming towards them through an archway. The other ladies followed her at a short distance; it was their voices which had attracted attention. Miss Phelps, startled, raised her eyes to follow the direction of his stare; for an instant they met Miss Selby's.

"If you have not discovered the Philosopher's Hall you must go there; it is beautiful and, I think, suggestive," said Miss Selby, approaching. "Also, there is a kind of underground arcade . . ."

The afternoon was hot; they flagged a little, returning; a film of vapour crept across the sky. The tram like a boat before the wind went rocking home across the empty Campagna. Mildred Phelps leant back, her hands before her face to shade it from the wide, bright glare; she said her head ached, she suffered terribly from headaches. Humphrey Carr read Mildred's Baedeker; his eyes were fastened to it in a kind of horror; all the interminable way he never once looked up, and never turned a page. Only Miss Selby, seated beside him, was eager, brilliant, indefatigable; she talked on, sketching out the skyline to her companions with a gesture, offering a thousand fugitive details of the wayside to their observation with a smile. Often the roar of the tram would rise to drown her voice, but they still saw her lips alive, her brain glowing through her features, while her dark glance flitted, stabbed and flitted from face to face. She made the gestures of gathering up some brightness and slowly for their approbation letting it trickle through her fingers. The American ladies, wound up in their veils, passively and smilingly marvelled at her. Afterwards, they said it had been a swansong.

That Miss Selby kept a diary (as a record, not as an outlet), entered her most trivial expenses in a notebook, and wore her keys round her neck, all proved that she was very methodical. From the account-book it was gathered that not a five-centesimi piece could have gone its way unconsidered; and from the diary that not a glance, a half-smile, an intonation, not the slightest interchange between any of them, had escaped her. She had charted the atmosphere of her company; she had been meticulously accurate.

Three days after the expedition to the Villa and the last appearance of Miss Selby, Humphrey Carr, alone in her disconcerted room, turned to see Mildred standing on the threshold looking at him like a stranger. Her eyes had purple circles round them; they looked past him to the ravished bureau, the wardrobe vomiting forth its dresses, the window open to the city and the sky.

"Will you come in?" he said courteously, in the tone of one already in possession; and she thought as she saw him standing among this litter of women's things that he might have been Miss Selby's husband.

"Oh no," she whispered, frightened out of her resolve by the sense of intruding on a privacy—*theirs*.

"But I beg of you—" he insisted, still in a sort of panic-stricken appeal to a stranger. A green Venetian necklace, straggling across the floor, crunched beneath his clumsy forward step.

"Oh, oh!" she cried, darting forward to tug at the end of the necklace. He tried to step clear of it, stood peering down through his glasses while she swept up the flakes of glass from about his feet. He brought waste and destruction with him everywhere. She got up and slipped the beads tenderly into a bureau drawer. Above, a photo of the tortured Laocöon had been slipped into the frame of the mirror. She asked, standing with her back to him, "Have you, did you—find out anything yet? There's still nothing?"

"No, she left nothing to tell us."

"Then she meant there should be nothing for us to know; and I think . . ."

"You think that wish is at *any price* to be respected? At the price, even, of a lost possibility of saving her?"

Her eyes wondered, quite intelligibly, "What do you want to bring her back to?" Aloud, she only said meditatively, "And she left everything. Her keys, her passport, all her money, her—her diary . . . ?"

"Yes. It will be *that* that will tell us. I do firmly believe now that we should be justified—"

She saw now plainly what had been there in her mind at the moment of her entrance, and knew that it was under Miss Selby's compulsion that she had come, tranced, quite unwillingly, to stand in the doorway of the room. The book lay by the dispatch-case, defenceless against outrage.

"*Me!*" she said, holding her hand out.

"No," he said. "There will be little there that *I* can't guess at, but something, perhaps, to offend *you*."

Her face, still, mild and pale as milk, did not alter; she was holding her hand out mutely.

"Forgive me," he continued, taking the book up, "but I have been longest her friend—from her youth. It is surely for me?"

"Never," she said, with an unperturbed reasonableness. "You were never that; you could never—" She broke off, and then, with a violence that by contrast with her remote elegance seemed that of an apache, sprang forward and wrenched the book out of his grasp. She retreated to the doorway with it pressed against a bosom that could never have been so convulsed.

The two friends of the injured lady stared at one another over an abyss. At last Humphrey Carr shrugged his shoulders: an Englishman's inept and clumsy shrug. "As you wish," he said. "If you're not frightened."

"It's for me as a woman. Frightened?—what right have you to imply—?" Again too much mistress of herself for speech, she subsided into a ruffling, preening, incoherent flutter, sat down on the edge of the bed with the open diary in her hands and began to read. He turned away and leant his elbows on the window-sill. After a few minutes of attentive silence he heard a quick movement behind him, the book sliding to the floor. He was startled to feel her shoulder brush his own as she leant out perilously far across the sill.

"Steady—steady," he cried. "It's a nasty height."

"A nasty height," she repeated, looking down as with

desire at the lemon trees, the fountain so far below as
to be inaudible. She looked for so long that he touched
her shoulder to restrain her, and, shuddering, she followed him back into the room. She watched him pick
up and begin to read the diary. He felt her eyes on him
all the time, but she made no movement of protest. The
book had lain open, face downwards, at the date of
Miss Selby's conversation with Mildred, in the evening
light, in that very window. Word for word, without
comment, their conversation had been recorded, white-
hot from the memory, in the fluent writing that did not
seem to pause. The entry closed with this: "*I wonder,
now that she has gone, why I have not pushed her
through the window. It was so much in my mind to do
this, and I see now it could have been done more easily
than I thought.*"

Humphrey Carr raised his eyes slowly, but Mildred
did not stay to meet them. With another of those wild
movements so foreign to herself, she was gone; he heard
the door swing to, and his isolation once more sifted
down upon him.

He did not see Miss Phelps again; she left that evening with her friends—he was told, for Florence.

Making Arrangements

S<small>IX DAYS</small> after Margery's departure, a letter from her came for Hewson Blair. That surprised him; he had not expected her to write: surely the next move should be his? Assuming this, he had deliberated comfortably —there was time, it had appeared, for sustained deliberation—and now Margery had pounced back upon him suddenly. It was like being spoken to when he was settling down to a stiff book in the evening; Margery had often done this.

He remembered as he scrutinized the postmark that the last time she had written to him was from Switzerland, last Christmas. She always said she found him difficult to write to—why write now, then, when she might be better occupied? Hewson never sneered; his face lacked the finer mobility and his voice the finer inflections. He turned over the unopened letter, felt that it was compact and fat, and pinched the corners thoughtfully.

He found the name of a riverside hotel printed on

the flap of the envelope, and re-read this several times with amazement, unable to conceive how a young woman who had gone away with somebody else to a riverside hotel—with white railings, Hewson imagined, and geraniums swinging in baskets, and a perpetual, even rushing past of the water—could spare some hours of her time there writing to her husband. Unless, of course, she simply wanted to tell him about Leslie.

Of course, she must have a considerable amount to say about Leslie after having lived with him under necessarily restricted conditions for the last six days. She had always told Hewson about her many friends, at greath length, and as he was not interested in these people the information went in at one ear and out at the other. He imagined that Leslie was the one with the 'cello, though he might have been the one with the golf handicap—he could not say.

If she wanted to come back—he was slitting open the envelope carefully, and this made him pause a moment —if she wanted to come back he must write briefly and say he was sorry, he could not have her, he had made other arrangements. His sister was coming to keep house for him tomorrow, and the servants were even now getting ready the spare-room.

Hewson had just come in, having got away a little earlier than usual from the office, where people were beginning to know, and to speak to him awkwardly with scared faces. He had not, of course, been near the club. In stories, people who were treated as Margery had treated him threw up everything and went abroad;

but Hewson did not care for travelling, and it would be difficult to leave his business just at present. He had never seen very much of Margery, his wheels went round without her; all this, if one could regard it rationally, came down to a few readjustments in one's menage and a slight social awkwardness which one would soon outgrow.

Parkins had just made up the library fire; she was drawing the curtains noiselessly across the windows. Hewson wondered what she had thought of Margery's letter as she enisled it, lonely, gleaming, and defiant, on the silver salver on to which Margery had so often flung her gloves. Margery would fling her gloves on to the salver and her furs across the oak chest and swing humming into the library to read her letters by the fire. She would settle down over them like a cat over a saucer of milk, bend and smile and murmur over each, rustling the paper; and one by one drop them, crumpled, into the grate. Margery was a person who dealt summarily with her husks; bit through direct to the milky kernel of things and crunched delectably.

Tonight the grate was very tidy. Hewson watched Parkins's back and felt the room unbearably crowded.

"That's all right," he said. "That will do. Thank you, Parkins."

He stood with his back to the fire, watching Parkins narrowly until she had left the room. Then he let Margery out of the envelope.

* * *

"It does seem funny to be writing to you again," Margery wrote. "I haven't for such ages—that note I left on the mantelpiece doesn't count, of course. Wasn't it dramatic, leaving a note like that! I couldn't help laughing; it just shows how true novels really are.

"Dear Hewson, there are several things, quite a lot, that I want sent after me at once. As I expect you saw, I didn't take more than my dressing-case. I know you will make all arrangements—you are so awfully good at that sort of thing. I suppose there are rather a lot of arrangements—I mean, like getting the divorce and sending my clothes on and writing to tell people; and I expect you would rather give away the dogs.

"We don't quite know how long a divorce takes or how one gets it, but as I told Leslie, who often gets rather depressed about all this fuss, you will be able to arrange it all beautifully. We are going abroad till it is all over; Leslie is so fearfully sensitive. We want to go quite soon, so I should be so much obliged if you could send those clothes off to me at once. I enclose a list.

"Leslie says he thinks I am perfectly wonderful, the way I think of everything, and I suppose it really is rather wonderful, isn't it, considering you always made all the arrangements. It just shows what one can do if one is put to it. Leslie would like to send a message; he feels he can't very well send his love, but he asks me to say how sorry he is for any inconvenience this will cause you, but that he is sure you cannot fail to feel, as we do, that it is all for the best. Leslie is fearfully considerate.

"Dear Hewson, I think you are too sweet, and you know I have always liked you. I feel quite homesick sometimes in this horrid hotel, but it's no good being sentimental, is it? We never suited each other a bit, and I never quite know what you wanted me for. I expect you will be fearfully happy now and settle down again and marry some fearfully nice girl and get the rock-garden really nice without my horrid dogs to come and scratch it up. Now, about the clothes . . ."

Directions followed.

As Hewson read this letter he remembered Leslie (though he still could not say whether he was the one with the 'cello or the golf handicap), a young man with a very fair short moustache and flickering lashes, who liked his port. It seemed quite right that such a fair young man should admire Margery, who was dark. Many people had, indeed, admired Margery, which gratified Hewson who had married her. Many more people praised her clothes, which still further gratified Hewson who had paid for them. When he married Margery he stamped himself as a man of taste (and a man of charm, too, to have secured her), and he rose still higher in the estimation of his friends; while even men who had thought him a dull dog in the army or at Oxford began coming to the house again.

It was all very nice, and Hewson often found himself arrested in a trance of self-congratulation; when he came in in the evenings, for instance, and found fire-light flooding and ebbing in the white-panelled hall and

more cards on the table, and heard Parkins moving
about in the dining-room, where through the slit of the
door the glass and silver on the table sparkled under the
low inverted corolla of the shade. Sometimes he would
have to put his hand before his mouth, and pass for
yawning, to conceal the slow smile that crept irresistibly across his face; as when he stood beside the really
good gramophone and changed the records of thudding
music for Margery and her friends to dance to. She
danced beautifully with her slim, balanced partners;
they moved like moths, almost soundlessly, their feet
hiss-hissing faintly on the parquet. Hewson's hand
brushed across the switchboard, lights would spring up
dazzlingly against the ceiling and pour down opulently
on to the amber floor to play and melt among the
shadows of feet. This had all been very satisfactory.

Hewson never conceived or imagined, but he intended; and his home had been all that he had intended.
He had a sense of fitness and never made an error in
taste. He was not amusing, he did not intend to be an
amusing man; but he had always intended to marry an
amusing wife, a pretty little thing with charm. He considered that Margery was becoming to him, which indeed she was. He had a fine fair impassive face with the
jaw in evidence and owl's eyebrows; he stood for dark
oak and white panelling, good wine and billiard-
tables. Margery stood for water-colours, gramophones,
and rosy chintz. They had made a home together with
all this; none of these elements was lacking, and thus
their home had, rightly, the finality of completeness.

Tonight he dined early, and, though eating abstract-edly, ate well. He knew the importance of this. They had taken out all the leaves, the table had shrunk to its smallest. Margery had often been away or out, and this evening was in no way different from many others. They brought his coffee to the table, and after coffee he went upstairs, slowly, turning out all but one of the hall lights behind him. He carried Margery's letter, and paused on the landing to look through the list again, because he had decided to get the things packed up to-night and sent off early tomorrow. As he did not wish to give Emily or Parkins Margery's letter (the list being punctuated by irrelevancies), he proposed to get the shoes and dresses out himself and leave them on the bed for Emily or Parkins to pack.

Yes, Margery was not unperceptive; he really did like making arrangements. The sense of efficiency in-toxicated him, like dancing. He liked going for a thing methodically and getting it done; jotting down lists on pieces of paper and clipping the papers together and putting them away in the one inevitable drawer.

"You can't think what Hewson's like!" Margery would exult to their friends, waving a glass dessert-spoon at him from her end of the table. "He does every-thing and finds everything and puts everything away and sends everything off. He's absolutely amazing!"

At this, all the way down the table the shirt-fronts and pink quarter-faces veered intently toward Margery would veer round, guffawing, toward Hewson, and be-come three-quarter faces, twinkling over with mirth,

while the ladies, tittering deprecatingly, swayed toward
Hewson, their mirth drawn out into a sigh. "You must
forgive us, Mr. Blair," they implied; "but your wife is
really *so* amusing!" And Hewson sat on solidly and
kept the wine going.

Margery's room sprang into light nakedly; the servants had taken away the pink shades. The curtains were
undrawn, and Emily, with a housemaid's one cannot
say how conscious sense of the dramatic, had dropped
a sheet over the mirror and swathed the dressing-table:
bowls and bottles here and there projected, glacial,
through the folds. The room was very cold and Hewson thought of ordering a fire, then recoiled in shyness
from the imagined face of Emily or Parkins. He had
not entered Margery's room since her departure—he
preferred to think of it as a departure rather than a
flight, an ignominious scurrying-forth unworthy of the
home and husband that she left. He preferred to feel
that if his wife sinned, she would sin like a lady.

Margery's directions were minute, though perhaps a
trifle incoherent. Hewson sat down on the sofa along
the end of the bed to study the list in the light of imminent activity. He must revise it systematically, making
it out into headings: "Contents of wardrobe, contents
of chest by window, contents of dressing-table drawers." Something caught his eye; he started. Margery's
pink slippers, overlooked by Emily, peeped out at him
from under the valance of the bed.

From the slippers, connections of ideas brought
round his eyes to the fireplace again; he had never seen

it black on a chilly evening; Margery had had everything, this was a really good room. She would never have a room like this again; Leslie would not be able to give it to her. What could have been the attraction? . . . Well, that was a blind alley; it was no good wandering down there.

She had written: "I never quite know what you wanted me for."

That statement amazed Hewson; it simply amazed him. He got up and walked round the room, staring at the shining furniture, challenging the pictures, thinking of the library fire, the dancing-floor under the downpour of light, the oval table in the dining-room compassed about for him always with an imaginary crowd of faces. Surely the sense of inclusion in all this should have justified Margery's existence to her. It was not as if he had ever bothered her to give him anything. He had assumed quite naturally that this sense of being cognate parts of a whole should suffice for both of them. He still could not understand where this had failed her.

He could not conceive what Leslie had held out to her, and what she had run to grasp.

Hewson advanced toward his reflection in the wardrobe mirror, and they stood eying one another sternly; then their faces softened. "Lonely fellow," Hewson condescended. The ghost of one of his old happy trances returned to his reflection; he saw the slow smile spread across its face, its fine face. That she should have fallen short of this. . . .

He tugged at the handle of the wardrobe door, and his reflection swung toward him, flashed in the light and vanished. From the dusk within, cedar-scented and cavernous, Margery leaped out to him again as she had leaped up out of the envelope. There were so many Margerys in there, phalanx on phalanx, and the scent of her rushed out to fill this room, depose the bleak regency of Emily, and make the pictures, the chairs, the chintzes, the shadows in the alcove, suddenly significant. He drew out his fountain pen, detached a leaf from his notebook and headed it: "Contents of Wardrobe."

If he had been a different type of man Margery's chameleon quality would, he knew, have irritated him; the way she took colour from everything she put on, and not only took colour but became it, while shadowing behind all her changes an immutable, untouched, and careless self. Now the black dress—Hewson took it down and carried it over to the bed, and its long draperies swept the carpet, clinging to the pile, and seemed to follow him reluctantly—you would have said the black dress was the very essence, the expression of the innermost of her, till you met her in the flame-colour.

He took down the flame-colour next, and could hardly help caressing it as it lay across his arms, languishing and passive. The shimmer and rustle of it, the swinging of its pendent draperies round his feet, filled him with a sharp nostalgia, though they stood to him for nothing in particular—there had been that evening in the billiard-room. He laid the dress down reverently on the bed, like a corpse, and folded its gauzy sleeves across its bosom.

He was less tender with the one that followed, a creamy, slithery thing with a metallic brilliance that slipped down into his hands with a horrible wanton willingness. He had always felt an animosity towards it since they drove together to that dance. It slid and shone round Margery's limbs as though she were dressed in quicksilver; more beautiful than all the rest, more costly also, as Hewson knew. He let it drip down from his arms on to the bed and creep across the counterpane like a river.

He was summary, too, with the velvety things that followed, weighed down by their heavy fur hems. They were evenings at home to him, *tête-à-têtes* with their faint, discomfortable challenge; Margery tilting back her chin to yawn, or lolling sideways out of her chair to tickle her dog in the stomach, or shuffling illustrated papers. She would say: "Talk to me, Hewson. Hewson, do talk. . . ." And later: "Hewson, I suppose evenings at home are good for one. I'm so sleepy. That does show, doesn't it, how I need sleep?"

He worked more quickly after this, carrying the dresses one by one across the room, laying them on the bed, and pausing after each to compare his list with Margery's. Sometimes the name of a colour, the description of a stuff, would puzzle him, and he pored above the two lists with bent brows, unable to make them tally. Reluctantly he would inscribe a question mark. He heard ten strike, and began working even faster. He had still to make arrangements with the chauffeur: he liked to be in bed himself by half-past eleven, and he didn't approve of keeping the servants late.

Then, leaning deep into the cupboard, he saw the red dress, melting away into the shadows of the cedarwood. It hung alone in one corner with an air of withdrawal. Hewson reached out, twitched it down; it hung limp from his hands, unrustling, exhaling its own perfume of chiffon. He stepped back; it resisted for an infinitesimal second, then, before he could release the tension on it, tore with a long soft sound.

It came out into the light of the room hanging jagged and lamentable, the long hem trailing. Hewson had torn it, torn the red dress; of all her dresses. He looked at it in fear and a kind of defiant anger. He assured himself the stuff was rotten; she had not worn it for so long. Had, indeed, Margery's avoidance of the red dress been deliberate?

With what motive, Hewson wondered, had this unique presentation of herself been so definitely eschewed? Did it make her shy—was she then conscious that it stood for something to be forgotten? He could never have believed this of Margery; he was startled to find that he himself should suspect it. Yet he returned to this: she had never worn the red dress since *that* occasion. He had watched for it speechlessly those ensuing weeks, evening after evening, but it had never appeared again. And here he had found it, hanging in the deepest shadow, trying to be forgotten.

Margery had put the red dress down on her list; she had underlined it. It was one of the dresses she wanted to take away to Leslie. Now it was torn, irreparably torn; she would never be able to wear it.

Hewson wondered whether Margery would be angry. He quailed a little, feeling the quick storm of her wrath about him; windy little buffets of derision and a fine sting of irony. She would certainly be angry when she knew, and go sobbing with rage to Leslie: Hewson wondered whether Leslie would be adequate. He debated whether he should pack the dress. Well, since it had admittedly stood for that to Margery as well as to himself, let her have it as it was! Hewson's wits stirred—this should be his comment. Why should he let her go to Leslie with that dress, the dress in which Hewson had most nearly won her? It had been pacific, their relationship; neither of them would have admitted a crescendo, a climax, a decrescendo; but there had been a climax, and the red dress shone in both their memories to mark it. He did not think he would let the Margery who lived for Leslie wear the red dress of his own irreclaimable Margery.

Smiling and frowning a little with concentration, he eyed the thing, then gripped the folds in both hands and tore the dress effortlessly from throat to hem, refolded it, and tore again. A fine dust of silk crimsoned the air for a moment, assailed his nostrils, made him sneeze. He laid the dead dress gently down among the other dresses and stood away, looking down at them all.

These were all his, his like the room and the house. Without these dresses the inner Margery, unfostered, would never have become perceptible to the world. She would have been like a page of music written never to be played. All her delightfulness to her friends had been in this expansion of herself into forms and colours. Hewson had fostered this expansion, as it now appeared, that Leslie might ultimately be delighted. From the hotel by the river the disembodied ghost of Margery was crying thinly to him for her body, her innumerable lovely bodies. Hewson expressed this to himself concisely and heavily, as a man should, as he stood looking down at the bed, half smiling, and said, "She has committed suicide."

From boyhood, Hewson had never cared for any thoughts of revenge. Revenge was a very wild kind of justice, and Hewson was a civilized man. He believed in the Good, in the balance of things, and in an eventual, tremendous pay-day. At once, the very evening Margery had left him, he had felt the matter to be out of his hands, and, wondering quite impartially how much she would be punished, had sat down almost at once to write and make arrangements with his sister. He had not, these last few days, felt sorrowful, venomous, or angry, because he had not felt at all; the making of these and other arrangements had too fully occupied him. He had always very lucidly and reasonably contended that the importance of mere feeling in determining a man's line of action is greatly overrated.

Now, looking down, he watched the dresses, tense

with readiness to fall upon them if they stirred and pin them down and crush and crush and crush them. If he could unswervingly and unsparingly hold them in his eyes, he would be able to detect their movements, the irrepressible palpitation of that vitality she had infused into them. They lay there dormant; only the crimson dress was dead. He bent, and touched the creamy trickle of the ball-dress; his finger dinted it and a metallic brightness spurted down the dint, filling it like a tide. He drew back his finger, cold yet curiously vibrant from the contact. The folds were cool; and yet he had expected, had expected . . . He brought down his outspread hands slowly; they paused, then closed on handfuls of the creamy stuff that trickled icily away between his fingers. The dress lay stretched out and provocative and did not resist him, and Hewson with dilated eyes stared down at it and did not dare to breathe.

He turned and crossed the room on tiptoe, peered out into the darkness of the trees, then drew the blinds down. He glanced round secretly and stealthily at the pictures; then he went over to the door and peered out, listening intently, on to the landing. Silence there and silence through the house. Shutting the door carefully behind him, he returned to the bedside.

It seemed to him, as he softly, inexorably approached them, that the swirls, rivers, and luxuriance of silk and silver, fur and lace and velvet, shuddered as he came. His shadow drained the colour from them as he bent over the bed.

Half an hour later, Hewson once more crossed the landing and went up to the box-room to look for Margery's trunk. He was intent and flushed, and paused for a moment under the light to brush some shreds of silver from his sleeve. He seemed unconscious that a wraith of flame-coloured chiffon drifted away from his shoulder as he walked, hung in the air, and settled on the carpet behind him. He came down again from the box-room breathing hard, bent beneath the trunk, and as he re-entered the bedroom something black and snake-like lying across the threshold wound round his feet and nearly entangled him. Approaching the bed, his steps were once more impeded; sometimes he was walking ankle-deep.

He pitched the trunk down in a clear space, propped it open and began to pack. Many of the fragments, torn too fine, were elusive; he stooped with the action of a gleaner to gather them in armfuls, then thrust them down into the trunk. The silks—they seemed still sentient—quivered under his touch; the velvets lay there sullenly, and sometimes, when he heaped them in, dripped out over the edge of the box again. Here and there an end of fur ruffled into deeper shadows under his excited breath. When he had amassed everything, Hewson beat with the flat of his hands upon the pile to make it level, spread tissue over it, and locked the trunk. Then he rang for Parkins and sat down to wait. He re-read Margery's list once again, folded it, and put it away in his pocket-book.

That night, Lippit the chauffeur received his instructions. He was to take Mrs. Blair's box to the station at half-past eight the following morning, and despatch it to the given address per luggage in advance, having taken to the same station a ticket to be afterwards destroyed. This extravagance Hewson deplored, but the exigencies of the railway company demanded it. The trunk was strapped and corded and placed in the back hall in readiness for its early departure, and Hewson, seated comfortably at his table by the library fire, printed out two labels in neat black characters, then himself affixed them to the handles of the trunk.

"Would there be anything more, sir?" inquired Parkins, standing at attention.

"No, not tonight," said Hewson courteously. "I am sorry to have kept you late, Parkins: you had better go to bed."

"Thank you, sir."

"And oh, Parkins!"

"Sir?"

"You had better ask Emily to sweep out Mrs. Blair's room again tonight. The carpet needs sweeping; she should pay particular attention to the carpet."

Hearing the hall clock strike eleven, Hewson turned the lights out, quenched the astonished face of Parkins, and went upstairs to bed.

The Storm

Don't come near me," she said, turning sharply. "I hate you! Why do you keep on following me about?"

He said, "Well, we've got to go down in the same tram."

"I'll walk."

"Not with those heels. You couldn't."

"If you had any decency, you would."

"I don't care for walking those long distances down hill. It shakes me up. Besides, I feel another blister coming."

He stooped to feel one foot, and the crimson of his face deepened.

"O-oh!" she shuddered, pressing her handbag with both hands to her bosom, and grimacing up at the sky.

He peered over the parapet. "Hush," he said, "there are people on the terrace just below us, listening."

"Danish women," she said scornfully, looking over at the three flat hats, but she dropped into silence, shifting away from him as he leant forward and spread his elbows out on the parapet with a prolonged "Phew!" They were high up on the terrace of a Villa; dizzily high.

The air was warm and tense, stretched so taut that it quivered. Breathing had become an affair of consciousness, and movement they both felt to be impossible. Behind the terrace, the doorways of the Villa grew solid with darkness, the high façade loomed. Colour faded everywhere, the hills grew livid; forms assumed a menacing distinctness, blade-like against the architecture of the clouds.

Immeasurably below them, the trees were clotted together in the unnatural dusk. Steps from the terrace descended in a series of inexorable zig-zags. If one went down the steps into the depths of the garden, one might never come up again.

"I can't bear the noise of the fountains," she said angrily. "Why doesn't somebody stop them?—they get louder and louder."

He did not answer.

"What makes them like that, all of a sudden? Look at that pale strip, along the horizon. That's the sun shining over Rome." She thought of the streets and the houses and the bright, safe trams. "Why didn't we stay in Rome—*Rupert?*"

His squared shoulders looked broader than ever, but did not inspire confidence.

"I don't know why we ever came up here," she continued miserably.

"Well, you wanted to come . . ."

"Now you're going to be sulky. Oh, I can't think why we ever came to Italy at all!"

As he did not answer, she dragged herself a little further away from him down the terrace, trailing her gloved hand along the parapet. She could not bear to look down at the view any longer, nor dared she face the blind-eyed Villa behind her, so she stood with eyes shut, increasingly afraid. She knew that they were caught up here, impenetrably surrounded, on the nakedness of the heights. She was still at times, irrationally, afraid of God. Like other outlaws, it was probable that He had taken to the hills, and she had never cared to venture far into the country of outlaws. He had hung once about certain elemental passages in her life, and had been brought down upon her, sometimes, by Rupert. Here in Italy, in the churches or out in the sunshine, she had been feeling recently a complete security. And now here was Italy turning luridly upon her the whites of its eyes. She felt that she had been led up here and betrayed.

With a succession of uncertain impetuses she had reached the corner of the terrace, where the whole world fell away from under the Villa. The murmur of the Danish women's voices faded here, and she was less troubled by the insistence of the fountains. The darkening skies contracted and the balustrade and the wall of the house looked ash-pale, brittle, and impermanent. She longed to return to the village, and meditated how she would slip away through the chain of empty rooms, defying the echoes, across the courtyard and out into the street. From here, she could see the houses toppling up the hill, the awnings of the cafés colourless and undefined by shadow, the steep street empty in the dusk. Life, however dormant, lay accessible behind her. She reassured herself that she was on a peninsula rather than an island. She craved the comfortableness of strange voices, the impersonality of casual contacts, the touch of hands that would be nothing but human. She wanted an abstraction of humanity. The further proximity of Rupert had become intolerable; he was a bundle of potentialities and grievances; inextinguishably Rupert. She already fatigued herself sufficiently, and was fatigued by herself, without the superimposition of Rupert.

Round the corner, she discovered that the terrace went no further. It was swallowed up into the darkness of an archway, diminishing from sight in an ascent of steps. One could enter the house here, by a doorway to her left; the dark room within was attentive, the mustiness of it stole out on to the terrace and hung here, even on the edge of this illimitable space. Other smells crept up from below, and hung too, unable to disperse themselves, thickening the close air: sultriness from the blossoming trees below, a dank breath from water, and decay, faint and very sickly, from, perhaps, the small dead body of some animal under those impenetrable branches.

Here was a way of escape open to her: she could pass down the long chain of rooms, link on link of frescoed emptiness with garlands duskier in the dusk, with little

bald, square windows, lashless eyes, staring out on to
the darkening sky. She could regain the courtyard and
the village without retracing her steps along the terrace,
and bewilder Rupert, and defeat the beleaguering
forces of God.

She could not do it; she was too much afraid of the
dark rooms and the echoes. She put up her hands to her
forehead because her head ached.

After the young woman in orange had passed her,
she wondered dully where she had been going, whither
she hurried so. Her urgency had cut like a knife
through the opaque twilight, and her dress had been
curiously brilliant in the drained-out colourlessness of
the evening. The chief impression of her passing had
been a rustling and a rushing sound, and though she had
not passed in an imponderable moment there had been
an effect of speed about her forehead and blown-back
hair. She left a coolness of displaced air, like the single
gesture of a fan. She had taken form out of the darkness
of the stairway, simultaneously emerging and descending. At its foot there had been a sort of hesitancy—a
gesture of return; then she had rushed forward with an
impetus that made her almost luminous. She had vanished round the corner of the terrace, one could not say
how long ago. Rupert would feel the wind of her
movement, she might brush against him as she passed.

Rupert's wife went slowly to the corner of the terrace, leaned her hand against the blunted angle of the
wall, and looking down the long perspective saw that it

was empty. Rupert was gone and the other—she could not remember what other she had come to find.

Then she felt the wall of the Villa tilt for a moment over towards her as she cried, "Oh, Rupert, Rupert, I have seen a ghost!"

Rupert had remained leaning forward on his elbows till the sound of her angry breathing from above him died away and the rustle of her dress diminished. The least sound twanged on the taut air. He turned his head with an imperceptible slowness to watch her down the terrace; she stooped badly and her head poked forward under that feathered hat. The contemptuous nonchalance of her trailed hand irritated him: she was not a person to have brought to Italy. Then the back of his eyes pricked as he remembered how ineffectual they both were, how they neither of them knew what they wanted, how suspiciously they watched one another, jealous of a gleam of certainty. Their journeyings were a forlorn hope, they never found what they had come to seek, nor even knew what they had come for. He bent down again to feel the blister on his foot, and when he raised his eyes she had turned the corner of the terrace. Round the corner, she would find nothing that interested her, and soon she would come slowly back again to tell him how there had been nothing, and to reproach him with Italy, and with the noise of the fountains. Although the whole afternoon he had been determined that she should not evade him, and had kept close on her heels, because she had been somehow eluding him in her displeasure, he now decided to evade *her*, to escape utterly, to walk through the village without her and be found sitting waiting for her in the tram. He would have liked, indeed, to follow the steep curves of that road down on to the Campagna, if it had not been for the blister on his foot.

Furtively, with a quick resolution he darted away across the terrace into the Villa, through air that impeded his movements as in a dream. The sound of his footsteps, suddenly intensified by the constricting walls, rose up startlingly around him. Softly!—she might hear him, even from the end of the terrace! To his left and right, opposite one another, doorways showed him empty doorways in diminishing perspective, and the nakedness of floors. In the windless dusk the painted garlands swayed, it seemed, a little on the walls. From some pin's-head vanishing point, where beyond the long perspective the ultimate blank wall had faded into darkness, steps began. "Hullo!" said Rupert nervously.

The shutter slammed. Black darkness drowned the room and the house shivered. "Hell!" screamed Rupert. He did not know that there was a wind; indeed, it had been more than negative, that windlessness. He ran to the next room, and, pressing back the shutters against the embrasure of the window (they shook a little under his hands), saw the tops of the three cypresses that rose above the terrace making wild gestures against the sky.

The taut clouds, he knew, would never stand this buffeting. Why, the very slamming of that shutter must have ripped through them like a bullet. In flight before an imminent Something that he did not dare to imagine, he determined to go further into the Villa and find the passage and the steps up to the courtyard. He could not go on like this for ever, from one to another of these infinite rooms—they were too like one another. Each, too, might crash again at any moment into darkness, and Rupert did not like the dark. So he took the exit that a little door offered him, low in the centre wall, and found himself in a half-familiar obscurity, like that of his own dining-room at home. It sounded small, and something facing him, as it were a sideboard, he understood to be an altar. He guessed, too, rather than perceived, a tall cross up above it on the wall. This meant something, anyhow. "This is the chapel," said Rupert.

He enjoyed patronage, and had at all times adjusted to their (he believed) mutual satisfaction his relations with his Maker. An Agency had made arrangements for his passage across Life, at the price of moderate concessions on the part of Rupert, and to its divine supervision Rupert trustfully consigned himself. God was everywhere, making arrangements, even as a Cook's official met him on every platform when he travelled. Rupert remained sublimely passive; he was not a fussy man. So this was a chapel—he sat down in it to wait.

He did not realize whom he was disturbing till they slipped away behind some curtains into an opaquer darkness. Their rosaries tinkled swinging from their fingers as they passed him; their gowns, drawing together, relieved the floor of its blackness as they rose from their knees silently, even faintly revealing the pattern of the tiles. Six faces, incredibly long, turned towards him— no, not faces, wimples; they were nuns. "Oh, pardon me," said Rupert, as they passed out quietly.

Now that the shadows fell into order behind them, he found, his eyes growing accustomed, that the place was not after all impenetrably dusky. Three shafts lighted it, striking down from the level of the court- yard; under one of them, even, candlesticks faintly glimmered. In the front of the Villa, in those rooms he had come from, a shutter slammed again, then quickly another; there was a long rushing, scudding sound that died away round the corner in a whistle. Rupert felt that it was good for him to be here.

The Danish ladies were also alarmed. This was not Italy as they had been led to expect her, nor, indeed, as she had hitherto displayed herself to them. Deep within them, the Teutonic decencies were outraged by this ex- posure. They turned their eyes from the livid hills and gasped a little beneath the pressure of the sky. Above, the peevish Englishwoman had finished quarrelling with her husband; he leaned over the parapet, looking down on them, and they wondered if he were going to speak. They were tired of taking photographs of one another beside the fountains, and for this, also, it was now too dark. They wearied of poking their umbrellas up the mouths of the dolphins to intercept the spouting of the water. The exhalations and the darkness of the trees rose toward them like smoke. They wished to return to the village and buy postcards and drink chocolate in a café. "Let us go up," they said. And when they were not yet half-way to the first of the many angles of the ascending stairs the stoutest of them sat down suddenly and said, "I cannot." Later, the others succumbed and sat down also, mopping their faces; having taken off their hats that the perspiration might not injure the linings. The youngest, who, still consistent, felt justified in demanding a certain consistency of Nature, said that she did not see why it should be so hot and yet so black. "Thunder," said the stout one, and the others looked at her incredulously for a moment, then agreed. They all stared up at the sky, inquisitorially, and one of them, by twisting her neck for a moment, was able to observe that the Englishman had vanished from the upper terrace.

One does not speak much while contemplating a too great expanse of country under the imminence of a storm. They sat close together, so that their mackintoshes creaked in contact; each one enclosed within herself, aloof, chaste, inviolable to emotion. It was sitting thus that they heard the Englishwoman scream.

There was excitement in the scream, they thought pleasurable excitement. They turned their heads, and one of them conjectured that she had picked up a bracelet on the terrace. By the prolonged sustenance of her highest note, it might even have been a diamond bracelet.

"She is calling her husband."

"The man Rupert."

"He has gone in."

They supposed that when she had finished screaming she would go in too, taking whatever she had found, and look for him in the Villa. But no, she came down the steps with her hands shaking; they heard the little loose coins jingling in her handbag. Her hat was pushed back from her forehead; she looked very white, not hot at all.

"I have seen a woman, a woman in yellow. She went round the corner and vanished. Did she come past you? She was a ghost."

They listened very carefully, looked at one another, and assured her in their careful English that they had seen no woman. She herself was the only lady whom they had encountered in the gardens of the Villa.

"Not a lady," she cried, pushing her hat back further from her forehead, "a ghost, a ghost!"

They agreed that the gardens might be full of ghosts, and that many things were possible. Meanwhile, was Madame seeking her husband? He had gone back into the Villa. Did not Madame feel that it was likely to rain? While they hung expectantly upon the silence of Madame the trees below them were sucked sideways with a roar. Pale gashes curled forward, slit and dissipated themselves like waves where the wind flung forward whole branches. Little eddies of sound sucked and whirled down in the shadows. Above it all, there was a high whistling.

The pillar of a fountain, solid as marble, swerved,

bent like a bow, and flung a cloud of fine spray into their faces.

"The wind has come," said the youngest lady, tucking away strands of hair behind her ears and putting on her hat. The Englishwoman stampeded like a horse: she cried, "My husband!" and went wildly up the steps again with an agility which surprised them, her skirts shrieking in the wind.

The wind caught the Villa full in the face, one stinging challenge like the lash of a gauntlet. Elegant, rococo, with an air of balance delicately perilous, it yet struck down deep into the rock, deep as a fortress. It braced itself, and now the assailing forces of the wind came singing between the pillars of the parapet. Row on row, the windows looked unflinchingly out into the sky, though here and there the swinging-to of a shutter was like the nervous and involuntary flicker of an eyelid. The attack begun, the clouds brought up their artillery; lightning, splitting the sky, shimmered across the flagstones of the terrace. The honey-coloured façade, soaked and languorous with sunshine, stood up, naked, sensitive as flesh, to the stinging onslaught of the rain that beat against the windows with a faint, fine, infinitesimal clatter.

Deep in the heart of the house, the man Rupert was sitting in the lower chapel. The light coming down from the shafts was darkened, the candlesticks no longer gleamed. Little rapiers of windy draught came whistling and stabbing at him, the curtains twitched audibly, then faintly and more continuously rustled. The chapel suffered Rupert, but did nothing to entice him. He remembered with an immeasurable nostalgia their bedroom at the hotel, warm, crude, actual; the patterned tapestry of the sofa, the painted ceiling, his wife's garments, straggling, be-ribboned, the thermos flask with the coffee that they had forgotten today. He remembered the talk in the lounge. "Going to the Forum?" "No, we've done the Forum . . ." "they give good coffee and milk here, but the butter is execrable . . ." "a postcard of the Dying Gaul," "Gladiator," "We must do St. Peter's—yes, yes, yes. . . ."

Rupert watched the darkness where the curtains were, and wondered if the nuns were coming back. Faintly envisaged, and thus more faintly desirable, was his smoking-room at home, full of the books he had never finished. Perhaps he had been sometimes too arbitrary in his refusals of hospitality—from books, places, people. He had been always hurrying on to a rendez-vous, afraid lest he should miss God and the expedition thus proceed without him. He had hurried his wife along with him, reluctant and suspicious, looking back over his shoulder at the destruction of her cities, trailing after him with slack steps.

She had trailed away from him down the terrace, and he was surprised to find that now he was wanting her. This darkness, potentially, this frightening darkness, made him protective; something passive and weak was wanting, to come and cower against him. A dog, even, or one of the children that they might have had; but better than all, his wife. Failing this, he was at a loss— even, he admitted, frightened, The great thing, he knew, was to stop thinking about oneself. He veered full round towards his wife, mentally and emotionally. She was a listless creature, but now she would be tense, horribly at bay and afraid, propped against a doorpost, clutching at it. She was a coward, he knew; his heart swelled with delight and desire as he felt what a coward she was. She had never been on the side of the angels; he had never been able to explain to her about God. She could not understand that she was being catered for.

Rupert's wife, having taken shelter, stood in one of the front rooms by the window, breathing hard and flinching away from the lightning She heard the Danes enter, and pressing herself back against the wall listened while they hesitated for a moment and turned, unconsciously, away from her; making their way through the chain of rooms in the direction of the village. Watching them, she observed something duck-like about their recessive backs. Rupert, she guessed, was somewhere near at hand, but might very possibly be inaccessible to her. She was now feeling very definitely in contest with an opposing will, and the storm slanting and flaring beyond the windows, darkness rolling up on darkness, set her tingling with the exultation of a definite encounter. The house enclosed her greedily; it impeded her, and yet it was an ally.

She also had it in her to project herself, to stamp on time her ineffaceable image. She had an urgency which made her timeless, like the woman on the terrace; which made her step clear of the dimensions. She had simply, as she now knew, beheld herself in a mirror as that other went past her; and stepped back, shaken, from her own reality. That was it: she was over-charged. She was too much for herself, and terribly in need of Rupert. He was a slight, dependent thing, and infinitely pitiable, trotting hard and a little hopelessly at the heel of his gigantic Somebody. She ached now with the consciousness of her own sufficiency for him, her potency to crowd out even God.

Crowd out? There was nobody there to oppose her. Up here in the hills she had parleyed, and made an alliance. Rupert had been sold to her; by a treachery of God, which would be inconceivable to him, delivered up utterly into her hands. She sought for and eventually found him, squatting on one of the stools by the altar, low and toad-like, and her own shadow darkened his white face upturned towards her as she stood in the square dull greyness of the open door. They contemplated one another's outlines speechlessly; self-sufficient, travelled, wary, and mutually pitiful.

Then: "Rupert," she cried, "where were you? I've been looking for you, looking for you everywhere!"

"I was waiting here. I knew if I went wandering about we would miss each other. I thought it would be better to wait here till you came to me—I didn't know where you had gone. This place, you know, is part of a convent. It is full of nuns."

"*Nuns?*" she said incredulously. She would not believe him, and when, feeling his way over to the corner of their exit, he drew back the curtain, he found that there was nothing behind it but stone: it was a blocked-up archway.

"Well?" came her voice with a smile in it. It was beautiful to her that Rupert had been making himself nuns.

"They *seemed* to me to be nuns," he faltered, "and they went away here where the curtain is. . . . A kind of archway. . . . But they may only have been shadows, black and white ones. You know, the wind was so terrible that I couldn't hear anything, and I couldn't see or think properly either. It was rather fine, I thought, to think of good women still living in this house and coming here and praying. It—it was a Testimony," he concluded huskily. "It seemed to me extraordinarily fine."

"Extraordinarily fine," her voice echoed, soft and kindly. "But, Rupert, I was afraid and lonely. I wanted you. I was alone."

"Afraid!" he cried gladly, clambering to his feet and making his way toward her tall shadowiness. His hand stretched out and touched hers and withdrew timidly: he did not often caress her. "I ought to have been with you . . . Darling . . ." he said rustily.

"I'm all right now. But let's go, Rupert, let's go up

to the village together, and soon we can go down in the tram." They heard thunder, a dull sound, low and enveloping, and the room behind her shimmered with two or three flashes. They thought the house trembled.

"Not yet: stay here," said Rupert.

"Does this make you feel religious?" she asked, shutting the door behind her.

"Well, God's everywhere."

They stood together by the musty canopy of the altar, shoulder to shoulder. His arm crept round her waist and lightly encircled her. "Poor darling!" he whispered, "poor dear!" She leaned toward him in the dark, her feathers brushed his cheek.

"You're very strong," she said.

"I think when one believes in an ultimate Rightness . . ."

"Yes . . ."

She was beginning to understand, he thought. He was beginning to be able to win her over. God with him, she was learning to cling to him. And she ran her hands over his tweed shoulders, stroking them, sighing ineffably, knowing that he was delivered up utterly into her hands.

Charity

WHEN RACHEL had done showing Charity the garden, they both sat down in a wheelbarrow beside the flowering currant-bush, swung their legs exaggeratedly, and looked away from each other. There was still another hour before tea. The fact was, they were still rather strange to one another in the relation of guest and hostess. All the effects Rachel had planned for this afternoon had come off; yet somehow not quite come off, because there was an incalculable strangeness about Home today that had altogether surprised her. Nothing seemed as usual. By the time they were half-way round the house she was beginning to feel, each time she opened a door, "Perhaps I am letting Charity in for more than I know?" When they looked into the bogey-hole under the stairs, and she told Charity by way of a joke that they kept the family ghost there, she felt horribly afraid. Even the currant-bush began to be affected; it smelt so hot and sharp that she felt she ought to explain it in some way. The zumming and bump of bees in and out of it filled up the silence embarrassingly. It seemed equally unlifelike to mention the bees and to ignore them, so she laughed aloud to herself unnaturally and kicked the wheel of the barrow.

Yet the strangeness perhaps lay in Charity. She wore a flowery hat from under which her nose came out at an unexpected angle, and when she took her hat off she patted her hair. When she talked to Father or Mother she had "a manner." She had got out of the train (backwards) in a bottle-green dress much longer than usual. Rachel had understood at once that there need be no fear of her not being a success at Home; on the other hand, she did not seem to be so much impressed by it all as one had expected. Her gaze ate things up and diminished them. Her own home and her unknown relations kept like a shadow behind her. She might almost have been one of the Little Daughters of Your Age that Mother invited to tea. Just now, as they slowly paraded the borders, Rachel had caught herself wishing that they were back in the garden at school. *There* it would have been thrilling to be walking about with Charity, arm in arm. . . . She did not show her the Secret Place. . . .

For this her heart smote her. "Did you know," she said, "that I had rabbits of my own now?"

"Show!" said Charity.

With a lovely feeling of release they rushed off.

Rachel had been praying days ahead that Adela might be out for tea that first afternoon. Yet even when the gong sounded she could not be sure. She thought it better to prepare the ground, so said to Charity coming across the hall, "You will laugh when you see my sister!"

"I thought she was grown up," said Charity, looking down thoughtfully into a brass pot that held, besides a palm, several of Father's and Adela's cigarette-ends.

"Still, she's pretty mad," said Rachel cautiously. She punched Charity in the small of the back to make her go first through the door, Charity punched her back, and they scuffled together on the threshold quite naturally, as at school. But Rachel was noticing how the dining-room and the round white table in the afternoon light looked somehow less like themselves than like their own reflection in a looking-glass. Mother and Father made a smiling pattern one on each side of it. What a cheery pair of little girls!

They sat down: Mother and Father, not too apparently watching them, talked to each other. They broke off now and then to say encouraging things to the Little Friend, who sat with her chin tucked in, taking long drinks and smiling politely. Having dining-room tea in the holidays gave Rachel the unfamiliar and pleasant feeling of this houseful of grown-up people pivoting round on herself. Nobody else liked it; there were plain kinds of dripping-cake and gingerbread that nobody else cared for; Father would drink his two cups straight off and go away quickly; Adela would cry out, "*Must* we all watch this child eat?" cross her legs and jerk back her chair. Sitting thus, she would smoke and say, "Oh lord! *Oh* lord!" and at last take Mother by the arm and march her out through the French window into the garden. Mother would go with her frowning and laughing, very much flattered, torn in herself and reluctant. Then it would be dreary sometimes, though not unprofitable, being left alone with the cakes.

Father was going over, for Charity's benefit, all his usual rather silly questions and jokes about school. "Do they cane you?" he kept asking her. "Do they make you talk Latin? Do you have dormitory feasts?" Charity gave little giggles. "Ooh, Major Monstrevor, you *are* . . . !" She ate a refined tea, and did not want jam, she said, because it was sticky. Rachel was proud of her father's appearance, she thought he looked "soldierly"; but she could not bear him to talk too much. In an access of nervousness and with some idea of causing a distraction, she leant over and said to her mother, "Where's Adela? Isn't she in?"

Her heart went up into her throat at the question, and stayed there till Mother, absent-minded, brought herself to reply, "Oh, Adela? Tennis."

This was an answer to prayer, but it might be more awful than ever when Adela did come in. To hear her talk of her tennis made one hot all over: she might have been Suzanne at least. One did not know where to look.

Mother came out with the inevitable. Getting up, she beamed at them. "And what are you two going to do with yourselves?" said Mother.

There was an absolutely blank moment: everybody looked at Rachel. Rachel remembered that *this* was the afternoon she had been saving herself up for since the middle of term; she could have wept. If only she could be back at school again, telling Charity . . . But *this* was Charity, looking at her aloofly with critical little clear pale eyes. Charity waiting to be entertained. It was an absolutely blank moment. "Oh, *I* dunno," said Rachel. "Just mouch round. . . ."

Mother smiled helpfully; the smile stayed on a minute or two while her thoughts wandered.

"Rabbits?" said Father.

"She's seen the rabbits. . . ."

So he took them into the study and showed Charity his butterfly collection. He took down cabinet after cabinet of the poor, brittle, bright-coloured creatures that one would rather die than touch. Rachel loathed the butterflies and the way they would all quiver suddenly on their pins as though coming alive again; she was certain Charity loathed them too, but she felt grateful to Father. To make things go off well she exclaimed loudly at them as though she hadn't seen them before, and asked their names eagerly. She hoped Charity didn't remember what she had once said about Father's butterflies, on their way to Gym. Charity, who didn't like her own father, had said that fathers were the limit. Rachel had agreed at once, though with a feeling of shock, and, seeking round for some shortcoming of her father's, thought of his collection. Wasn't it atrociously cruel, she had said, to stick a butterfly, still quite living, through with a pin! Anyhow, when she had said "atrociously cruel" she hadn't *meant* anything to do with Father.

He thought of something important, put away the butterfly-cabinets suddenly, and turned his back on the two of them, bored. So Rachel pushed Charity through the door (she seemed to have been pushing Charity through doors all day, but no solution yet offered itself), and they went back to the garden and played French-cricket there with a tennis-ball.

Charity played a brilliant game and couldn't be got out. Rather flushed, she began to enjoy herself, and soon with her eyes (apparently) quite tight shut she was scornfully knocking Rachel's bowling all over the place. At last she sent the tennis-ball in at the drawing-room window and knocked over a pot of azaleas.

"Crikey!" she said. "Will They mind? Let's tell Them afterwards. . . . I call this a silly old game!"

The rude way she said this made Rachel see light. It was this politeness that had been the matter all day. Inspired, she shouted, "Silly fool yourself!" and came charging at Charity full tilt, in the rôle of Laughing Tomahawk. Charity, unprepared, lost her balance forthwith and rolled over. She lay kicking at Rachel with both feet for a moment or two, and it seemed as if things were going all right. Then she jumped up suddenly (that green frock!), stood dusting herself, and said in a cold voice, "Shut up; I wish you wouldn't." She was an absolute stranger; the green frock had pleats down the side and bobbly brass buttons. *What* one must have looked like, with one's scarlet yelling mouth, being Laughing Tomahawk! . . . Rachel was quenched.

"Shall we climb up," she said, "and sit on the roof of the bicycle shed?"

"I don't mind," said Charity. "Do you often?"

Rachel did. It was here that she read her books, designed cathedrals, made a new will every holidays, and kept the key to a terribly secret cipher under a flowerpot. It was here that she would lie pulling an elderbranch up and down above her head like a punkah, and dinting the roof with her heels while she thought about Charity. She felt embarrassed as she hoisted up Charity into this ring of terribly secret thoughts; she wished that she had gone up first to get the place into order. Sometimes the thoughts would simply be conversations, or sometimes the school was on fire, or there was nearly a bathing fatality. Sometimes there was a war on, and, as none of the men were brave enough, they were both going to fight.

"This must be awfully bad for the roof," said Charity, jumping about. "Just look at those dints. Do They mind?" But Rachel took out the cipher, and suddenly, effortlessly, unknowingly, like falling asleep at last when one has been trying and trying, they were together again. The evening went terribly fast.

Presently they heard a bicycle being rattled along and branches brushing against a bicycle wheel. Adela coming home. Adela's red felt hat was pulled right over her eyes like a sombrero; the top of her looked

Spanish, and the rest, muffled up to the mouth, like an Antarctic explorer. She came back from tennis like this in the hottest weather because, one could only suppose, it looked rather professional. She managed to look languid and sinister, even pushing a bicycle down a narrow path through syringa bushes. "Crikey!" said Charity audibly when she appeared.

Adela looked up at them darkly from under her hat, but kept her chin in her scarf and said nothing. They both rolled over on to their stomachs, and watched her over the edge of the roof while she put her bicycle away.

"You know that's bad for the roof," said Adela in her dead-sounding voice as she came out again.

("There!" said Charity to Rachel.)

"*Are* you," said Adela, "Faith, or Hope?" Charity giggled. She did not know that Adela had been talking about her, before she came, as the Charity Child, and asking Mother in Rachel's presence to have her thoroughly disinfected. "You never know," she had said, "with Charity Children . . ."

Standing still in the path underneath them, like a pillar of salt in the six o'clock sunlight, Adela began to unwind (very guardedly, for fear of pneumonia) some of her wrappings. Her chin came out, chalky white like the tip of her nose, and her long thin jaw like rather a beautiful crocodile's. She grinned to herself; the joke was for neither of them, but she did not mind them seeing she was amused. "I've heard the most *terrible* things about you," she said, looking at Charity, and, shaking her head in a horrified way, walked away through the bushes. She left behind a fatal gash in the peace of the afternoon. When they kicked the roof it gave out a dungeony, clanking sound, and down in the shed underneath Adela's bicycle rattled.

Charity could not give her mind to the cipher again; she was very pink. "What *have* you been telling her?" she asked, in an agitated, pleased voice. Rachel said, "Nothing"; she never told Adela anything. "Well, I must say I didn't expect her like *that*," said Charity sharply.

Adela did not seem to Rachel to have gone off so badly. This revived a particular hope that the awfulness of Adela might be simply her own delusion, and that she would seem just an Elder Sister to anyone else. "She isn't really so bad," she said comfortably, deep in the cipher.

"Well, I must say . . . She isn't what I'd call very Good Style."

Rachel was so angry, she did not know with whom, that she was hardly able to speak.

People were coming to dinner, so Rachel and Charity were to have "a tray" in the spare-room. This felt very select, especially when one spread a lace handkerchief over the table in the window and imagined this was a restaurant; though there had been an uncomfortable moment when Rachel saw Charity unpack two beautiful evening dresses and hang them up in the wardrobe without saying a word. Was this, she wondered, the only house in the world where girls of twelve didn't come down to dinner? The spare-room was a magnificent room (like in somebody else's house), all mirrors; they danced a pyjama ballet surrounded by their reflections. The room got so dusky that when the tray with their poached eggs was brought in and put down they did not see it, and forgot that supper was there.

They sat in the window-sill, outside, told each other stories and listened to the rooks going to bed. There would be a sudden cry, a tree shaken, and the sky would be dark with them; then calling to one another again and again, they would drop back into the branches. Fewer rooks rose each time, and this gave one a feeling of great peacefulness, as though the whole earth were being hushed-up and reassured. These were the evenings that Rachel missed most when she went back to school.

The happiness that she had been waiting for all day seemed to have something to do with light behind the trees, the rooks, and the dry chintzy smell of the curtains when she leant back her head against them into the room. Also, there is something very heroic about dangling one's legs at a height.

Suddenly they remembered supper and dived into the darkness to look for the poached eggs. They lit one candle, and Charity, who could be very funny, sat languishing in the light of it, fluttered her lashes and ate off the tip of her fork. Rachel was a Guardsman, very adoring, and kept offering her champagne and cocktails. "A *mushroom* cocktail," she said coaxingly, and they both thought that sounded delicious. They imagined cocktails to be little red things like prawns, that sat at the bottom of glasses with their tails turned up.

Rachel, still in the character of Guardsman, jumped up, flung an arm round Charity's neck and kissed her violently. "Oh, be *care*ful, Captain de Vere," squeaked Charity; "you are dripping champagne from your moustache . . . *Oh*, my Reveille and Rossiter!" She mopped the champagne from Captain de Vere's moustache off the front of her pyjama-jacket, and wrung out her handkerchief into her plate.

Then she stiffened up and pushed Rachel away. The expression was wiped off her face suddenly, leaving it blank. "Do *listen*," she snapped out, listening herself all over. Rachel heard nothing at all for a moment; it was creepy, as though Charity were hearing a ghost. To encourage herself and hear better she lighted more candles, padding round the room in her bare feet and trying not to shake the matchbox. All she heard then was Adela moving about next door, pulling drawers open and pushing them shut with a rattle. For a moment she wondered what Adela could be doing at midnight —she felt like midnight, miles from the ordinary, delirious, rather guilty: then she remembered the gong hadn't gone yet; it couldn't be more than eight. That could only be Adela dressing for dinner.

When Charity heard this she got up and swaggered about the room. It is wonderful what one can do on cocoa and a little imagination. She made Rachel feel as a matter of course that everybody else in the house was their enemy.

"Let's make a raid," said she; "let's tie up Her door handle!"

"Coo . . ." wavered Rachel, greatly attracted.

"No, let's go in and pretend to be sick on Her bed."

"But Mother'd—"

"Who cares for your mother?"

They took off the ropes from the waists of their dressing-gowns and crept into the passage. Adela's door was ajar and her lights lighted; she was humming, and seemed to be prowling about like a panther. As though she had heard them, she pounced and appeared in her doorway. She was tall, and every inch of her glared in the gaslight. Rachel immediately curled up inside like a woodlouse, because she felt Adela was going to "rasp." They stood there at bay rather foolishly, the ropes of their dressing-gowns coiled up in their hands like lassoes. But Adela's best "Evening" manner had been finally arranged and put on with her pearls and her earrings; she wasn't going to take it off again, even for them.

"What the devil—" she began pleasantly, as though to her own friends.

Having nothing ready they stood curling up their bare toes, each wondering what the other was going to do. Evening dress still filled Adela's mind as she stood above them; frowning down as though they were not there, she touched delicately, inquiringly, one long earring after the other with the tip of a finger, and, with head a little sideways, screwed one tighter. Having done this she shook her head, at first very cautiously, but though the earrings wagged violently they did not come off. Relief at this made Adela still more pleasant. "What *do* you want?" she said, and raising her eyebrows smiled despairingly, as though she must be very kind to a little idiot sister.

Charity moved. "We came," she said in an awed and breathy voice, "to ask if you would come in and say good-night to us?"

"Soppy," said Adela, pleased. The gold fringe round her dress swung as she stepped back into her room to close a cupboard door and turn the light off. Saved, it seemed that they were.

"You have got a nerve!" said Rachel in a shaky whisper. But Charity's features rolled up into an appalling "face." "Come on; come now!" said Rachel, quite unnerved and tugging at the skirt of Charity's dressing-gown. "*Back* from the jaws of death, *Back* from the gates of Hell," she was saying to herself, half aloud. She knew she must be what they all called "very excited." She was so excited that something throbbed in her ears, and she wanted to scream and rush back across the passage before a something that was worse than Adela put out a long arm and grabbed her into the dark room. She wanted to slam the spare-room door in the Enemy's face and barricade it, perhaps with the wardrobe. "You won't get us," she was prepared to call out, "not if you burn the house down." She felt like staying up all night. She tugged with all her might at Charity's dressing-gown.

"Leave go!" An unknown, scornful person flashed round suddenly. A dressing-gown was wrenched from her. "Let *go*, you fool!" Full of wild suspicion and enmity, lost to one another, they scuffled, skidding on the oilcloth. Rachel cried, half sobbing from breathlessness, "No, listen, Charity . . . Charity, don't be a beast." Charity grew a year older each moment, her protests grew shriller and more reasonable. . . . "No, seriously, *listen*, Charity. . . ."

"It's you that are the beast," said Charity in a remote voice, as Adela showed up again in the dark doorway. With a wave, as though they had been sparrows quarrelling, Adela dispersed them. She put an arm round Charity's shoulders, and they walked off into the spare-room. "My friend and I," their two back views, short and tall, said of each other.

"*You* must go to bed," said Adela, looking back. "*You're* excited."

Rachel sat on her bed in the dark and thought over her day. Her door was ajar, and she heard a continuous murmur and mumble and laugh coming out of the spare-room. Then Adela came out, keeping on the same smile with which she had said good-night to Charity, to do for the visitors down in the drawing-room. She paused at the top of the stairs, touched her earrings again, and shook out the fringe of her dress. Then she turned the gas low and went down. "Well, I just hope," thought Rachel, "she *likes* being tucked up by Adela.

I've never known anyone tuck up so rottenly." She felt contemptuous and, in a queer sort of way, happier than she had been all day. She knew Charity would be expecting her back, and presently, sure enough, she heard "Coo-ee?"

"Coo-ee, Coo-ee," Charity kept repeating, every few seconds. Rachel lay with her eyes shut, taking no notice, and then there began later a puzzled and angry silence. "I shall go to sleep," thought Rachel, beginning to count sheep. Then she began to believe she heard Charity sobbing. She lay listening for the irregular vague sounds, watching the circle of light from the gas-bracket wobble and fade on the ceiling over the spare-room door. When she was nearly asleep, Charity, hugging her elbows, crept out and stood on the landing.

"Oh, I can't sleep," moaned Charity. "Oh, I'm so homesick. Oh, I'm so lonely in there. Oh, what a *horrible* way to behave to a visitor. . . ."

"Homesick?"

"Of course," said Charity, shivering in a dignified way. "Wouldn't you be homesick, away from your father and mother?"

Uninvited, she groped through the dark room and got into Rachel's bed, sobbing and shivering.

"Well, I must say, Charity," said Rachel, making room for her, "I don't understand you at all."

The Back Drawing-Room

M<small>RS.</small> H<small>ENNEKER</small> having taken her place among them, inevitably they had begun to discuss the larger abstractions. They did not even hesitate to challenge the mortality of the soul, and Miss Eve, the violinist, said with that slight vibration her voice had caught from her fiddle-strings that she believed one was born doubting everything, and that *she* even doubted sometimes whether death meant extinction at all. Survival—

"Survival," said Bellingham, the man in the low chair beside Lois, who had up to now been talking about Greece, "simply isn't a matter of fitness, I consider; it's a matter of tenacity."

Lois, who was getting sleepy, nodded at the fire like a mandarin, and after a pause said weightily, "I should think that is very true"; but the young man with the horn-rimmed glasses challenged this remark of Bellingham's, sitting bolt upright and staring inexorably at him like an owl. He said in a deep drawl: "Surely the two are synonymous?"

Bellingham was less well in hand than the rest of Mrs. Henneker's pack; he did not want to discuss the larger abstractions, he wanted to talk about Greece, which he had lately visited, and Greece itself, in its actuality, not, as Mrs. Henneker would have directed, Hellenism. Now he saw her leaning back and drawing herself up and narrowing her eyes for utterance, and he realized that if he took any notice of that young man they two would be left skirmishing in a back alley while the talk swept by without them. However brilliant his repartee, however remarkable his agility, it would be unnoticed by Lois, who even now hung passionately on the lips of Mrs. Henneker.

So he repeated generally, with an inclusive glance challenging the semi-circle, that survival was a matter of tenacity. Now in Greece—

"Tenacity to what?" Lois asked the fire.

"*Ah* . . ." said somebody. "Yes—"

"Well," he hesitated, "it depends what plane we're on. On the purely physical—"

The word attracted two young women in the corner, who leant forward, suddenly illuminated, thinking he was going to talk about sex. Of course, the word had not always this connotation, but having read widely they knew it to be a word of possibilities.

"—On the purely physical alone," said Mrs. Henneker, "there's always, isn't there, a slackening of the grip?" She illustrated this with her hands. "Fitness and unfitness is such a purely objective way of pigeon-holing. Besides, all that is *circular*, isn't it? Fitness for what? To survive. But to survive what? What is one fit for?"

They all wondered. She swept a glance round them smilingly, to glean up any wandering attention. The little fair, plump man did not even look up at her; he did not seem to realize who she was. He sat with his legs crossed, his hands clasped on his knee, looking around him modestly and unintelligently, with an air of not having realized anybody. Somebody who came in late had brought him, with an apology, and had whispered an explanation into somebody else's ear. They had seated him, and he sat, looking propped-up and a little dejected, like an umbrella that an absent-minded caller has brought into the drawing-room. Once or twice, when the conversation prior to the entrance of Mrs. Henneker had veered dangerously near the comprehensible, he had volunteered remarks —oh, quite intelligent—quoting a friend, a banker who sometimes wrote to him from Modern Athens. He obviously belonged to one type of club, read the confessions of eminent diplomats' wives, and lunched with friends who considered him an entertaining fellow. Now he submitted, looking up at Mrs. Henneker with his little, perplexed blue eyes: "It's extraordinary, isn't it, what one does survive . . ."

"After death," said Mrs. Henneker, hanging poised for a moment, then sweeping forward over him, "the only criteria of our reality for those who have not passed over are the senses—*their* senses, or perhaps what I always think of as that finer internal fabric of the senses: I mean the soul."

"But surely," said the young man with the horn rims, deferentially, but as one having authority, "the soul doesn't exist."

"That's just the point of it," said Lois, a little too bluntly; "*does* it?"

"Exist *when?*" said Bellingham crossly. "Now, or when we're dead? I don't quite see what we're getting at."

Mrs. Henneker looked at him sideways like a wounded dove. "The survival of the soul after death," she said gently, "the survival of the *us*—oh, surely, Mr. Bellingham, of the *you* and of the *me*, is a matter, it always seems to me, that we are unable to consider, to weigh up for ourselves clearly, because in considering it we can only represent the thing to ourselves in terms of the *physical*. We stand aloof from the after life of the spirits of our friends, from that persisting essence of them which we call the spirit, in *giant ignorance*. It is like shutting out, if such a thing were possible to imagine, the sensuous appeal of music because we have not the score under our eyes to analyse—"

"Analysis?" said the young man with the horn rims, holding her up politely. "Ah, there you interest me very much, Mrs. Henneker. Now, you contend that there does exist in us a consciousness, an apprehension of the—er—people in the after state which will permit of quite definite analysis, like our power of ap-

prehending music, or our sense of smell? A consciousness quite apart from the sensory manifestations of the
spiritualist—table-rapping, gramophone horns, plan-
chette?"

"Oh, Spiritualism!" said Mrs. Henneker, shrinking
into herself. "Oh, that's horrible, I think, that is so
horrible! No, Mr. Mennister, that way of approach, if
it could or did ever mean anything, is vulgarized. Besides, have we need of verbal communication? No, I
think we attain our consciousness of *them* as one attains
that finer intercourse, if you like, *telepathic*, of two
people, any two of us here, maybe, who are closely
knit together, emotionally, or by unity of interest."

"Ah," said several people, rustling; "yes . . ." Lois
leant sideways and fingered a fold of Mrs. Henneker's
dress.

"By a prolongation," she continued, "by an ever-
increasing frequency of this intercourse, in presence
and in absence, we possess within us and have access
to a more and more complete personality, grafted on
to our own. When that personality has emerged wholly
from the muddle of our unperceptiveness, like Galatea
out of the marble, a given relationship is complete."

Her voice dropped beautifully from sentence to
sentence, lingered over the peroration and was still.

"I don't quite see," said Bellingham, and the young
man with the horn rims looked at him in despair. Lois
let a sharp little sigh escape her, and the little man beyond the fire brightened visibly.

Mrs. Henneker was infinitely patient. "I mean," she

said, speaking very slowly, "that such a complete cognizance of one being by another must give the one *known* a second distinct vitality apart from that either of the known or of the knower. You know how during those rather terrible séances a face or body sometimes takes form out of the psychic fluid generated by the medium. This face or body may become detached from her, liberated, and has then its own vitality and is definitely *objective*. . . ." She leant forward, spreading out her hands.

"Objective," said Mennister. "Ye-es. You contend that imagination, memory, cognizance, have the power of carrying themselves over from the *sub*jective into the *ob*jective?"

"Because you remember a thing," said Lois diffidently, "or even imagine it, or from loving it very much really know it, it *exists* apart from itself and from you, even though you don't remember it, imagine it, or know it any more?"

"Yes," said Mrs. Henneker simply, "that is what I meant. I grope. I don't express myself very clearly, I'm afraid."

They dissented murmuringly.

"That," Mennister informed them, leaning back and putting the tips of his fingers together, "is very interesting. Though we're not, of course, covering new ground. What it all comes down to ultimately is: a question of the visibility or—er—perceptibility of thought-forms. What Mrs. Henneker contends for is: their indefinite or their even infinite survival. Mr. Bellingham finds that survival is a matter of tenacity—though he hasn't yet distinguished tenacity, in this particular sense, from fitness, or given us any reason why we should oppose them. If we are to go all the way with Mrs. Henneker"—he pulled out a stop in his voice and it became richly humorous—"we accept that we may only hope for immortality in so far as we have attracted favourable attention, and become somebody else's thought-form. We then survive, not by our own tenacity, but by somebody else's. We—"

"In so much of Hardy's poetry—"

"Quite," said Mr. Mennister, suppressing the young woman who had contributed this remark. "The idea is not a new one; it becomes increasingly popular, doesn't it? In fiction—"

"Popular fiction is not my line, of course," said Bellingham swiftly. "I know very little about it, but"—Mennister's glasses blazed at him, he looked up blandly at the ceiling—"but, getting down to the ghost story, the ghost story pure and simple: well, I remember saying to a man only a few weeks ago, as we walked in the streets of Athens—"

Something stirred beyond the fire; the little man came alive from his torpor, uncrossed his legs and sat up, clearing his throat. "Ah," he said, "ghosts! Yes. What a fascinating theme for speculation!"

Everybody turned to look at him; it was as though the umbrella had spoken.

"Very," said Mennister dryly.

Mrs. Henneker turned her mournful eyes full upon him and inquired, "It *does* interest you?"

"Oh, Mrs. *Hen*neker!" said one of the young women, sobbing with laughter.

"One cannot fail to be interested," said the little man earnestly, looking from Mrs. Henneker to Lois, as though they were of equal importance, and even including Miss Eve and the two young women in the opposite corner—"one cannot fail to be interested if one has *experienced* . . ."

He was getting out of hand, quite suddenly. Mennister hummed softly and raised his eyebrows, and Lois slid to the floor from her chair and sat at Mrs. Henneker's feet, leaning up against her friend's knee protectively. Only Bellingham secretly and cynically grinned.

"Because I *have* had experience," said the little man, looking at them in surprise. "I can't, I really cannot account . . ."

Lois said "Hell!" under her breath. "Bring in the Yule log, this is a Dickens Christmas. We're going to tell ghost stories." Mrs. Henneker laid a hand on her shoulder and said, "Hush, Lois!" and Miss Eve, who had been waiting for some time to catch Bellingham's eye, smiled at him with an air of secret understanding. Back and behind the artist, the woman in her was enchanting: this was what Miss Eve liked to convey.

There was something very guileless about the little man; he thought they were all so clever. "I expect some of *you'd* make it fit in at once," he said trustfully. "I think it would fit in with some of that you've just been saying: about memory, or perhaps about love. May I tell you what occurred? It was very curious.

"A cousin of mine has property in Ireland. He is a sporting man; we have little in common, though I think all the world of him, he is a very nice fellow; and I have the greatest admiration for his wife—she is one of the few people I know who really makes her poultry pay, or she did so, at least, until these civic disturbances began. I have seen very little of them lately; they were worried about the place, and had several times been raided. Lately, since things in their part of the country began to improve, my cousin began writing again to say, 'Do come over.' My previous (and only other) visit there had been very pleasant; there was a good deal of croquet in the neighbourhood, and I am an enthusiastic player. I bicycle a good deal, too, and when my cousin wrote to say the roads, those pretty roads round there, were really safe again (not *good*, they are never good), I was greatly tempted to accept his invitation, and at length did so—that was last year. So I went over to Ireland."

"Ireland," said Mrs. Henneker, "unforgettably and almost terribly afflicted me. The contact was so intimate as to be almost intolerable. Those gulls about the piers of Kingstown, crying, crying: they are an overture to Ireland. One lives in a dream there, a dream oppressed and shifting, such as one dreams in a house with trees about it, on a sultry night."

"Now *that*," said Bellingham, "just illustrates what I said about tenacity. Compared with Greece—"

"Quite," said Mennister. "A beastly country, I thought. Of course, their plays—"

The little man, having looked wistfully from one to another of them, at last raised his voice and continued:

"I went to Ireland, and found my cousins much as ever, and the place looking very well. Several dozen of her chickens had been stolen, but it turned out to be a case of an ill wind—she had since introduced a new strain of Leghorns, which were doing very well indeed. My cousin was as busy as usual, but he had arranged for me to borrow a bicycle belonging to the cook's brother: a new bicycle, which was supposed to be very good.

"The first day after my arrival I went out for a ride. We had not had time to talk very much the night before, but they had told me a certain amount of what had happened in the neighbourhood, and warned me that I should find the country around them dilapidated and rather depressing. And it did look indeed very sad. Sad, I should say, when one passed ruined cottages along the roadside, and a poor police-barrack like a box with its lid off, with the sky staring through the windows. When I got clear of these, however, my depression forsook me. I am always sensitive, I believe, to the beauty of landscape, and the country did that day look very beautiful in a pale-coloured, early-autumn way which is, I think, peculiar to Ireland. It was a very smooth, clear day, quite windless; with a pale grey sky, and no lights or shadows anywhere. The only accents in the landscape were the mountains; these were dark and grew darker—a bad sign, almost invariably portending rain. My bicycle went well for some hours, and I went easily along, free-wheeling a good deal, and perhaps a trifle absent-minded. I must have been absent-minded, for I rode right over a patch of sharp stones which had been put down (but not rolled) to mend the road. I am seldom so careless, and I acknowledged myself punished for it as with sinking heart I felt my back tire go completely flat."

"Quite," said Mennister. "You should write your cycling experiences—er, er—'Potters on a Push-bike.' It is not impossible that they might be published, even read." The others acknowledged by involuntary glances that Mennister had spoken with unnecessary sharpness; but the little man took correction with humility.

"I do perhaps linger," he admitted, "over the not quite necessary preface to my story. I will now proceed to the point of it, which is very curious. Well, my tire, you must understand, went really flat, and after having tried to ride, and descended to re-pump it every two or three minutes, I began to feel that my plight was a miserable one. I am not a good walker, and I was a very considerable distance from my cousin's house. Though I could have retraced my way, I had no idea of my whereabouts; I was in strange country where I had never been before. To increase my embarrassment, the sky was growing perceptibly darker, and I had that uncomfortable feeling of being overtaken and closed in upon, which I—and I find several of my friends also—often experience in open country when heavy rain is imminent. I was greatly cheered, therefore, to gather from certain indications—hewn-stone walls along the roadside, good though dilapidated iron gates into the fields, and two avenue-like rows of beech-trees making a tunnel over the road—that I was skirting the boundary of a gentleman's demesne, and that it was not impossible that I should pass the gate. I walked quickly, wheeling my bicycle, and heard now and then a big drop of rain fall—plop—into the leaves above my head. Soon, sure enough, I did come to the gates: they stood wide open with an expression of real Irish hospitality —it is whimsical of me, but I do always feel that people's gates and doorposts have expressions—and I walked in, after a glance at the lodge: there was a trickle of smoke coming out of the chimneys, but the door was barred across and the windows shuttered. I remember thinking this curious.

"Along the avenue the trees were planted closer together, and it was as dusky as evening. It was overgrown with moss, too, so that I could scarcely hear my own footsteps, only the rattle-rattle of my bicycle. Judging from the width of the avenue, it must be a big place I was coming to; and how I did hope somebody in it would understand repairs, or perhaps lend me a bicycle, or even offer to drive me home in a trap or a motor! In England, of course, one would not think of this, but the Irish, I find, are always unconventionality itself."

"Quite," said Mennister.

"*I* entirely agree," said Bellingham.

"From now on," said the little man, looking at Bellingham, Lois, and Mrs. Henneker, "I would like you to believe that all my impressions were distinct, quite distinct, but perhaps a little isolated from one another. In the intervals of these distinct impressions my mind was a little blurred; things slipped past it rather; as they do when one is tired, worried, or put out. I felt—"

"Oh, forgive me," Miss Eve vibrated, releasing Bellingham momentarily from her eyes, "but I *do* know how you felt, I *can* imagine! You felt an extraordinary sense of foreboding as you came up to that house with its great dark windows. You longed to fly, and something held you, gripped you, drew you in. You looked along the front of the house, expecting, expecting . . ."

"You had a sense of immanence," said Mrs. Henneker authoritatively. "Something was overtaking you, challenging you, embracing yet repelling you. Something was coming up from the earth, down from the skies, in from the mountains, that was stranger than the gathered rain. Deep from out of the depths of those dark windows, something beckoned."

"Like in that poem of de la Mare's—"

"Exactly," said Mennister, again suppressing the young woman who had spoken. "It has been often described. Let Mr.—Mr. . . . er . . . proceed to the point of his story." His voice regretted that there was one.

"Well, no, do you know," said the little man politely, with the reluctance of a Washington, "I cannot say that I experienced, that I remember to have experienced, what you have described, though of course I possibly may have. I walked very quickly down the avenue and across the gravel sweep to the steps of the house, and I remember thinking humorously, as I hunted for the bell, that if the bell *were* out of order (as bells in Irish houses often are—the Irish don't mind, they are the soul of unconventionality)—that the noise my poor bicycle made coming across the gravel would quite sufficiently advertise our arrival."

"And what was the house like?" asked Lois. "Was it very obviously haunted? *Weren't* there any dark windows?"

"I don't quite understand you. Dark windows? I cannot remember that the windows looked any darker than windows seen from the outside, in daylight, usually do. I did not look in, of course. The house seemed very large and high. I heard a dog running on a polished floor and skidding, the way dogs do. The hall door was open, and I could swear I did hear the bell tinkle, somewhere down below, but still nobody came. I felt no more raindrops; the rain held off, but the air was cold and heavy with it, and the trees were very quiet. The place was completely and very closely encircled with trees, and it was all so quiet I could hear myself breathe. Only, now and then I heard the ping-pong of tennis-balls, somewhere beyond the trees, and people calling to one another in the game. Sometimes this sounded very clearly, sometimes as though a long way away. I guessed that they must be having a tennis-party, and I felt a little shy of presenting myself—unconventional as I knew they would all be—all dusty and in my cycling knickerbockers. So I propped my bicycle up at the foot of the steps, and presently, as no one came, I walked into the house. I had never walked into anybody's house like this before."

"And the hall?" they cried.

"Hall?" he repeated, looking at them mystified. "It was a very ordinary hall, like in other country houses. There was a window on the staircase, which sent down a little light; otherwise the place was dark."

"And the *smell?*"

"And the *sound?* Didn't you hear an echo? Hadn't you a queer foreboding? Didn't you want to go but yet have to go on?"

"Well, no," he hesitated, carefully considering. "I do remember that I felt a little awkward, coming in like that—well, even in Ireland people might have wondered. And the misapprehensions . . . these bad times, you know. Why, anybody seeing me suddenly might have shot me, in their impulsive, simple way. I was really worried, and I'm afraid I don't remember that I noticed anything particular. Well, the smell, yes. People evidently hung their mackintoshes there, and there were dogs in the house. I imagine, too, that they didn't throw away their old tennis-balls, but kept them somewhere on a tray, possibly for the dogs. I stood in the hall and coughed a little and rapped with my foot —like in a village shop, you know, when it is empty. I was very much ashamed of myself and felt very nervous, but I was really desperately worried about my poor bicycle and how I was going to get home. So I stood there, tapping with my foot."

"Yes," said Mennister, "exactly. But, my dear fellow, you're an expert in the finer forms of torture. Don't you see, we're . . . ? Tell us about the ghost. Something gripped you, rattled at you, made itself unpleasantly visible. For one who does not profess the modern manner—well, *mes compliments*—you've hit something quite distinctive for your *décor*. But all ghost stories have one of three possible climaxes, A, B, or C, and every climax has its complementary explanation. Get on to the climax, and I'll guarantee you the explanation pat—"

"Or is it possible he might care to finish his own story for himself?" suggested Bellingham, with detachment. "One never knows."

"Quite."

"Oh, *hush*," appealed Mrs. Henneker. "Won't both of you hush? We are so *intrigued*. And then?"

"Well, I just stood there, tapping with my foot. No one came. Then a door at the back of the hall opened, somebody looked out. It was a lady's figure, standing right against the light, so that I could only see her outline, which was tall and pretty. I said something, began an explanation, but without speaking she turned and went in again, leaving the door open. I—I don't know what came over me. I—I followed her in."

"Ah," said Bellingham, with appreciation. "Yes?"

"I followed her into a drawing-room, a back drawing-room, with an arch with a curtain over it, and a window looking out into some trees. It was nicely furnished, I thought, but a little sombre, because of the trees outside the window."

"And smells? And sounds?" cried Lois and Miss Eve, while the others peered curiously, as though through bars, at the little man who sat perplexed and baffled, knowing nothing of atmosphere.

He said at length: "It smelt chiefly of geraniums. I remember them, some fine tall plants in pots, standing on a table by the window. And the wallpaper smelt a little musty; I remember thinking as I stood there (among many other things) what an improvement central heating would have been. I looked round and could see nobody; then I heard sobbing, really a pitiful sound. Well, you may imagine—here was I, unintroduced, in a back drawing-room, really quite an intimate room, where I believe only favoured visitors are usually admitted, with a lady sobbing on the sofa. I saw her head move where I thought there was just a pile of cushions; it made me jump. The room received less and less light from the windows, probably because of the rain, which was now coming down heavily, and partly because of the thick lace curtains—really thicker than one cares for nowadays. I do not know for how long I listened; then I said (I remember saying it), 'My dear lady,' I said; 'really, my dear lady!' I felt so terribly sorry for her, do you know, I couldn't go away, though I had no right to be there, of course. I may say that I am not an impulsive person even for an Englishman, and that I am as a rule quite singularly loth to intrude. When she looked up I was quite startled—"

"—As though you had not known she had a face—"

"Why, ye-es, as though I had not known she had a face. She looked up at me, and her expression was—was like . . ."

"Drowning?"

"Drowning," he accepted, with a grateful side-glance. "Drowning, and I could do nothing for her. Do you know, it quite appalled me. I don't know whether drowning people are frightened: I submit that they are —I know I should be. I don't think that if my life did pass before me then, I should glance at it. I should be too much afraid, looking forward to all that was going to happen to me."

"No, to the world," amended Mrs. Henneker, "to the whole of a world, your world. Because it is the quenching of a world in horror and destruction that happens with a violent death; just as one knows a whole world is darkened when one sees a child crying its heart out. Even a good death means a world quenched, but beautifully, like a sunset. So she looked at you like that —with fear?"

"Yes, fear. It was terrible. She had not a young face; the way she was crying was not young either. I am not a *nervous* man; I tell you that up to now I felt nothing but embarrassment. But I could not look away from her eyes. I did not wonder what she thought of me; it did not seem as though there were room for her to think. And she was looking at where I was, not at me."

"She was menaced . . ."

"Yes. It was terrible, more than distressing. It would have been no more than that if I had remained outside it, but I didn't. I make no bones about it—I was terrified. She made me feel the end of the world was coming, and I felt myself beginning to perspire all over, as I had not done the whole summer. I couldn't speak to her again; she—she . . ."

"Beat it back."

"Beat it back. I stood there, and she put down her face again, all wet, among the cushions that were crumpled and faded and smelt musty from even where I stood. So I went back into the hall, thinking only of one thing, to get away quickly before something had actually happened. Every step seemed dangerous—"

"—Like the House of Usher—"

"—Terribly dangerous. The hall was as empty-sounding as ever, and I rushed down the steps, seized my bicycle, and wheeled it as fast as ever I could down the avenue again, simply not caring if they did think I was a burglar or a Republican, and fired at me from the bushes. Once I paused for just a second to listen, and the tennis-balls had stopped, and the voices too. There was nothing to say where they had all gone. It was quite quiet."

"Except for the rain?"

"Yes, I heard the rain in the trees. The lodge was still shut up when I passed it; I was relieved at that—didn't want them to see me. Well, I just turned up my collar and trudged it. Nothing passed me, no conveyance, scarcely even a soul, except an old woman driving two cows—she looked at me queerly. Not a walk I should care to do again, wheeling a bicycle. Mercifully, the days were still longish; I got back to my cousin's before it was quite dark, and even so they were worried—I met them walking about on the avenue. They said (I remember), 'Well, you have been keeping up a pace, anyway!' and I was surprised to find myself panting, till I found I had done that big distance in under the two hours.

"I had a hot whisky at dinner, and told them where I'd been. I told them exactly, and my cousin seemed puzzled, kept on contradicting. 'No, no, you couldn't have been *there*. No houses along that road.' That irritated me; I made him get his motor map, and I traced where I'd been, every turn. Just where I expected there was a place marked Kilbarran, and I put my thumb on it at once and said, 'That's the house!' He laughed and said, 'That's impossible, there isn't a house there.' I said, 'Why?' and he said there hadn't been one for two years. 'Oh, there *was* one,' he said, 'and this marks it; this is an old map.' I can't tell you how angry I felt—for no reason. He said, 'There was a place, you see, until two years ago—very fine it was; then they came one night and burnt it, the winter before last. We had expected it would have gone sooner, and the Barrans—the people themselves—did too, though they never said a word. Those women went about looking green.'

"Well, he didn't say much more, and of course I didn't; but his wife sighed, then started off talking. She started talking about the people at Kilbarran—an old gentleman with two daughters, not young, and a gay, pretty niece who had been often there. She spoke as though they were dead; I rather assumed it, but asked. She said, 'Oh no; they're in Dublin, I think, or England.' I couldn't help saying she seemed to have lost interest in her old friends, and she looked at me (quite strangely, for such a practical woman) and said, 'Well, how can one feel they're alive? How can they be, any more than plants one's pulled up? They've nothing to grow in, or hold on to.' I said, 'Yes, like plants,' and she nodded. Then it was time for her to go and shut up the chickens."

"That illustrates exactly—"

"Quite."

But Mrs. Henneker was silent, staring at the fire. She did not raise her lids when Lois rose, and only held her hand out, offering it vaguely in perfunctory valediction as others rose to go. Someone collected the little man and took him away quietly—in the confusion he protested, but was overruled. He lingered, looking round the room, and even escaped once and got half-way back to Mrs. Henneker, his lips wide for further speech. But she was petulantly blind to him, and he was led away. When the rustle of departure had subsided and the street door down below had faintly slammed, the broken semi-circle drew closer together, intimately. They asked each other, with raised eyebrows, "Whose importation?" And this remained unanswered; no one knew.

"Dunno," said Lois to the last inquirer. They all looked up expectantly at Mrs. Henneker, but Mrs. Henneker was silent. And the silence lasted, because Mennister was gone.

Recent Photograph

A MR. AND MRS. BRINDLEY lived for some years quietly and unknown to history in one of the more rural of London's outlying suburbs. One spring evening Mr. Brindley, returning from business, cut his wife's throat with a razor, and afterwards turned in for the night with his head inside the gas oven, having mitigated the inside's iron inclemency with two frilly cushions. Towards evening of the following day their privacy was broken in upon, a paragraph announced them in a morning paper, and the villa, the avenue, and the entire neighbourhood arose and shone. The News Editor of the *Evening Crier* was on to the thing like a hawk; it was decided that the man they wanted on the job was young Lukin. So they sent down Lukin into Hertfordshire.

Mr. Bertram Lukin had joined the staff of the *Evening Crier* some months before, having presented himself at a moment of crisis with a letter of recommendation from a provincial editor of standing. He was young and immeasurably keen, and he directed himself to the essentials of journalism with an intensity which kept him always strung to the tautness of a slight vibration, so that his pince-nez, fugitively poised, were always just perceptibly a-shimmer. He read a good deal of American literature, said "Git!" and advised people to "hustle." He was getting on very well with the *Evening Crier*, the News Editor had his eye on him; but it had been a slack time lately, older men had unavoidably taken precedence of him with the only two murders, and nothing bigger had so far fallen to the share of Bertram Lukin than a city fire, extinguished with deplorable rapidity, in which no lives had been lost. Now, the very second the News Editor unleashed him, he was downstairs in one streak and into a taxi. "Git like hell!" he told the driver feverishly, bouncing on the shiny cushions.

The streets were silver in the sunshine; London in the April morning glowed like a pearl. It was a morning for children to come to birth, and poems to be written, and the creative soul of Lukin stretched its wings out and leant breast-forward to the wind in an ecstasy of liberation. The back of the taxi was open, and he nodded sideways with a blind benevolence to the roofs of London fleeing behind him. He clasped across his knees the morning paper rolled into a baton, nothing but a symbol, for the paragraph was burningly engraved into his brain. "A Mr. Joseph Wellington Brindley, resident at Moyallo, Homewood Avenue, Elms' Hopley, Herts . . . discovered . . . is believed to have . . . the head being partially severed from the body . . . in comfortable circumstances, and had been married some years." It was copy, Bertram Lukin's copy. God was in his heaven and all was right with the world. The taxi took the corners of the still empty residential streets abruptly, and Lukin's little exultant and forgotten body bounced and swayed.

The brickwork and the stucco faltered, the streets broadened out and lay open to the sun, and fields and allotments interspersed themselves among the houses. Clumps of trees stretched up their branches all fretted over with green; here and there a field was ridiculous with lambs, and above them larks surcharged with song went wobbling up into the blue. The world became too small for Bertram Lukin, who felt himself expanding infinitely; nowhere could contain him for self-sufficiency and happiness. He did not think the man was pressing hard enough on the speed-limit; and, glancing down continually at his watch, he began to beat upon the glass behind the driver's head, and make forward gestures at him, indicative of urgency.

Elms' Hopley was the sort of place where murders usually do occur; that is to say, the last place on earth that seems appropriate to such occurrences. The enterprise of the Metropolitan had already embraced it: the interior of the big blue-and-white station yawned at them as the driver drew up by the kerb to ask the way to Homewood Avenue. The sunshine had brought out all the awnings over the shops; trees were planted along the pavements and many bicycles were propped against the trees. In groups about the doors of shops people stood talking, while rival terriers, affecting ignorance of one another, sniffed sedulously along the gutters. A lady buying geraniums off a barrow sighted a friend, signalled wildly, waved away the vendor, and darted across the street under the very bonnet of Lukin's taxi, her eyes dilated and lips wide for speech. The whole place was vital to Lukin, everybody was significant; a light burnt through it, making every detail poignant. It was like arriving at a house where there is a party going on.

He had his notebook out, and his neat writing sprawled and staggered a little as, the taxi making full speed to its bourne, he recorded here and there an observation. Homewood Avenue was the kind of road where many people love to live; it was flanked by innumerable little gates, and laburnum boughs dripped languorously over the pavement, slanting from among the sprightlier grace of Japanese plum. Lukin, one hand on the door, crouched against the side of the taxi; his eyes ate up the numbers on the gates. His heart leapt up as he saw, before one house, two or three people loitering. At the gate a very big policeman stood, impassible and blue. The police were in possession.

Lukin stopped the taxi at a short distance from this little group, told the man to wait at the end of the road, and descended with an air of unconsciousness. He glanced at the loiterers with a sort of unconvinced contempt, and drew in upon himself; an iota of his light was quenched. Then he turned his head resolutely down the road, and tried to look like a young man who happens to be visiting an aunt. His eyes went down to the faintly stirring shadows of the branches on the pavement, then stole gradually, cautiously, paving-stone by paving-stone, towards the feet of the police-man, very large and planted very square. He felt confident that he could be pleasant enough with anybody; he had a "good manner," and he wished the police-constable to know it, but he could not remember, some-how, how one should begin on a policeman. And this was so very important, Lukin knew. Then he saw an-other pair of feet, too familiar, in orange-leather Amer-ican shoes, advancing cautiously, diagonally, towards the constable. The *Evening Query* man was down here too. He spoke American even better than Lukin, had been three years on his paper and written up all their murders; and he had the sort of eye one could not pos-sibly like. Lukin, quite dispassionately, did not think that the fellow had at all a good manner. By the un-usual hesitancy of his movements, it was possible that the constable had already rebuffed him. Lukin stepped back, crossed the road, and, sauntering as though cas-ually along the opposite pavement, cast up a rapid and devouring glance toward the windows of Moyallo, naked of muslin and unmasked by trees. Sinister blue curtains, a little arty, framed them all, and in a bay window of an upstairs room one saw the back of a mirror, an oval mirror. They had been that kind of people. Sheltering his notebook from observation, he jotted down "artistic," faintly, with a query mark.

Then he walked on very slowly, further down the road. The *Evening Query* man sighted him and hailed. Confound the fellow, he was coming across.

"You won't do much *here*," he remarked, with malicious complacency. "Sick'ning having that long run down, and in a taxi and all."

"Oh, no," drawled Lukin, with the polite indifference of one already informed.

"I s'pose you didn't expect much," said the other odiously. "Well, I daresay it was a nice run down. I must be off now and write my stuff up." He was evidently on to something; he was licking his chops. He was a spotty man, the spottiest man Lukin had ever met; it must be very distressing for him.

"Well, s'long," said Lukin, very preoccupied, turning on his heel.

"*So* long," said the *Evening Query* man, who could make anything he said sound unpleasantly significant. He patted his breast pocket with complacency and swaggered off in the direction of the High Street. He was a very spotty man. Lukin wondered what he really had got in that notebook. He sauntered on again in the opposite direction, down the road.

A large lady in an emerald-green jersey was leaning over a gate, her arms along the top bar folded comfortably beneath the abundance of her bosom. Her hair, with which the breeze dared take no liberties, was piled high above her forehead *à la* Pompadour. Her eyes dwelt amicably upon Lukin and caught his own as he advanced towards her; he felt himself grow great again with resolution. The one thing now was to get some-how, anyhow, into conversation with someone, anyone. He would talk to this lady. The lady was willing to be talked to. A fringe of laburnum dipped and danced above her head; she was like somebody at a party, happy and very much entertained.

"Too *dreadful*, isn't it?" she said brightly, nodding across the road towards Moyallo. That was the hub and centre of the entertainment, and the host and hostess were behind those windows with the blue curtains, barred away by the policeman, very indifferent and cold.

"Dreadful!" he said eagerly, coming to a stop before her, and gleaming incredulously at her through his glasses. This was just the sort of lady to get into con-versation with—he knew all about her; this sudden manifestation of her was too good to be true. "A very great shock for you all, I'm afraid?" he hazarded.

"Oh dear, oh dear!" she sighed luxuriously. "*Shock!* —I should think it was. I really thought I should have fainted when my maid came in and told me. 'What nonsense!' I said to her; 'don't talk such absolute non-sense. I know her quite well; I was talking to her only yesterday.' It was quite a time before I could believe the girl. Oh, I was upset!"

"Terrible," he murmured, covertly unscrewing the top of his pen. "Most painful, if you knew the unhappy couple well."

"Oh yes, I did know them. Not very well, of course:

one hardly likes to say it now, but I did not care much about her. I couldn't take to her, though she seemed very bright. As for *him*—well, as I was saying just now to another lady, we really ought to have known."

"Ah!" he said profoundly. "Drink? . . ."

"Nothing like that. Nothing you could put your finger on. But we all said at once: that was just what we might have expected. Now my little girl was in there quite a lot at one time; she had quite an infatuation for Mrs. Brindley this last year, the way girls do. She had seen her just the other day, and been talking to her about a blouse pattern. My little girl is very much upset. I hardly knew how to tell her; I knew she'd be upset. And she was, *very* much upset."

"Too bad. And your daughter *knew* Mrs. Brindley intimately?" He now made no further effort to conceal his notebook, and she glanced at it with interest.

"You're the Press, aren't you? I *thought* you'd all be coming down. And this road used to be so quiet; I don't think we've ever had any trouble of any sort, not even a burglary. What a *sad* life for a young man, going from tragedy to tragedy! . . ." She paused, absorbed momentarily in an attempt to read what he had written. "You know, I simply couldn't stand it. Of course, I am tender-hearted, even for a woman. I can't stand horrors and tragedies. My little girl quite laughs at me. I can't bear to squash a beetle."

"One gets used to it," he said, shaking his pen. "A profession's a profession, after all."

"I suppose it *is*," she sighingly conceded. "And I know it doesn't do to be too tender-hearted. So many sad things happen, don't they?"

"Yes, indeed. Now, I wonder if you'd be so kind . . ." They both felt happy and important; he was the Press and she was being interviewed. They smiled at one another across the gate. She told him a great deal, and the leaves of his notebook, black with information, were flicked over one after another. She caught herself up and paused once to sigh and say that her maid was the most fearful gossip. She deprecated this, and complained that in vain had she set her face against it. There was nothing those girls did not know, she said, and nothing that they had not got the face to come and tell one.

He glanced through his notes. She had told him everything there was to tell about the Brindleys, every fact. He wanted something now that wasn't fact, he wanted a bit of colour. The personal touch. Recollecting his good manner, he expressed aloud a hope that he was not taking up too much of her time, and regretted inwardly that she had taken up so much of his. He had got to get his copy written up and in by midday. It was now half-past ten.

"I'm very much obliged to you indeed," he said again. "You've been most kind. . . . There was one thing—let me see: you said they had been married quite a short time? Mrs. Brindley was quite *young*, I gather?"

"Well, they'd been married four years, really. She was not so very young: thirty-two."

He considered that this was quite young enough to justify his headline. Nothing went so well in a headline as a Young Wife—except, of course, a Bride or a Girl Mother.

"I wish my little girl was in," the lady sighed. "Of course, it's all been very painful for her, and I hardly think she'd care to talk about it, but if she *could* bring herself to talk about it I expect she'd tell you things that would be very valuable. You know—quite an inside personal impression."

"Very painful for a child," he said politely, anticipating further incoherencies.

"Ah, well," said the mother tenderly, "she isn't what you'd call a child, you know; she's only that to me. To me she'll be always just my little Totsie; it is so difficult to realize how they grow. But the young fellows don't seem to consider her a baby. She's had quite a number of admirers since she was fourteen. She's just put her hair up. She's gone out this morning to her music; nothing would prevent her, though it seemed to me dreadful somehow, though of course there's nothing one can do. She's very musical, she loves her music. She really might be home at any moment now."

Even as she spoke, the mother's eyes, looking vaguely up the road beyond his shoulder, focussed themselves and brightened. A young girl came walking briskly towards them, like a picture of the Primavera, but preoccupied; with a tight little mouth. She edged scornfully past the now augmented group about the gate of Moyallo, and advanced indifferently, swinging a portfolio. She was fair and plump and dapper, and walked as though she had no opinion of the pavement. She eyed Lukin comprehensively, dwelt a moment on his note-book, then glanced from him to her mother. "Well?" she said.

"This is my little girl," said the lady in the green jersey. "Verbena, this gentleman is the Press."

"So I see," remarked Verbena, acknowledging the introduction with a nod. "Please!" she said imperiously, as neither of the two made way for her. "*I* must be getting in, mother. I should have thought *you'd* have been busy this hour of the morning, too."

The mother relieved the gate of her bulk, and stood aside dubiously, and Lukin receded unwillingly as Ver-bena swept between them. Pausing to hiss something into the ear of her mother, the friend of the late Mrs. Brindley turned to Lukin a demi-lune of furiously crim-son cheek. She disappeared into the house indignantly, her rigid back implying that though she did not think that this was much of a house, it was at least a sanctuary from outrage. Verbena, her mother deprecatingly ad-mitted, did not think that a so public intimacy with the Press was, under the circumstances of her bereavement, altogether nice. Verbena preferred that they should go into the house. Would Lukin . . . ?

Lukin, replete with information, did not really want to, but he was sucked irresistibly forward in Verbena's wake. It seemed impossible that she could be so ever verdantly a little Totsie, even to a mother, as she now leant nonchalantly against the dining-room piano, sprawling her elbows across the top and turning over leaves of music. As they came in she knitted her eyebrows and began absorbedly to hum. She said that she supposed Mr. Lukin would like some information, and looked coldly at him out of china eyes that were set in level with her face.

"It has all been very painful for Verbena," said her mother, sitting down expectantly in an armchair.

"Your mother has already been most kind," said Lukin, temporizing wildly, looking at the clock on the mantelpiece.

"Ho, well," she laughed, on a high single note of scorn. "If you want to publish a whole pack of servants' gossip—"

"Oh, darling!"

"—Of course I know some papers wouldn't mind."

"Your mother has been most good," repeated Lukin with finality, even preparing to put away his notebook. He didn't want two stories, after all, and he knew perfectly well that Verbena was only going to contradict her mother's. He had the stuff half-written in his mind already; it was beginning to rise in his brain like a cake in an oven. The whole truth was, for the purposes of his profession, a thing of too various dimensions to be easily encompassed.

"Oh, well," she murmured. "I should have been sorry to part with it. I only *thought*—"

"What's that?"

She patted her back hair complacently, while her mother started, looking round at Lukin. The young

man was like a bandit, suddenly, holding her daughter
up. There was an impersonality about him one could
hardly like. "Just a little photograph I have," said Verbena dreamily. "A snap I took. *Of them.*"

To Lukin's vision the whole room shifted and light-
ened; he heard the clock stop ticking, and the silence
bulged, swelled like a bubble from the bowl of a pipe,
and burst in a flash of sound. The clock started ticking
again wildly in his very brain. "Yes?" he whispered.

"Yes," said Verbena, and, licked about with silver
light, like a nymph, divinely, she crossed the room and
vanished through the door. The clock ticked on interminably, registering the flight of hours.

They were sitting on the sofa together, and Verbena,
her brief little skirt strained tight across her plump little
knees, had the photo lying on her lap. His eager hand
stretched out for it, but with a quick movement she
fended the hand away. So he just gazed down over the
barrier of her arm so burningly at the photograph that
the glazed print might almost have curled up beneath
his eyes and shrivelled away to ashes. The tartan pattern of Verbena's skirt danced and shifted kaleidoscopi-
cally around it. A couple stood with arms entwined,
their faces black with sunshine, in a garden, among
spikes of leafage. The male figure had a faintly perceptible outward slant.

"I remember very well the day I took that snap,"
Verbena said.

"Indeed?" said Lukin, with a look that yearned to
violate her memory. She had a fat little white throat,

and she bent back her head and shut her eyes in an
ecstasy of reconstruction. Laughter, laughter had been
the motive of that day, it seemed. She and Mrs. Brindley
had laughed as they pursued Mr. Brindley round and
round the garden. He never smiled, so he did not smile
then, though he was a kind man, Verbena knew, but
ambled uncomplainingly and unamusedly round and
round the little zigzag gravel paths like an old billy-
goat, with Verbena in pursuit with the camera, and
Mrs. Brindley endeavouring to head him off. It had
been a Sunday morning. He was a near-sighted man,
and his glasses had leaped from his nose and swung at
the end of their chain wildly. So blinded, he had
headed straight into an apple-tree and cut his lip, and
Mrs. Brindley, who couldn't stick the sight of blood,
had turned momentarily a queer pale green. Verbena
had gone into the house with Mr. Brindley and stuck a
strip of plaster on his lip. She pointed out to Lukin,
now, the strip of plaster in the photograph. He had sat
grey and passive beneath her ministrations, stretching
up his queer long neck. As they were going back to the
garden he had turned and said to Verbena, "No one else
but me would do a thing like that, would they? Have
you ever run straight into a tree?" and Verbena had
laughed and said, no, she hadn't, and that she didn't suppose anybody but Mr. Brindley ever would. She had
learnt from his wife that that was the way Mr. Brindley
should be treated, just chaffed and laughed at, else he
got so morbid. He was a clumsy man; he never laid
hands on anything but it broke, or at any rate tumbled

over, and then his wife would laugh. She was ever so good-tempered with him, Verbena said; she would only shout, "You are an old duffer!" and sometimes she could hardly speak for laughing. This infected Verbena, and they had had some very cheerful times together. Mr. Brindley never said anything; he would just stand there, looking shyly at his wife out of the corner of his eye. Once they had found him burying some broken china in the garden.

"She was ever so cheerful," repeated Verbena, staring with her round eyes out of the window. Her mother's armchair creaked in a great pang as the lady shuddered irrepressibly. "If people only knew . . ."

So they had caught Mr. Brindley that morning, Verbena continued. Look, you could see in the photograph how he was tugging away. Stupidly—it showed, didn't it?—like an animal.

"What a long face!" said Lukin, peering down. Yes, a long face, and it was never different. He was very humble, and when he had knocked over anything or broken china he would go for a long walk alone and not come in till his wife was asleep. "Joseph never does anything right," she used to say, as cheerfully as anything; and among her friends it had been quite a by-word. Verbena had never seen her out of temper; look, in the photograph you could see her smiling—there, that white bit; she had rather big, white teeth. Once when she and Verbena had been coming home from the cinema they had seen Mr. Brindley, back from work, walking with his bag in his hand up and down in front of his own house, and sometimes stopping to stare up at the windows. You would have thought it was a strange house that he was afraid to go into.

Verbena's mother here interposed that she, too, had on several occasions noticed this. It gave her the creeps, somehow; it didn't seem right. She had felt inclined to put her head out of the window and shout at him.

"Gee!" said Lukin meditatively, biting his upper lip. "Nothing else? Nobody? Then why did he, and why particularly then—?"

"Oh, but of course—didn't mother tell you? He had lost his job a week before. His wife rang him up at the office *that* afternoon and discovered it. He had been going out every day just the same, goodness knows where to, and coming in later and later."

"But they were in comfortable circumstances," said the mother wonderingly. "They had Incomes. *His* work was not worth very much; she told me so in front of him. They wouldn't have been seriously reduced. *I* can't see that that was a reason."

"*I* can't see that it was a reason, either," said Verbena; "when he came home, she wouldn't have said very much to him. She would only have laughed."

Verbena made Lukin a present of the photograph, and he received it reverently, and tucked it away in his notebook. He was burning now to be back at the *Evening Crier* offices, burning to be there; his impatient mind tugged at its moorings to his less mobile body. He discovered that he and she were sitting very close together, and he looked down, as though through a mile of ether, at the two blunt, smartly-shod little feet that she stuck straight out in front of her.

Wife's Discovery Precipitates Tragedy of Disappointed Man. That was the vital stuff the *Evening Crier* wanted. And he had Recent Photograph, showing plaster over the scar that the Coroner might still discover on Mr. Brindley's lip. It was patently Recent. He caught the eye of the clock, and was reminded that, though all this was excellent, he should have been by now half-way to town. "I'm ever so obliged to you," he said, rising. "You've been just fine. You can rely on my discretion—absolutely."

The face of the mother, upturned to him benevolently, was faintly clouded, as she realized what his absolute discretion meant. It had been, however, a delightful morning, and she held out her hand to him amicably at parting. She invited Lukin to pay them a call some Sunday afternoon, and said that they were always in for tea. "You *are* always in for tea on Sundays, aren't you, darling?"

"Oh, occasionally," said Verbena, very much detached, and tapping the barometer. The green lady, standing at the door, called out after him that their name was Thomas, and their house The Glen, as Lukin scuttled wildly down the steps.

He fled blithely up the road to find his taxi, without so much as a side-glance over to Moyallo. His heart was like a singing bird.

A NOTE ON THE TYPE

This book was set on the Linotype in Janson, *a recutting made direct from the type cast from matrices made by Anton Janson some time between 1660 and 1687. Janson's original matrices were, at last report, in the possession of the Stempel foundry, Frankfurt am Main.*

Of Janson's origin nothing is known. He may have been a relative of Justus Janson, a printer of Danish birth who practiced in Leipzig from 1614 to 1635. Some time between 1657 and 1668 Anton Janson, a punch-cutter and type-founder, bought from the Leipzig printer Johann Erich Hahn the type-foundry that had formerly been a part of the printing house of M. Friedrich Lankisch. Janson's types were first shown in a specimen sheet issued at Leipzig about 1675. Janson's successor, and perhaps his son-in-law, Johann Karl Edling, issued a specimen sheet of Janson types in 1689. His heirs sold the Janson matrices in Holland to Wolffgang Dietrich Erhardt, of Leipzig.

Composed, printed, and bound by
Kingsport Press, Inc., Kingsport, Tennessee.

Vermilion

Vermilion Campus Library
Arrowhead Community College
1900 E. Camp Street
Ely, MN 55731